# Elemental Forces

## Book Three of the Oracle *of* Light

Cil Gregoire

*PO Box 221974 Anchorage, Alaska 99522-1974*
*books@publicationconsultants.com—www.publicationconsultants.com*

ISBN 978-1-59433-495-5
eBook ISBN 978-1-59433-496-2
Library of Congress Catalog Card Number: 9781594334955



Manufactured in the United States of America.

# Dedication

To my son Israel.

# Books by Cil Gregoire

Oracle of Light series:

*Crystalline Aura*
*Anthya's World*
*Elemental Forces*

Visit her website at:

www.cilgregoire.com.

# Acknowledgments

Special thanks to my wonderful team of reader mentors who faithfully kept me on course through the writing of this novel. Most have worked with me from the creation of the Oracle of Light starting with Book 1, Crystalline Aura. They are: Renamary Rauchenstein, John Connolly, Becky Smith, Herman Thompson, and Dawn Rinehart.

Also I wish to express special gratitude to Evan Swensen for how he magically makes publication happen.

And finally, I offer special heartfelt thanks to all my fans for encouraging me to continue writing.

# Table of Contents

## EARTH

Distance from sun: 91.3 – 94.4 million miles
Length of day: 24 hours (1 Earth-day)
Orbital Period: 365.26 days (1 Earth-year)
Closest star: Proxima Centauri (4.24 light years)

## AAIA

Distance from sun: 90.9 – 95.6 million miles
Length of day: (app. 6 Earth-days)
Orbital Period: (2.5 Earth-years)
Closest star: Seaa (0.008 light years)

# Chapter 1

# Earth

A long thin serpentine life form dashed away through the murky dark water as Brakalar thrashed about to regain his feet. Once on his feet, he found himself standing in shin-deep mucky water dimpling with the actions of hidden life forms lurking unseen below the surface. The musky odor of rot and decay toiling with the striving aroma of green growth and bloom filled his nostrils. Tall fluted trees guarded by stalagmite sentinels of woody growth grew in the dark blackish soil as well as the muddy watery quagmire. Dry land may be a preference, but apparently it wasn't a necessity. Overhead, dark gray turbulent clouds scudded across a lowering sky.

Brakalar's usually darkly reserved, unruffled demeanor dissolved in the dirty swamp water, the threats from living creatures unraveling his composure. Frantically he looked about seeking dry land, and then spotted some just a few strides away, his feet stirring up the fetid stench of decomposition with each sluggish step. He found upon reaching ground that the land wasn't really "dry" by definition; it just wasn't covered with water. It also harbored life forms that chirped and twittered and flapped and scuttled all about him; most were small and unseen, but not all. He had taken only a few steps when he encountered a long thick-bodied, short-legged scaled monster of a beast with long tooth-lined jaws openly threatening. The end of its long stout tapering tail lay hidden behind a thicket of trees, dark muddy mulch, and woody underbrush. Discovering quickly that here, unlike on the Devastated Continent, he could freely draw from the abounding elemental energy surrounding him, Brakalar teleported out of range of the gaping jaws… into more swamp water.

Brakalar didn't know what would happen to him when he dove for the energy field Rahlys had detected in the Crystalline Landscape. He didn't really care what happened to him; he had to get away from the accusing glances from the rest of the expedition, an expedition he led until the tragic incident. Death would have been welcomed. Poor Zayla! He hadn't intended to kill her…it was the Rod of Destruction…. He fought to drive the memory of the horrible scene in the ruins of the Temple of Tranquility out of his mind and focus on survival.

The wind began to pick up, stirring the humid air. Carrying the pack with the sealed chest containing the Rod of Destruction snuggly in one arm, his heart pounding frantically in the muggy oppressive heat, his body and clothing dripping with sweat and swamp water, Brakalar teleported what he hoped were safe jumps ahead in one direction. Eventually he reached terrain more consistently above water.

It wasn't long before he encountered a humanoid life form. The lanky bearded male stooped at the shoulders wore tattered clothing that hung loosely over his thin frame. Noticing Brakalar's approach he straightened somewhat eyeing the strangely dressed intruder suspiciously. When the man spoke to him, he didn't recognize the language at first as English, it sounded so different from what Rahlys and Ilene spoke.

"Wat dat ya got dare?" The thin raggedly dressed man asked with awed curiosity, his long bony fingers pointing to the pack Brakalar carried. Before Brakalar could answer, the dark gray angry clouds burst open and rain poured down. "Ya betta come in out o' duh rain," the man said with concern when Brakalar failed to answer. "I got a pot o' alligator sauce piquante to heat up, if ya hungry."

"Thank you," Brakalar managed as he followed his benefactor to a wooden structure that blended in with the rest of the woods. He later learned that the welcomed meal had been prepared from one of the reptilian beast he had encountered earlier.

---

Summer warmth anointed the cold, freshly thawed soil of Alaska's northern Susitna Valley, urgently encouraging myriad seedlings to rapid growth and fruition before winter's quick return. Robins, redpolls, chickadees, and swallows flittered about flustered with mating, nest building, and snatching up the awakening, droning, buzzing flies, bees, and beetles that zoomed by Rahlys' head. Cheeky little ground squirrels scampered after each other along the way, running up and down tree trunks and jumping from branch to branch in frolicking abandon. Even the air seemed restless, gently fanning the spring green leaves of the emerging forest, to keep them awake and growing.

The openness of the woods made for easy walking, as she made her way with a full picnic basket to the site in the woods where Quaylyn had been diligently working on something he called a traw playing field. Today she and Ilene were to begin their training in the traw arena.

As she followed the newly scratched trail, Rahlys reflected back to her first meeting with Quaylyn five years ago when the High Council of the Crystal Table sent Quaylyn to Earth to help her in confronting Droclum. Although a highly trained warrior and master of the elemental forces, Quaylyn had seemed endearingly innocent at the time with his tousled golden brown hair, twinkling dark blue eyes, and dimples when he smiled, which had been often back then.

For Quaylyn, the mission had been a rite of passage into full standing in Aaian society, a culture that placed servitude to others according to their needs – and your talents – over individual choice and personal goals. In the end, Quaylyn left the battle, and Earth, in a state of unconsciousness; but Droclum had been defeated. Quaylyn had reached the sought after status of Accepted One, but he went through a period of bitter despair after learning that Droclum was his father.

Three years went by before Rahlys saw Quaylyn again, this time on his own world, for she had joined an expedition to the Devastated Continent in search of another expedition that never returned. On that adventure she had helped Quaylyn heal his emotional wombs and the start of a relationship had formed. That journey had ended abruptly when she and Ilene were transported home to the upper Susitna Valley without warning from the Crystalline Landscape.

Two months later, Quaylyn had appeared in her yard, professing his love. What's more, he had come of his own free will, without an assignment from the High Council. She waltzed along the greening path of dappled sunshine lost in her own exuberance, like a schoolgirl of sixteen instead of thirty-six, her long braid of honey brown hair swinging across her t-shirt clad back. It had to have been a tough decision for him to make, Rahlys knew. Such a decision goes against the customs and culture of his world in which individual freedom and the pursuit of personal happiness are generally frowned upon.

As she approached the clearing, Rahlys spotted Quaylyn and Ilene through the trees and underbrush not yet dense with summer growth. At last night's dinner gathering Quaylyn had challenged Ilene to train as a warrior alongside Rahlys, after all Quaylyn had pointed out, she was Theon's daughter. Ilene had been quick to agree.

Rahlys paused, still unnoticed, and watched quietly, her heart swelling with warmth and contentment. She watched as Quaylyn handed Ilene one of two wands made of local birch and explained its function in the game of Traw. Ilene listened attentively to his instruction. Then Quaylyn inadvertently looked up as he demonstrated proper wand action and spotted Rahlys.

"Good, you're here!" He waved her over. Upon reaching them, he handed her a well-crafted birch wand, smoothly rounded, shaped to fit her hand at one end and tapering to a blunt point at the tip, and whipped out a third from his back pocket. His glacier blue eyes twinkled with controlled excitement over his project, the sunshine accenting the golden highlights of his hair. The old khakis, borrowed from Vince, hung loosely over his lean, muscular frame.

"I brought lunch," Rahlys said, setting the basket down.

"Work first; lunch later. What do you think?" Quaylyn asked spreading his arms wide.

Rahlys turned her attention to the traw training field spread out before her. "It's finished?"

"Isn't it awesome?" Ilene exclaimed as Rahlys took it all in.

According to Quaylyn, traw was an ancient discipline designed to train warriors in self-defense using speed, focus, physical agility, and mental dexterity in a confrontation. Rahlys gazed out over the field of play, a large diamond nearly a hundred feet to a side, bisected into two triangles. Each triangular court had areas of sand, sod, and outcrops of rock protruding from the earth.

"I can imagine the questions anyone flying over might ask."

"There is no need for concern. An invisible shield protects the playing field, reflecting back the surrounding forest. It won't be seen."

"That's good to know. So how do we get started?" Rahlys asked, taking on a warrior's stance.

"I'm ready," Ilene agreed, vibrantly enthusiastic, her wildly curly, grayish-brown hair charged with the lively spark that lit up her dark gray eyes. Rahlys recalled the quiet, timidly shy young woman of just a few years ago working in her mother's gift shop when she brought in her paintings to sell.

"We'll start by practicing with the wands," Quaylyn began. "Let's spread out a little." Ilene and Rahlys stepped back putting distance between them until Quaylyn indicated for them to halt. "That's good. Now hold your wands up and I'll activate them." Following Quaylyn's example, they extended their arms, the tips of their wands reaching for the sky. Then to their surprise, a streak of light shot out from the tip of Quaylyn's wand connecting with Ilene's wand, then Rahlys', before streaking back to Quaylyn, momentarily forming a glowing triangle before winking out.

"Wow!" Ilene exclaimed, obviously impressed.

"Now each wand has twenty-four shots."

"What kind of shots?" Ilene asked, lowering her arm and studying the wand with fascinated interest.

"They look like this." To demonstrate, Quaylyn gently flicked his wand in Rahlys' general direction and a translucent ball of light slowly arched its way toward her. "Now, using your wand, try to draw the shot in."

Rahlys cautiously approached the incoming glow globe. When her wand tip drew near, it pulled in the ball of light, taking it out of play.

"Good job. That's a point for you. Now try sending a shot toward me, both of you. You are in control of the speed, arc, and direction of the glow globes; it's all in the wand action. The harder you flick the wand, the faster the glow globes travel."

Soon, two awkwardly released glowing globes were speeding Quaylyn's way. He dispatched them both with ease and quickly released two more, sending Rahlys and Ilene chasing after them. Before they could recover from their hard-earned success, Quaylyn had two more glowing balls hurling their way. He kept the two women so busy running after the shots he released, with most of the glow globes falling teasingly short, or long, or off to the right or left, Ilene and Rahlys forgot all about firing off shots of their own. Finally Quaylyn's wand was spent and two winded, sweating women, surrounded by several missed glowing orbs that had landed on the ground, glared angrily toward him.

"Go ahead, fire off the rest of your shots," Quaylyn shouted, knowing the women were steaming for revenge.

"Let him have it," Rahlys shouted to Ilene - and they did! Rahlys and Ilene released one shot after another, as fast as they could, in every direction imaginable.

Quaylyn twirled around gathering the barrage of fire with agile grace, his wand swirling and swooshing through the air as he leapt about drawing in the spread of glowing globes in a steady stream of light. Soon it was all over and not a single shot had landed un-retrieved! Rahlys and Ilene gawked in stunned disbelief.

"Well, that's a start, but the idea is to send out shots while retrieving those from your opponent, keeping your opponent busy." Quaylyn didn't notice their silent, open-mouthed stares, or chose not to. "Now you are ready to try it on the field. The playing field adds boundaries and obstacles. Choose a side; I'll play against the two of you."

"We can do this," Rahlys reassured Ilene, trying to sound convincing.

"Yes, we can," Ilene agreed for reinforcement. Rahlys and Ilene chose the nearest court and proceeded to inspect it while Quaylyn made his way to the other end. Granite boulders of varying size and shape protruded from the ground, creating irregular areas of playing surface that had to be dodged or clambered over to defend. The front of the court was mostly loose sand, the back sod.

"Now stand on the area of sod at the back of your court," he instructed from across the field, and we will re-charge our wands. I'll go a little easier on you this time, giving you a chance to fire off some shots and get familiar with the course."

"How sporting of you," Rahlys said sarcastically. Rahlys and Ilene held up their wands, standing away from each other on the diamond of sod at the back of their court and looking up in anticipation of the stream of light that would connect them.

"As soon as we are connected, you can commence firing," Quaylyn warned, "so be alert." A streak of light zipped from wand tip to wand tip in a flash, connecting them, and then winked out in an instant. Quaylyn made sure both women had released a shot before sending over a couple of easy volleys. He was pleased when he noticed Rahlys release a second shot before drawing in one of his. Then she released two more before he could get another one to her. Ilene was holding her own, releasing a shot after every one she drew in.

So far, he had placed his glow globes within easy reach, while theirs sent him dashing all over the court. Now he aimed his shots over the outcrops of granite, forcing them to watch their footing and in some cases climb over boulders to reach the bright orbs before they touched the rocks. Then he sent them jumping down into the sand pits, the deep sand dragging at their feet. But true to his word, he always gave them time throughout to fire off shots of their own. The women missed drawing in only a few of the glow globes, although suffering many scrapes and bruises for their effort. When the game finally ended, Quaylyn glowed with pride over their progress.

"Excellent!" he shouted from across the field.

Ilene and Rahlys slumped, exhausted, to the ground.

"Great job; that was a good start," Quaylyn gloated, joining them. "What's for lunch?"

"Aaaarrrk…! Aaaarrrk…!"

Just the mention of the word "lunch" brings that bird calling.

Raven circled overhead cawing in puzzlement over the scene below. His telepathed images to Rahlys of Quaylyn standing over their sprawled out bodies explained his concern.

"Aaaarrrk…! Aaaarrrk…!"

*We're all right,* Rahlys reassured her familiar, even though every muscle in her body ached. Raven had once been like any other raven; sly, raucous, predacious, and content with life as a raven. But his perspective on life changed when one day, sitting on an old tree trunk washed up on the bank of the mighty Susitna River, he spotted something shiny drift to shore. An investigative peck at the shiny object had altered his life forever, but the trade-off had been worth it.

Raven flew in lower and landed on a nearby rock, this time sending Rahlys telepathed images of the picnic basket.

"You and Raven are on the same wavelength," Rahlys moaned, forcing her way up to a sitting position. She drew healing energy to the places that hurt while Ilene brought over their picnic lunch.

"A true warrior does not waste precious energy to heal minor wounds," Quaylyn informed her, sensing her draw on energy. "A true warrior embraces her wounds as a reminder of her shortcomings and her need to improve."

"I'll keep that in mind," Rahlys reassured him with a weak smile.

---

"It's time we moved the twins out of our bedroom," Maggie announced, standing next to one of two cribs that lined a wall of their crowded, cluttered bedroom. She completed the finishing touches to Crystal's diaper change and lifted her out of the crib. "Now you smell sweet again," she said, nuzzling her little daughter.

"You're right, it's about time we had our bedroom to ourselves," Vince agreed. "How about you, my little fellow, are you and your darling little sister ready to move into the children's room?" Eight month old Rock, his diaper already freshly changed, cooed in response. "I know you understand Mommy and Daddy need their privacy. After all, we men have to stick together." Vince turned back to Maggie. "But what about Melinda, won't rooming with three little ones be an invasion of her privacy."

"I've been thinking about that. When we added on the children's room, we planned on later dividing it into two. We can still do that. Then Leaf and Rock would share a room and Melinda and Crystal would have their own."

"We can do that. Let's go and take a look at it. By the way, Leaf is awfully quiet."

Maggie and Vince carried the babies into the children's room to find Leaf building a tower of stacking blocks, books, toys…anything he could find… held together mostly by levitation. His parents' unexpected entrance broke his youthful concentration, causing all to tumble down with a loud crash.

"Leaf Bradley…." Maggie began and paused, saying no more. Vince's gentle squeeze of her hand had alerted her to proceed with caution.

Maggie decided to let it go. Maggie and Vince were greatly concerned about their toddler's incredible abilities, especially after Leaf killed a wolf to protect his mother. Even Quaylyn, after interacting with Leaf for a while, was astounded by the ease with which Leaf could draw energy from the elemental forces.

Three-year-old Leaf, aware that his parents didn't fully appreciate his talents, bowed his little head in contrition. All three children had inherited some shade of Maggie's red hair; Leaf a bright orange carrot top, Crystal a strawberry blonde, and Rock burnished reddish brown. All had Maggie's emerald green eyes. Vince felt colorless around them with his less descriptive brown hair and eyes.

"I'll get a tape measure," Maggie said, placing Crystal on the floor.

Ignoring the mess, she headed for the kitchen where she kept her own stash of tools…hammer, screw driver, tape measure, etc.…that she could always find when she wanted them. Crystal crawled over to investigate the assortment of items that littered the floor. Rock, noting his twin sister's freedom, squirmed in protest. Vince set Rock down on the floor to join her. His arms now free, Vince started moving a box of toys so he could roll back the rug that covered the middle of the painted floor.

"What are you doing, Daddy?" Leaf asked, full of curiosity.

"We're going to measure the room to find the center."

"Why?"

"So we can divide the children's room into a girls' room and a boys' room."

"Why?" Leaf asked, his angelic little face creasing in concern. Hoping to avoid a long string of "whys," Vince searched for another strategy. Then Maggie returned with the tape measure relieving Vince from the interrogation.

Handing Vince the tape measure, Maggie sat on the floor and beckoned Leaf toward her. "Come here," she said and gently took him into her lap. "It's time for Rock and Crystal to move out of Mommy and Daddy's room and move in with you and Melinda." She brushed back his carrot orange hair, only a shade brighter than her own, with her fingers. "Won't it be fun for you and Rock to share a room? We'll put up a wall in the center of the room, and then instead of having one room, we will have two."

"I want to be with Melinda," Leaf said, his emerald green eyes staring searchingly into her own. Maggie had anticipated something like this. Leaf and Melinda were deeply attached. Melinda was more a big sister in spirit to Leaf than any biological big sister could ever have been. They were strongly connected, always aware of the other's emotional state and physical whereabouts.

"Melinda is a girl and Crystal is a girl and girls are supposed to share a room," Maggie explained.

"Why?"

Vince, watching bemused, arched up his eyebrows in anticipation, but to his amazement, Maggie sailed right through.

"You and Rock are approaching the age when the two of you will want your own boys' space, without the girls."

"Do you want to help us?" Vince interceded. "We need a crayon to mark the wall and floor."

"I'll get it," Leaf said, jumping up. After clearing away toys and furniture along the long east wall, Maggie and Vince stretched out the tape measure locating the center of the room and Vince showed Leaf where to make a mark. Leaf excitedly marked the wall and floor where Vince indicated.

"The wall will go here," Vince explained when they were done. "I might have enough lumber on hand for this little project." They heard the front door open and close and soon Melinda walked into the room.

***'What's going on here?'*** Melinda sent telepathically. She looked with dismay at the room in shambles; she usually ended up being the one to pick it all up. Melinda, a ward of the Order of the Oracle, was a stunning beauty, looking summery in cut-off jeans and a red sleeve-less top. The gleaming sunlight streaming in through the window, reflected warmly off her dark brown hair and silky smooth light brown complexion, but her almond-shaped eyes reflected remembered pain and horror. Four years ago Rahlys rescued her from Droclum's clutches, but the encounter with Droclum had left Melinda orphaned and mute.

"We are going to have two rooms," Leaf sputtered excitedly, his body animated, "one room for you and Crystal and one room for Rock and me!"

'***Is that true?***'

"The wall is here," Leaf added, running to the spot he had marked. Up to now, the twins had played quietly with the toys scattered about, but Crystal soon lost interest and wanted to be fed. Rock quickly followed her example.

"Feeding time," Maggie said, picking up Rock. Melinda picked up Crystal and she stopped whimpering immediately. Holding the baby in her arms, she walked about the room trying to picture the change being proposed. She had enjoyed the larger space and didn't really want to see it go, but of course, she and Leaf could not share a room forever. If she left, the house wouldn't be so crowded, she reasoned, but she wasn't ready to bring up the topic of her leaving just yet. There was no telling how Maggie, Vince, and Rahlys, not to mention Leaf, would react to the news.

***'When is this going to happen?'***

"Well, we can frame in the partition wall tomorrow. I might have to mill some boards to cover it. Even so, we could have it done by the weekend," Vince calculated.

"Great, we will have a guest room for your friend coming up on the train Saturday," Maggie decided. Jack Faulkner, known to Maggie only through stories, was an old marine buddy of Vince's; she was anxious to make a good impression. "Leaf can sleep on a pallet on the floor in Melinda's room and we can wait till after the weekend to move the twins."

"I'll take some more measurements and see what I have on hand in the line of materials," Vince concluded.

Crystal, who had become quiet in anticipation of being fed, started to whimper again over lack of progress in that direction, forcing Melinda to follow Maggie out of the room. Leaf watched quietly as Vince took the measurements he needed, jotting them down on a piece of paper from Melinda's desk. The children already occupied opposite sides of the room; they wouldn't have to move beds or much furniture. The babies' cribs could go against the new wall.

When Vince left the children's room to head out to his workshop, Leaf sat in his youth chair to ponder what he had gleaned from Melinda's mind.

---

*"Taku...."* It was just a whisper of a thought or sound, a sigh of breath. Melinda shuddered with cold fear, detecting an ephemeral whiff of soul cringing evil. Her father's boat had been called *The Taku;* it had also been Droclum's name for her. *"Come closer,"* the disembodied thought coaxed her. *"I have something for you."* The memory of an unspeakable evil veiled over her senses. She broke into a sweat, her heart pounding in her ears, fear paralyzing her. She struggled desperately to wake up, to stop the approaching, unrelenting horror, but she couldn't move; she couldn't scream, or even breathe.

*Help me,* her mind cried out.

"*Rahlys cannot hear you....*"

*Help! Please, someone, help me,* Melinda screamed mentally. She could feel Droclum's evil drawing closer, intensifying.

"*I will find you....*"

Leaf bolted awake and jumped out of bed; Melinda needed his help. For a moment he was disoriented, not understanding why he couldn't see her across the room in the semi-darkness. Then remembering the newly constructed wall that divided their bedrooms, he bypassed the wall by teleporting to her bedside.

"Melinda, wake up!"

She felt someone shaking her, "Wake up, Melinda, please!" To her relief, a wave of consciousness pulled her away from the horror. She opened her eyes to Leaf's shaking, sobbing pleas, perched on the edge of the bed beside her.

*Oh, Leaf....* She grabbed him into her arms, hugging him.

"Are you okay?" he asked with concern beyond his tender years.

*Yes,* she sobbed, her head nestled on his tiny shoulders. *It was just a nightmare.*

"I heard you screaming."

*You heard me?* The essence of Droclum had said Rahlys could not hear her mental nightmarish screams. Nothing had been said about Leaf. The thought that Leaf could hear her when no one else could was somewhat comforting, but it was a terrible burden to place on someone so young.

"Do you want to play a game?" Leaf asked when things seemed back to normal. Melinda glanced at her clock, four twenty-three.

*Sure, whatever you want to play.* She wouldn't be going back to sleep. Pulling on her robe, she got up and opened the heavy brown curtains covering her east facing window. The early summer sun sparkled through the tree tops. In no time at all, Leaf was back with a box of dominoes, noisily spilling them across the floor.

*Quiet,* Melinda warned him, *Mom and Dad and the twins are still sleeping.* At least the twins hadn't been moved yet into their rooms. Melinda and Leaf both froze listening for sounds coming from their parents' room. All was quiet.

*You can't play dominoes; you're only three. See, ages five and up.*

"I'm three and a half."

*Dominoes requires math.*

"I can do math," Leaf argued.

Two hours and many games later when Maggie peeked in after putting coffee on, Leaf had just won by seventy-five points.

## Chapter 2

# Aaia

Theon sat in the hot sun on an outcrop of bedrock in the high rocky valley outside the entrance to his private rooms, carved into the cooler interior of the surrounding mountain. He closed his eyelids to the bright sun, golden sky, and rose and lavender rocks draped with orange and blue-green foliage, and let his mind wander to a distant world with blue skies, gray stone mountains, and green forests. In the warm orange glow that still reached his retinas behind closed lids; he enjoyed remembered images of his daughter Ilene, across the galaxy. Born of an Earth mother, he had thought Ilene would never see his world, a world she was half descendent from, but he had been wrong. Recently she had joined him on an expedition to the Devastated Continent. His last memory of her was Ilene and Rahlys' sudden disappearance from the Crystalline Landscape a season ago. Then by means still unexplained, he and the rest of the expedition had been returned half way around the globe, across the Golden Sea, to the Community of the High Council.

It was only later, through her connection to the Oracle of Light in Rahlys' possession on Earth, that Councilor Anthya was able to reassure Theon that Ilene, Rahlys, and Raven were all alive and well back in Alaska. *Will I ever see my daughter again?* It was doubtful he had to admit to himself with a heavy heart. *I miss her....*

'***Warrior Theon, you are wanted at the Academy.***'

The telepathed message seared through Theon's thoughts like a laser cutting through steel. Groggy from the sun, he forced his mind back. *The Academy can be demanding at times, but I guess I do have a debt to pay to this society,* he sighed in guilt-laden resignation. Of course, no amount of service was ever going to pay for Droclum's catastrophic destruction of their world and his own role in that destruction.

"Warrior Theon…"

"I'm coming," Theon sighed, opening his eyes to see Kiril standing before him.

"I came to take you to the Academy, Sir," Kiril spoke with formality. Kiril, his thick tan wavy hair, always wildly tousled, exuded youth and misguided enthusiasm. He was studying to become a research historian and explorer. Theon was sure he spent more time shadowing him than he did studying and training.

*Is it voluntary on Kiril's part or has he been assigned to keep an eye on me? Do I ready want to know?*

"I'm not that old and feeble; I can teleport myself to the Academy gardens," Theon growled. "Don't you have anything more important to do?" Kiril appeared to give his question some consideration before answering.

"No, Sir, you are the most important thing on my list."

"Ah…" Theon exhaled to cover up a painful groan as he stood. "What's on my agenda today?"

"You have a meeting with Rojaire followed by a history class. Then later today you and Rojaire have a meeting with Councilor Anthya."

"Rojaire…yes," Theon said, seemingly energized over the prospect. "We had better get a move on."

"I'll take you there; you need to reserve your strength for healing instead of teleporting." It was obvious Kiril had seen through his little cover up.

They arrived to find Rojaire already waiting in the little alcove in the Academy gardens that had been designated for the meeting.

Rojaire and Theon shared a common goal; they wanted to return to the uninhabited Devastated Continent – to be free, beyond the easy reach of the Academy and the High Council of the Crystal Table. Unfortunately, these governing bodies controlled access to the continent with the portal guarded by Captain Setas on Limitation Island, so named because it marked the closest point to the Devastated Continent in which one can still draw energy from the elemental forces. It is now known that a blocking force field produced by an enormous landscape of crystals in the center of the continent is the reason.

"There you are," Rojaire greeted them. Rojaire's strong facial features, fathomless dark eyes, orderly shoulder-length black hair, and tall muscular build seemed chiseled in stone. A rugged adventurer, Rojaire lived many years on the Devastated Continent as a rogue explorer, his activities not sanctioned by the High Council. For a share in any relics Rojaire might find, Councilor Brakalar had secretly arranged passage to the forbidden continent by bribing Captain Setas with rare plants and seeds for her horticulture project on Limitation Island. Now Brakalar was gone, and Rojaire had earned Accepted One status.

"Thanks for the ride," Theon said, turning to Kiril. Now, don't you have a class to go to?"

"Ah...no, my next class is history...with you."

Rojaire shrugged. "Let the boy stay; you know he wants to."

Theon relented, easing onto the ornately cut crystal bench in the shady shelter of a triangle fruit tree. The tree was as ornate as the bench, boasting smooth pink and white marbled bark, curvy branches densely foliated with large waxy blue green pink-veined leaves. Lemon yellow triangular fruit, resembling tiny paper lanterns, dangled from its branches on spindly spiraled stems.

"Are you sure you are strong enough to make the trip," Rojaire asked with genuine concern as he joined him on the bench. A light breeze made the heat in the shade tolerable.

"What trip?" Kiril asked, dropping to the ground, his hands gripping his knees. Theon stared at him, declined to answer, and turned back toward Rojaire. Kiril decided it best to just be quiet and listen.

"I don't expect to come back," Theon said, definitively. "I have lived far beyond any reasonable life expectancy. On Earth, I got used to watching generations of humans come and go, their lives so tragically short, but now I have outlived many generations even on my own world." Theon could see that Rojaire didn't know how to respond to that and changed the subject. "How are we going to present our case to Councilor Anthya when we meet with her later today? What do we have to convince her and the High Council to let us return to the Devastated Continent?"

Before the Dark Devastation, Aaia's two continents had developed burgeoning civilizations driven by greed and hunger for power, with the world population over two billion. Today the main continent, covering most of the planet's western hemisphere, is sparsely populated. Far to the east the smaller, but substantial, island continent in the middle of the Golden Sea remains uninhabited. Sorcerer Droclum's death-defying spell, a spell of such great evil it ripped the fabric of the elemental forces, resulted in the catastrophic eruption of Mt. Vatre, an eruption that nearly tore the planet apart. In the heat of the maelstrom, Droclum's evil essence was encapsulated in a dark orb and hurled across the galaxy. From Aaia, the dark orb landed on Earth where it lay dormant for twelve thousand Earth-years. When the ground and sea finally settled and the clouds eventually parted, a population of only a few thousand remained on the main continent. Many plant species and nearly all animal species had become extinct, and the land, especially in coastal areas, had changed dramatically.

But the island continent across the sea had been wiped clean, the turmoil and devastation so complete the continent's land features had been transformed.

"The Devastated Continent…! You're going to the Devastated Continent?" Kiril had jumped to his feet, his tousled hair and sandy eyes electrified with excitement.

"We said you could stay; no one said you could speak," Theon told him. Kiril settled back down. Rojaire pulled a note out of an inner pouch of his light and airy, green and white tunic.

"I've jotted down some arguments to support our position."

"Let's have them."

"Well, there are still members of the lost expedition whose whereabouts remain unknown. For instance, what happened to Ollen after he buried Cremyn? He never returned to the beach to meet up with Captain Setas. Also there's still a lot of unmapped territory to be explored. And let's not forget, there may be more historical artifacts to be found. I even offered to map the passage through the Crescent Mountains to the interior of the continent; the route is quite complicated."

"We've already brought up these ideas; do you have anything new?"

"Just one," Rojaire said, with a smile that brought out his roguish grin, "we could search out the best location to establish a colony."

"Crystal shards – a colony…!" Kiril shouted. The two men stared him back down to silence.

"You think the High Council will go for that?"

"We won't know until we try."

It was then they saw Councilor Anthya strolling down the garden path toward them. Her porcelain white complexion, long white gold hair, and satiny white gown gave her the appearance of an apparition in the glaring morning sunlight. It quickly became apparent that this was no casual encounter. Her clear grayish blue eyes hinted at welcome news.

"Please remain seated," Anthya said, as the men began to rise. "I came to let you know that I submitted your proposition to the High Council, and they have already made a determination." Rojaire, Theon, and Kiril held their collective breaths in anticipation of her next words.

"Basically, you got what you asked for, with some conditions of course." A synchronized exhale accented her words as the three men breathed again.

"What conditions?" Theon was quick to ask.

"You, Rojaire, and Traevus, who has also requested to return to the continent, have been given the assignment to map the passage Rojaire claims to have found through the Crescent Mountains." Traevus had been a member of the lost expedition, and Rojaire and Theon had been on the mission to find them. It turned out; Traevus had been separated from the rest of his group when kidnapped by the Band of Rogues. He was the only member of the lost expedition their search had found, if you didn't count Cremyn's grave. Theon didn't mind Traevus joining their team; he would be an asset instead of a hindrance.

"Is there anything else?"

"Kiril has been assigned to hands-on training as your assistant to record all details of the journey." Kiril let out a barely suppressed whoop of joy and disbelief. Theon rolled his eyes in resignation.

"Also your classes at the Academy have been reassigned," Anthya continued, "leaving you free to focus on getting ready to depart."

"Is that it?" Rojaire felt they were getting off easy.

"No…there is one more thing. Tassyn and Edty have been assigned as laborers…."

"Oh, no…" Rojaire and Theon moaned together. Tassyn and Edty were what remained of the Band of Rogues. Rojaire, especially, knew them quite well.

"I think you will find the two willing, hard workers. I'm highly doubtful they will give you any trouble," she reassured them with a knowing nod. "You have a full rotation to get ready. I suggest you use the time wisely," and then she was gone.

"We're going to the Devastated Continent!" Kiril exclaimed, breathlessly. "I'm going to the Devastated Continent," he whispered to himself, still not quite believing it. *I didn't even have to beg to go along!* Councilor Anthya had said he was going, so it would be.

"It's good we'll have Traevus at least; we can put him in charge of the labor force since the Band once enslaved him," Rojaire suggested. "Justice can be sweet sometimes."

"Good idea. That's less we will have to deal with them," Theon agreed.

"What about me?" Kiril broke in.

"What about you?" Theon asked, irritably. "You heard the councilor; you're a Recorder. Gather your notepads, writing implements, and a change of underclothes, say good-by to anyone you are inclined to, and we'll see you tomorrow."

"Yes, Sir," Kiril said. He jumped up quickly and dashed away, jubilant over the unexpected development. As he left, they heard fading in the distance, "I'm going to the Devastated Continent…!"

---

*Caleeza….*

The summons gently entered her consciousness. She raised her eyes from her work, looking about the crystalline landscape for Sarus' projected image of himself, but found none. From the high crystal boulder on which she sat the crystal formations stretched to the horizons before her, glittering in the starlight. Only to the north was the beauty and purity of the landscape marred. There, Mt. Vatre still smoldered, a dark shattered reminder of a world destroyed. It was Caleeza's habit to emerge after sunset from her cave deep below the surface mass of crystals, which protected her from the heat and blinding light of day, to enjoy the cool night air and soft glow of the massive crystal formations under the stars.

"What is it, Sarus?" she asked the emptiness around her.

"Are you lonely?"

Startled by his question, she dropped the crystal spindle she had been filling with the silken crystalline threads she had spun to her lap. Brain waves were all that was left of the flesh and blood Sarus Caleeza had known and loved. Only her presence, which served as a constant reminder of who he had once been, saved Sarus from becoming totally disconnected with his former humanity.

"Are you?" she asked in return, without answering, her moody violet eyes making it hard to conceal her deeper thoughts.

"No, I don't think so, but I have less need of human contact than you."

"Sometimes I feel lonely," Caleeza admitted quietly, "but I am learning so much here and I don't want to leave you."

The soft music from an underground stream of cool clean water flowing through the crystals filled the silence. "Tell me again the story of our lives together," Sarus requested, "so that I may feel it."

Caleeza picked up her spindle again, spinning the fine crystalline filaments she had gathered into a fine silky thread. Later she would weave the threads into the luxuriously soft bluish white fabric from which she made the comfortable, loose-fitting garments she wore. Her shimmering bluish white knee length tunic, creamy rosy white skin, and soft violet eyes camouflaged well with the softly glowing colors reflected by the crystal field around her. Only her dark red hair, longer now than she usually kept it, stood out in the pastel background.

"Please…?" Sarus asked gently when her response lagged.

"Of course…" *It's why I am here she reminded herself….* "Come sit with me and I will tell you the story of our love and hopes and dreams." An image of Sarus appeared beside her. Her heart seized momentarily at the sight of his tall lean frame, dressed in the coal gray tunic, breeches, and cloak he wore when last she saw him – in living form. She wanted to reach out to him, to run her fingers through his richly burnished dark brown hair and gaze into his deep midnight blue eyes, but having her hand pass through his body would ruin the illusion. She desired to hold him, embrace him, feel his warmth, but he had no warmth to give.

"We grew up together, raised by the Community of the High Council," she began. "Your chosen mother and father and mine were best of friends." Caleeza let her thoughts flow through memories of an idyllic childhood for him to read. She described family gatherings, shared friends, and joint adventures, imbuing the stories with all the associated emotions the memories conjured up. She recalled the years of study, training, and discipline they had endured at the Academy; and the dream they eventually shared to take an expedition across the Golden Sea to the Devastated Continent.

"We failed," Sarus said solemnly. It seemed that failure was the only emotional experience Sarus remembered. "Please, tell me about the expedition that I may experience it all again."

Caleeza knew Sarus could recall the facts; it was the emotional attachments he lost track of. He tended to forget what friendship, desire, love, hate, fear, joy, pain, and sorrow, the whole array of human emotions – except for a deep-rooted sense of failure - felt like, if she didn't repeatedly remind him. Loss of the emotional "why" behind a human-driven activity could render it meaningless to Sarus.

"There were seven of us in all," Caleeza began and she named them off; Traevus, Ollen, Cremyn, Caponya, and Selyzar. "You were the leader and I your second in command. Most of us had trained together at the Academy;

we all looked up to you as our leader." She told him of their arrival on the Devastated Continent, full of curiosity and wonderment, disembarking from Captain Setas' ferry onto the lavender beach. Looking back, that was probably the high point of the entire expedition. Their misfortunes had started lightly. "Only a rotation into our journey, you sprained an ankle in the rifted valley."

"Yes, I remember. There was pain - lots of pain - and because we were unable to draw energy from the elemental forces, the ankle took long to heal. I was angry and disappointed over the inconvenient delay."

"There were disappointments all along the way," Caleeza said. Together they recalled the discovery of the ruins of the Temple of Tranquility and the subsequent disappearance of her best friend Cremyn. Caleeza had been sick with fear and worry over Cremyn's whereabouts and safety during that awful time. They spent many rotations searching for her, in and outside the foreboding ruins, the expedition refusing to move on until they found her.

It was even worse when eventually they did find Cremyn, hidden deep within the temple ruins, an empty shell of her former self, her body sound, but with no mental connection to the exterior world around her. Ollen had sacrificed continuing the mission to escort her back to the Community of the High Council.

"It was a hard decision for Ollen to make," Sarus said, indicating he understood the value of the sacrifice Ollen had made.

"Then Traevus disappeared while we were crossing the interior plains."

"Traevus lives," Sarus was quick to bring up. "He was returned to the Community of the High Council along with the members of the expedition that came to find us."

Their numbers were further decimated when first Selyzar and later Caponya mysteriously vanished while crossing the Crystalline Landscape. At the time, they hadn't realized the crystals were causing the disappearances. Now Sarus and Caleeza knew with certainty the disappearances were caused by the inadvertent triggering of powerful, but invisible, force fields produced by the landscape of crystals.

"What about Selyzar and Caponya? Where are they?"

"I still have not been able to locate them," Sarus admitted.

Shortly after Caponya's disappearance, Caleeza had been transported, without warning, across the galaxy, to a cold northern region of Earth, leaving Sarus all alone, the only remaining remnant of the expedition he once led.

What happened to Sarus after that? Caleeza had no way of knowing, but somehow he had become part of the land of crystals. After his strange metamorphosis, Sarus was able to draw on the crystals' collective power. He had directed energy from the crystals to mentally locate her on Earth - and eventually bring her home.

Caleeza smiled as memories of Vince and Maggie and the house full of children they were raising flooded her mind. It had been fascinating to watch so few Accepted Ones guide so many new persons. Caleeza had enjoyed helping Maggie out while learning about Earth-style family living. Caleeza longed for a family of her own in a community of her own making. She felt empty inside. The image of the intangible man sitting beside her could never fulfill those dreams. Suddenly she wanted to be alone, if she wasn't already.

"I need to gather food," Caleeza announced, putting her spinning aside.

"I will send you to an area where food is plentiful."

"I will need light to see by," she reminded him; "it will be dark away from the crystals."

"I will provide light. Call me when you wish to return."

No sooner had he spoken, and Caleeza found herself in a shallow valley that cut into the central plains, a glow globe floating beside her. It was far too hot to venture out in daytime during the scorching summer, even for food gathering, and the absence of Seaa, the brightest star in the night sky, made for dark summer nights.

Caleeza wasn't really very hungry, but she pulled her harvesting bag from a deep pocket and grazed while she filled it with zan fruit, pinkberries, leafy vegetables, spicy nuts, and sweet fruit. When her bag was full, she climbed out of the shallow moist cut to the drier plains above and sat on the sun-seared grasses. A comfortable cool night breeze fanned out her sweat-dampened hair from her hot neck and shoulders.

"Light out," she said toward the glow globe hovering near her and immediately the light went out. It was through no magic of hers that it did so; Sarus had programed it to respond to her commands. Once gone, she could not bring it back. Her eyes adjusted to the darkness, the stars increasingly lighting up the night. The distant Crescent Mountains rose darkly in the starlight to the west. With primordial wonder she gazed into the brilliant star-studded heavens and sighed deeply, trying to ease her mounting anxiety.

*Why do I feel so uneasy*, she wondered? *Is it fear? If so, what am I afraid of?* She thought about her life with Sarus in the Crystalline Landscape. *Is what I am doing really necessary? I love Sarus, but Sarus is....* She no longer knew how to refer to him, but certainly he was no threat to her safety. Nevertheless, what "is" or "was" Sarus' mind can now wield a tremendous amount of energy from a very powerful renewable energy source. *Could Sarus become a threat to us all?*

She whispered the question to the universe, but the stars offered no answer. Caleeza felt lonelier than she had ever felt before.

*What should I do?*

# Chapter 3

# Earth

After the shower squall passed, Pierre the alligator hunter took Brakalar by boat to the nearest landmass connected to a road. The man was definitely deranged Pierre had decided based on some of the questions Brakalar had asked. A person has to be pretty confused to be roaming the swamps of Louisiana and asking if he is in Alaska. When Pierre edged his boat up to the launch ramp, Brakalar disembarked climbing the ramp that rose out of the water to the road beyond. He turned around to see Pierre back away from the ramp, obviously relieved to be rid of the peculiar stranger. Pierre never did find out what was in the bundle the man carried so possessively.

Two men backing a truck and trailer down the ramp to launch their boat gave Brakalar strange looks; one actually burst out laughing. There could be no doubt Brakalar stood out comically in his gray tunic and breeches, the conical pack containing the rune-covered chest slung across his back. Ignoring the men, Brakalar hastened away on foot.

Brakalar was not as clueless to his predicament as the alligator hunter may think. He had studied Earth culture in general and the English language in particular in preparation for the mission which had included the Sorceress Rahlys and Theon's daughter Ilene; and Quaylyn had shared his experiences in great detail upon returning to Aaia after helping Rahlys defeat Droclum.

One thing was certain, before he could blend in with the local population; he had to find some different clothing.

He followed the road out of the heart of the community to stares, finger pointing, and car honks, the hot sun steam drying the rain-drenched terrain. Eventually he came to a road junction. To prevent drawing so much attention, he took what appeared to be a less traveled route. The narrow road curved through dark woods with wooden dwellings crowded in along the way wherever the swamp didn't encroach. Scanning the buildings for human signatures, he found to his surprise that most of the shelters were empty. Brakalar chose a secluded empty structure and approached it for closer inspection. Walking around to the back porch, he peeked in through a window, then teleported inside. Here he found everything he needed; food, clothing, and a place to rest. Through experimentation he soon discovered that the apparatus above the deep basin near the food storage released clean water when manipulated correctly. After locating some suitable clothing, he stripped off his filthy garments and washed away the stench of the swamp. Once clean, he wanted rest. Before crawling into one of the beckoning sleeping areas, as a precaution, he drew energy from the elemental forces to place wards around the place that would alert him in time if the owners returned. He needn't had worried; the owners of the camp lived and worked in a large city a long ways away and would not be back for some time. For once exhaustion took over and Brakalar slept without dreams haunted by the images of Zayla's death.

---

Ilene and Elaine were enjoying a last cup of coffee before descending the stairs to open up their gift shop of locally-made items below. A beautiful day already full of sound seeped in from the open window. "People are walking the streets and it's not even seven yet," Ilene commented as she and her mother stared out the kitchen window overlooking Main Street. The sun had long been up, in fact, it had barely gone down, not enough to create darkness anyway. It was summer in Alaska with summer solstice, the longest day, just a few weeks away.

Elaine didn't respond to her daughter's comment; her thoughts were elsewhere. Her lackluster eyes and pouty expression indicated a deeper disquieting concern.

"What are you thinking about?" Ilene finally asked, noting her mother's distraction.

"Oh, nothing..., it's time to open the shop," Elaine said, rising from her seat. Without another word, she grabbed the keys from the rack in the kitchen and headed down the stairs.

Ilene grew up not knowing she had a father living close by who loved her until the holographic image of the Oracle of Light from Rahlys' painting revealed the truth. She knew her mother lived in constant fear that Ilene would leave again to rejoin her father across the galaxy.

Ilene rinsed out their cups at the sink and before following Elaine down, looked in the little mirror over the sink to see if at least the bulk of her thick curly mossy brown hair was still contained in its tieback. When she approached the painting of the Oracle of Light hanging by the door, the holographic image glided out of the two dimensional image to hover in front of her.

"Is my father still alive?" Ilene asked the hologram. The ephemeral crystal zipped through the room like a miniature comet blazing out an answer.

**YES.**

"Will I ever see him again?" She knew it was a worthless question to ask, but the longing in her heart caused her to ask it anyway. The holographic crystal flashed out the answer and returned to the painting.

**UNKNOWN...**

The hologram is only capable of telling what is, not what will be. Giving the painting, that appeared once again to be just an ordinary painting, a final glance; Ilene left the apartment and headed down the stairs.

"Is Angela coming in today?" Ilene asked Elaine when she arrived. Her high school friend, now a wife and mother of a baby boy, had moved back to the little end-of-the-road town in the upper Susitna Valley. Angela's husband had a job for the summer building a new school, so rather than Angela and the baby staying in Anchorage; they had sub-leased their apartment and moved in with her mother. Elsie was only too glad to watch her little grandson while Angela took a job at Elaine's shop.

"Yes, she'll be here at eight...why?"

"I was just wondering..." Ilene strolled about the shop fluffing, tucking, folding, arranging items for optimal visual appeal while her mother toyed with paperwork near the cash register.

"I haven't forgotten you have plans for this afternoon." A few customers ambled through the shop. Elaine approached the ambling shoppers.

"Are you interested in anything in particular?" she asked.

Ilene watched as Elaine tried to interest the visitors in various items, all locally made over the long cold winter in hopes of making enough money to buy supplies to make it through another long cold winter. As she watched, Ilene felt a sudden pang of sorrow for her mother. She never really seemed happy; she had no close friends, no real hobbies or interests, and she looked like she was just shrinking and graying out of existence.

"Thanks for coming," Elaine called after them as they walked out the door without making a purchase.

"I've been thinking," Ilene said when they had the shop to themselves again, "why don't you come up the tracks with me this weekend? Rahlys has repeatedly invited you to join us."

Before Elaine could respond with an outburst, the shop door tinkled open again. She glared at her daughter in silence, angry that Ilene even brought the topic up. She thought she had made it clear she did not want to party with that group up the tracks.

"Good morning," Ilene greeted the visitors. Two women, apparently traveling together, nodded and smiled in response. Ilene pointed out several popular items that she thought might interest them.

Elaine's emotions grew in intensity as she held back her words, waiting for the shop to empty again. The customers took all the time in the world, finally purchasing a knitted cap and a pair of earrings. Finally the shop door closed behind them.

"Have you lost your mind…?" Elaine exploded with pent up rage. "I told you I don't want to get involved with those people up there."

"You really need to get away for a while…," Ilene countered immediately, but Elaine didn't give her a chance to finish.

"I can't leave…," Elaine sputtered exasperated at having to explain the obvious. "Why would I go...?"

"It's time you have an adventure and make new friends. You would have fun."

"I don't belong among…"

"We would have our own little cabin…," Ilene pressed on, "and Vince and Maggie have a guest coming from…."

"I can't possibly leave. Who would take care of…?" Just then the door opened.

"Good morning! Am I interrupting something?" Angela asked entering the room like a burst of sunshine. Elaine and Ilene's tirade came to a halt.

Then two women who could have been sisters their features were so alike entered the shop. Letting the potential customers browse a bit before stepping in, Angela sidled up to Ilene.

"Now, what is this all about?" she whispered.

"I want to take Mother up the tracks with me this weekend. Do you think you can mind the store? Tourist season isn't in full swing yet."

"Absolutely, I think the challenge will be getting your mother to agree to go. It would be great for her to get away. I'll help any way I can." Angela walked over to offer her assistance to the lady who was looking through racks of homemade quilts. "We have many talented quilters living in the area; there are more quilts in the back if you would like to see them," she informed the lady.

Elaine and Ilene watched Angela win the customer over with her natural abundance of cheerful optimism.

"Oh, yes, I'm looking for a wedding present for my niece."

"Where are you from?" Angela asked, showing genuine interest.

"We're from Anchorage. It's been so nice out, we decided to take a drive north and get out of the city for a while. Do you have anything more formal and traditional, like a wedding ring pattern? These are mostly appliqued."

"Yes, I believe we do. I'll be right back." Angela ducked into the little storage room behind the desk and quickly returned with a beautifully stitched quilt.

"Oh, yes, this is what I had in mind," the lady exclaimed when they spread it out.

"This lady lives here in town and has won several ribbons at the state fair," Angela said telling the potential buyer a little about the quilter.

What do you think, Mildred?" she called to her friend who was studying Rahlys' paintings.

Mildred turned and walked over. "That's gorgeous!" Mildred agreed. "Holly should love that." Then she pointed to a painting on the wall of a girl and a black bear surprising each other in a blueberry patch. "I like that painting; it's so full of life."

"It's called *Berry Pickers*," Angela said, quick to jump in with confirming praise for Rahlys' abounding talent and whimsical style. Soon what would probably be the largest transactions of the day were complete and the two ladies walked out the door jubilant with their purchases.

"Case closed; it is obvious Angela can handle things here. We're going up the tracks this weekend," Ilene said, breaking the ensuing silence.

"Fine," Elaine said, her voice still argumentative, "but I won't enjoy it!"

*I will find you.*

The sinister words, tainted with the faint essence of Droclum's signature, crept into her mind taunting her. Melinda looked for someplace to hide, but her surroundings were featureless. She ran on without seeming to go anywhere.

*You cannot run and you cannot hide. There is nothing that can conceal you.*

A dark spectrum coalesced from the darkness coming toward her. Melinda's heart seized up in terror.

*There is no escape from me.*

She strained to scream, but no sound came out. She struggled in an effort to run, but her feet would not move.

"Melinda sweetie, wake up," Maggie said repeatedly. Melinda continued to thrash around in her bed not hearing.

"Come on, sweetie, wake up."

Gradually Melinda detected a softer, gentler voice trying to reach her. It also spoke her name. If only she could reach it. She fought to break through the unseen bond that held her, reaching out frantically to pull herself up out of the abyss.

Melinda gasped and opened her eyes to find Maggie by her bed with loving concern written on her face. Melinda sat up and reached for Maggie who held her in a consoling embrace.

"You're safe; it must have been a terrible nightmare the way you were thrashing around. Do you want to tell me about it?"

Melinda glanced about the room, safe in Maggie's arms. Moonlight filtered in through the curtains and Crystal slept in her crib across the room. All was as it was supposed to be, with the threat of Droclum gone.

*It was just a stupid dream.* Melinda cried silently.

---

"Good morning!"

Rahlys opened her eyes to brilliant sunshine streaming into the room and Quaylyn standing before her in cut-offs and a t-shirt holding a breakfast tray.

"I fixed you a healthy breakfast…" Rahlys heard as she struggled for alertness. Slowly she sat up.

"What is that?" she asked puzzled when Quaylyn set the tray down before her.

"Oat cakes, I made them myself. You also have mixed nuts, apple wedges, and Chaga tea…a warrior's diet; traw practice commences in one hour."

Maggie, Melinda, and Quaylyn had found a new interest, wild medicinal plants, which they pursued together. Their proudest discovery so far has been Chaga, a black fungus that grows on birch trees, reputed to be a cure for cancer and a valuable herbal supplement for maintaining good health. Once harvested, the Chaga is dried, ground, and brewed into a dark tea.

"Aren't you having any?" she asked when he sat down in the cushioned wooden chair to watch her eat.

"I've already eaten. I've been out and about for some time now. It's an incredibly beautiful day. Vince and Maggie have company coming this weekend," he added after a pause.

"Oh, so that is where you had breakfast, you sneak. What did you have?"

"Maggie made her fabulous biscuits and gravy," he admitted.

"You're eating biscuits and gravy, and you're feeding me fruit and nuts?"

At least he had the decency to feign being apologetic, although the effect was quickly erased by the boyish dimpled grin that followed.

"Ilene and her mother, Elaine, are also coming up for the weekend. They will be using the guest cabin," Rahlys said, changing the subject.

"Ilene's chosen mother?"

"If that's how you want to look at it." Rahlys carefully adjusted her position to sit up straighter, without upsetting the tray. "Even though Elaine knows about…our connections with another world...I'm sure she will be more comfortable if she doesn't witness proof. Vince's friend knows nothing, and Maggie is adamant that it stay that way."

"Yes, I know, it was nearly all she could talk about."

"Maggie's greatest worry is Leaf. She fears he may, without thinking, do something that would be hard to explain. Leaf's talents are a constant challenge for Vince and Maggie." Rejecting the oat cakes after one bite, she concentrated on the apple and nuts, washing them down with the tea.

Glancing at Quaylyn, Rahlys couldn't understand Quaylyn's puzzled look. "What is it?" Rahlys asked. "You look bewildered."

"Maggie has been asking me how parents on my world cope with raising children who can do amazing things. But on my world, a new person as young as Leaf doesn't usually have such talents. As a race, we don't generally acquire the ability to even telepath a message, much less draw energy, until at least Melinda's age, if not older."

"Are you serious?"

"I'm afraid to tell Maggie that; she is already so worried, and it wouldn't change the reality of the situation."

"I see your point, but if she asks the right questions, you have to answer honestly. Did Maggie happen to mention Melinda's nightmares?"

"Yes, she said they started around the time you and Ilene returned from the expedition."

"I've been giving the matter a lot of thought lately looking for a connection," Rahlys said making a move to put aside the breakfast tray. Quaylyn jumped up from his seat to take it. "What if…?" Rahlys paused and chose a different approach. "Look, we know that through Droclum, Melinda was imbued with telepathic ability and Droclum also made the rune-covered chest, which has summoning powers of its own; so what I'm trying to say is maybe Melinda's nightmares are somehow connected to the chest containing the Rod of Destruction." It was a bone-chilling thought; she hoped it would not prove to be true.

"So you are assuming Brakalar arrived on Earth after vanishing from the Crystalline Landscape." Quaylyn gave it some thought. "It's worth considering."

"Anyway, as for this weekend," Rahlys said returning to the previous topic; there is to be no drawing of energy from the elemental forces, no inexplicable events while we have guests up here in the woods."

"Understood, I'll help you set up the guest cabin for Ilene and her mother… after our workout on the traw playing field."

"Do we have to train today?" Rahlys asked, grateful for his offer of help. "I want to just lounge around and be lazy," she said trying to ease sore muscles that had been wedged under the breakfast tray.

"We work first; there will be plenty of time to be lazy later. There is no predicting what dangers may lurk ahead. Besides, I would be devastated if anything happened to you," he added sweetly. "You must be prepared for the unexpected at all times."

"And playing traw will prepare me for the unexpected?"

"Yes. You are doing great, by the way," he added for encouragement. "But what you haven't quite grasped yet…and you will…is that traw is actually more a mental challenge than a physical one. We will focus on that concept today," Quaylyn said carrying away the tray. He paused at the head of the stairs before leaving. "I'll meet you on the playing field."

Reluctantly, Rahlys eased out of bed and dressed, her mood darkened with concern for Melinda.

*If Brakalar is on Earth I will find him,* Rahlys vowed silently before limping stiffly down the stairs.

## Chapter 4

# Aaia

Once dismissed by Theon, Kiril wasted no time returning to Galeza, the tiny community that raised him. Nestled in a hilly valley many leagues north of the Community of the High Council, Galeza seemed far removed from academic politics. Before him lay a quaint village of lavender, rose, and cream stone huts and walk ways, cradled by colorfully foliaged hills. A small stream, crossed by numerous picturesque stone footbridges, wriggled a course through the village on its way to the Golden Sea only a league away. The rocky terrain was not the best farmland, but a natural abundance of fruit and nut trees grew in the hills, and the land that could be cultivated produced whole grains for breads and porridges, and for brewing beverages. All was as Kiril remembered it; nothing had changed. He didn't want it to.

The inviting stone pathways and footbridges were deserted due to the intensity of the sun. Searching for his chosen mother's signature, he teleported to the stone workstation by the stream outside the village where his mother worked the rare milky blue porcelain clay into vessels of rare beauty.

"Kiril!" his chosen mother Zaloka exclaimed with pleasure, rushing out of the shelter to greet him. "What brings you here?" she asked, her gold flecked eyes searching his face for answers. He smiled at her efforts to brush back the escaped strands of her unruly auburn hair sparking golden in the sun.

"Only pleasure," he said, taking her clay-crusted hands into his momentarily, "and to say goodbye…for a while."

"Where are you going?" she asked with concern. "Your training at the Academy isn't over."

"My journey to the Devastated Continent is part of my training."

"You're going to the Devastated Continent…alone?" Now she *was* concerned.

"With five others; there's nothing to worry about. I will be recording history as we map out a route to the interior through the Crescent Mountains."

"One expedition didn't return," she reminded him.

"Actually, one member of that expedition was eventually found. He will be going with us." The summer sun beat down with intense heat.

"Come, we can't stand around here without expending a lot of energy to keep cool. You have a whole community to visit and I have a celebration to plan…in our son's honor."

Kiril found his chosen father on a sheltered floating platform a short distance offshore from the beach, the pale golden waters of the bay reflecting the golden white brilliance of the sky. He drew energy to teleport himself from the shore out to the floating deck. Wessid didn't notice his son's presence; he was too intent on pulling in the invisible webbed net of energy that bulged with fish to the waiting hold built into the fishing platform.

"Let me help you, Father," Kiril said, mentally latching on to the net of force, adding his strength in pulling. They pulled together straining to bring in the full net. When they finally brought in the haul, it nearly filled the hold's capacity.

Unlike the land animals that became extinct, a few small edible species of fish had eventually recovered from the Dark Devastation that had nearly destroyed the world. By the time edible plants and fish in the sea thrived once again, a culture of low procreation had evolved. With the human population kept unnaturally low and predation from larger species equally low, fish abounded in the Golden Sea.

"Thank you, Son. Welcome home."

"Unless there has been a population explosion in Galeza that I haven't heard about, I think you have enough fish here to feed the whole village."

"That's the plan, my son. Your mother already telepathed me that you were here. There was something about you going to the Devastated Continent." Kiril could detect pride in his father's voice. "There is much to celebrate."

While they cleaned fish, Kiril regaled his father with tales of life at the Academy and expectations of the eminent journey. Word quickly spread that

Kiril was here, and soon others joined them to help, filling the fishing station to capacity.

"Devastated Continent...," Drak spat with disgust, "when will the High Council and the Academy get over what can't be changed and call the continent again by its real name?" Drak, his long silvery hair and weathered skin suggesting a longevity status not yet reached, was normally a man of few words and highly respected in the village. His unexpected outburst about the Devastated Continent brought momentary silence to the merry crowd that had gathered.

"Come with me; I want to show you something," Drak said to Kiril, "there are enough helpers here to finish up without us."

Kiril cleaned off his hands and Drak teleported them to his stone cottage at the far end of the village. Drak led him inside. The rooms were invitingly cool and offered basic comforts. "I'll get the maps and pour us some refreshment," Drak said.

Kiril strolled about the familiar room revisiting the historic relics displayed on shelves and in cubicles worked into the stone walls. He watched Drak through the open archway to an adjoining room fill two tall milky blue porcelain tumblers with a clear bubbly liquid and retrieve a large rolled map and a small cloth bundle from a concealed storage cabinet. Kiril helped Drak carry the drinks and the maps to a low oblong dark wood table before settling into a cushiony chair nearby.

"A man gets thirsty cleaning fish," Drak said. Kiril declined to mention that Drak hadn't actually cleaned any fish.

"I can certainly agree with that," Kiril said, feigning familiarity with brewed refreshments. He took a quick gulp from the tumbler and swallowed. *Crystal shards,* Kiril swore silently, breaking into a sweat. His insides burned as the effects of the fiery liquid cruised through his body. "What did you want to show me?" he asked the tremble in his voice revealing his discomfort.

Drak did not answer. Instead, he unrolled an aged map of Lynnara, otherwise known as the Devastated Continent. Kiril helped lay it out, placing his drink on a corner to hold it down. Drak did likewise at his end. The map labeled thousands of towns and villages that no longer existed. Only the mountain ranges made the continent recognizable. Ruins of the Temple of Tranquility had been found, but little else. Even the outer shape of the continent had changed where coastal areas had eroded away up to the Coastal Mountains during the Dark Devastation. Off the coast of Lynnara lay Alaia Island, now known as Limitation Island since it marks the closest point to the continent in which energy from the elemental forces can be drawn. Only a small portion of island, shown here, still remained above water today. The map was old and had been copied from one that had survived the devastation.

Kiril's eyes roamed over the names of towns and villages; these names were all that remained of a civilization gone. He was nearly as familiar with the names as Drak. Although a wood carver by trade, Drak was a historian at heart. It was through Drak's teachings that Kiril's interest in history had been ignited.

"Why doesn't the High Council call the Devastated Continent Lynnara?" Kiril asked trying to imagine what it had been like to live in those times.

"I assume it is because the Lynnara that was, is no more and they feel they are being respectful toward the millions who died. If you ask me, and no one from the High Council ever will, Lynnara needs to be resurrected. At least give the continent back its name. To do so would be a sign of healing. Where exactly is your mission headed?"

"We will be mapping a route to the interior through the Crescent Mountains," Kiril explained and noted a sudden tension in Drak's face. "Rojaire knows the way," he added, reading Drak's expression as concern.

"Then what I have to show you is more important than I thought."

Drak unfolded the little bundle he had brought over with the map. To Kiril's surprise, the little bundle turned out to be another map, this one printed on a smoothly textured fabric yellowed with age.

"What is it?" Kiril asked staring at what appeared to be a map of a valley surrounded by mountains. It differed from the first one in that it had no place names, only crudely drawn landmarks stitched into the fabric.

"It's a treasure map. See all these little circles? They're caves. The map claims the existence of a great hidden valley, deep within the Crescent Mountains. An enormous fertile valley completely surrounded by mountains and riddled with caves rich in gemstones ...once highly prized, long ago."

"Who discovered the valley? Who drew the map? Was it your father?"

"No, my grandfather; he was a career adventurer, his chief interest, the Crescent Mountains. According to my father, my grandfather was adept at scaling cliffs and crawling through caves, but had very little telepathic ability, and would venture off for many seasons at a time. Every time my father felt certain that his father had vanished forever, he eventually returned yet again with tales of exploration and discovery. My father carried this treasure map with him when he fled Lynnara during the Dark Devastation."

"How can that be? This fabric looks old, but it can't be that old," Kiril said, reaching out to touch it.

"The cloth is made of crystal floss. And yes, it is really that old."

"And you believe this valley still exists?" Kiril asked, fascinated.

"Perhaps that is something you can find out." Drak took another sip from the tumbler his expression becoming quite sober. "I had planned on giving you this treasure map after you completed your first mission and became an Accepted One, but under the current circumstances I've decided it would be wise to give it to you now."

Kiril understood the treasured value the map held for Drak; he also understood the great hope and faith Drak had in him. Kiril tried to speak, to express his gratitude, but his throat choked with emotion.

"It has always been my hope that after becoming an Accepted One, you would one day explore Lynnara," Drak continued without waiting for Kiril to recover. "It seems you will be fulfilling that dream sooner than expected."

---

"Where is Kiril? He should be back by now. When you don't want him around, you can't get him out from under foot," Theon grumbled.

"He's not officially late till morning," Rojaire reminded him.

The High Council had decided on a chain of command for the mission and since Rojaire had been handed the list, he was obviously Command One. It had surprised Rojaire to see his name at the top of the list. *Has my standing with the council come up that much, or is it because I know the way?*

"So, who's your second?" Theon asked casually as he and Rojaire made their way down the stone hallway; logically it should be Traevus.

"You are."

"What...?" It was Theon's turn to be surprised. "Has my past been forgiven, or is this just such a misfit bunch there's not much to choose from?"

"Perhaps a bit of both...."

Having been summoned by the Academy; Traevus, Tassyn, and Edty were already in the great east wing hall when Rojaire and Theon arrived. The men were seated at a large glowing map table which provided the only lighting in the open-aired room. A three-dimensional map of the Devastated Continent glowed on display. Through the archway portals to the adjoining balcony, daylight faded into evening. Mercifully, a light breeze brushed away the heat of the day. Theon chose a seat and sat down, but Rojaire remained standing.

After taking a deep breath, Rojaire cleared his throat. As first in command, it became his job to conduct the meeting. "Greetings...," he started feeling a bit awkward, but he forged on. "The High Council has assigned an order of command for the mission; I'll read off the list: First Command, Rojaire; Second Command, Theon; Third Command, Traevus; Fourth Command, Kiril. That's it," Rojaire said, showing them the list.

"What about us?" Edty asked softly, a bit uncomfortable in an academic environment.

"We are here to serve," Tassyn reminded his short-witted follower, "not to lead."

"Yes, of course," Edty said, his voice trembling, "but what if something happens to them?" His scrawny little body and thin face expressed earnest concern.

"If that happens, I will take care of us," Tassyn assured him.

Tassyn cleaned up well, as they would say on Earth, Theon noted. He had also grown more solemn in mood and expression. What rigors had the council put these two through? Theon couldn't help but wonder. With Stram's death, Rojaire's acceptance into society, and Tassyn and Edty "reformed," there was no longer a Band of Rogues …at least not that anyone knew of.

Rojaire noticed the room had grown quiet and, as leader of the mission, all eyes were turned toward him …waiting for him to speak he now realized. Again he cleared his throat.

"I wish to welcome all of you to the mission," Rojaire said, a little embarrassed by the formality. "I will do my best to keep everyone safe. Tomorrow we will teleport to Limitation Island. From there Captain Setas will ferry us across the strait to the Devastated Continent where we will disembark at what is now called Lavender Beach. My biggest concerns for us are shelter, food, water, and light," Rojaire said, getting right into it. "The cloaks you will be issued can serve as protection from the scorching summer sun if at some point we are unable to find shelter. The plan is to cover the stretch of our journey from Lavender Beach to the Crescent Mountains during the cooler parts of the day and at night, using stored energy for light. That won't be a problem as long as we can recharge using energy from the sun, but when we are passing through the mountain range, there will be long periods of time when sunlight won't be available."

"Couldn't we carry extra power crystals?" Traevus asked.

"Yes, but we will also need to carry a large supply of water and food when we enter the mountains, enough to last for many rotations. Therefore, personal items are to be kept to a minimum. Finding something to eat won't be a problem at first; the hot summer temperatures and nearly daily rains in the coastal area produce a lush abundance of food at this time of season. Much of the passage through the mountains is above ground, weaving around peaks; but there are also long sections of the passage that bore through the mountain. It's a maze with plenty of dead-end detours. Also Councilor Anthya has informed me," Rojaire added remembering to include her title, "that dehydrated food bars and nutrition tablets are being prepared for us as emergency rations, should we need them."

"Have you decided on what route we will take?" Theon asked.

"I have," Rojaire said, picking up a short thin pointer. Using the pointer, he aimed a narrow blue light at Lavender Beach where the Zayla River spilled into the Golden Sea. "We will disembark from Captain Setas' ferry here and follow the Zayla River inland until we reach the confluence of a second river with the Zayla coming out of the north." Rojaire moved the pointer along the newly named Zayla River, marking the location of the confluence of the two rivers about a third of the distance inland to the Crescent Mountains.

"From here we will take a more northern route than previous expeditions, following the second river north, crossing the hills where the river flows through a deep narrow gorge into another large valley, and then head east toward the mountains." With the pointer, Rojaire indicated approximately where the eastward turn would take place. "The opening to the mountain passage is located near the head of yet another stream that follows the contour of the base of the mountain range for a ways before flowing west. From here we will weave and tunnel our way through the mountains to the other side," Rojaire concluded.

The projected map depicted the Crescent Mountains as an impregnable crescent-shaped fortress of mountain peaks. What lay beyond the outer peaked sentinels remained a mystery.

"And you have been all the way through the passage before?" Traevus asked Tassyn and Edty with genuine enthusiasm.

"We have," Tassyn said, "it's not a place you want to get lost in."

---

Kiril arrived from Galeza in the Academy gardens, wishing his head wasn't so cloudy; it had been a long night of celebration. *I should have returned before now.* Rubbing his head, he searched mentally for Theon's signature and found him with Rojaire and Councilor Anthya in the Academy kitchens where several food technicians were at work preparing the nutritional food bars for their trip.

With his head throbbing, Kiril stood back, watching and listening, but not wanting to interrupt. At least his concern over having been left behind could be eliminated.

"They are almost finished here," Anthya informed Rojaire and Theon. "Your packs, protective clothing, harvest bags, water containers, lanterns, and supply of charged crystals are ready; you can pick them up at the supply room. "Is there anything else you can think of that you may need?"

"Do you have a star stone?" Theon asked.

"I'm afraid not," Anthya said. "What happened to the one you had?"

"I gave it back to Rahlys."

Anthya smiled her approval. "You have just confirmed my faith in you. Perhaps you will find another star stone." A wistful expression crossed her face. "I would like to see more of the Devastated Continent myself someday," she confessed. Zayla's death on the mission to find the lost expedition had been hard on Anthya, it had been hard on all of them, but Zayla had been Anthya's closest friend and mentor.

"I wish you a safe journey," Anthya said after a moment of silent respect and teleported away.

"There you are," Theon said, scrutinizing Kiril after the councilor left. "Where have you been?"

"You told me to say goodbye…," Kiril stammered.

"Welcome back," Rojaire said, giving him an understanding wink. "I hope you had a successful visit. Now it is time to get to work." A food technician brought over the last of the wrapped food bars and tablets adding them to the pile.

"We made them as tasty as we could," the tech said almost apologetically. "Here's a sack to carry them in."

"Thank you, we appreciate it," Rojaire reassured him. "Kiril, I want you to gather the others and see to it that they are supplied and ready. Take this with you," he added, indicating the sack of food.

"Yes sir." Kiril glanced at Theon as though reluctant to leave his side.

"Rojaire is Command One," Theon explained. Kiril turned back toward Rojaire.

"What about *your* packs, sir?"

"Theon and I will tend to our own."

"Yes sir." Grabbing the food sack, Kiril hurried from the kitchens.

"By Seaa's light, Rojaire, if you keep that boy busy for me …why, I'll share my recipe for zan fruit wine with you."

"I'll do my best, Theon. Come, we have a meeting with Sulyan."

"You mean Sulyan, the mad inventor?"

"He wants to show us some devices he thinks could prove helpful where elemental energy can't be drawn."

Society saw very little of Sulyan who lived mostly in the exciting realms of his own mind. Inventor Sulyan designed devices for people who had limited ability to draw energy from the elemental forces, a category he himself fell into. That did not mean that Sulyan lacked talent, for he possessed an abundance of creative imagination. Unfortunately, not all of his inventions were successful, or even useful, and more than once the roof of the inventor's abode had to be replaced and the inventor healed from an experiment gone bad.

Theon followed Rojaire from the kitchens located at the back of the Academy, down a stone pathway that led into the forest of scattered trees and tall, dense underbrush. The pathway soon led them to an isolated stone and mortar structure choked in flowering vines.

"Inventor Sulyan," Rojaire called softly, seeking out his signature. Eventually they heard the soft shuffling of approaching footfalls inside.

"Come in, come in," Sulyan repeated upon opening the heavy wooden door as far as it would go. A paving stone that had worked its way out of its setting over time stopped the door from opening wider.

"I've got to fix that some season," Sulyan mumbled under his breath.

Rojaire and Theon wormed their way in around the partially opened door into what looked more like a tinker's workshop than a home. Tables, benches and shelves filled with all sorts of strange looking gadgets flashed, beeped, hummed, and steamed around the room from the level of the stone floor to height of the timbered rafters, and in some cases protruding through the roof.

"Greetings, Inventor Sulyan, I'm Rojaire and this is Theon. We were sent by Councilor Anthya. Theon and I are leading a mission to the Devastated Continent…."

"You're the ones going to the Devastated Continent…" Sulyan muttered drifting away, his bright red hair sticking out in all directions as though charged with static electricity. Hunched over, Sulyan shuffled around the work room, mumbling frequently to himself, his attention seemingly challenged to stay focused on visitors with so many other thoughts in his head. "I could do that," Sulyan whispered, already forgetting they were there, finally resolving a long debated problem only he was aware of.

"Councilor Anthya said you had something for us," Rojaire said, informing Sulyan of the purpose for their visit.

"You are still here," Sulyan murmured, noticing them again. "Yes, oh yes," he said picking up a small crystal disk that glowed softly to his touch. "Here," he said handing the tiny disk to Rojaire.

"What is it?" Rojaire asked, examining it briefly, before handing it to Theon.

"It's a helodahlectodoleste…" Sulyan mumbled as he distractedly moved things about on a nearby worktable, lost again in his own thoughts. "Here it is…" Sulyan breathed softly upon finding a notepad and he began writing.

Holding the disk in his hand, Theon turned his body around, noticing that the lit area in the disk always pointed in the same direction no matter how he moved.

"It's a compass," Theon realized.

"That's probably a better name for it," Sulyan mumbled in agreement.

"This could be helpful mapping the passage through the mountains," Theon said, handing the crystal disk back to Rojaire.

"Simple, but effective," Rojaire agreed after further examination. Sulyan had already drifted away again, tinkering with a wooden box housing gears, wires, and crystals. "Was there anything else you wanted to show us?" Rojaire asked, drawing Sulyan's attention back to awareness of their presence.

"Oh, yes…something else…." Sulyan pondered a moment then started looking around. "Oh, here; this is it." Sulyan brought over a small plain wooden box that could fit inside a closed fist. "That's it," he said handing it to Rojaire. "Now, please, I have much to do," he said dismissing them.

Rojaire and Theon didn't resist. There didn't seem to be any reason for staying longer.

"Well, that was interesting," Theon muttered, once the door had been closed behind them. They started walking back toward the Academy. "What's in the box?" he asked.

Pausing along the path, Rojaire cautiously opened the lid of the box while holding it out away from them in case it contained an explosive surprise. The actual surprise though was a welcomed one. Inside the box was a stone, seemingly possessed of an inner light …a stone as smooth and round and golden as the star Seaa in the winter sky …a stone capable of reversing the effects of the Crystalline Landscape, making it possible for the bearer to draw elemental energy …to an extent… on the Devastated Continent. Sulyan had handed them a star stone!

## Chapter 5

# Earth

Another gorgeously warm, even hot, summery day in a long string of warm sunny days blossomed over the northern Susitna Valley. Ilene could hardly believe their good luck. The gift of sunshine greatly improved the chances of her mother actually enjoying the trip up the tracks.

As one would expect on such a beautiful weekend, the train loading platform buzzed with activity. Children romped around older couples, younger couples, and individuals holding dogs on leashes, chatting with acquaintances, and stacking boxes, bags, packs and ice chests along the platform's loading zone. Beyond the tiny train station, the more distant sound of children playing in the park, vehicles looking for parking spots, and small planes taking off and landing on the village airstrip rounded out the summer melody. A light breeze, warm to the touch, stirred the leaves of the trees, sending showers of fluffy white cottonwood seeds flying through the air, the fallout covering the ground after the breeze subsided resembling snow. It was too beautiful a day to stay indoors after the long Alaska winter.

"Isn't this exciting?" Ilene asked her mother with all the happiness she felt.

"What's so exciting about standing around waiting for a train?" Elaine asked from under a baseball cap that nearly concealed her face. Ilene had to work at not laughing every time she looked Elaine's way. It had taken a lot of convincing on Ilene's part to get her mother to agree to wear jeans and walking shoes instead of skirts and heels for the trip. While practical, the change was so drastic it struck Ilene as comical.

"Where are all these people going?" Elaine asked backing away from a large muzzled dog on a lease that kept nudging her for attention.

"Some of these people live in Anchorage or Wasilla and have cabins that they retreat to on weekends. Others live in the woods full time and are on their way home with supplies. And then there are a few tourists who take the train ride up to Hurricane Gulch and back to view the scenery," Ilene explained.

"Vince's friend should be in this crowd," Ilene said, surveying the options milling around.

"Do you know his name?" Elaine asked.

"Jack something, I think."

"Could it be Jack Faulkner?" Elaine asked, reading the name on an unguarded, strapped box next to a backpack in the line of baggage sitting next to theirs.

"Yes, that's it," Ilene recalled upon hearing it again. Finally the long-awaited train blew in the near distance, signaling its approach. A lone male figure strolled up to the unguarded boxes and pack from the direction of the park.

Short of stature with a bulbous nose, sagging jowls, and bulging waistline, Jack Faulkner wasn't much to look at, but Betsy would tell everyone who would listen how she had the world's greatest husband. He had tried hard never to prove her wrong …right up to her death less than a year ago. Jack had salmon fished in Bristol Bay for most of his life. Now doctors were telling him he should start taking it easy or he wouldn't be in this world much longer. Forced to turn over running the fishing boat to his son, he had decided the best thing to do was to leave for a while, giving his son Mike a chance to make decisions on his own.

"Hello …Jack, is it?" A female voice startled him out of his reverie. Two women, definitely mother and daughter Jack decided, were looking him over.

"Howdy, ladies," he said in response to their scrutiny. He lifted his cap in greeting, exposing a bald pate.

"Are you Vince and Maggie's guest for the weekend?" Ilene asked.

Jack eyed the two women with increased interest. "You know Vince and Maggie?"

"Yes, we're good friends. I'm Ilene and this is my mother, Elaine."

"Nice to meet you," he said, shaking their hands. "Are you also Vince and Maggie's guests for the weekend?"

"No, but we are certain to visit. We will be staying at a cabin not too far away," Ilene explained.

Further conversation became nearly impossible as the rumbling train approached the platform, clanging nosily in warning to all to stand back. Offering more in quaint character than speed and sleekness, the train pulled up to the platform, rousing a beehive of activity. A few passengers from Anchorage and Wasilla disembarked carrying daypacks. Baggage was unloaded and the disembarked passengers trickled away barely noticed. There were far more items waiting to be loaded than what came off the train. These supplies were for families living off the road system, beyond the little end-of-the-road town, who limited their trips to town ...and liked it that way.

Ilene handed up their backpacks, stuffed with more food than clothing, to the man in the baggage car and led her mother over to the steps to board the train. Jack, following her example, handed up his items giving the mile post destination before heading for the passenger door.

The long aisle running down the center of the passenger car revealed more empty seats than even the little crowd on the platform would be able to fill. "Anywhere you want to sit, Mother. The river and views of the mountain will be on this side," she said, indicating the left.

They weren't seated long before Jack Faulkner entered the passenger car and chose a seat across the way from them. The rest of the passengers settled in up and down the long car and soon the train eased away headed north, slowly picking up some speed. The quaint little end-of-the-road community immediately disappeared around the bend. Spring green boreal forest of birch and spruce, shimmering in the warm sunlight, glided by, occasionally opening up to vistas of Denali and the Alaska Range towering over the braided Susitna River. Ilene recognized the too friendly, too plump, too talkative conductor waddling down the aisle collecting and selling tickets.

"Miss Ilene," the jolly conductor said, recognizing her. "Any word about what happened to your friend Half Ear?" he asked in a more serious demeanor.

Ilene heard her mother catch her breath in reaction to the conductor's mention of Theon's local identity. Ilene didn't like the direction the conversation had taken and feared an embarrassing outburst from Elaine. She shook her head hoping that would be the end of it, but the conductor kept talking.

"For a while it was believed you may have disappeared with him," he chuckled, "but obviously you're not missing." Ilene smiled in response, not knowing what to say. To her relief, Elaine didn't say anything. "Are you going up to see Miss Rahlys?" the conductor asked.

"Yes, my mother and I are going up for the weekend; so I will need two tickets, please." She gave him the milepost number, and when the transaction was completed, the conductor turned to Jack seated across the aisle from them.

"One ticket, please," Jack said, giving him Vince and Maggie's milepost, less than a mile away, thus launching the conductor into another dialogue.

"So, you're a friend of Vince and Maggie, wonderful people! What a beautiful family they're raising! Well, then, you must know Miss Rahlys, too."

"No, I've never met her," Jack said.

"Well, have you met these fine ladies?" the conductor asked, stepping back and turning sideways to include Ilene and Elaine.

"We met while waiting for the train," Jack said, startled by the conductor's personal service. Jack paid for his ticket, and finally, the conductor moved on.

"He's a bit nosy, isn't he?" Jack said, indicating the conductor with a nod of his head.

"He must think he works for NSA, the way he interrogated us." Elaine grumbled releasing a tad of pent-up fury. Jack wanted to ask about the person the conductor had called Half Ear, but feared doing so would equate him with the nosy conductor.

"He does tend to keep tabs on people's comings and goings," Ilene said. "So, how did you and Vince meet?" Ilene asked intentionally changing the subject.

"We were in the Marines together, but I didn't make a career of it."

"So what do you do?" Ilene asked.

"I'm a commercial fisherman, Bristol Bay, at least I was; my son is running the boat this summer, and you?"

"Mother and I have a gift shop on Main Street."

"In the little town we just left?"

"Yes, I was born and raised here." Ilene glanced out the window as the train emerged from the forest following the eastern bank of the mighty Susitna River. Denali and the Alaska Range rose majestically before them in full panoramic view. The train slowed for the benefit of visiting passengers eager to take pictures of the spectacular sight.

"Beautiful..." Jack gasped not making the effort to move for a better viewing of it. Soon the train resumed speed as the rails led deeper into the woods.

"We're almost at our stop," Ilene informed Elaine shortly. As though on cue, the conductor appeared again.

"I'll let you out back here," he said in passing. "Do you have anything in the baggage car?"

"Two packs," Ilene informed him. The train slowed down as Ilene and Elaine followed the conductor to the exit.

"I'll hand you down your backpacks," Jack offered taking up the rear.

"There's no one waiting for you," the conductor noted, as the train came to a stop.

"Are you sure Rahlys is expecting us?" Elaine asked Ilene, not liking the idea of getting off the train where there was nothing but woods.

"I'm sure."

They descended the steps the conductor put out for them and Elaine followed Ilene along the outside of the waiting train to the baggage car. Jack handed their backpacks down to Ilene one at a time.

"Thanks," she shouted up over the rumble of the train's engine. "We'll probably see you tonight. I think Vince and Maggie have planned a cookout."

"See you then," Jack shouted as the train pulled away.

Elaine watched with dismay as the tail end of the little train click-clacked away around a curve leaving only woods and the soft murmur of the river barely visible through the trees across the tracks. "Now what do we do?" she grumbled, not at all happy.

"Aaaarrrk…!"

"Ah…!" Elaine jumped, startled by Raven's unexpected, piercing cry as he made a low sweep overhead before climbing again, and then arching high into the sky. "Ah…!" Elaine exclaimed again as bird's eye view images filled her mind. To her amazement she could see from high above a wide sweep of the forested valley, the train following a curve of the river in the distance, and two people heading down the trail toward them. The overhead views of the surrounding forest came to an end as the largest raven she had ever seen circled around and landed in a nearby birch tree.

"Hi, Raven, good to see you again," Ilene greeted him.

Elaine stared in awe at her daughter not knowing what to make of it all. "You're talking to that bird like you expect it to answer you."

"Aaaarrrk…!"

"He did," she said. Before Elaine could object, Rahlys and Quaylyn stepped out from under the canopy of the forest.

"Hello, welcome!" Rahlys greeted as she hurried toward them. "I see the train was almost on time. Glad you could make it, Elaine," she said, trying to put her at ease. "Elaine, this is Quaylyn; Quaylyn, Elaine."

"Greetings, Elaine, chosen mother of Ilene; it is my pleasure to serve," Quaylyn beamed, bowing respectfully.

"Hello," Elaine responded curtly, scrutinizing him. *He's one of the extra-terrestrials. At least he has manners.* With a bit of effort, she managed a handshake and a smile which broadened contagiously as she looked into Quaylyn's friendly startling blue eyes.

"Here, let me carry your pack," Quaylyn offered, taking it from her.

"Thanks," she said, nodding her approval, grateful to be relieved of the burden. Elaine wasn't sure how far she could hike carrying a pack; she hadn't done anything like this in a long time …ages in fact. Ilene donned her own pack and the group started down the trail with Quaylyn in the lead, Elaine following her pack, and Rahlys and Ilene bringing up the rear.

The woods were invitingly beautiful; the trail unmistakable in the dappled sunlight. Violets and watermelon berry sprouts bloomed in the soft mulch along the trail's edge. "Did you have much trouble convincing Elaine to come?" Rahlys asked Ilene?"

"Not too much." Rahlys raised a questioning eyebrow. "Well, it took a little convincing," Ilene admitted, "but I think she is enjoying the trip so far; of course, she would never admit it."

Rahlys chuckled in response. "Well, we'll try our best to show her a good time. The weekend isn't over yet. Did you see Jack on the train?"

"He was on the train, seems to be nice enough; he looks a little sickly though."

When Quaylyn turned to check on the others, he noticed Elaine had paused, winded and facing an uphill climb, a short distance away. Rahlys and Ilene lagged even farther behind, doing more talking than walking. Quaylyn stopped and backtracked to Elaine. "Let me give you a hand," he said, lightly touching her elbow.

"Oh," she said smiling shyly, not sure how he could help short of carrying her. She didn't want to appear weak. With his hand on her arm, they continued on. Quaylyn slowed the pace and she noticed that somehow his touch made walking easier, requiring less exertion on her part. *Surely, that cannot be; I must be imagining it.*

By the time they crested the last hill the other two women had caught up. Rahlys' log home shone golden in the sunlight. "Nice place," Elaine commented, glancing around. The log building proved far more substantial than she had visualized. For some reason she had expected a tiny falling down hovel.

"The cabin we will be staying in is right through those trees," Ilene pointed out. "We can take our packs there, but we have groceries to empty out first."

"Oh, good," Rahlys said. "Thank you so much for the delivery. What do I owe you?"

"Nothing," Ilene assured her, "we'll help you eat it, too."

---

Waiting at the foot of his trail, Vince heard the train blow its whistle upon leaving Rahlys' stop and listened to its approach coming slowly around several river bends. When the train finally appeared around a corner, he spotted Jack standing in the door ready to disembark as soon as the train came to a stop. "Hi, there," he greeted Vince, handing him a couple of strapped cardboard boxes before descending the steps wearing a backpack.

"Good to see you," Vince said. "What do you have in here, bricks?"

"Mostly beer; I didn't want us to get thirsty."

"Have a good weekend," the conductor called out as the train pulled away.

"You certainly like living away from things," Jack said, scanning the vast wilderness that surrounded them. "This is beautiful. You're a lucky man to live in the peace and serenity of the woods."

"It's a rough life, but someone has to do," Vince said with a grin.

"I see you have wheels to get around on; you're not roughing it too hard."

"You'll be surprised to see how comfortably we live out here," Vince said strapping Jack's boxes to the luggage rack on the back of the four-wheel ATV. When he was done he reached for Jack's pack. "I can strap the pack down on top of the boxes," he said. Jack eagerly handed it over.

"How's your son doing out on the boat?" Vince asked, while working.

"I talked to him last night. He says the last opening was really good. I expect he will probably end up a highliner. I just hope his zeal doesn't get him into trouble."

"You trained him well. It's time to let him make his own mistakes."

"I know; that's why I'm here, to make it easier for me to let him make his own mistakes."

Vince laughed with understanding. "I hear you. Are you ready for a little ride? Maggie is probably wondering what's taking us so long."

"I'm ready when you are; riding sure beats walking."

The ride wasn't as smooth as Jack thought it would be, not like running a four-wheeler up and down the beach on the coast. The birch and spruce that dominated the growth grew much larger and taller than he had expected so far north, dwarfing the scrubby growth that strove to survive in protected valleys along stream beds on Alaska's west coast. The going was slow with the trail winding up and down hills and tree roots creating speed bumps all along the way. Jack found himself straining to ease the impact on his back, leaving him wondering if walking wouldn't have been easier after all. Fortunately, the distance wasn't great and soon they arrived in the yard. Maggie, looking radiant dressed in her best pair of jeans and favorite white blouse, stood waiting for them on the porch.

*She's even wearing the gold nugget necklace and earrings I gave her,* Vince noted when they came to a stop. He knew she wanted to make a good impression. *Maggie is stunning no matter how she dresses,* he smiled knowingly to himself. When their eyes met, he gave her an admiring wink.

"Maggie, this is an old buddy of mine, Jack Faulkner."

"It's so good to finally meet you," she said, coming down the steps to join them. "Vince has told me some fascinating stories."

"Yes, well, don't believe everything Vince tells you. Besides, I've mellowed out of late," Jack said, extending his hand. "It's certainly nice to meet you, too." Maggie took his hand and gave him a warm hug.

"You are one lucky man," Jack said, turning to Vince.

"That I am," Vince agreed, unhooking the pack and placing it on the porch before grabbing a box. "Where're the kids?" he asked Maggie.

"They're inside, planning a special surprise. Come on in." The men followed her up the steps, Vince carrying the box. The children certainly did have a surprise waiting.

Upon opening the cabin door wide for Vince, carrying in the box Jack Faulkner brought up with him on the train, no one was more surprised than Maggie. The scene before her made her heart stop. Barely managing to stifle a scream, Maggie gaped in horror at the sight of Rock and Crystal suspended upright by invisible forces, cackling with laughter as they strolled unnaturally back and forth across the room, their feet barely touching the floor.

Caught in the act, Leaf gently eased the twins down, the pre-toddlers still laughing, with Crystal's laughter turning to hiccups, as they fell over into a roll upon settling to the floor. Quickly Leaf and Melinda each grabbed an end of the brightly painted welcoming banner and stood guiltily at attention. All looked normal by the time Vince moved away from the door, no longer blocking Jack's view. Jack remained unaware of Maggie and Vince's internal turmoil as he followed his hosts into their wilderness home and was greeted by four charming children, gathered to greet him with the thoughtful welcoming banner they had painted.

"Surprise," Leaf shouted out for all of them, accented by Crystal's hiccups.

Vince already doubted they would make it through the weekend without something happening. He placed the box on the table and seeing that Leaf was about to drop his end of the banner, decided to take action.

"You're a lucky man," Jack told his friend for the third time. "What a beautiful family you have here!"

"Why don't we staple the banner to that log over the entrance to the kitchen," Vince suggested, relieving Leaf of his end just before he dashed off to inspect their visitor.

"I'm Leaf," the friendly little lad said, introducing himself to the stranger.

"Nice to meet you, Leaf," Jack responded with suitable drama. "Give me five," he said stooping down and holding up his hand so Leaf could reach to slap it with his own, which he did with surprising strength. Of course, when Jack tried to stand up again, he realized he didn't stoop like he used to, especially after that pounding ATV ride.

In response to Jack's sighs and slow rise, Leaf extended him an invisible helping hand. No one knew about it but Jack who had felt the force that helped lift him and relieve his pain. Had this small child really helped him straighten up; surely he must have imagined it. Leaf met Jack's gaze with ease, assessing him. Jack sensed there was something special about the little guy.

Vince, Maggie, and Melinda finished securing the banner over the archway into the kitchen and came to join them.

"And this must be your big sister," Jack said indicating Melinda. Vince had informed him their adopted daughter was mute.

"Yes, Melinda is the best big sister in the whole world," Leaf said with unquestionable love and loyalty.

Melinda smiled, holding up a hand to Jack for a high five of her own.

"It's nice to meet you, Melinda; and thank you for the wonderful artwork." Jack looked again with admiration at the beautifully rendered banner. Forest and mountains filled the background with a variety of Alaska wildlife peeking around the wording. "I think you were probably a main player…considering the ages of the rest of your team. I can see real talent here."

His understanding comment lit her face with an even warmer smile. Melinda decided she liked Jack Faulkner and sent him the faintest mental *thank you.*

*Did I hear her whisper "thank you?"* Jack looked toward Melinda puzzled. *I could have sworn I heard "thank you."*

"And these are the twins, Crystal and Rock," Maggie said, under control again. "Do you have anything in the box that needs tending to?"

"There are two half racks of beer in the other box still out on the bike," he said opening up the box Vince had set on the family room table.

"I'll set the beer in the spring box to get cold," Vince said stepping out to take care of it.

That left only presents to be dispersed.

"Well we're down to the good stuff, Leaf," Jack announced cheerfully to his new sidekick, confidentially. Leaf climbed up on a chair to peer inside the box. To his surprise, the box was filled with presents wrapped in Christmas wrapping paper …even though it was summer!

"Presents…!" Leaf cried out in delight. Not yet truly appreciative of the joy of presents, the twins crawled over toward the sofa where they could work on pulling themselves upright.

"Let's see, here is something for the lovely lady of the house," Jack said handing her a small carefully wrapped package.

"Thank you," Maggie said graciously accepting the gift. "How thoughtful of you," she added unwrapping the unexpected present. Inside the box, she found an ivory pendant carved into an eagle in flight that hung from a golden chain. "Oh, Mr. Faulkner…"

"It's Jack, and you're welcome."

"…it's beautiful," Maggie said as Melinda helped her put it on.

Not interested in necklaces, Leaf gazed with intense patience at the remaining presents, his blazing carrot orange hair outlining his delicately angelic little face. What had Jack brought for him, he wondered? He tried probing Jack's mind for a clue, but didn't turn up anything.

Jack messed around with the remaining gifts for a while; lifting them and shaking them, as though trying to figure out what was in them, when Vince walked back in through the door carrying in Jack's pack.

"This is for you," Jack said handing Vince a small gift wrapped box.

"Thank you," Vince said shaking the box before quickly opening it to find an ivory pocketknife with a walrus scrimshawed on it.

"Nice…" he said examining it carefully, "I can certainly use this." Dropping the pocketknife into his pocket, Vince reached into a small change dish they kept on a shelf and took out a penny. "…so it won't cut our friendship," Vince explained, tossing it to him.

There were only four presents left; one more little present and three bigger ones. Leaf knew this as a fact, because he could now count all the way to four and beyond. He was already three years old and on his next birthday he would be four. He watched as Jack lifted the last small package from the box and handed it to Melinda.

Melinda nodded her thanks and again Jack felt he could "hear" her say "thank you." Upon opening the present, she was surprised to find a gold nugget necklace. Her very own gold nugget! *Thank you so much. I love it.* The message was unmistakable.

"You're welcome," Jack said in response.

There was only one other person Jack knew of who could do that ...speak telepathically that is... and that was Kaylya, but she couldn't have any connection with Melinda. Or could she? Melinda was not one of the Bradleys' natural children.

"Where are those twins?" Jack asked, grabbing a gift in each hand and taking them over to the sofa. He sat down and Crystal immediately moved one hand from the sofa to his knee and gazed up at him with interest.

Excited, Leaf jumped down from the chair at the table and followed Jack into the living room area. After all, the twins might get something good and will need some help to unwrap their gifts.

"Come on up here," Jack said, placing the packages down on the sofa beside him and pulling the little girl with strawberry blonde hair and hazel green eyes into his lap. Rock inched over closer using the sofa for leverage, another redhead. With reddish brown hair and brown eyes flecked with green, Rock resembled Vince the most out of the three young children.

Crystal reached up to touch Jack's grizzled face. "I could use a shave," he agreed when she pulled her hand away. "Here we go; this is for you."

Taking advantage of Jack's immersion in the children, Maggie and Vince retreated with Melinda to the kitchen for a moment. Hidden from Jack's view by the wall extension between the two rooms, Maggie and Vince quietly confronted Melinda over the incidence that had just occurred.

"How could you just stand there, Melinda, and let Leaf physically manipulate the twins like that? You knew Jack was coming. What if he had seen the twins floating upright across the floor? They are living babies, not toys. Leaf could hurt them by dropping them or worse," she whispered in harsh reprimand.

Melinda was getting tired of being blamed for everything Leaf did. *Why do I have to stop Leaf from doing things all the time? Leaf is always doing things. Besides, the twins like it.*

"Well, I don't," she hissed.

"Now hold on, Maggie. We can't always hold Melinda responsible for Leaf's actions," Vince said, putting a hand on Maggie's shoulder to calm her, "but, Melinda, you did know we could enter the cabin at any time," Vince reasoned.

*I'm sorry,* Melinda apologized. They could hear Jack enjoying the company of the children in the other room. *But what is to stop Leaf from doing anything unusual right now?"*

Maggie gasped in horror at the thought and hurried out the kitchen to check on the state of affairs in the living room. She arrived to find Jack happily surrounded by a captive audience. They had unwrapped more of the generous gifts Jack brought, a set of large rubber building blocks that squeaked when squeezed and a spinning top on a stand. Jack and Leaf repeatedly built a tower with the blocks for Rock to knock down while Crystal sat enthralled by the motion and sound of the spinning top. Jack looked up at Maggie when she entered the room.

"Jack, can I get you anything to drink?" she asked, playing the hostess and trying to relax. Vince was right behind her.

"Are you ready for a beer?" he asked.

"Oh, no, it's too early yet; but I could use a cup of coffee. I got a late start before catching the train."

"I'll put on a fresh pot," Maggie said pouring the last of the water into the kettle. Melinda, wishing to be alone, took the opportunity to escape by heading out the door with the empty five gallon water container.

"Mommy, look what Jack brought for Crystal and Rock!" Leaf exclaimed touting the merits of each toy.

"You have been so generous," Maggie said graciously. "Thank you."

"Is there anything I can do to help?" Jack asked.

"Relax," Vince said, taking over as host while Maggie made coffee, "you can tell us stories about life on Alaska's west coast. Later you can help me with the barbecue."

"What are you grilling, Vince?" Jack asked.

"…a fresh king salmon, caught this morning." It had been a joint effort between Vince and Quaylyn; Vince knew where to go and Quaylyn could get them there, and back again, fast.

"There's another present in the box," Leaf reminded Jack.

"Oh, yes, there is," Jack said rising carefully from the sofa. Again, Leaf gave him a secret helping lift. Jack wasn't sure what to make of this, but decided it would be best not to say anything …for the moment. "The last present is for the whole family. Would you like to open it?" he asked Leaf.

"Yes!"

"In that case here you go. Open it, but remember you have to share it with everyone."

Leaf eagerly dropped to the floor to better facilitate the ripping off of wrapping paper, step one of opening presents. He speedily unveiled an unmarked cardboard box taped closed. Opening a taped box required resourcefulness. Before Leaf could come up with solutions of his own, Vince quickly brought out his new pocketknife putting it to use for the first time by slitting the box open. Leaf took over from there, opening the flaps and removing a bit of packing.

"Candy!" he exclaimed with joy over a treasure box full of chocolates in colorful individual wrappings.

"Whoa, there," Maggie intervened when Leaf grabbed a handful. "Everyone gets one piece."

Vince and Maggie held strict control over the consumption of what they called junk food. Living in the woods made that task easier for them, than it was for most parents. Candy was a rare treat in the Bradley household.

Then Jack picked up his pack. "You can put your pack in here. Leaf volunteered his room," Vince said leading him to Leaf's bedroom.

"Then where will Leaf sleep?" Jack asked, dropping his pack on the bed.

"He'll sleep on a pallet on the floor in Melinda's room."

Jack opened his pack and pulled out a large gift wrapped box. Vince shook his head grinning. "That must be for Leaf?"

"And this is for the ladies," he said, pulling out a bottle of wine. "That's quite a boy you have there, Vince; smart as a whip …and so aware. That one is really special I'm telling you."

"Thank you; we think he's pretty special, too." Vince hoped he wasn't verifying more than Jack should know. Had something happened after all?

---

Melinda took the water container down to the spring and angrily shoved it under the water pipe to fill. *I should take off walking toward town right now. Why is everything Leaf does my fault? We were just having a little fun; no one was hurt.* The container filled quickly with the summer spring flow. Melinda caped the container and stood it off to the side, then took off down the trail with tears in her eyes. This is foolish she told herself, wiping her eyes with the shoulder of her blouse. *I'm too big to cry. Instead of crying, I should be taking action.*

Melinda touched the little gold nugget dangling at her throat. *Would it pay for a ticket on a plane or a boat? What would I do for ID? What would happen if I were to suddenly appear in my home village after four long years?*

*What would it be like to return to the outside world where I am documented, "Missing; presumed dead?" How can I explain my survival during the intervening years without exposing Rahlys and all the others? I'm mute; perhaps I could also claim memory loss.*

The day, so inviting, made the surrounding woods look like a setting from a fairytale ...one with a happy ending. The leafy green forest glittered in warm sunshine under a crystal blue cloudless sky. Flowering high bush cranberry and wild roses lightly perfumed the air. Birds, mostly hidden in the trees, chirped out to one another ...a bee buzzed by on its way to another patch of blossoming undergrowth. Melinda felt the anger gradually sloughing off as she hiked; it was difficult to remain upset with the forest so alive.

The trail eventually broke out of the trees onto the open railroad corridor, the thin ribbon of railroad tracks that wove its way through the forested valley. The mighty Susitna River, a short distance away, murmured softly in her banks, whispering a tale of ages to those receptive to her story. Melinda crossed the tracks and headed for the river. She made her way down the steep bank, holding on to alder and cranberry bushes in case her feet slipped out from under her. With the river running high in its banks, there was little beach to walk on when she reached the level of the water. The destination she sought was not the river itself, but a garden shed sized boulder on its shore that jutted out into the river. To her disappointment, the heavy spring melt made the landmark boulder inaccessible with rushing water flowing all around it.

Then to her horror Leaf suddenly appeared upon the big rock, the glacier chilled water running deep far below him. Melinda's heart fluttered in dreadful fear that Leaf would fall to his death. With his little frail body numbed by cold; he would be unable to save himself even with magic.

*Leaf...! What are you doing here?*

"What are *you* doing here?" he asked.

This wasn't going well. Melinda took a deep breath.

*I'm thinking.*

"I'm thinking, too," Leaf responded, and sat down in a classic pose to think. It was a good thing she had taken a breath, because when Leaf moved to sit, her heart stopped in dread. It wasn't until he successfully completed the move, that she allowed herself to breathe again.

*Please, come and think with me down here.*

"It's better up here."

Then suddenly Melinda's perspective changed and she was standing on the giant boulder. She nearly lost her balance adjusting to the new setting.

Melinda let out a silent screech that only Leaf could "hear." Far below the frigid river rushed by. Gingerly, she lowered herself down next to Leaf and grabbed ahold of him. At least if he fell now, they would die together.

*Oh, Leaf, we are going to be in so much trouble if you don't take us home right away.* She hugged him to her, perhaps as much for her own safety as for his. *Please, Leaf...* she pleaded with him.

"I don't want you to leave."

So Leaf knew; she could not hide her thoughts from him.

*I'm not leaving.*

"Promise you will never leave."

*Now, Leaf, that's not reasonable. You will leave one day, too. I promise I won't leave until after my eighteenth birthday, when I will be an adult.*

"Okay." That seemed reasonable to Leaf; birthdays were always a long ways away.

Then to Melinda's powerful relief, she and Leaf were sitting on the pallet on the floor of her bedroom, where Leaf would sleep tonight. They were home safe ...and hopefully... not yet missed by Maggie and Vince.

---

Having put the younger children down for their nap, Maggie joined Vince and Jack sitting outside in the shade. "I wonder where Melinda went," Maggie said, finally expressing her concern out loud. "She's been gone a good while."

"She filled the water container and left it by the spring; I brought it up," Vince informed her. "It's a nice warm day; she probably went exploring." It was not unusual for Melinda to spend large blocks of time searching for rock samples and rare plant specimens.

"I know she is nearly a grown woman, but I worry about her hiking the woods alone. She could encounter a bear."

"Give her a few more minutes; if she isn't back soon, we will start looking for her."

"Well, then, I'm going to go and pull some rhubarb for a rhubarb crisp," Maggie decided to ease the worrying.

"Rhubarb...! My wife planted rhubarb around our place; it's the only thing that grows out there on the coast. Too bad the stuff isn't worth eating," Jack said.

"Oh, but you haven't tried Maggie's rhubarb crisp; it's like eating candy."

"Well in that case, can I help?" Jack asked, still skeptical.

"Sure, follow me."

"I'll chop some wood for the cook stove," Vince volunteered and Maggie led Jack to her rhubarb patch.

"Look at the size of these rhubarb plants; they're huge," Jack exclaimed when he saw them. They pulled out a half dozen stalks from each plant, breaking off the leaves and the tough bottom ends where the stalks had been attached to the root system, and threw the discard off to the side to compost. Soon they had a harvest of rhubarb stalks ready to be made into dessert.

Melinda walked out the house just as Maggie and Jack reached the door.

"There you are," Maggie said sounding relieved. "I didn't see you come in. How was your walk? Are you all right?"

Melinda smiled and nodded and Maggie put a reassuring arm around her before taking the rhubarb inside with Jack following. Melinda breathed a sigh of relief; she had made it through another incident with Leaf without Vince and Maggie knowing about it.

# Chapter 6

# Aaia

Captain Setas glided through her gardens, gaily lit with lanterns. Her slight withered form dressed in white moved wraith-like along the garden paths. She paused to bend an exquisitely sweet smelling blossom to her wrinkled face; the flowers always seemed most fragrant before sunrise. As an experienced horticulturist, she was certain that flower blossoms in general had become more fragrant over the intervening span of time since the Dark Devastation. It was as though the plants strove to improve their fragrance in an increasing effort to attract insects that no longer existed, but were once relied on to carry pollen for fertilization. Perhaps the flowers produced the extra fragrance to attract the humans they now depended on for survival, for only plants that didn't need help from insects, or had the advantage of helping human hands could thrive and multiple.

Today another group was scheduled to arrive from the Community of the High Council. Her ship was ready for the trip across the strait; before sunset she would ferry them to the mainland. Something mysterious had happened to the last expedition; they had returned home without her assistance. Setas reviewed the roster of names the Academy had sent from memory; it was an unusual blend of renegades and straight line followers. She was familiar with everyone in the group except for the student Kiril. Strange that the High Council had never questioned her on how Rojaire and the Band of

Rogues, included in the group arriving today, had reached the Devastated Continent in the past. Her services were reserved for the High Council and the Academy only. Traevus, a member of the lost expedition, was also on the list. But most importantly to Setas at least, Theon was one of the members of the group coming; she would see him once again. Why did that please her she wondered? Probably because Theon was the only one in the universe who could possibly understand her inner feelings at this stage of their life. Only the two of them were ancient enough to truly remember what their world had been like before.

The sky gradually lightened to pale gold, revealing the jungle covering the island, thanks to all her hard work, and laying a smooth golden sheen over the calm waters of the bay. It was going to be a beautiful day.

The hot summer sun arched high overhead by the time Rojaire and Theon arrived with their team on Limitation Island. Captain Setas usually received her passengers on board her ferryboat …she didn't like the High Council snooping around her island… but there were no councilors in this group. Today she made an exception, receiving them in her cultured gardens.

"Greetings, Captain Setas, Lady of the Ferry," Rojaire addressed her formally.

"Greetings, Rogue Leader, or should we pretend we've never met," Setas said saucily, her sunken diminutive figure staring him down. Intimidated, Rojaire struggled to stand his ground; he didn't want to show weakness by stepping back.

"It's good to see you again, Setas," he amended truthfully. Setas nodded her agreement. She knew Rojaire faced life boldly, but she could still sense the subtle aura of sadness that welled up from down deep since the loss of Kaylya.

"Apparently the High Council's estimation of your worth has changed," Setas said looking him over. Without waiting for a response from Rojaire, she turned toward Theon.

"So, you return, Earth Traveler." Shocked to see how much he had aged since she saw him last, only two seasons ago, Setas led him to the shaded pavilion where refreshments awaited them. "We'll sit," she said, taking on a gentler tone, "then you can introduce the others."

"You may remember, Traevus, from the lost expedition," Theon said once they were settled with cool drinks in their hands …might as well continue the introductions in their assigned pecking order. "He is the only member of that expedition we actually found, alive anyway."

"Yes, I received the Academy's report, welcome explorer. It is strange that you now travel with some of your former captors."

"Thank you for your gracious hospitality, my lady," Traevus said, bowing respectfully. "I can assure you that we are a team with no residual animosity between us."

"May that always prove to be true," Setas bespoke as though bestowing on them a protective spell.

Outside the pavilion Kiril gazed in amazement at the lush, tall, dense growth; vines, ferns, fruiting bushes, vegetables, and flowers of every color, shape, and size sparkling under a golden sky covered every available inch of ground and then some. Huge trees, some with spreading blue-green fronds and dark red ribbing, others with leafy crowns of pink and gold towered to the sky and covered the island to the very edge of the Golden Sea. As far as Kiril could tell, there were even plants growing on plants; he had never seen anything like it before.

"And the young snapper staring around all goo goo-eyed out there is Kiril; a bit of a nuisance, but he usually means well."

Upon hearing his name, Kiril came to attention and rushed over.

"Greetings, gracious lady," Kiril said bowing low. "Thank you for inviting us to Alaia Island; it is extraordinarily beautiful."

The shock of hearing her island called by name was too great for Setas to fully disguise. She stared open-mouthed for countable seconds before recovering sufficiently to respond.

"Who are you, new person, to boldly proclaim my island's name?"

"I am Kiril of Galeza, my chosen mother is Zaloka, a ceramist; my chosen father is Wessid, a provider. In the community that guided my upbringing lives Drak, a historian not recognized by the Academy." Theon signaled for Kiril to cease talking; he was getting into dangerous territory. Unfortunately, Kiril wasn't one for discretion. "I will be keeping a journal, recording the details of our mission to the Lynnaran continent."

Frantically Theon gave Kiril the cut throat signal to shut up. Although unfamiliar with the Earth based signal, the intensity of Theon's expression finally got across to him. This time, taking the hint, Kiril's vocal chords came to a halt.

All was quiet.

"Please forgive the boy, my lady. He's rash and undisciplined," Theon said, giving Kiril a *talk-to-you-later* look.

"I see," Setas said when no more was forthcoming. She gazed upon Kiril with intense interest. "May you use this knowledge you possess wisely."

"And as you have noted, we have Tassyn and Edty," Theon said, hopefully changing the subject.

"The rest of the rogues, minus one," Setas said looking them over. These were originally Rojaire's followers and later Traevus' prison guards.

"Your pardon, my lady," Tassyn said, speaking for both of them, "we are here to serve."

"Good, then I have a task for you; one of great importance. It will give you a chance to prove your dedication to serve."

"What is that, my lady?" Tassyn asked.

"I have a bag of seeds ...very special seeds," she added with intensity. "These seeds will grow into trees that will produce shade as well as food. It will be your task, the two of you, to see that all the seeds are planted along the way from the Golden Sea to the Crescent Mountains. I will give you specific instructions and the tools you will need."

"We're going to be gardening?" Edty piped up.

"Trees are an argument for preserving life that most humans will never equal," she said sternly, staring Edty down.

"We will succeed," Tassyn assured her quickly giving Edty a quieting stare.

"I will make sure the seeds are planted," Traevus offered as added insurance.

"See that you do."

"Come with me," Setas said turning to Theon. "We will go for the seeds. The rest of you are to enjoy the cool shade and refreshments while we are gone." No one dared to argue.

Setas led Theon away from the pavilion. They were quickly lost from sight as they followed a curving pathway through dense foliage.

"Seek heart, not soul," Theon said when the silence stretched.

"Are you playing games with me, Earth Traveler?"

"I'm guessing there is another reason, besides seeds, that you have pulled me away from the others. I've ruled out intimacy," Theon said, raising a questioning eyebrow.

"Something washed up on the beach in the last storm," Setas said not taking the bait. "I think you may be interested in seeing it."

"Oh...?"

Theon didn't see Setas' dwelling until they were standing at the door. It was impossible to determine the nature of the other walls; its surface was completely overgrown with plants. Following her inside, he was surprised to find real living space enclosed with highly polished amber wood walls. The room was comfortably furnished and artfully decorated in a floral theme that included carvings, fabrics, paintings, and sculptures.

Setas crossed the living space and Theon followed her through a living arch that led to a back room lined with tables, cabinets, and shelves filled with bits and pieces of pottery, glass, and rusted and tarnished metals. "You have your own museum," Theon commented upon seeing it all.

"I have collected every piece of our lost civilization that I have found throughout the ages during my stay on Alaia Island." Theon didn't miss her reference to the island's historical name. Just what kind of rebellion was Kiril stirring up? "It doesn't add up to much," she said indicating the piles of rubbish. "The land and sea are reluctant to relinquish relics of the past. At least that is how it's been in the past. Recently things have changed." To prove her point, Setas pulled out a large deep drawer revealing more treasures. There were several obviously old, but well preserved items ...a tarnished goblet with intricate etchings, a dented but serviceable platter made of an old but nearly indestructible metal alloy, and... Theon grabbed his chest; his heart momentarily stopped beating.

"It can't be...," Theon gasped, laboring to breathe. But every etched detail was exactly as he remembered it. *It can't be* he told himself. There in the bottom of the drawer looking as ordinary as could be lay Droclum's wand.

Setas lifted the metallic wand from the drawer and handed it to Theon. "I see you recognize it; I thought you might."

Even holding it in his hands didn't seem proof enough of its existence. The use of a wand had been more fashion than common practice; like fashionably carrying a cane when you didn't need one for walking. But Droclum's wand was like no other. Forged for a specific purpose, had the plan worked, this wand would have changed Earth's history.

"Where did you find this?" Theon asked obviously shaken.

Instead of answering his question verbally, Setas teleported them to the spot where the wand had been found. Suddenly they were standing on the high tide line of a narrow pale lavender beach pebbled with pink and blue-violet rocks. The beach was exposed to the open ocean, unprotected by a bay. Tall dense jungle hung over them leaning toward the gentle waves lapping the shore. "I found it here," she said pointing down at their feet.

Theon crumbled down to the sand, his legs buckling beneath him. Setas sat down beside him, but said nothing. Fortunately, they were shaded from the cruelly hot sun by the overhanging forest. After a few moment of contemplation, Theon began to speak.

"Droclum's wand...," he began. For thousands of years I have wondered what happened to it. I thought I still had it with me when I followed the Dark

Orb to Earth, but when I got there, the wand was missing. Somehow I lost it in the chaos that followed Mt. Vatre's eruption. I was to use the wand to locate the Dark Orb containing Droclum's essence. I never found it. Twelve thousand years of searching the planet for the Dark Orb and, without the help of the wand, I was unable to find it." Theon paused and Setas didn't push him. His breathing was easier now, she noted with some relief.

"It took me a while to realize, that the loss of the wand was a good thing," Theon admitted after a while.

"Your life would have been very different, not to mention Earth's cultural development, if you had managed to take the wand with you."

"…very different," Theon agreed, shuddering over what might have been.

*At what point in my life did I come to view the loss of Droclum's wand as fortunate? Was it early enough on to even begin to redeem myself? I spent most of those centuries looking for the Dark Orb to destroy it.* He tried to console his troubled mind, but Theon was resigned to the fact that he would never know inner peace; his crimes had been far too great.

"My longevity is coming to an end," he informed Setas quietly. His voice choked up causing him to pause for a while. They listened quietly to the soft whisperings of the surf. "It has been a long life …a long time to live with the guilt over my role in the nearly total destruction of my own world and the death of millions. As penance, I made it a point to do no harm to Earth and her people." Suddenly Theon was overwhelmed with grief. Setas placed a comforting hand on his shoulder.

Setas quietly cried with him, shedding tears for the loss of their world so long ago. Together they sat oblivious to the passage of time, the lengthening of shadows, the changing of the tide. Together they traveled back in time in their hearts and in their souls, reluctant to don again the cloak of the present.

"Have you shone the items you've found to the Academy or the High Council?"

"Of course not…. I don't communicate with those fools at the Academy any more than I have to." She spat disdainfully.

"So what are you going to do with it?" Theon flicked the wand he still held lightly; nothing happened.

"I'll put it back in the drawer; unless you want it."

"No, keep it in your archives; it's no use to me now; besides, it's dead." … *as is Droclum*, he added to himself.

The broiling summer sun arched toward the west by the time the group boarded Captain Setas' ferry. There were no seats on the empty wooden oval deck, only the control pedestal where Captain Setas stood before the long pointed bow. Powered by solar energy stored in crystal, the ferry basically operated like an airboat, sucking in water under the deck and spitting the water back out behind the stern. To Theon's relief, a rigid domed canopy had been mounted into the deck railing to provide shade and later shelter from the approaching rainstorm, if the dark orange cloudbank on the southern horizon was any indication.

"What did you and the captain talk about," Kiril asked brimming with curiosity once they were underway.

"We talked about the past," Theon said wistfully watching rainbows in the boat's spray. Then he remembered he wanted to have a discussion with the boy.

"And what was that all about, using the island's former name like that?" he asked turning to address Kiril. He didn't mention that Setas had spoken the name again in his presence. "The establishment doesn't take kindly to that sort of thing."

"I didn't do anything wrong," Kiril protested. "What harm is there in calling a place by its true name?"

"You would be wise to practice discretion if you want to get ahead."

"I believe Lynnara and Alaia Island should be called by their real names. Drak agrees with me; and I would wager, so does Captain Setas."

"What if, let's say Traevus, for instance, were to inform the High Council of your unorthodox views?"

"I don't care what the High Council thinks; I want to be like you and Rojaire. I want to stand up for what I believe in." Kiril's voice became louder and bolder as he passionately expressed his views. "I am a free thinker."

"You're not thinking at all; that's the problem," Theon roared over the rush of water gushing out from behind the stern of the ferry. "You're not considering the far-reaching consequences of your actions."

"What's going on here?" Rojaire asked drawn to the noise.

"Nothing, we were just talking," Kiril said and slipped away. Rojaire filled the space Kiril vacated at the railing.

"He wants to be like you and me," Theon explained.

"Well, that's not good; the boy needs a lot of talking to," Rojaire agreed. "So, where did you and the captain wander off to?"

"We went to the beach and talked about things that can't be changed." Rojaire looked at his second with concern. Theon looked tired ...the kind of weariness that no long rest, no matter how long, can cure… and their mission was just beginning.

"Are you alright?" he asked simply.

"I will be," Theon sighed.

At the start of the journey to find the lost expedition, Rojaire and Theon's positioning had been adversarial at best. But the two men were more philosophically alike than either cared to admit and over time the traded vocal jabs at each other had become increasingly more playful and admiring rather than disdainful. Now deep seated respect bonded them into valued friendship.

"Setas found Droclum's wand," Theon said after a while. Rojaire didn't fully understand the significance of the find, but he could see clearly that it had taken an emotional toll on Theon. "She has found a treasure trove of relics from before the Dark Devastation," he added. "She claims they are washing up on the beach."

"Where do you suppose these relics are coming from?" Rojaire asked with interest. "Where was the wand lost?"

"I don't know, somewhere in Lynnara." Theon shook his head. "Now he's got me saying it." Rojaire knew Theon was referring to Kiril.

"Did Councilor Anthya give you any feedback about Sorceress Rahlys' report that Caleeza had been to Earth?" Theon asked Rojaire after a while.

"She said the High Council was still discussing the significance of the report."

"Typical bureaucracy," Theon moaned.

"Do you believe the report?" Rojaire asked. "After all, Sorceress Rahlys didn't actually see Caleeza; she was on the Devastated Continent with us."

"I know the family that took Caleeza in; they did not lie," Theon confirmed.

"But the report said Caleeza claimed to be in mental touch with Sarus in the Crystalline Landscape and he was working to bring her back. Do you believe that too?" Rojaire asked.

"I believe Vince and Maggie reported the facts as they understood them," Theon said.

"How could Sarus have been in communication with Caleeza across the galaxy when we couldn't send a telepathed message to each other ten feet away?" Rojaire asked. "Even a star stone wouldn't give him that ability."

Rojaire and Theon had decided to keep the star stone Inventor Sulyan had given them a secret for now. The star stone would be a valuable asset in case of an emergency, but they did not want anyone fearing an unjust wielding of power.

"Maybe Sarus has found a way to safely tap the energy stored in the Crystalline Landscape," Theon suggested. "He's been there for a while now, assuming he's still alive."

Traevus, Tassyn, and Edty sat together center deck and studied the instructions Captain Setas had given them for planting the trees. Kiril, bored with the discussion on planting seeds, moved to the starboard side railing to watch the approaching rain. The breeze picked up, refreshingly cool, adding a chop to the water in the channel. Then suddenly rain came pounding down, drumming on the dome above them and splaying out on the starboard deck.

"There are flaps you can drop and tie down to keep out the rain," Captain Setas croaked, steadfastly anchored at her pedestal control panel near the bow.

Kiril went to work immediately dropping the flaps; Tassyn, Edty, and Traevus jumped up to help. Soon they had the flaps tied down on the starboard side of the boat, blocking out the rain and the view in that direction.

With little to do and a long boat ride yet to endure, most of the explorers curled up in their cloaks and went to sleep, despite the pounding of the rain and the humming and gushing of the boat and sea. Rojaire sat on the dry port side of the boat, his back propped up against the railing, to think.

His early years of exploration had been shared with Kaylya, the only woman he could ever love. They had been raised by nearby communities and had been inseparable long before attending the Academy. He and Kaylya were the first to discover the crystal landscape and Kaylya had been its first victim. Now Kaylya was gone and he blamed himself. He had lured Kaylya away from her community and the Academy, lured her away from the life course the High Council would have chosen for her, lured her off track from becoming an Accepted One in Aaian society. If Sarus really dwelled in the Crystalline Landscape and he was capable of recalling Caleeza from Earth, might he also be able to locate Kaylya, wherever she might be, and bring her back to Aaia.

He thought about the Crystalline Landscape and all the people who had vanished from there, tallying them up. If you counted Caleeza and Sarus as well as Selyzar and Caponya, a total of four members of the lost expedition vanished in the extensive, mysterious field of crystals. No one knows for sure what has become of them. Then there's Brakalar who intentionally exited the landscape, with the Rod of Destruction in his possession, through a crystal energy field Rahlys had discovered. Where did he vanish to? With the deadly weapon in tow, Brakalar would be a formidable threat to any world. And finally there was Kaylya ...his own sweet Kaylya. Six people in all; where were they now, he wondered?

---

*Caleeza….*

*Please, Sarus, find a way to bring me home,* Caleeza cried in her sleep.

*You are already home, Caleeza.*

With that, Caleeza jolted awake. She was not in the little cabin in the woods in the Susitna Valley, even though she was wearing the light blue nightgown Maggie had given her, but on her crystal floss bed beneath the surface of the Crystalline Landscape. *I'm still not home,* she told herself, disappointed.

"Sarus, why did you wake me?"

He answered her question with a question. "Do you wish you were still on Earth?"

"No, why do you ask?"

"You often dream about your experiences there. What is it about Earth that intrigues you so?"

Caleeza could block her thoughts from Sarus when awake, but there was nothing she could do to lock him out of her dreams while she slept. She gave his question some thought as she lay back against her pillows nestled on her crystal bed in a crystal cave; it was a lonely crystalline existence. Caleeza didn't bother to ask Sarus to project an image for her to talk to. His image was only hollow, empty companionship.

"There were a couple of things that impressed me," she began, speaking to the emptiness around her.

"Such as…?"

"Well, I found the family unit on Earth particularly interesting. A couple can choose, at their own discretion, to produce several new persons close together in time and raise them as siblings." On Aaia it was rare for a joint community effort to raise more than one new person at any given time. "But that wasn't true all over Earth since over-population had also become a problem. There was at least one country I read about, that didn't allow more than one reproduction per family unit because they already had so many millions of people."

"And does this family unit system work?" Sarus asked.

"It does if the mother and father are good at parenting. But what I really found interesting was everyone's ease with abundant personal freedom. People decided for themselves what they wanted to do with their lives."

"Is this good? It is my understanding Earth's population is in a state of chaos."

"Much of the printed material I read while I was there supports that supposition, but the people I encountered were peaceful enough in the limited region of the planet I visited. Strangers took me in and fed me when I was hungry. Why do you ask these questions, Sarus?"

"I wish to understand...," Sarus hesitated as though searching for the right words, "...why you are unhappy," he concluded.

Caleeza didn't answer becoming lost again in her own thoughts. Sarus' mental presence waned; whether it was to ponder this, or something else he deemed more pressing, she had no way of knowing. Caleeza did not rise and dress, but continued to lie on her crystal bed thinking through her situation. She sensed something had changed in her relationship with Sarus, something she had been picking up on for some time; she felt that he was distancing himself from her. Was her time in the Crystalline Landscape nearing an end? Sarus had promised to send her back to the Community of the High Council with the next expedition.

---

"I will check the beach every three rotations should you need me," Captain Setas croaked down to them from the bow of her ship. Rojaire, Theon, Traevus, Kiril, Tassyn, and Edty had already disembarked. A short distance away, the Zayla River flowed into the bay. The clouds had moved on and the sun, although low on the horizon, had begun to steam dry the landscape. Beyond the beach; pink, blue-green, orange, and gold foliage anchored in coarse lavender soil glistened brightly, freshly washed by the rain.

"Good luck!" Captain Setas shouted and gunned the boat in reverse, pulling the low thin pointed prow from its anchorage in the beach's lavender sands. "Plant my seeds!" she added as she turned the boat around. "Make sure you plant every one!"

The group stood quietly watching as Captain Setas steered the ferry toward the mouth of the bay and out to sea.

"Well, we have some daylight left; let's get moving," Rojaire said, ready for action.

"Shouldn't we plant some seeds?" Edty asked even before Captain Setas rounded the point.

"We will go a few paces inland away from the coast before starting the tree planting project," he said.

"You have to drop one of these little tablets in with each seed," Edty informed Rojaire taking the project to heart. "Captain Setas said the tablets will feed the little trees for a time to give them a good start. And we have to water the seeds in."

"We will follow the instructions," Rojaire reassured Edty gently.

"Lynnara, we have arrived!" Kiril cried out un-expectantly. Kiril could hardly believe he was finally here. Throughout his formative years he and Drak had fantasied going to Lynnara and exploring the continent. If only Drak could be here now! "Never again will you be called the Devastated Continent," he proclaimed over the quiet open land that stretched out before them. "From this moment on you will once again be called Lynnara."

"What are you, a rebel?" Theon roared. Theon knew from long association that landing on Lavender Beach was a dream come true for Kiril, but he shouldn't let it go to his head. "I can see our little talk did a lot of good."

"Kiril is right," Rojaire intervened.

"You too…?" Theon asked dumbfounded.

"As Command One of this mission, I declare we are exploring Lynnara. Let Kiril express that fact in his journal. Are there any objections?" No one objected, but there were several glances toward Traevus. Traevus didn't have a rogue history and had always been a loyal member of the Academy and a true follower of the dictates of the High Council. Traevus couldn't help but notice the attention he was receiving.

"Why is everyone looking at me?" Traevus asked clearing his throat.

"What about you?" Rojaire asked. "How do you feel about Lynnara?"

"Ah…, t…that's fine with me," Traevus stammered not really knowing what to say to reassure them.

"It really is," he added when the group's continued stares insinuated they were not totally convinced.

"Lynnara…!" Traevus roared for all to hear. "I greet you, Lynnara!" Traevus bowed low to the vast land and slowly the others turned away satisfied.

Theon just shook his head, not saying anything. It really didn't matter, he decided. The High Council and the Academy were a long ways away.

Rojaire donned his conical backpack and led his team up the broad valley that funneled away from the beach, following the little stream. A variety of low and shoulder height bushes, flowering plants, tufts of grasses, and clusters of trailing vines with thick pointed red and gold leaves bearing large green and orange striped fruit grew along the stream bed. Sparser foliage of blue, pinkish green, orange, and gold grew on the rolling lavender hillsides. Rojaire led the group a short distance away from the stream and up a gentle rise to an open meadow that overlooked the valley and came to a stop. From their vantage point, they could see a long ways across the uninhabited valley. Isolated copses of zaota trees with their long streaming leaves of blue-green and gold could be seen in the distance.

Rojaire gazed out over the terrain with new vision. In his heart, Lynnara was a new country, with new possibilities, free and independent from the shackles abroad. Lynnara was his country, although he wasn't claiming it for himself; it belonged to all who would stand up to the High Council and proclaim their freedom. Together they would embrace this land and give it new life. Rojaire dropped his pack to the ground.

"Let's plant some trees."

[illegible]

# Chapter 7

# Earth

Rahlys would have offered to teleport Ilene and her mother over to Vince and Maggie's, or at least take her closer to their place, if she thought it wouldn't freak her out to even offer. Theon and Ilene had revealed everything to Elaine over a year ago before they left for Aaia in search of the lost expedition on the Devastated Continent, but Elaine still had a hard time taking it all in. Rahlys didn't want to push her. Coming up here this weekend was an effort toward acceptance.

As it turned out, Elaine loved the hike. Quaylyn's attentiveness along the way contributed greatly to her enjoyment. He related all he had learned about the plants, birds, and insects they encountered along the way. When the trail climbed a hill, he graciously offered her a helping hand. There were moments when Elaine felt she was floating, with her feet barely touching the ground. When they came to places where the brush hung over the trail, he held it back for her to pass.

"Thank you," Elaine said after each kind service he rendered.

"It is my pleasure to serve." Quaylyn bowed to her gently, offering her his endearing dimpled smile. Elaine found herself becoming comfortably trusting of him despite his ET status.

Rahlys and Ilene hung back on the trail, letting Quaylyn work his magic.

"Your mother seems to be enjoying herself," Rahlys pointed out.

"How could she not with Quaylyn so attentive; and look at this day, will you? Mother might not have found the experience of coming up here so pleasant, even with Quaylyn's support, if it were cloudy and drizzling."

"Look at them…," Rahlys grinned as they watched Quaylyn assist Elaine up another rise.

"I won't be able to thank Quaylyn enough for this; I owe him huge," Ilene said. "How is traw practice going? I've missed quite a few sessions."

"It's been tough, especially when you aren't there. Quaylyn says he doesn't have a mission, but I'm not so sure."

"What makes you say that?"

"Well, the intensity of my training may be a clue."

Ilene pondered on this for a moment. "I think about the Devastated Continent and the expedition all the time," she said after a moment of quiet. "The continent was so beautiful, so vast …so empty, but I don't think the people of Aaia should call it devastated; at least not anymore."

"I remember how Theon kept tabs on you whenever you were near Rojaire," Rahlys added laughing.

According to Quaylyn, Theon and Rojaire were doing public service by teaching classes at the Academy. Theon covers the Devastated Continent's history before the Dark Devastation and Rojaire shares his extensive knowledge of the Devastated Continent today.

"I want to see him again."

"Rojaire or your father…?"

"Both …and I want to return to the Devastated Continent with them and build a cabin …or a cave, or something …and live happily ever after."

Rahlys could only smile. "What about your mother?"

"I'll have Quaylyn convince her to come with us," Elaine said, making them both laugh.

"Have you heard anything new from Anthya …about Father?"

"There has been no communication since Quaylyn's arrival."

"What did the High Council have to say about Vince and Maggie's claim that Caleeza, Command Two of the lost expedition, was here in Alaska while we were searching for her and the rest of them in the Crystalline Landscape?"

"There hasn't been any response."

By the time they arrived at Vince and Maggie's, the children were up from their naps, the rhubarb crisp was out the oven, and Vince and Jack had started on the beer.

"Jack, these are our neighbors Rahlys and Quaylyn," Vince said, stepping up to make the introductions. The men shook hands. "And I believe you met Elaine and her daughter Ilene on the train."

"Yes, it's nice to see you again. I hope you have been enjoying this day as much as I have."

"It hasn't been bad," Elaine agreed. Ilene was glad to hear her mother respond in the positive.

"We've set out chairs in the shade; it's been such a hot day," Maggie said, her face red from the sun. Leaf came running, circling around them in greeting.

"Well, since everyone's here, I guess it's time to start up the grill."

It wasn't long before a full-fledged party ensued. The salmon went on the grill, the cork in the wine bottle was popped, and conversation peppered with merry laughter drowned out the bird song in the surrounding woods. The crawling babies were confined to a play pen where they could be easily watched since everything they picked up went into their mouths. Leaf divided his time between entertaining the babies, visiting with the guests, and running wildly around the yard.

"I wish I would have brought Betsy here to visit," Jack said wishfully.

"So why didn't you?" Elaine asked sitting next to Jack.

"She passed away a year ago."

"Oh, I'm sorry."

"Vince invited us up here repeatedly," Jack said sadly. "I was always too busy and made excuses, postponing it. I thought we could always do it later, at another time. Now there is no longer another time."

Jack and Elaine sat quietly for a while. Elaine thought about all the times she had declined to make this trip up the tracks with Ilene, even though she knew how much it meant to her daughter. Suddenly Elaine was glad she had finally relented. If something happened to her or Elaine tomorrow, at least this wouldn't be a regret they would have to bear.

"So tell me, who was this fellow named Half Ear the conductor on the train said was missing?" Jack asked Elaine now that they were relaxed and had gotten a chance to know each other better.

"He's Ilene's father …and he's not missing. He just returned to his own world," Elaine said unaware that Jack wasn't fully informed of the true nature of the tiny community in the woods.

"Dinner's ready," Maggie and Vince announced gaily before Jack could recover and question Elaine further. Hungry from the outdoor exertion, Elaine was first to rise to the call of food.

---

Vacating the camp on the edge of the swamp before the owners returned, Brakalar sought a new hideout, an abode where he could dig in until he figured some things out. There were no mountains or caves in the surrounding terrain, and more water than land. Brakalar spent days wandering through cane fields, woods, and swamps, skirting communities to avoid human contact. He slept in sheds and ate out of gardens, needing to be alone with his thoughts.

He still had in his possession the sealed rune-covered chest containing the Rod of Destruction ... the rod that had killed Zayla. No, he corrected himself, momentarily overcome with grief; I wielded the rod ... I killed Zayla.

Brakalar stumbled, momentarily blinded by tears, down another headland between cane fields. Quickly regaining control he wiped his eyes before jumping across another muddy drainage ditch. On the other side, he entered more damp woods of cypress and palmetto palms. But then surprisingly he came to higher ground and cypress and palms gave way to willows and oaks. Suddenly as Brakalar weaved through the brush a hopeful possibility stood before him, a large weather-beaten wooden structure slowly being reclaimed by the encroaching woods.

Brakalar scanned the area for life and found only the ubiquitous small life forms that slithered and scurried away. The shelter didn't look like it had been occupied by humans for a long time. Still he approached cautiously, but it was obvious no one was around. The rotting steps and porch leading up to the front door appeared incapable of supporting his weight. To remedy the problem, he drew energy from the elementary forces that abounded in the elements around him and directed the energy to the rotting wood planks. The drawn energy strengthened the molecular bonds of the wood filling in the gaps, rendering the steps and porch safe for him to tread. The wooden front door leaned askew, nearly rusted off its hinges. When he tried to open the door wider, it came loose in his hands as the rotting wood and rusty metal gave way. He set the door off to the side and walked in.

Inside the structure the wooden flooring fared better where the roof was still intact. Four large rooms, each opening on to the next, followed in succession. The house was empty, void of any furnishings, with only broken glass, rusty bits of metal, animal droppings, and bits and pieces of natural materials brought in by the same creatures that left the animal droppings. The first three rooms were in better shape than the last one which was less substantial and appeared to have been added on as an afterthought. The inner two rooms shared a fireplace that opened into both rooms.

Brakalar strengthened the back steps and stepped out again into the bright sunshine. Close to the back of the house stood a large crumbling structure of brick and cement that reached to the roof's eave built to capture rainwater. On the other side of the house, amidst tall grass and much younger trees, lived the largest tree Brakalar had ever seen. With its massive trunk and long thick sprawling branches, the tree was as wide as it was tall. Its thick canopy of dark green leaves produced a wide umbrella of shade.

The old dilapidated house was just what Brakalar had been looking for. It was deserted, forgotten, and hidden. Of course someone had to know it was here, but he could make certain it wasn't rediscovered. Brakalar drew energy, putting up wards to warn of approaching unwanted visitors and invisible protective shields that reflected back the surrounding woods. Then finally, draining his energy reserves, Brakalar wove a powerful spell, protecting him from detection by the Oracle of Light.

*The day will come when Rahlys, Ilene, and possibly even Theon, return from the expedition. Let them search for me if they wish; they will never find me.*

---

"Good morning," Vince whispered in Maggie's ear, snuggling her awake.

"Umm...," Maggie moaned, not yet alert.

"Look, no babies," he pointed out, indicating the vacant space across the room." Mention of the babies did it; Maggie's eyes shot open.

"I should check on them," she said making a move to get out of bed.

"Wait, Maggie," Vince stopped her, "what's the hurry; the kids are fine."

"You don't know that," but she let him detain her longer.

"Have I told you lately how much I love you?"

"Hum...I could stand to hear it again." Maggie rolled into his arms. "Tell me, how much do you love me?"

"I love you more than all the sunshine produced by all the suns in the galaxy."

"Nice, is that all?" she asked, kissing him softly on his ear ...then his cheek...then his neck...."

"I love you more...," a baby's waking cry pierced the silent morning. Maggie made a move to answer the call, but Vince held her a little longer, "...more than all the cries of all the babies in the universe." The cry grew louder.

"Good try," Maggie said, breaking from his embrace. "I'll take a rain check though," she added, grabbing her robe as she headed for the door.

Vince laid his head back down, a smile adorning his face. *I am indeed a lucky man.* The baby stopped crying, and he could hear sounds of Maggie putting coffee on in the kitchen.

Yesterday afternoon, they put Jack Faulkner, Ilene, and her mother Elaine back on the train headed for town without any extraordinary events in between ...that they knew of. He and Maggie hadn't realized how much stress they had been under during Jack's visit until they watched the train pull away. That evening they moved the baby cribs into Melinda and Leaf's rooms.

"Someone's here to see you," Maggie sing-sang carrying Crystal in on one arm and depositing her on the bed. "She's freshly changed; I'll get us some coffee."

"Come here little girl," Vince said, pulling his little daughter up to sit on his chest. "How do you like your new room?"

Crystal sat bright eyed and morning fresh on her father's chest and cooed and babbled a series of sounds complete with hand expressions.

"I can see you are going to be a talker." Vince said, smoothing down the wreath of strawberry blond hair that encircled her earnest little face as she chattered on for her captive audience of one. Her little mannerisms as she babbled on were so cute, Vince couldn't help but chuckle.

"You don't say; is that a fact?" Vince said holding up his end of the conversation. "And is Crystal a pretty little girl?" he asked smiling at her. Crystal touched her disheveled strawberry blond hair and cooed.

*Crystal pretty....* she said telepathically!

---

Jack Faulkner parked his battered red pick-up truck at the end of the approach to the weather-beaten cannery dock built near the mouth of the Naknek River on Alaska's west coast. He leaned against a steady stiff breeze that buffeted him with grit and fish scales as he slowly walked the dock's length, the sound of the surf drowned out by the wind. An extreme low tide had drained all but the main channel of the river leaving only the far end of the dock reaching out over the edge of the water. As far as Jack could tell, the tide was still going out. To the right, far below the level of the dock, a raft of boats sat slightly askew, listing this way and that in an effort to tilt. Each boat helped hold up the next, as their keels settled in the muddy river bottom with insufficient water beneath their hulls to keep them afloat.

Jack spotted the *Betsy Mae* third boat out on the string from the ladder. Then he looked directly over the dock's edge at the long descent down a long narrow metal ladder that ended slightly above the boat deck below. In his day he could dash up and down that metal ladder without a thought to it. Now a sense of vertigo made him step back before the wind blew him over the edge. He was fairly certain his son Mike was down there, but how could he get his attention? He tried shouting out, but the wind drowned out his words.

Finally, someone stepped out of the wheelhouse of the boat next door. The young crewman recognized Jack and jumped over onto the deck of the *Betsy Mae* to inform Mike he was here. The briny fishy odor of the exposed muck below wafted up on the breeze.

Mike's head quickly popped out of the door to the cabin on deck. Seeing his father up on the dock, he signaled he was on his way up, and then darted back into the cabin to grab a jacket. Almost immediately, Mike reappeared with hat and jacket, made his way across boat decks, and scurried up the long ladder with the agility of muscled youth.

"Good to see you; how was your trip?" Mike asked. They took shelter from the wind against the leeward side of the fuel shed built on the dock. Looking at them, anyone would say Mike was a younger version of Jack; his stocky muscular build not yet overburdened with fat and his abundant dark brown hair not yet overburdened with gray.

"The trip was wonderful, very relaxing. You wouldn't believe how big some of the trees get where Vince lives, trees suitable for cabin building. How's the fishing going?"

"We did real well this last opening." Bristol Bay's salmon fishery was closely monitored by Alaska Fish and Game who determined when and how long fisherman could fish. "There's another opening in the morning so we will be going out tonight at high tide to anchor out in deeper water. We don't want to risk getting caught in a low tide during a fish opening."

"Is there anything you need?" Jack asked his son.

"No, but thanks for offering; everything is taken care of. We're just waiting for the tide to come back in so we can fuel up and move out; meanwhile we were coming up with a little shopping list for the store." Jack could sense he was not needed and there was really little reason for him to hang around.

"Have you seen Kaylya lately?" he asked.

"Yes, she's in town; I saw her this morning. She said she would be around for a few days."

"I'll locate her." Seagulls squawked around them, sailing on the wind, squabbling over delectable morsels exposed by the retreating tide. "Well, good luck tomorrow morning," Jack said preparing to depart. He couldn't think of anything else to say.

Father and son shook hands and Jack placed a hand on his son's shoulder. "I know you're a good fisherman; just be careful while you are proving it to the rest of the world."

"Thanks, Dad; I'll keep you updated on the radio now that I know you are back." A marine radio was mounted on the kitchen wall at home to communicate with the boat from shore.

Walking back to his truck Jack lifted up one corner of his jacket to shield his face from the gritty wind. He was almost there when a four-wheeler with two passengers sped by on the dusty trail that crossed the entry road to the cannery dock. He stopped just in time to prevent being run over, the added grit stirred up by the ATV increasing the buffeting power of the wind. When the gritty air cleared enough for him to see, he made it to his truck and got in, wrestling with the forces of nature to shut the door. Finally managing to do so, welcomed calm and quiet reigned in the enclosed cab. Just fighting the wind had been a workout. After a few moments to catch his breath and slow his heart rate, Jack started up the truck and drove a short distance toward town before turning onto a dusty gravel and dirt road through scrubby trees and brush going through the throes of short-lived rapid seasonal growth and bud development before going dormant again for the duration of another exceedingly long frigid windblown winter.

He pulled up to a small weathered wood-sided house, the tiny yard landscaped with rhubarb, and parked. He was home, but he felt no desire to go in; there would be no one to greet him. Slowly he got out of the truck, unlocked the front door, and walked in. Betsy's collection of travel memorabilia crowded the rooms that felt so empty without her. Would he ever get used to her being gone?

There was a message on the answering machine; it was probably for Mike, but he pushed the button to listen. It turned out to be for him and it was from Kaylya.

"Call me when you get back from your trip; I want to hear all about it," Kaylya's voice said.

Jack dialed Kaylya's cell phone number, posted on a small corkboard by the marine radio. While waiting for her to answer, he stared out the kitchen window at the heavy gray sky that hung over the windblown tundra a short distance away.

"Jack, welcome home," finally replaced the ringing. "How was your trip?" followed the inevitable question.

"The trip was good; I'm glad to be back," he added automatically, although he wasn't really sure that he was.

"Why don't you let me come over and cook dinner for you tonight so you can tell me all about it?" Kaylya suggested.

"Well, you don't expect me to turn down an offer like that, do you?"

"I'll see you in about an hour."

"That'll give me time to shower and unpack," maybe even put a load of laundry on, he added to himself. There was no need to bring up the news he wanted to share on the phone since she was coming over.

"See you then."

As Jack put his clothes to wash, he thought back to fourteen years ago. He and Betsy were returning from a party traveling on two snowmachines across a stretch of frozen snow-covered tundra. In the middle of their journey, far from any settlement, they came across a woman, without a coat, seemingly lost and confused, stumbling in the snow. They assumed she was inebriated …he and Betsy were a little tipsy themselves… but they were well aware of the danger of the woman freezing to death if they left her behind. Jack placed the coatless woman behind Betsy and they took the poor woman home with them.

The story that would eventually unfold …a story he now believed and for good reasons… would prove more far-reaching than the Bristol Bay area.

Kaylya came from a distant world across the galaxy. She had been transported to Earth by an energy field powerful enough to warp time and space …generated by a landscape of crystals. Of course these specific details had to wait for Kaylya to gain a sufficient grasp of the language, but Kaylya's off world origin was quickly established by her demonstrated ability to draw energy from the elemental forces.

Kaylya didn't drive up to Jack's house in a vehicle; she simply appeared suddenly standing in the living room, her long golden-brown hair undisturbed by wind, her smooth chestnut skin exposed in tank top and shorts, her golden eyes with only a hint of brown free of windblown grit. She looked about twenty-seven, but Jack knew that measured in Earth-years she was closer to three hundred years old …or so she claimed.

"I brought a pizza; did you really believe I was going to cook?" she asked, placing it on the table. "Come and get it while it's still hot; too expensive to let get cold." A freshly made pizza in Naknek can cost forty dollars.

"I'll get the cheese and napkins," Jack said, rising to the task.

"The trip seems to have done you some good; you're looking better."

"It was my first time to visit that part of the state," Jack said when they were settled eating. "The upper Susitna Valley is really beautiful." He described the train ride into the remote river valley and the abundance of trees that grew there. "We took a four-wheeler ride up to the cabin. That was a rough ride." Then he described in detail the log cabin Vince built, Maggie's garden, and their bush lifestyle. "Maggie gave me her recipe for rhubarb crisp; you wouldn't believe how good rhubarb can be." He got up, retrieved the recipe from his wallet, and handed it to her. Kaylya looked it over.

Maggie's Rhubarb Crisp

¾ cup uncooked rolled oats
1 cup brown sugar, firmly packed
½ cup melted butter or margarine
1 cup all-purpose flour
4-5 cups raw rhubarb, cut into ½ inch chunks
1 cup sugar
2 tablespoons cornstarch
1 cup water
1 teaspoon vanilla extract

Preheat oven to 350° F. Lightly grease a 9x9-inch baking pan; set aside. Mix together the rolled oats, brown sugar, melted butter and flour. Press three-fourths of this mixture into bottom of prepared pan. Cover with cut rhubarb. In saucepan, mix together sugar, cornstarch, water, and vanilla extract. Cook over medium heat, stirring constantly, until mixture is thick and clear. Pour over rhubarb. Crumble remaining oat-flour mixture over top of rhubarb. Bake 45 to 60 minutes, or until sauce is thick and bubbly and the crust is nicely browned.

"Sounds good, let me know when you make it," she said, placing the recipe on the table. "So now you want to be a woodsman?" Kaylya teased.

"If only I were younger ...and healthier," Jack moaned. "What I really want to tell you about has to do with Vince and Maggie's kids."

"What's wrong with their kids?"

"Nothing is *wrong* with them; quite the opposite. The oldest, Melinda, is a teenager, a girl they adopted. She's mute, but she spoke to me telepathically, just like you do." Kaylya's mouth fell ajar, but she quickly rationalized an explanation.

"You think Melinda is from my world? There are well documented cases of humans on Earth with sporadic telepathic capabilities."

"There's more."

"Really...can she teleport, too?"

"No, not that I know of, but their second child named Leaf, a little boy just three years old, can levitate objects." Kaylya's heart pumped with excitement.

"Are you serious? What did you see him levitate?"

"I suspected this small child was giving me a helping hand to stand up from a sitting position. After all, I know what it feels like; don't think for a moment that I don't know it when you give me a little power lift to get me going. But the real proof came when I spotted him alone in the back yard playing with a toy train I had taken as a gift. Thinking no one was watching, without even touching it, he sent the train flying through the air, making wide twirling loops like a colorful dragon.

Kaylya didn't know what to say; the implications were tremendous. "How old did you say this child is?" she asked finding the claims incredulous.

"Three ...maybe four...."

"That young...!"

"I know what I saw. Leaf is definitely their offspring; well, Maggie's for sure, and I'm fairly certain that Vince is Earth human."

"So you think Maggie is from my world? Didn't you say there were four children?"

"The younger two are twins, still babies. They seemed normal enough ...as far as that goes, so did Maggie."

"Like I said before, there are documented cases of people here on Earth with telepathic and telekinetic abilities." Kaylya didn't want to build up any false hopes. "Perhaps these are just especially talented children."

"Well, I would have to agree they are talented," Jack said, "but Earthlings with these abilities are rare. Since the only other person I've ever heard of with these talents is you; I strongly suspect there must be some level of connection." His tone had become heated in an effort to make his point. Because he couldn't confirm it, Jack refrained from telling her what Elaine said about Ilene's father.

Could he be right, Kaylya wondered; had Jack really come across a connection to her world?

"What do you propose I do?" Kaylya asked Jack seeking guidance. "I could go to the woods where Vince and Maggie live with their family and spy on them, and if what you say proves true, introduce myself," Kaylya offered as an option. "Or I could approach them directly and ask them if anyone from Aaia lives among them, or you can introduce me to them as your friend from another world."

"Yes, I see your point; let me think on it. We don't want to upset anyone. Maybe what we need is a plan that combines several of the elements you brought up."

"How do Maggie and Vince react to their children's abilities?"

"That's the strange part; they either don't know about their children's talents or they are just pretending not to know."

"That detail helps support your theory. If Maggie and Vince have connections with my world, they would probably work toward keeping it secret."

"I can see that would be wise. Are you staying in town tonight?" Jack asked, closing the box on the almost demolished pizza.

"Yes, I have a food shipment coming from Anchorage that I'm waiting for."

Kaylya found a purpose in life even far away from her home planet. Since languages come easy for her she learned Yup'ik Eskimo, Aleut, and Athabascan as well as English. She was also quick to grasp the principles of economics and capitalism which had been totally foreign to her before. She spent most of her time in the villages helping the elders while learning their dialects, customs, and crafts. In return she helped with the chores, gathered food, brought in supplies, and found markets for the carvings, baskets, and clothing products they produced, providing the villagers with income, necessities, comforts, and luxuries they would otherwise have been unable to afford.

"You can stay in Mike's room tonight; he'll be out on the boat," Jack informed her. "You might want to wash the sheets though," he added after some thought.

"Hmm…good idea; I'll go and strip the bed now and put them to wash."

"Do you want to move my clothes to the dryer?" Jack called out to her.

"Sure." Completing the chore, she returned to find Jack staring at a portrait of his dead wife that hung over the sofa.

"When are you going to find love, Kaylya?" Jack asked, turning to face her when she re-entered the room.

"I already found the love of my heart, Jack. I just need to find a way to return to him."

"It's been fourteen years. Do you really believe this Rojaire fellow is still waiting?"

"My people do not consider a mere fourteen Earth-years a very long time," she accentuated, "Rojaire will be waiting for me, and he will come to take me home as soon as he knows I am here." Jack could detect no hint of doubt in her statement.

Hours after Jack turned in for the night the arctic summer sun still hung low on the horizon. Kaylya lay awake, her mind too active with recalled memories to sleep. She fantasized returning to the Devastated Continent to live with Rojaire on their own terms, free from the dictates of the High Council. She visualized them building a dwelling and raising a family, sons and daughters that would embrace the empty continent and call it home.

# Chapter 8

# Aaia

Over several rotations Rojaire's mapping team slowly made their way deeper inland following the Zayla River until they reached a second stream that emptied into it from the north. Already a routine had been established ...and over a thousand seeds had been planted. A thousand trees, assuming they all sprouted and grew, amounted to little across such a vast continent, but the tree planting project had given the group unity and purpose beyond their assigned mission by the High Council. Even Traevus envisioned with enthusiasm thousands of little trees one day marking their passage. Planting trees definitely slowed their progress down, but all agreed they were in no hurry.

The terrain had changed some over the distance; the hills became steeper, the valleys narrower, and the foliage, though still abundant, offered less variety, with zan fruit and the fruit of the zaota tree that fell to the ground when ripe replacing the meaty orange-striped melons that could be cut up and cooked as a vegetable, or even roasted on a stick, as well as many of the other coastal fruit, nuts, and vegetables that they had been enjoying.

"We turn north here," Rojaire announced guiding his team. Following the secondary stream, he led them into the narrow valley.

"Are we going to be able to pass through here?" Theon asked skeptically after an extended hike, eyeing the rocky purple and rose cliffs that were closing in on them.

"We will have to traverse a couple of hills where the canyon narrows, but eventually we will reach a broad valley," Rojaire said taking him aside while the others planted a few more seeds. "We should reach it before dark." He could see that Theon needed to rest and led him to a place where they could sit in the shadow of the hill. "Here, take the star stone," Rojaire whispered, slipping him the stone hand to hand without exposing it. "Use it to help you up and down these hills."

True to his word, when the group finally crested the second ridge the men looked down upon a broad valley enclosed by distant ridges stretching to the horizon to the north. The unnamed stream they had been following cut through the valley sparkling like a golden ribbon as it reflected back the last rays of golden sunlight. But it wasn't the grand panoramic view that held their attention. For there in the valley set back from the stream stood a crude stone shelter with a brush roof…and a lone man sitting by a campfire.

"Who is that…?" Kiril gasped putting the question on everyone's tongue into words.

As though sensing their presence, the man by the fire looked up, and then cautiously rose to his feet upon seeing six human forms standing on the southwest ridge silhouetted in the light of the setting sun. Rojaire raised his hand in the accepted sign of peace. The man down in the valley responded by doing the same.

"He looks familiar," Traevus said after a while. "Why…I do believe it's Ollen!"

Traevus and Ollen had both been members of the lost expedition. According to Traevus' report to the High Council of the Crystal Table, Ollen had volunteered to escort Cremyn, whose mind had been affected by the dark forces encountered in the ruins of the Temple of Tranquility, to Lavender Beach. Once there, they were to wait for Captain Setas' next regularly scheduled trip to the beach to check for possible passengers. But Ollen and Cremyn never rendezvoused with the captain. Cremyn's marked grave was found by the last expedition headed by Councilor Brakalar. There were no clues indicating what had happened to Ollen …until now!

As the group moved down the hill, the man believed to be Ollen approached. Traevus nodded to Rojaire confirming the man's identity when they were closer. His charcoal black hair was longer and his darkly tanned face hairier, but there was no mistaking Ollen's loose-jointed gait.

"Greetings Traevus and friends," he said, speaking first when they came together.

"Greetings, Ollen," Rojaire responded, "and we are indeed friends."

"Well, that's good to hear," Ollen said jovially, not really showing any concern. "I was just about to cook a meal; it will be a simple matter to increase the portions if you will join me."

"It would be our pleasure," Theon accepted wholeheartedly, his stomach growling. The hike had been arduous for him even with the help of the star stone. Traevus made the introductions and Ollen led the group to his hearth.

"Here, wise one," Ollen said indicating Theon, "have a seat. I'm sorry I don't have more chairs to offer." The unusual chair Ollen offered Theon had been fashioned out of hacked zaota tree limbs bound together with vines. A mat woven from the tree's long slender leaves served as a cushion. The others found comfortable places to sit on the ground. Meanwhile, the sun had set behind the ridge casting the valley in shadow.

Ollen's fire had burned down so he added more branches from the stack he had stockpiled off to the side. This would give him time to enlarge the dish he had been preparing to accommodate his unexpected guests. Crude but functional purple clay ceramic bowls sat on a rough low table chipped from an outcrop of stone. Did Ollen have his own kiln, Kiril wondered?

"I've had to learn to improvise," Ollen said before darting into his stone shelter and returning with a harvesting bag filled with grain. "Life has gotten more comfortable over time."

Ollen lined a large ceramic dish with large pliant blue-green and pink leaves harvested from the tall leafy stalks that grew near marshy areas. On top of this he piled high a mixture of grains, herbs, and chopped up vegetables he had prepared before company arrived. Then he added a couple more handfuls of grain to the mixture and some more dried herbs from a small stoneware jar. "I've never made such a large amount before, but it should work the same," he chatted on as he chopped up more herbs and vegetables that were still readily at hand, stirring the mix with a hand-carved wooden spatula. The men, still stunned to have found another member of the lost expedition, watched fascinated as Ollen prepare their meal. There were so many questions they wanted to ask, but didn't know how to begin.

"We found Cremyn's grave marker," Traevus finally ventured. Silence ensued. "Can you tell us what happened?"

"What do you say, we get our feast cooking and then I will tell you my life story, what little there is to tell. I'm sure you fellows have a lot to share with me as well." Ollen added water and covered the nearly full bowl with more of the fruity smelling leaves. He then walked over to the fire and scratched out a bed of coals to place the dish on. Once set in place, he dragged more coals around it. "Now, fellows, we can have our little chat," he said taking a seat on the low stone table.

"How long have you been living here?" Rojaire asked amazed by the budding homestead.

"Oh… I've been here at least a couple of cycles through the seasons," Ollen admitted. About five Earth-years Theon figured in his head.

"A long time for a person to be alone," Edty said, as though fearful of it happening to him.

"Why didn't you return to the expedition or to Lavender Beach?" Traevus asked puzzled.

"After Cremyn died my heart was no longer into the expedition so there was no point in returning. I wanted to be alone, and I didn't want to leave the continent. Cremyn was my soul mate, the love of my heart," Ollen tried to explain. "When she became lost in the ruins of the temple, life became torture for me. When we found her, an empty shell without a mind, a part of me died. All I could think of upon leaving the expedition to take her home was finding her help. I pushed her hard the first leg of the journey and she compliantly followed along. When we stopped to rest, she went to sleep right away." A piece of wood popped loudly surrendering to heated pressure. Ollen paused in his story telling; they could hear their meal sizzling on the coals.

"She never woke up," Ollen said after a while. "Perhaps her death was merciful in the long run, but I was devastated. To me, my own life had also ended. I scratched a shallow grave right there in the hillside where we had slept under the stars." No one knew what to say. Rojaire felt once again the sharp pain of losing Kaylya; he had no problem understanding Ollen's desire to be alone.

"I wandered around aimlessly for a long time after that," Ollen said picking up the narrative again. "And then one day I stumbled on this valley; I've been here ever since. And doing quite well I might add until you folks came along," he said, wiping his eyes.

"So, Traevus, you must have made it to Mt. Vatre and back," Ollen said, becoming jovial again. "I haven't heard a tale of adventure in a long time; it's time you filled me in. What did I miss?" The men realized it was going to take some time to fill Ollen in on all that had happened.

"Things haven't worked out as you think," Traevus began. "I never made it to Mt. Vatre, nor has anyone else that I know of."

Traevus explained how he had been abducted in the interior by a band of rogues led by a madman in possession of a stone that made it possible for him to draw energy from the elemental forces, even on the Devastated Continent. "Stram had visions of ruling the continent and wanted me to help him capture the rest of my expedition and enslave them." Traevus did not point out that Tassyn and Edty had been part of that band.

"So what happened?" Ollen asked anyone who would pick up the tale, his curiosity whetted.

"Well, eventually the High Council sent out another expedition with Councilor Brakalar as Command One to look for you," Rojaire said taking up the storyline. "Theon and I were members of that expedition. Also with us were Councilor Zayla, Councilor Anthya, and Quaylyn. These were people Rojaire was certain Ollen would know.

"Such important people coming to look for us…!" Ollen exclaimed amazed.

"Sorceress Rahlys, Guardian of the Light, who by the way has defeated Droclum if you haven't heard, my daughter Ilene, and Raven, all from Earth, also joined the search for your lost expedition," Theon added. They could now smell the delicious aroma of the cooking food and stomachs began to growl.

"What…? Are you telling me that Droclum has been destroyed?" Ollen asked astounded. Theon, the only one among them who had actually been there when Rahlys battled Droclum related the story to a spellbound audience.

"Quaylyn is the son of the legendary Sorceress Anthya and Droclum? How can that be?" Ollen questioned when Theon got to that part of the story.

So then Theon explained how baby Quaylyn had been stolen by Droclum from his mother so very long ago and encapsulated in suspended stasis in the Sooty Caves. It was now common knowledge that baby Quaylyn had been found by Brakalar and Zayla on the very first expedition to the continent after the Dark Devastation. He described how the tiny necklace Sorceress Anthya had forged with protective powers to protect her infant son had changed during the battle between Rahlys and Droclum into a lethal golden serpent, searing Droclum into ash.

"So where is Quaylyn now?"

"…On Earth, romancing the Guardian of the Oracle of Light."

Each bit of news seemed to Ollen more astounding than the last. How could he have missed so much? The smell of food was becoming overwhelming. "I do believe it is time we eat," Ollen announced finally, getting up to check on the baking dish. "Let's see how it came out."

Carefully he raked away the coals then lifted the leaves on top the dish with the wooden spatula to prevent escaping steam from burning his hand. "Oh, yeah," he said when he got a peek inside; "this looks good." Using woven bundles of folded leaves for hot pads, Ollen moved the hot dish to the stone table where he had been sitting. "Grab your food bowls and utensils; it's time to eat," he announced cheerfully.

Ollen stirred the fire and added wood to bring up the flames, providing more light to eat by, while everyone scrambled for their packs and dug out bowls and eating tools. They crowded around Ollen as he removed the top leaves from the baking dish releasing mouth-watering aromas that wafted up their nostrils. The mixed grains had expanded and fluffed out as they had absorbed the water, overfilling the baking dish; but after Ollen served everyone, the baking dish was empty. For a while there was only the sound of eating.

"So how did you escape from the Band of Rogues?" Ollen asked Traevus when their hunger had been abated.

"I was rescued in the Crystalline Landscape by the expedition looking for us," Traevus explained.

"Crystalline Landscape…?" Ollen asked puzzled. Of course Ollen wouldn't know about the vast landscape of crystals, ground zero of the Dark Devastation, Traevus realized. Except for Kiril, everyone else in the group had been to the Crystalline Landscape and they excitedly took turns at describing the incredible expanse of crystals, ending with Edty telling how Stram incinerated and blew apart.

"Who's Stram?" Ollen asked confused.

"He was the mad leader of the Band of Rogues we told you about," Theon explained. "We believe the crystal fields are capable of storing great amounts of energy and when Stram drew energy with the help of the star stone to hurl at Councilor Anthya, he burned himself up. But that's not all. We have also learned that the crystal fields can cause people to vanish."

"Is there much more to this tale?" Ollen asked, already overwhelmed with new information.

"Oh, lot's more," Traevus assured him.

"Then I propose an after dinner drink to soothe the mind. I have a special brew that is in need of sampling," Ollen explained seriously.

"Of course, we would be happy to help you out, there," Theon spoke for everyone. Ollen darted into the stone and sod structure a second time and brought out a stoneware jug. Cups retrieved from packs were quickly filled with a dark red fruity fermented drink.

Kiril sniffed the contents of his cup with uncertainty. His previous hangover still loomed vividly in his memory. Rojaire, Theon, Tassyn, and Edty didn't hesitate taking a satisfying gulp. Traevus sipped the liquor with caution.

"Well, in my expert opinion," Theon announced after smacking his lips, "this is brewed to perfection." The others voiced agreement.

"Now, to get back to your story," Ollen said, refilling their cups, "tell me, who has vanished in this crystal landscape you described?"

"The rest of our expedition, I'm afraid," said Traevus.

"All of them…?" Ollen asked shocked, trying to absorb the information; Sarus, Caleeza, Selyzar, and Caponya vanished in a land of crystals. With Cremyn in her grave that left only Traevus and himself as survivors.

"It is not for certain they are truly gone," Theon said. "While we were on the expedition to find you, Sorceress Rahlys' warriors back on Earth say Caleeza was with them for a time."

"What…? Are you saying these fields of crystals can teleport people across the galaxy?"

"It's a viable theory," Theon agreed.

"Has anyone else besides our expedition disappeared?" Ollen asked.

"Yes, Councilor Brakalar…" Theon cleared his throat, holding out his cup, "that's another long story…" Ollen quickly picked up on the hint and poured another round. After taking a generous gulp, Theon related the story of the rune-covered chest containing the Rod of Destruction that Rahlys found in the Sooty Cave. Without divulging the fact that Rojaire had found the key initially, he explained how Brakalar claimed possession of the chest because he held the key that would open it. "After knocking me on the head, Brakalar took control of the weapon and brandished it, either accidentally or intentionally releasing its deadly force …ending Councilor Zayla's longevity.

"Councilor Zayla is dead?" It was yet another incredible bit of information for Ollen to take in.

"The Zayla River that empties into the bay at Lavender Beach is named after her," Kiril informed him; then he had a great idea. "We should name the stream that flows through this valley the Cremyn River."

"Excellent idea," Rojaire agreed solemnly. "Record it as so, scribe."

"So what happened to Brakalar?" Ollen asked.

"Council Anthya removed him from duty and we took him with us, but eventually he escaped," Theon said, describing how they managed to locate one of the Crystalline Landscape portals by tossing pebbles before them. "Brakalar took advantage of the exit; to what end no one knows."

The friends became contemplatively quiet; weariness, good food, and what was amounting to excess drink were starting to take their toll. Unnoticed by the gathering during all the story telling and camaraderie, dark clouds crept in blanketing the stars. Dark became darker and suddenly the men were pelted with heavy rain. The dying fire sizzled angrily and smoked out.

"Gentlemen, indoors…!" Ollen ordered grabbing his grain bag and stoneware jars of dried herbs. The men gathered their packs and rushed into the dark shelter filling it to capacity. Once inside, they discovered that woven mats covered the floor. "Take off your boots and find a spot to lie down; it'll be tight, but there should be room for everyone."

A couple of crystal powered lamps were brought out as the rain continued to pound beyond the open shelter. Ollen's guests found their spots, grateful for the accommodations. Light from the lamps revealed small stone shelves, mortared into the walls, that held numerous stoneware jars. Larger stoneware vessels and woven baskets filled with stored food lined the walls along the floor. There was no furniture. Once everyone settled in, the lights were extinguished. With little left to say, one by one the men drifted off to sleep, weary and content, to the soft rhythm of the rain.

"Our seeds are getting watered," Edty said sleepily to the dark quiet.

---

When Ollen awoke the stars were out again and the night sweltered hot and muggy. Human snores reverberated off the stone walls of the shelter. For the first time in so long he was not alone. With the aide of starlight that poured in through the open entrance and through tiny windows created by the omission of strategic stones from the walls, he gingerly stepped across sleeping bodies and exited the shelter.

His thoughts weighed heavily on his mind, a little cloudy from the drink, but even more burdened by the vast amount of information his new friends had imparted. There had been so much news to digest all at once; he hadn't even asked the purpose of their current mission. How strangely stimulating it was to be among people again!

Ollen headed toward the stream to bathe in what was now the Cremyn River. *Do you hear that, love of my heart; there's a river named after you …* but by what authority? Could Rojaire and his team name a river and make it stick. On the bank of the Cremyn River he peeled off his tunic and trousers and immersed himself into the cool refreshing water. *What should I do?*

He asked himself as he swam, considering his options. Rojaire and his men would probably want to leave soon in order to cover another leg of their journey before another long scorching hot day came their way. *Am I ready to return to the world of the living?*

*Or should I return to the community of the High Council and present my report? How would they respond to my long self-removal from society? If all I've been told is true, the composition of the High Council has changed some. Does that mean it has become more tolerant ... or less?*

As he headed back toward the shelter another thought occurred to him. *Will I still want to be alone after my visitors leave? Perhaps I could join their mission, depending on what their objectives are?* When he returned to the shelter he found Rojaire standing in the doorway rubbing his eyes.

"Rojaire, just the man I wanted to talk to," Ollen greeted, digging under a pile of zaota branches for his protected stash of dry kindling. "We'll have tea shortly," he said, striking a fire in the burn circle.

"I have to say, Ollen, you have done an incredible job homesteading here," Rojaire said, joining him by the fire. "As an independent explorer I've survived countless seasons on this continent, but I never picked one place to settle."

"You are an independent explorer?" Ollen asked astonished. "Then what were you doing on an expedition with the High Council? Don't they frown on anything independent?"

"I guess you could say I've become compliant for a while. Things are always subject to change."

"So what is your mission now?"

"Long ago, after many dead ends and false turns, I found a passage through the Crescent Mountains to the Interior. Theon and I presented a proposal to the High Council to return to the continent to explore and map that passage."

"And you were given the authority to name rivers?" Ollen asked.

"No one said we couldn't name rivers," Rojaire said after some thought. After placing a container of water on the cooking stone, Ollen collected two rain-washed cups and entered the shelter to retrieve the dried herbs he used for tea.

"Excuse me for saying so," Ollen said upon returning, "but I'm a bit surprised that a man with such an independent streak would so willingly give up strategic information like a secret passage through the Crescent Mountains to the High Council," he said sharply. "Or have I misread you?"

"It was an excuse to return to Lynnara," Rojaire admitted. "Theon just wanted to return home to die."

## Chapter 9

# Earth

In the Susitna valley, the peak of summer faded into an early fall with the fireweed blossoms spent, their seed pods releasing streams of white fluff on the cooling breeze, and the first golden leaves appearing on the birch trees. The sun hesitated making an appearance with a dull gray dominating the sky. Safely perched high above in his tree, Raven watched mama black bear give her twin cubs their first fishing lesson. Down below the creek widened, running shallow, thus making the area a favored fishing spot for bears, with the salmon's bellies skimming the gravel creek bottom, their backs sticking up out of the water as they wriggled by. It was easy enough fishing even for a baby bear.

I will return later when the bears are gone, Raven decided. He knew the bears were picky eaters, devouring the tender flesh and leaving behind tasty morsels that clung to the discarded head and backbone. There would be plenty to eat with very little expenditure of effort when he got back. Spreading his wings, Raven took off following the creek then glided over the forest to the magically shielded warriors' training field that Quaylyn had built. Rahlys had invited Raven to attend a meeting of the Order of the Oracle and to watch a traw tournament. Soon Raven was circling over the gathering at the strange field of angles. Crude flattened log benches had been built for the spectators and placed along the sideline at center field.

"Aaaarrrk…!" Raven cawed announcing his arrival. He spotted Rahlys among the gathering; Quaylyn was right there by her side as usual. It seemed to Raven he never had time with Rahlys alone anymore. Vince and Maggie were there with the children. And Ilene had also come up for the weekend, this time without her mother. There was an air of festivity about the place; Raven even spotted a couple of picnic baskets. In anticipation, he landed in a nearby tree, a safe distance from the young Bradley children.

"Welcome everyone to our first traw tournament," Quaylyn announced taking upon himself the role of master of ceremonies. The gathering burst into enthusiastic applause. As though on cue, the thin layer of clouds overhead dissipated and a late summer ray of sunshine lit the battlefield. "Contestants, take your places!" To applause and cheers and another caw from Raven, Rahlys and Ilene waved to the crowd and approached their starting positions at the back points of their respective triangular playing fields, the two triangular courts joined at the center line along their longer side.

"In the east court," Quaylyn announced, enunciating slowly, loud and clear, his voice amplified over the cheers of the supportive spectators, "we have the Guardian of the Oracle of Light and defeater of Droclum, Sorceress Rahlys," Everyone cheered with Leaf, who was getting into all this rowdiness, cheering the loudest; the twins stared in amazement at everyone's unusual behavior, not quite sure what to make of it all.

"And in the west court we have defender of peace and healer of the weak, Warrior Ilene," Quaylyn announced. Then to the delight of the younger children, everyone made even more noise for Ilene.

"Ladies, raise your wands!" Quaylyn instructed when the cheering died down. Ilene and Rahlys lifted their arms, wand tips reaching for the sky. "When the wands connect; the game begins." The audience watched in silent anticipation.

With their wands held high, a thin streak of bright bluish-white light flashed briefly from wand tip to wand tip and Ilene and Rahlys flew into action. Both contestants immediately released several shots to engage her opponent, sending balls of light streaking like meteors in every direction as the contestants jumped, ran, climbed, rolled, flipped, and dove for incoming glow globes. The unexpected speed and intensity of the competition ignited the audience into an excited shouting frenzy.

"Go Ilene! Go Rahlys!" the spectators cheered, unable to favor one over the other. Quaylyn's unbiased shouts of encouragement joined the others. When Rahlys tripped and fell the audience moaned in sympathy as glow globes landed around her. When she quickly regained her feet, the spectators went wild. Then it was Ilene's turn to take a spill. With youth on her side, she was up in a flash, not missing a shot. The crowd roared, Raven cawed raucously, and Leaf jumped up and down in the excitement. All too soon the game was over without a clear winner. Glow globes that weren't captured in play continued to glow long enough to be counted before finally winking out. With the points tallied, the game ended in a tie with a score of 18 – 18.

The exuberant spectators rushed out onto the field to congratulate the players. "You two have come a long ways; that was amazing," Vince praised with intensity.

"You sure have improved since the last practice I watched," Maggie agreed.

"I want to play! I want to play!" Leaf shouted repeatedly, jumping around the huddle of fans. "Can I play ...please?" he asked hoping the added "please" would do the trick.

"Sure, I'll play a game with you," Quaylyn said.

"Yeah...!" Leaf cheered, yet to come to a standstill.

"This should be fun; do you want to do the announcements, Ilene?"

"Oh, by all means," Ilene agreed. "Good, luck," she said, handing Quaylyn her wand.

"Ladies and gentlemen, there will be a second match today," Ilene announced excitedly.

Renewed cheering broke out from the group.

"Contestants and spectators please take your places," Ilene continued, giving everyone time to reorganize. Rahlys led Leaf, now seriously calm, to center court position, deferring to his diminutive size. After some quick instructions on holding the wand and flicking it, she handed him her wand.

Quaylyn also took a center court position in the opposite court and Ilene proceeded with the formal announcements.

"In the east court we have second in command of our expedition to the Devastated Continent and renowned traw instructor, Warrior Quaylyn," Ilene announced mimicking Quaylyn's earlier performance. The group standing on the sideline whooped and cheered wholeheartedly. Maggie and Vince held Rock and Crystal to prevent them from being accidentally trampled on.

"And in the west court we have the apple of his mother's eye and the littlest warrior, Leaf Bradley." The applause and caws and cheers were as deafening as a crowd of seven in an open arena could manage.

"Gentlemen, raise your wands!"

Following instructions, Leaf held his wand high, but tilted. Rahlys reached over and straightened his hold, then stepped back farther.

"When the wands connect; the game begins!" Ilene shouted. Moments later, light shot out connecting the wand tips.

"Whoa!" Leaf cried out in amazement at the streak of light overhead.

Quaylyn flicked his wand sending Leaf a long gentle shot carefully launched to reach him, then waited for Leaf to intercept his first shot before sending another.

"Flick your wand, Leaf!" the spectators shouted. "Send Quaylyn a globe."

Leaf waved his wand erratically, releasing one, then another glow globe, both of which fell far short of Quaylyn's court.

"Here comes a ball of light, Leaf!" Maggie called out to him. "You have to catch it with your wand."

Leaf held out his wand and closed his eyes as the globe of light came directly for him causing everyone to laugh. His wand drew in the glow globe and the crowd cheered over a point scored.

"Move up some, Leaf," Vince advised, "You need to get closer. Hurry, send Quaylyn another shot. He's looking bored over there."

Taking his father's advice, Leaf climbed up on a rock outcrop, an obstacle built into the game toward the center of the court, and tried again to flick his wand to release a ball in the right direction, this time with more success. The glow globe made it across the center line …just barely… sending Quaylyn diving for it, which he did with gracefully theatrical success. Once again the crowd roared over a point scored.

Getting the hang of it, Leaf's next shot was even better. Laughing over Quaylyn's antics, he quickly fired off several more shots in opposing directions sending Quaylyn scrambling for them. Leaf cackled over the acrobatics he put Quaylyn through.

Quaylyn retaliated by sending over a couple of spread out shots of his own.

Leaf climbed down off the rocks to intercept one while the other globe landed on the ground to join the ones that hadn't cleared the center line. Again he sent a barrage of glow globes Quaylyn's way.

Refusing to let the littlest warrior get the best of him, Quaylyn managed to get in a few shots of his own as he collected the in-coming globes.

Leaf continued to receive advice from the cheering squad on the sideline; advice which he no longer heard as his concentration on the game intensified. With wand held high, Leaf ran around collecting a glowing ball here and there, but the majority of the globes landed on the court, glowing like little fallen moons all around him. Nevertheless, Leaf's skill level increased exponentially with every passing moment ...which steadily increased the crowd's cheering.

"Go, Leaf!" they all roared.

No one offered Quaylyn encouragement.

Leaf quickly emptied out his shots and it didn't take long for Quaylyn to collect them all. Now he had Leaf where he wanted him. Quaylyn slowly released the rest of his shots, making Leaf work for them, but with reasonable probability of success. As Leaf's speed and success rate increased, Quaylyn pushed him even harder. Leaf's natural talent stunned the spectators. The faster Quaylyn released his shots, the more rapidly it seemed Leaf's ability improved as fewer and fewer globes landed on the court. He watched stunned as Leaf captured the last two shots making a telekinetic jump from one to the other. The game ended with Quaylyn the clear victor, but the group rushed to Leaf to congratulate him.

The day will quickly come when Leaf will beat me at traw, Quaylyn realized.

*Oh, Leaf, you were wonderful!* Melinda praised him, easily planting the thought in his mind as the others crowded around him.

Maggie wasn't quite as jubilant, although she praised him highly. Her heart swelled with pride, but she worried about where Leaf's talents were going to lead him down the long road ahead? It was a future she couldn't envision ... and it terrified her.

By now throats were raw from all the cheering and shouting; thankfully there was an ice chest of cold sodas which were quickly passed around. Then picnic baskets were opened offering sandwiches, cookies, fruit, and chips.

Raven moved in closer, taking a position on the ground.

Vince and Maggie had an important correspondence to share now that they had quieted down to eat. "We received a letter from Jack Faulkner," Maggie said bringing up the topic. "The letter presents a bit of a mystery."

"What do you mean?" Rahlys asked opening a root beer. Vince pulled the letter from his back pocket.

"He asks if he may return for another visit ...and he wants to bring a friend with him ...a woman named Kaylya."

For some reason the name "Kaylya" triggered a spark in Rahlys' mind. She wasn't sure why; where had she heard that name before?

"What's wrong with that?" Ilene asked, also thinking the name sounded familiar.

"There's more," Vince said unfolding the letter. "He includes a strange paragraph about his friend that uses some interesting word choices. Shall I read it to you?"

"Yeah," they agreed, their curiosity roused. Vince located the paragraph and began to read.

"Kaylya is from far, far east, from a land of crystalline beauty and lasting longevity. I know she greatly misses the golden sky and seas of her homeland...."

Ilene gasped audibly. An emotion she didn't like gripped her heart. Was the Kaylya in Jack's letter, Rojaire's Kaylya? Had she really hoped Rojaire would one day be hers? Vince continued reading from the letter.

"...She hadn't planned on coming to Alaska fifteen years ago, but circumstances beyond her control brought her here and she has made the best of it. I've described the beauty of the Susitna River valley to her and she longs to see it, so I've promised to take her there. But since she is a talented traveler she will probably end up taking me. She has been watching over me since Betsy's passing. Her love for life gives me healing strength. Should I bring her by for a visit? I think you will find you have much in common."

"Wow..." Rahlys breathed in the silence that followed. "I have to say Jack did a clever job of informing us. If we had been unaware of the significance of his choice of words, they would have just passed right over us."

"I've never met Kaylya, but it does sound like she is from my world," Quaylyn said. "Imagine Rojaire's reaction if we have actually found the long lost love of his heart? How did Jack make the connection, I wonder?"

"Well, we may have a chance to ask him. Vince and I have been wondering about that also. How should we respond to the letter?" Maggie asked bringing everyone to task.

"We invite them to visit, of course; what else can we do?" Rahlys asked. "If Kaylya is really Rojaire's lost love, we want to help reunite them."

"Should we indicate, in any way, that we understand the clues...?" Maggie wanted to know, "...or pretend to know nothing?"

"We might as well be up front about it and agree we have much to talk about," Rahlys suggested.

"I agree with Rahlys, if Kaylya is from Aaia and she and Jack are on to us, there would be little point in pretending," Quaylyn said. "There is one thought that troubles me though; if Kaylya came to Earth through the Crystalline Landscape, and so did Caleeza, who else may be here from my world?"

"Brakalar...," Rahlys answered instantly, the dreadful possibility chilling her heart. "Brakalar could be here somewhere with the Rod of Destruction in his possession."

"It does seem to be a possibility," Quaylyn agreed.

When the picnic baskets were opened, Raven had flown down to the ground to be closer to the food. Over each passing minute he inched closer and closer to the group, not to contribute to the dialogue, but to keep a careful watch on things, especially the portion of a meat and cheese sandwich precariously held in ten-month old Rock's left hand. Rock's other hand rested on his mother's knee, a crutch to maintain balance as he stood beside her and ate. Raven stepped closer to the anticipated drop site, ready to snatch the bit of sandwich up as soon as it hit the ground.

"Ah..." Rock said to his mother, pointing at Raven with the hand that had been holding onto her knee.

"Yes, that's Raven; he wants your sandwich," Maggie told him in response.

"Look," Ilene whispered to the others, "Rock is standing by himself."

The group watched quietly excited as Rock took two small cautious tottering steps toward Raven and handed out his sandwich, dropping it on the ground. Accepting the offer, Raven obligingly scooped it up and flew off with it. Fresh salmon for dessert waited for him down by the creek.

---

Acquiring the things he needed to set up his domain certainly didn't pose a problem for Brakalar. His first acquisition was a bed, followed by a table and a chair. After finding a location that offered these items, he quietly made his choices, then after the store closed, he teleported the furnishings to his den. Soon he had all the basic comforts he needed. Aaian culture held honesty as the greatest of virtues, and the credence ran deep. Brakalar's conscience twanged disturbingly over each item he commandeered, but compared to the guilt over ending Zayla's longevity, the pangs of guilt over stealing were minimal.

It was time he turned his focus to opening the rune-covered chest.

The key to the chest remained on Aaia on the Devastated Continent. It had been absorbed by the stones of the temple ruins, the Temple of Tranquility, guarded by the swirling dark tattered forces that haunted the place. Since recovering the key was no longer an option he would have to figure out another means to open the chest. There had to be a way.

Brakalar set up shop in the add-on room at the back of the house, supplying it with an assortment of work benches and tools acquired in the same fashion as the furniture. Since he was capable of drawing energy from the elemental forces, he didn't need power company supplied electricity for light or for power tools. First, he tried using some of the crude hand tools he found at a hardware store. When that didn't work, he experimented with using some of the electrical energy power tools these people who could not draw energy from the elemental forces used. With the chest firmly secured in a vice, he applied a high speed circling cutting blade to the outside of the chest, the blade sending up sparks on contact. He held on continuing to apply pressure, but the teeth on the blade wore down without leaving a mark on the rune-covered chest. Nothing he had tried had even put a dent into it.

Brakalar had tried every means at his disposal to crack open the rune-covered chest containing the Rod of Destruction, but to no avail. His frustration became uncontrollable. He threw tools, kicked workbenches, stomped and cursed in vernacular he recently learned on Earth, as well as his own. Frustration mounted to the point of explosion. Furious over his failure, he drew in energy from the elemental forces, more energy than he had ever controlled before. Strengthened by his fury, he drew all the energy he could hold …and hurled it angrily at the mocking chest. The chest blasted through the wall of his workshop and impaled the trunk of the majestic old live oak tree several yards away.

*Perhaps it is time to give up on opening the chest, at least for now,* Brakalar considered after a cooling off period, *and turn my focus on what I am going to do with my life on Earth. I don't really need the rod to get ahead, not when these people have such limited mental ability. It is only if and when I am confronted by Sorceress Rahlys or a warrior sent by the High Council of the Crystal Table that I will need the rod for protection.*

*There is a world of possibilities here; I just need more information on the planet's history, sociology, economic structures, and politics to make some informed decisions about my future. Theon lived most of his longevity on this world. Surely, I can do as well with my talents and magical deceit.*

*It's time to do some research.*

# Chapter 10

# Aaia

With Ollen's enthusiastic consent, Rojaire's team planted hundreds of tree seeds in the Cremyn River valley in the region around his shelter. Then they packed up some of his dried grains and herbs to take with them, as Ollen had decided to accept Rojaire's invitation to join them on the journey through the Crescent Mountains.

Frequent showers and persistent cloudiness over the next rotation brought welcomed relief from the overbearing summer sun; making significant forward progress possible even during the day, but cloudy nights were exceptionally dark without the multitude of stars and the planet's small moon to light the way. Their trek through the broad flat river valley had been relatively easily going. They reached a small stream …what would be called a creek in Alaska; Theon noted …cutting a path through the rolling hills that hemmed it in, directing it in its course to join the Cremyn River. Following this smaller stream, flowing full from the recent rains, the group turned east toward the mountains with only a narrow rocky shore on which to walk.

"We'll take a break here," Rojaire announced after a reasonable stretch of ground covered. "This stream flows out of the Crescent Mountains close to where the mountain passage begins. With luck, we could reach the mountains in another rotation."

"It looks like the sky is clearing," Tassyn predicted. No sooner said, the orangey-gray cloud cover thinned, letting golden rays of sunshine shine through, glittering off the water of the unnamed creek.

"We still have quite a few seeds left to plant," Edty said in all seriousness. After each rest they had planted more of the bag of seeds they had been entrusted with; it was finally getting low. "Captain Setas said we were to plant them from Lavender Beach to the Crescent Mountains." It was obvious Edty wouldn't accept anything short of success.

Rojaire looked out over the surrounding hills dotted with zaota trees and low brush. Distant hills faded out in the rising haze of water vapor steaming up from the drying ground.

"There's lots of space here; get to planting."

Edty didn't have to be told twice. Despite the long hike they had just completed, he dashed off to unite seeds with soil and water in the hope of a miracle. Tassyn and Kiril went to help him.

"I'll gather some wood for a fire to make tea," Traevus volunteered in lieu of planting tree seeds.

"Do you really believe all those seeds are going to sprout and grow?" Ollen asked Theon and Rojaire.

"Have you seen Alaia Island?" Theon asked before Rojaire could answer, and then walked off after spotting a dry place to sit on a rock by the creek. His use of Limitation Island's original name was a direct result of Kiril's continued campaign to do so.

"Only from the deck of Captain Setas' ferry," Ollen said turning back toward Rojaire.

"Perhaps one day you will be granted the privilege of seeing it up close," Rojaire said. "It suffered the same devastation as the Main Land, but it is completely reforested."

"I guess I could give Traevus a hand with the wood," Ollen said.

After a quick glance Theon's way to assure he was all right, Rojaire decided to join Ollen. They walked off together to collect the dry dead under branches of a near-by zaota tree.

"There is another person I didn't tell you about that also disappeared in the Crystalline Landscape," Rojaire said after breaking off a stack of wood to carry to the spot where Theon still rested. "Her name is Kaylya and she is the love of my heart."

Ollen noticed that Rojaire spoke of her as though she was merely missing as he described the many seasons he and Kaylya explored the continent together, and the painful memory of the circumstances surrounding her disappearance.

"You really were a rogue," Ollen exclaimed.

"It depends on your philosophy; I thought of myself as free and independent," Rojaire explained. "Long after I lost Kaylya, I returned to the Main Land and made an effort to 'conform.' It didn't quite work out. Eventually, I managed to bribe Brakalar once again with artifacts for access to the Devastated Continent in order to continue my work."

"Lynnara…," Ollen corrected him in Kiril's absence.

"Yes, Lynnara…," Rojaire chuckled.

He told Ollen how he brought Stram, Tassyn, and Edty with him, but eventually left his companions to work on his own after a falling out with Stram.

"I didn't know it at the time, but Stram found a star stone somewhere and after I left he took control. They called themselves the Band of Rogues and later took Traevus captive. You've heard how the story ends from there."

"So Tassyn and Edty are rogues, too?"

"No, they have been reformed. They never were evil in the first place. It was Stram who was out of control."

"And why are you telling me all this?" Ollen asked as they prepared to head back with their bundles.

"Well, it is all common knowledge among the rest of us and you are one of us, so I thought you should know," Rojaire explained.

"What else haven't you told me?" Ollen asked playfully, following Rojaire back to camp. But Rojaire didn't answer.

---

"Crystal shards, I still can't understand why a man would choose to live so long totally removed from society," Kiril chattered on while hiking close to Theon who wished he would stop jabbering and take a breath. "And he seems so sane …as though he has been enlightened by his solitude! I thought prolong solitude was supposed to drive a man insane."

There were three heartbeats of silence.

"I can understand why you decided to continue on with us, Theon, instead of staying behind at the shelter like Ollen suggested," Kiril started up again, the brief silence shattered. "You would be alone forever!"

It had been a long hard journey for Theon and he wasn't quite sure if he had made the right decision after all to continue. He wouldn't have made it this far if Rojaire hadn't played his little game of deception when cliffs and a waterfall blocked further progress forcing the group to traverse several hills.

"Solitude isn't for everyone," Theon said, wishing for just that, "but to some of us it is golden." Kiril wasn't sure what he meant, but didn't push for an explanation. The lavender and rose colored pebbles of the stream bed crunched nosily underfoot, the flow of the stream greatly reduced as the dry weather continued.

"Theon and I will scout ahead," Rojaire announced after calling for a rest stop at the foot of another waterfall.

As soon as they were out of sight from the others, Rojaire took possession of the star stone and teleported them ahead. They made several jumps until the land finally dropped back down again to the level of the creek. Then leaving Theon on its bank in the shade of pinkberry bushes to rest, Rojaire turned back to rejoin the others.

Theon laid back in dappled sunlight and basked in peaceful quiet, the smooth feel of the star stone in his fingers. He drew just a little energy to soothe the worse of his aches and sighed in contentment. Without the star stone it would be a long time before Rojaire and the rest of the group arrived.

As he lay there warm and content Theon thought of dying.

*It would be so easy to close my eyes right now and be no more. It is time for me to explore a new plane of existence.*

He didn't know how when he fell asleep. He groggily awakened to the sound of Kiril's voice a hand span away.

"Are you all right, Theon?"

The grogginess was deep, it had been a long nap judging by the lengthening shadows, and hard to shake off.

"I'm still here," Theon answered realizing he hadn't yet left his current plane of existence.

Suddenly, the ground beneath them began to shake. "Earthquake," Theon shouted in English.

"You are a long ways from Earth, wise one," Kiril said worried, not understanding the meaning of what Theon had said.

The shaking almost subsided, when unexpectedly it built up again in intensity nearly knocking them to the ground.

"It's a strong one," someone shouted. The scattered brush swayed without wind and the little stream jiggled. After several long moments of uncertainty the shaking finally died off. Kiril pulled out his notebook to record the event.

"And we're planning on going underground?" Ollen questioned.

"We will have to wait and see if there are any following shakes before entering the mountains," Rojaire admitted. "Good that the seismic event occurred now rather than later." Soon they were up and moving again.

"You don't look too good," Kiril said at the end of another long hike, hanging behind the rest of the group with Theon.

"I just need a rest; we are almost there," he said pointing to the mountains.

Before nightfall they reached the Crescent Mountains looming tall as they drew near. The dwindling creek they had been following turned north and only a stretch of grassland separated them from the leading dark-purple sword blade shaped stone peaks that rose abruptly out of the grassland. Taller, darker serrated mountain peaks rose behind them forming an impregnable barrier to the interior. Dark reddish purple scars marked areas along the mountains' steep jagged slopes where recent slices of rock gave way, probably dislodged during the earlier ground shake.

"I wouldn't want to get caught in a ground shake like the one we just had in there," Traevus pointed out.

"We'll set up camp and gather food for the next leg of our journey allowing some time for any following seismic activity that may occur," Rojaire announced. "I want everyone well rested before we start out again."

They established camp at the edge of a stretch of prairie grass near a clump of zaota trees which could be used for shelter in case of rain and built a fire to prepare tea and a hot meal. Sitting together around a campfire heighted the spirit of camaraderie as darkness descended, as did their sense of achievement in finally reaching the Crescent Mountains. Ollen pulled out a flask from his pack that got everyone's attention. Cups still containing tea were quickly emptied and Ollen doled out the contents of the flask carefully; life was good.

"Well, my friends," Ollen said after filling their cups, "humor me for a bit and tell me; what do you think the High Council of the Crystal Table intends to do with the information you will provide them from this mapping expedition?" Ollen spoke like a man who had become used to his personal freedoms and envisioned any mapping of the territory as a possible threat. "After all, to find the entrance to the passage you say exists, all they will have to do is follow a trail of trees, assuming all those seeds you planted sprout and grow."

To everyone's genuine relief, except for maybe Edty, the last of the tree seeds had finally been planted.

Ollen's words taunted Rojaire, making him feel untrue to himself. *If the High Council is the enemy, then I am a traitor.* "I see your point," he said cautiously. "Just what are you suggesting?"

"Before I answer that, let me ask another question ...and this question is for every one of you. What do you plan on doing when you return to the

Community of the High Council? Most of you have been classified as rogues at some time. What about you, Tassyn; what are your plans for the future?"

Stunned by Ollen's sudden direct attention, Tassyn didn't know what to say.

"Do we have to go back?" Edty whispered to him in anticipation of his turn. "You said we could stay; I don't want to go back. Who would take care of my trees?"

"I reckon we won't be going back," Tassyn said finally. "At least, we would rather stay here," he amended, less he no longer sound reformed.

"Well, I definitely don't plan on returning to the Community of the High Council." Theon chuckled, taking the focus off of Tassyn and Edty. "The High Council can come looking for me if they want to. Rojaire and I suggested the mapping expedition to regain access to the continent, but probably in all honesty, only Rojaire, Kiril, and Traevus will return. What about you, Ollen? Now that you have been found, what are your plans? Or do you expect these fellows to keep your existence secret?"

"You didn't do me any favor by finding me," Ollen said. It was the first time Theon detected bitterness in his voice. "I have to admit that I'm enjoying being social again; I don't really want to go back to being alone, but on the other hand, returning to the main continent means sacrificing a lot of personal freedom."

"Which brings us back to my question," Rojaire said. "What are you suggesting?"

"I'm suggesting we declare Lynnara a free and independent country not subject to the dictates of the High Council," Ollen said earnestly.

"The High Council would laugh in our faces and then arrest us for treason," Traevus said the practical voice of reason. Ollen's suggestion was incredulous. "Plus there are several practical issues you haven't considered. For one, the High Council controls access to Lynnara through Captain Setas."

"It hasn't stopped me from gaining access to the continent before," Rojaire pointed out.

"We're not in a position to colonize and grow; in case you haven't noticed, we have no women," Traevus added. "Don't misunderstand me; I'm not opposed to colonization and freedom from the demands of the High Council. I'm just saying we aren't ready yet."

Kiril said nothing through all this; all his focus was on taking notes. This little meeting by a campfire could be history in the making. He didn't want to miss a word.

"I think a formal statement of independence would be a little premature at this time," Rojaire said. "And all I can say at this point about mapping the passage through the mountains is that in the end we control the results."

Traevus, noticing Kiril recording their words, jumped up in alarm and tore the paper out his hand crumpling it and tossing it into the fire. Kiril watched in horror as his precious notes quickly caught fire, flared up, and turned black.

"What did you do that for?" Kiril cried out in dismay.

"What do you think you're doing?" Traevus shouted back. "Have you lost your mind? You can't write this stuff in your journal to turn over to the High Council!"

"I wasn't writing it in the journal; I was recording it for us, the founding history of New Lynnara."

"Still, the High Council could find it," Traevus retorted.

Ollen laughed uproariously. "What ...are you afraid? Do you believe the High Council is going to come scooping down on you at any moment?" Theon was starting to wonder if Kiril's assessment of Ollen's sanity could be questioned after all.

"We have brought up some very serious and maybe even dangerous ideas here," Rojaire said rising to put more wood on the fire. "Let's say for the sake of discussion that we are all for a free and independent New Lynnara, if you will; how do we work together to make that happen?"

"Are you serious?" Tassyn asked. Tassyn speaking up indicated the degree of passion that had been stirred up.

"Stram thought he was going to take over the continent too," Edty added. "It didn't end so well for him."

"Stram was a fool," Rojaire said simply. "I'm talking about seven reasonable men founding a country and defending it. Right now we have legitimacy with the High Council which is a valuable asset; it gives us a chance to work for our cause undercover."

"You'll need colonists," Theon offered.

"Then we need to convince the Runes of the Crystal Table that the continent should be opened for colonization," Traevus said.

"And how are you going to do that?" Ollen asked. There's no shortage of space on the Main Land for people to live."

"There is a shortage of freedom," Rojaire said.

"There's an argument that will go over well with the noble ones," Tassyn mumbled.

"Building a colony is labor intensive, especially without the ability to draw energy," Theon reminded them. "My guess is you would find few, if any, who would be willing to make the necessary sacrifices for freedom in exchange for a hard life."

"Which makes this land even more special," Ollen said to that. "It's not for everyone, but despite the hardships, it has a way of growing on you."

"There's a need for healing," Kiril said. It was his first contribution since the destruction of his notes. "Drak said it's time for people to get over the Dark Devastation. A new Lynnara, opened to settlement, would be an important first step toward that healing."

"The need for healing idea may go over better than the shortage of freedom stance," Ollen said with some sarcasm.

After much discussion and little in the way of solutions, the companions became quiet. The fire died down to dusky coals and the men curled up in their cloaks to sleep long before the future of Lynnara could be determined. Nevertheless, Kiril fell asleep with happy visions of people building villages, raising new persons, and pursuing dreams of their own choosing.

---

A new day dawned. There had been little in seismic activity over the long Aaian night, only one small tremor since the large ground shake …that they felt. After the lengthy break, Rojaire's team was well-rested and raring to go. They harvested and packed all the fresh food they had room for and could eat before it went bad, as well as the dried food from Ollen's cabin, emergency food rations, and water. The men were in high spirits, the long rest having prepared them for the challenges of the passage through the foreboding mountains.

The sky lightened as they crossed the grassland and soon they reached the base of the mountains. Rojaire lead them through what looked like a funnel between two mountain peaks that narrowed as they progressed forward. Then surprisingly, when they came around a bend in the passage, the space widened into a large area invitingly carpeted with thick blue-green grass.

"The sun reaches in here eventually," Rojaire said, noting the surprised looks on some of their faces. Though the day had brightened, the great orb had yet to climb above the mountains that enclosed them. "It will be easy going for a while."

As the day progressed and the heat intensified, the men were thankful to be in the mountain's shadow. Broken slabs, chunks, and boulders of rock, shaved off the steep rugged slopes over ages, littered the narrowing passage. The men doggedly moved on panting in the heat.

"By the time the sun hits us, we should be entering the tunnels," Rojaire said, offering them encouragement. After a long span they came to what appeared to be a new rock slide. Fortunately, the blockage wasn't extreme. While the others busily climbed over the rock rubble, Rojaire used the star stone to help Theon over in a series of tiny jumps without the others even noticing. As they continued on, the passage continued to narrow closing them in tightly. Eventually, like a burning torch, the arching sun blazed over them.

"We're almost there," Rojaire reassured them urging them on. Then finally they faced a slit in the mountain and slipped through into a large round tunnel. The air inside the tunnel was considerably cooler. Everyone dropped their packs and sat in the welcomed shade to rest.

As their eyes adjusted to the dim light near the entrance to the tunnel they could make out more detail around them. They were actually in an old lava tube where molten rock flowed long ago. "The passage is a network of lava tubes?" Theon asked.

"For the most part, yes," Rojaire confirmed, "but there are also sections of the passage that are above ground and a couple of cave systems too."

"And you think you can find your way through all this again?" Ollen questioned.

"We were lost for a long time," Tassyn admitted, "but eventually we found a route that led to the interior." It was easy to forget that Tassyn and Edty had been with Rojaire during that exploration.

"So what was it like?" Ollen asked.

"Mostly, it is a dark maze," Edty said putting in a few words.

"I marked every turn and return we took along the way," Rojaire said taking up the narrative. "We won't be clueless. I'm just concerned how seismic activity may have changed things. We will want to conserve light crystals; it may be a long time before we will see sunlight again to recharge them, even if things go well."

After everyone had cooled down and rested, ate and drank, Rojaire mustered his team back up. "Let's get moving; we have a long way to go yet." Using a couple of crystal powered lamps to light the way, they moved deeper into the mountain. It was easy going; the tunnel was high and broad enough to walk two abreast. The walls and ceiling, surprisingly dry, had started to crack and break and crumble with the pressures placed upon them, leaving an occasional pile of rock debris littering the floor.

"What happens if the volcano goes off?" Kiril asked after a long spell of quiet, not altogether comfortable about being in the path of moving lava.

"This lava tube hasn't seen lava for a long time. The odds should be in our favor," Theon surmised walking by his side. To have a little fun he added, "But keep a look out, will you?"

It wasn't long before they came to the first intersection of lava tubes. "Now which way do we go?" Ollen asked.

Rojaire inspected the walls near the entrance of first one tunnel then the next. "We go this way," he said with certainty when his inspection was complete.

"How do you know?"

"Come and have a look at this; you will see I have it marked," Rojaire said. Everyone crowded over to see.

"This mark ">" carved on the wall here means we went this way. The small mark roughly carved into the stone was hardly noticeable until Rojaire pointed it out. Since there is not a second mark beside it, we didn't have to backtrack. The other walls are unmarked. "We go this way," he concluded.

Kiril turned on his head lamp, pulled out his journal, and made an entry which made Rojaire think of the crystal compass. He pulled it out of his pouch and handed it to Kiril.

"What's this?" Kiril asked puzzled. The compass glowed softly in Kiril's hand as he studied it wondering over its intended purpose.

"Theon called it a compass. The brighter spot here indicates magnetic north," Rojaire explained leveling it in his hands, "so the beginning of this tunnel bears northeast," he showed him.

"I'll add these directions to my notes," Kiril agreed seeing the merit of it.

It wasn't until they reached the second lava tube intersection that Rojaire was able to show them a marking on the wall made long ago indicating a dead end. "Here we have a backward arrow following the forward one "><." That means this tunnel came to an end and we had to backtrack to this intersection. We need a tunnel marked with a forward arrow only." The team looked for marks at the entrances of the rest of the tunnels.

"Here," Traevus called out. A forward arrow ">" clearly marked the wall where Traevus stood. "We go this way."

Kiril pulled out the compass and entered some directions into his journal. "This is working out great, Rojaire," he offered in praise.

It was with a great deal of confidence in the eventual success of the mission that the group settled down in the wide intersection of the two lava tunnels to get some sleep. The men slept long and hard in the perpetual darkness; neither light of sun or shine of star marked the passage of time.

Edty was the first to eventually stir and unwilling to sit alone in the utter darkness, he reached for Tassyn and shook him.

"Hey Tass, are you awake?" he asked his voice quivering slightly.

"I am now," Tassyn groaned rolling over.

Hearing movement, Theon woke, his senses on alert, and then relaxed when Edty spoke again.

"Can we turn on a light?" Edty asked Tassyn pleadingly, whispering in the darkness.

"Keep the light dim, and don't point it into anyone's eyes," Tassyn warned. By now Rojaire woke up and it was a domino effect from there. There was no way to make tea without revealing the star stone, which Rojaire wasn't willing to do yet. They ate the fruit and ground nuts they had collected before entering the tunnels, and were soon on their way, checking again for Rojaire's mark to assure they were going in the right direction.

Sometime later, the floor of the tunnel took on a noticeable downward slope. "We're heading for the first cave system," Rojaire informed them. "There will be several twists and turns going through them; we had to do a lot of backtracking to find our way through the first time."

As they advanced, the floor of the lava tube sloped ever steeper ahead of them; at this rate, it would soon be too steep for comfort. By all appearances, the lava tube was about to take a dive, taking them on a long plunge to their deaths. "I'm ready to exit this route," Theon said starting to fear he would slide down to the molten depths, despite the rough stone floor. Fortunately Rojaire found what he had been looking for; a small jagged hole in the tunnel wall to their right.

Rojaire crawled through the tight opening that led into a large cavern beyond and after finding a secure rock to stand on turned back toward the entrance. "Alright, Theon, I want you to come through first. It's a rocky slope from the entrance to the cave floor. I will help you get your footing when you come through." Since it was necessary to climb down rocks to the cavern floor, Rojaire had Theon follow behind him so he could stealthily levitate him down without the others noticing.

"Careful now," he instructed Ollen as he crawled through the cave entrance after Theon. Rojaire stayed by the entrance lighting the way and requesting caution as they entered. When everyone safely reached the cavern floor, they turned on more lights to study their new surroundings. Thick glittering veins of gold and crystal sandwiched in bluish-black stone reflected back the light of the lamps.

"Crystal shards…!" Kiril exclaimed and brought out his journal.

Walking around was not easy, but they could stand upright as long as they kept to the center of the cave. The ceiling quickly dropped off to the sides and the floor of the cavern was more a jumble of stones than a floor. Moisture dripped from the ceiling and dampened the stones making them slippery.

"I can see this isn't going to be easy going," Ollen commented.

"It's going to be tough going for a while," Rojaire admitted.

Progress was indeed slow and laborious as they made their way through the long glittering cavern. "Do you have any idea what all this gold would buy on Earth?" Theon asked Rojaire when they finally stopped to rest.

"Food, shelter, and clothing..?" Rojaire guessed from what he had learned from Ilene, Theon, and Rahlys about Earth's monetary systems.

"Gold will buy the best food, mansions for shelter, the finest clothing … and fancy cars…; but gold also buys services."

"What kind of services?" Traevus asked his curiosity whetted.

"Services like people waiting on you, serving you food, taking care of your clothes, body, and everything you own. Gold will buy women to satisfy men, and vice versa, I'm sure."

"You can trade gold for love?" Kiril gasped when he caught on to Theon's meaning of "to satisfy."

"That would depend on your definition of love."

Progress suffered even further when the group reached the end of the main chamber and had to crawl on hands and knees through several long spans of low damp rocky tunnels that twisted and turned in tight bends and curves before finally entering another large chamber. The soft sound of flowing water greeted them as their lights fell on the trickle of water that seeped in through one of several cave openings along the cavern walls and out another.

Kiril and Traevus scouted around the many openings leading out of the cavern searching for the route they would take. Tassyn, Edty, and Rojaire knew they would be perplexed when the search was completed, but said nothing. Every tunnel entrance had been marked with both a forward arrow and a turn-around arrow.

"Where do we go from here," Kiril asked baffled when there were no more tunnel entrances left to search.

"From here we climb up," Rojaire said, surprising them all, except Tassyn and Edty.

"Up…? What about all these tunnels," Traevus asked.

"False leads every one," Rojaire said, shaking his head.

Intrigued the men lifted their faces, their eyes searching the walls and the high arched ceiling for an opening or a clue. Then Kiril spotted it, a tiny arrow pointing up "^" carved above a tumble of rocks that led toward the ceiling of the cave. It wasn't until he reached the top of the climb, the rocks serving roughly as steps, that the opening into another lava tube was revealed.

"How long did it take to do all that backtracking before you found this?" Theon asked.

"Several rotations; it's hard to keep track of time underground. Fortunately, there is water here, but we nearly ran out of food," Rojaire said telling the story. It was Edty who climbed up there and found the entrance back into the lava tubes. Still it was a risk at the time to continue forward instead of turning back and resupplying our food stocks.

"It was after this part of the journey that Stram started to act differently, I remember," Tassyn said. "He gradually became more aggressive. I can't help but wonder if he found the star stone somewhere in these caverns."

"You're right," Edty confirmed, "Stram was acting strange by the time we reached the interior."

Theon definitely preferred the lava tubes to the caves. Despite the unsettling threat of being overrun by molten rock, the lava tube made for comparably easy travel. The large tunnel ran nearly level, with Rojaire's carved arrow of long ago pointing in the direction of the slight incline, thankfully, with "up" being the preferred way to go in Theon's opinion.

The incline, though slight, took its toil over time. Theon held to the back of the group relying heavily on energy drawn with the help of the star stone to keep him afloat. "It seems to be getting lighter," Edty said; the first one to notice. As the tunnel gently curved to the left, they could also sense the intrusion of fresh air.

"But we shouldn't be anywhere near the exit by now," Rojaire said with some alarm over the incongruity. The explanation was revealed when they rounded the next bend.

"By Seaa's light…!" Rojaire said as they gazed with wonder at the refreshing sight. This wasn't here before."

Several paces of the tunnel wall before them had collapsed, most of the debris spilling down the side of a rocky hill, leaving an enormous opening that looked out over a small grassy valley just a few feet below. A bright early morning sky greeted them with the promise of another hot day, while the valley lay in shadow, the sun not yet peaking over the surrounding mountains.

While the rest of the men continued to gaze out at the valley, Theon glanced down at the dust on the cavern floor and couldn't believe what he thought he was seeing. He moved over to where the men had not yet trampled the dust for a better look. The tracks were unmistakable, little hoof prints were leading into the other end of the lava tunnel and coming back out again.

"Tracks…!" Theon announced his voice hoarse.

"Tracks …what kind of tracks?" Rojaire asked pulling his attention from the scene before them to where Theon pointed. Then he saw them; "What makes tracks like that?" By now they had everyone's attention.

"That looks like some kind of animal track," Ollen said. "It looks like it came in from out there," pointing to the opening to the valley. "It probably came in here to investigate."

"I wonder what could be living in these mountains," Traevus said. "It probably isn't very big with little tracks like that."

"We didn't come across anything in the tunnels when we passed through here last time," Edty said worried.

"True, but this wall wasn't busted open then," Tassyn explained.

"Are we going out there?" Edty asked, obviously fearful of whatever made the tracks in the dust on the floor of the lava tube.

"We're due for a break …and we certainly don't want to pass up an opportunity like this to explore. Aren't you curious to see what made these tracks?" Rojaire asked.

"No."

Rojaire, Ollen, Traevus, and Kiril were already heading down the rocky slope with Theon following slower behind. Tassyn moved to join the others encouraging on a reluctant Edty.

The valley of tall blue-green grass was about the size of a traw field and funneled toward them to a narrow rocky cut between two dark purple mountain peaks under a golden sky. As the group moved away from the rock slide from the collapsed tunnel wall and into the tall grass, the grass began to move. In fact, throughout the windless field of grass there was movement and something …make that lots of things… were moving unseen toward them …fast! Everyone noticed the movement but Kiril who was too engrossed in taking notes when the men began scrambling back up the rocky slope to what they hoped would be a defendable retreat to the lava tube.

Sensing something going on, Kiril finally looked up and then froze in terror as a herd of ten, twenty, maybe more small rotund silver-furred creatures only a couple of hand spans tall came rushing out of the tall grass, stampeding toward him on spindly hoofed legs.

"Ahhhh…!" Kiril yelled to the capacity of his lungs, expecting to be stampeded, attacked, and devoured. But just inches from Kiril, the flow of creatures parted like a silver stream flowing around a granite boulder; the flow of creatures closing again behind him as they made their way up the slope to the narrow cut between two peaks a short distance away.

Theon being slower than the others hadn't made it very far up the rocky slope to the tunnel. Following his honed hunting instincts, he picked up the largest rock he could muster and from where he stood dashed it down on the head of one of the escaping creatures, cracking its skull as the silvery herd dashed by before disappearing up and over the narrow rocky cut through the mountains.

The men watched in shock as Theon yelped with glee at his success. He rushed to the site with more life in his step than they had seen in a long time, and picked up the bloodied limp body.

"Meat…!" Theon salivated, proudly holding up his kill before a circle of astonished faces.

# Chapter 11

# Earth

Ilene stared out the gift shop window at the cold September rain attacking the remaining golden leaves still bravely clinging to birch boughs that were becoming increasingly bare. Between showers a cold breeze took its toil sending the leaves into a downward spiral. Several customers browsed through the gift shop but Ilene made no attempt to entice them to make a purchase, her mind too preoccupied with thoughts of Rojaire and her father so far away on a distant world; a world she had miraculously once visited. She rehashed the details of Jack Faulkner's letter in her mind and pondered on the mystery it alluded to. So often since returning to Earth she had fantasized seeing Rojaire again, their relationship going beyond mere friendship. Ilene had hoped he would eventually let go of his loss and accept that Kaylya was gone forever, but if what Jack's letter implied was true, his long lost love had been found.

"Move over and get out the way if you aren't going to work," her mother whispered shooing her aside so she could check out a customer. "Aren't you supposed to be getting ready to catch the train?"

"I'm packed."

The shop door opened again and Jack Faulkner walked in. He was accompanied by a young woman who looked only a few years older than Ilene. She was beautiful with long auburn hair, radiant golden brown eyes and flawless chestnut skin.

"You might as well go and greet them," Elaine said finishing up with the customer. Ilene had filled her in on everything that had happened on the expedition, except the fact that she had a crush on the Rojaire fellow involved; this Elaine had been able to surmise on her own.

"Well, Jack Faulkner, it's a pleasure to see you again," Ilene said with forced high spirits walking up to them.

"I assure you, the pleasure is mine," Jack said obviously happy to see her again. "I would like for you to meet, Kaylya, a dear friend of mine."

"Hello, Ilene; Jack's told me wonderful things about your little town and the surrounding area and the wonderful people he met." Elaine came over to join them.

"And this is Elaine, Ilene's mother; a charming lady if ever there was one."

"Thanks," Elaine said joining them, "but I hardly think that holds true. Hello, Kaylya. You picked a chilly wet day to go up the tracks."

"I am so looking forward to the trip regardless of the weather," Kaylya said. "Are you coming too?"

"Ilene will be going with you. Someone has to stay and mind the shop."

"I want to take a look around the shop before we have to catch the train," Kaylya said, her eyes already wandering over all the eye-catching merchandise.

"Of course," Elaine said always looking for a sale. "If you have any questions about anything you see, please let us know."

"Do you have any paintings by Vince and Maggie's neighbor, Rahlys?" Jack asked Ilene as Kaylya wandered off.

"Yes, of course, this way," Ilene said, finally deciding to work. There were several of Rahlys' paintings on display in the gallery area of the shop; Rahlys was their biggest selling artist.

Jack looked over the vibrant works of art on display. His eyes were particularly drawn to a painting of a little carrot top boy in a winter landscape with a stick for a wand and a small blanket for a cloak playing wizard, which he was sure was modelled after Leaf, and Raven seemingly dropping down from a snowy branch to do his bidding.

"Nice work," Kaylya commented, joining them.

"I like the one of the boy and the raven," Jack said looking at the price.

"That's a great painting," Kaylya agreed.

"I'll take this one," he told Ilene. "Can I pay for it now and pick it up when we get off the train Sunday afternoon."

"Absolutely," Elaine said stepping up eager to make a sale. "Excellent choice; and soon you will have the pleasure of meeting the artist," she told Kaylya.

Jack paid for the painting and looked at his watch. "We better head down to the train depot," he said. Elaine tagged the painting sold and Ilene headed upstairs to grab her pack.

"Have a good time," Elaine called out to them as they left for the station.

The drizzle had let up, but it was still cool and damp out. Ilene was glad she had grabbed a warm hat and jacket. They heard the train whistle blow in the near distance as they approached the platform. Jack and Kaylya retrieved a pack and a strapped cardboard box from the car they had parked close to the train station and carried them to the platform as the train came in sight ...on time!

"What a charming train!" Kaylya exclaimed, delighted by the journey despite the uninviting weather. As the train came to a stop the rain started to come down harder. Passengers quickly loaded their baggage and boarded to get out of the rain.

Ilene sat across the aisle from Jack and Kaylya and starred out the window at the drab fall scenery; the brilliant colors of just a couple of weeks ago were already faded and gone. Ilene's thoughts focused on Kaylya. Now that she met her, she could easily picture Kaylya and Rojaire together; they were perfect for one another. Kaylya's strong pleasant honest demeanor was alluring ... making it difficult for Ilene to even pretend she didn't like her.

By the time the train pulled up to their drop off, wispy rays of sunshine filtered through the clouds. The whole gang was waiting at the foot of Vince and Maggie's trail to greet them, including all the Bradley children, Rahlys, Quaylyn, and even Raven! Both Melinda and Maggie wore child carriers, but the toddlers, in little yellow rubber boots and raingear, had been released from confinement during the wait for the train. Leaf kept them entertained watching him play swords with dried wild celery stalks, knocking rainwater off the tall seeded grass that grew along the tracks.

"A welcoming party has come out to meet you," the cheerful rotund conductor said as the train came to a stop. Ilene darted into the baggage car to hand down their packs and the cardboard box to Vince and Quaylyn then followed Kaylya and Jack out the passenger door. Everyone stood away from the tracks as the train pulled away; then there was a free for all of greetings.

"Ilene, Jack, Kaylya, welcome," Maggie cried out going around giving hugs.

"Maggie, Vince, thank you so much for inviting us," Jack said.

"Aaaarrrk...! Aaaarrrk...!" Raven squawked taking part in the greetings.

"Hi there, Jack," Vince said walking up and shaking his hand. "I brought the four-wheeler down to carry up packs and whatever."

"Good thinking, my friend, but this time I will walk," Jack chuckled remembering his last ride up.

*Well...?* Rahlys sent Ilene in a tight telepathed message. *Is she Rojaire's Kaylya or not?* Ilene hunched her shoulders in I-don't-know-fashion.

Quaylyn gazed at Kaylya as though looking for clues to her origin. Finally he walked up to her and greeted her in his native language. Without hesitation she did the same. "It's a pleasure to meet you, Kaylya; welcome to our little community. I will request that from here on we speak English for the benefit of the others. We have no secrets here. "

"This is wonderful, thank you for letting me come," Kaylya said with warm gratitude, her eyes tearing up.

"We're pleased to have you," Maggie said, putting a comforting arm around her while balancing Crystal, who had tired of watching Leaf battle grass, on her opposite hip.

"Jack told me about all your beautiful children," Kaylya said replacing tears with a smile as she gazed into Crystal's little angelic face.

"Why, thank you. This is Crystal and her twin, about to put a rock in his mouth," Maggie said, "is Rock."

*Don't put rocks in your mouth; you can't eat rocks.* Melinda sent to her little charge, easing the small stone out of his hand. She picked a dried stalk sword for Rock and put it in his hand instead.

"Their older brother is Leaf and their big sister is Melinda." Upon seeing Rock get a sword, Crystal squirmed indicating she wanted down.

"Over here is Maggie's husband, Vince," Jack said introducing them.

"Hi, Kaylya, nice to meet you," Vince said taking time out from strapping the box and packs onto the four-wheeler to shake her hand. "So you have been living in western Alaska all this time?"

"Yes, I've particularly enjoyed learning about the cultures along the coast." Kaylya glanced around. "This is certainly different. Jack said it would be." Vince followed her glance. Very few leaves still clung to the trees making the forest look empty, the underbrush already dead and brown from early frost.

"You should have seen it a couple of months ago when it was green," Vince said.

"And this is Rahlys, the love of my heart and the light of my soul," Quaylyn said with feeling. He did not mention the Oracle of Light; they had agreed that they would let Kaylya tell her story first.

"Thank you so much, all of you, for inviting us to your community," Kaylya said to intrigued stares. "You can't imagine what it means to me to be here."

Again there were tears in her eyes. "I've waited so long to make contact with my world." Jack had never seen Kaylya shed a tear before.

"We should get a move on," Vince said looking at the lowering clouds, "It looks like it could rain again."

Leaf ran up to him. "Can I ride with you Daddy?"

"Sure, I have room for you."

Crystal and Rock were loaded into their carriers and the party followed Vince far ahead driving the loaded four-wheeler up the trail. Grayness had already closed off the brief sunshine and by the time they reached the porch of Vince and Maggie's log home, it had begun to rain in earnest.

The cabin was welcomingly warm and dry and soon they were all comfortably nestled in the large family room.

"Did you bring us presents?" Leaf asked Jack, when he had a chance, his tone hopeful.

"I brought something even better than presents, smoked salmon."

"Wow, what a treat," Maggie exclaimed truly excited. Leaf screwed up his little face and shook his head in disagreement.

"Did you get your moose this year?" Jack asked Vince.

"I sure did; Maggie is preparing a moose pot roast for our dinner tonight."

"I tried your rhubarb crisp recipe, Maggie; it came out great!" Jack told her.

"It sure did," Kaylya said. "I had some; it was delicious."

"Are you an alien?" Leaf asked Kaylya.

"Kaylya is from Quaylyn's world," Maggie explained a little embarrassed by Leaf's frankness.

Vince and Melinda set out platters of fruit, vegetables, meats, cheeses, pickles, crackers, and dip for lunch while Maggie settled the children down to play quietly in a corner with special toys she kept in reserve for this purpose. Rahlys and Quaylyn served coffee and tea.

"See what I mean; everything falls into place like clockwork around here," Jack said to Kaylya.

"So tell us about yourself, Kaylya," Quaylyn said when everyone was settled.

Kaylya had anticipated telling her story and didn't hesitate to begin.

"I awakened on Aaia in the community of Utaya, on the Golden Sea, many leagues south of the Community of the High Council. I have to admit, despite all the wonderful guidance my community bestowed upon me I never made it to Accepted One." Kaylya bowed her head briefly in humility that only Quaylyn fully understood. "Perhaps a large contributing factor was a man you wouldn't know named Rojaire." Ilene gasped softly at the mention of Rojaire's name, but only Rahlys heard her; no one said anything.

"Rojaire was nurtured equally well in Nellin, a nearby village upriver from Utaya. We saw each other often growing up; over time we became inseparable. Together we dreamed of going to the Academy to train as warrior adventurers and spent every opportunity we had exploring the territory that surrounded our villages. Eventually we were accepted at the Academy."

Leaf crept up to Maggie's chair, "Can I have some cheese and crackers?" he asked quietly.

"Of course, love; you have to share," Maggie whispered. She wrapped some treats in a napkin for him and he dashed back off to play. When she looked back to check on the children he was sharing the snacks with the twins.

Kaylya continued her story. "After several seasons of grueling training Rojaire was groomed to undergo a mission to Earth to find the Dark Orb." She hesitated wondering how to explain the significance of the Dark Orb.

"Long ago our world was nearly destroyed...."

Quaylyn gently interrupted. "Everyone here, except maybe Jack, knows the story of the Dark Orb," Quaylyn said. He did not tell her that Droclum was dead; there would be time for that later.

"I've told Jack everything I'm telling you."

"Yes, Betsy and I heard the story long ago," Jack confirmed.

"So what happened to Rojaire's plans to come to Earth?" Quaylyn asked to put her back on track.

"I'm not certain, but for some reason the High Council scraped the plans and the mission was cancelled. Rojaire was terribly disappointed, but he did have another goal; more than anything, he wanted to explore the Devastated Continent. Do they know about the Devastated Continent?" Kaylya asked Quaylyn.

"Yes, go on," he said coaxing her.

"Well, the High Council was not in favor of a mission there. Rojaire grew angry and decided to leave the Academy. I let him convince me to also leave the Academy and go with him on an exploratory journey across the Main Land. I loved him; the choice was easy. We spent many seasons, totally removed from society, traversing uninhabited wild lands, exploring, and finding relics of our past. It was a long and fascinating journey; we learned much about what life must have been like before the Dark Devastation. Eventually we returned to the Community of the High Council to report our findings.

Kaylya's expression which had been one of excitement over the journey she and Rojaire had shared turned to sadness.

"When we returned, we found out we had been branded as rogues. The Academy wasn't interested in our discoveries and we were refused admittance. We appealed to the High Council, requesting an expedition across the Golden Sea to the Devastated Continent, but the High Council determined we needed reforming.

Since access to the continent is controlled by the High Council, it is impossible to go there without permission. Eventually though, Rojaire managed to make some kind of secret deal with one of the councilors, Councilor Brakalar, I believe; Quaylyn may know him."

Rahlys had to suppress a gasp of her own at the mention of Brakalar's name. So far Kaylya's story matched what they already knew, or in Brakalar's case, suspected.

"I have met Council Brakalar," Quaylyn confirmed. "So you and Rojaire made it to the Devastated Continent."

"Yes, we had a whole continent to ourselves. For many seasons we explored between the coast and the Crescent Mountains where food is more plentiful. It was the happiest time of our lives; we vowed never to return to the Main Land. Eventually we ventured deep into the interior. You would never believe what we found."

"The Crystalline Landscape…," Quaylyn said.

Kaylya gasped …astounded! "How could you know this…?"

"Finish your story, please, Kaylya, and then we will give you some updates," Quaylyn promised after a moment of quiet. "What happened at the Crystalline Landscape?"

"You already know what happened, don't you?" Kaylya asked softly. "Is that what happened to you?" she asked Quaylyn.

"No …please, finish your story," Quaylyn urged gently. Kaylya collected herself and continued.

"The Crystalline Landscape was the most spectacular thing we had ever seen. We entered the glowing landscape of crystals cautiously; there were no obvious dangers. It was slow going, but so beautiful. The crystals refract sunlight into pastel colors by day and softly illuminate the sky at night. We were deep into the Crystalline Landscape when I found a small crystal wedged in tightly between larger ones. I knew Rojaire carried a handy tool that would help in extracting the crystal so I asked to borrow it. When I took a step forward to catch the extracting tool Rojaire tossed my way, I went through a …

space warp …energy field …wormhole …something…," Kaylya said trying to find a word that could describe what had happened. "I ended up on the frozen tundra in western Alaska."

"That's where Betsy and I found her fifteen years ago," Jack said. "She was confused, alone, skimpily dressed in the freezing cold, miles from a village."

"Wow…." Ilene summed it up for them. She had been deeply moved by Kaylya's story. *Will I ever find love like that?*

"So how do you know about the Crystalline Landscape? Rojaire and I were sure no one else knew of its existence." Kaylya couldn't contain her curiosity any longer.

"At the time you were right," Rahlys said speaking up. "After you disappeared, Rojaire was the only one left who knew about the Crystalline Landscape until Sarus led an expedition headed for Mt. Vatre."

"And Rojaire was alive and well and planning another expedition to the Devastated Continent when I saw him last about six months ago," Quaylyn informed her.

Kaylya would have staggered if she had been standing, as stunned shock paralyzed her mind. She had worried about Rojaire for so long. When she vanished he was left alone in the Crystalline Landscape in the center of an uninhabited continent. He would grieve her loss and wonder what happened to her, and there had been no way for her to let him know that she was okay.

"You've seen him…?" She fought back tears; the overwhelming relief in her voice unmistakable.

"Here, dear, it's alright to cry," Maggie said fetching a box of tissues. "After all, you just found out that someone you've been worrying about for fifteen years is alive and well."

"Thank you," Kaylya said, accepting the tissues. "It is such a relief to hear he is all right; it was a terrible way to leave him. I've worried and wondered what happened to him ever since. He will always be the love of my heart. You said he was planning another expedition to the Devastated Continent; does that mean the High Council finally caved in?"

"We have so much to fill you in on," Quaylyn sighed, "I'm not sure where to start."

"I do," Rahlys said and conjured the crystal from the beaded pouch that hung from her waist. The crystal appeared instantly hovering before her, turning slowly, radiating a soft glow of multicolored light from within. Rahlys sent the crystal spinning into the center of their gathering. The only one more shocked than Kaylya by the appearance of the crystal was Jack.

"Well, in all my days I've never seen anything like this."

"It's the Oracle of Light…!" Kaylya breathed softly, "The prophecy is true."

"Rahlys is the Guardian of the Oracle of Light," Quaylyn said.

Kaylya looked at Rahlys with astonishment and alarm. "You will have to face Droclum."

"Droclum is dead," Rahlys said.

This statement above all others left Kaylya speechless.

The gathered members of the Order of the Oracle waited silently giving her time to recover. Leaf, always awed by Rahlys' crystal, crept over quietly to gaze upon it. He looked up at Rahlys pleadingly. Knowing what he wanted, she nodded, and Leaf extended his hand palm up in front of him. Concentrating mentally he drew the crystal to him. It responded readily settling just above his outstretched hand.

"The High Council eventually changed its stand against sending an expedition to the Devastated Continent. Unfortunately the expedition led by Sarus never returned," Quaylyn told Kaylya. Going into considerable detail he related how they…he, Rahlys, Ilene, Raven, and Rojaire had joined an expedition led by Councilor Brakalar. Their mission: to search for the lost expedition.

"Rojaire was with you? He's been accepted by the High Council?" To Kaylya this was the best news yet. It meant that Rojaire was no longer an outcast from society. Of course, it would not help her own status, but her only concern was for Rojaire.

"Rojaire's knowledge of the continent proved a tremendous asset to the mission," Ilene found herself offering to the discussion.

While Quaylyn continued the story of their adventures describing how Rahlys found the Rod of Destruction in the Sooty Caves and how Councilor Zayla died in the ruins of the Temple of Tranquility; Maggie, Rahlys, and Ilene prepared the young children for a nap. Rahlys directed the crystal to lead Leaf to his bed, which he cheerfully followed. Ilene and Maggie gathered up the twins for a diaper change.

"How do you make a magic crystal, Aunt Rahlys?" Leaf asked after she tucked him in. Sparkling green eyes gazed up at her earnestly, waiting for an answer.

"I don't know," Rahlys said truthfully, "but I'm sure it's very difficult or there would be a lot more of them."

"Are you and Quaylyn super heroes like Batman and Cat Woman?"

"Not quite, but you don't have to wear a costume to be a super hero; anyone who sees a wrong and makes it right is a hero."

"I will be a super hero one day," Leaf said.

"You already are," Rahlys said blowing him a kiss. With the toddlers already in their beds, Rahlys conjured the crystal back to its pouch and left Leaf to dream about a magic crystal of his own.

---

Overnight the sky cleared and by morning a heavy frost covered the forest community, but now the sun was shining brightly gradually melting back the frost. Frosty sunshine was a great improvement over yesterday's rain. Jack had spent the night at Vince and Maggie's. Ilene and Kaylya shared the little cabin in the woods behind Rahlys. They sat across each other at the little table watching the frost melt. Ilene laid out some fruit and trail mix she carried in her pack for breakfast. She also pulled out a magazine she had packed for reading material.

There would be no need to wait for the train today; Kaylya could teleport her and Jack and Ilene back to town whenever they were ready.

The overnight arrangement had been a bit uncomfortable at first for Ilene who was still battling remnants of jealousy, but by morning the two women were bonded sisters. Ilene and Kaylya found they were more alike than different as they talked through the night and they shared much.

Kaylya now knew that Theon was Ilene's father and that he had also been on the expedition to find the seven missing explorers. Ilene told her she found out Theon was her father through a mystical portrait of the Oracle of Light that Rahlys had painted and how her former boyfriend Aaron had tried to steal the Oracle from Rahlys and ended up mauled by a bear. But mostly Ilene spoke of her concern for her father and her desire to see him once again.

Ilene learned of Kaylya's concerns for her future if and when she returned to her own world and the depth of commitment and respect a couple can have for each other, deep and everlasting, even a galaxy apart. Ilene now knew for certain that no one would ever come between Rojaire and Kaylya.

"You are so lucky to have someone who loves you so much," Ilene told Kaylya as she leafed through the rag. "When we neared the Crystalline Landscape Rojaire cried as he told us how you had disappeared. He tried to talk us out of entering the landscape of crystals warning us of the dangers, but we wouldn't listen."

"I have long dreamed of Rojaire and I being together again, but I must not get my hopes up; I still have to make it home."

"I wish I could see my father again; I miss him so much," Ilene said. Having him here would help relieve the hollowness she was feeling.

“Maybe you will see him again,” Kaylya said optimistically. But Ilene was not so certain. Her father had been losing strength; it would have to happen soon if it were to happen at all.

An article title in the magazine she had been casually leafing through jumped out at Ilene. She started reading it; its content giving her a feeling of unease.

“Listen to this!” Ilene read out loud:

CAMERAS CAPTURE VANISHING MERCHANDISE

> Security worker, Fred Landry, just happened to glance at the live-feed video screen in a department store when a flat screen TV vanished before his eyes from a store shelf, or so he claims. “Playback of the video feed would seem to verify his claims,” Louisiana State Police officer Gerald LeBlanc commented in a statement to the press, “but the video could have been tampered with.”
>
> A second incident in a different part of the state was also reported. A furniture store owner claimed furniture vanished from his store overnight even though there was no evidence of a break-in. Surveillance cameras around the outside of the building showed no disturbance; unfortunately, there were no cameras inside the store directed on the furniture that allegedly disappeared.

“What if it’s Brakalar who took those things? It’s possible that he is here on Earth,” Ilene said speculating. “After all, you arrived here; and so did Caleeza.”

“We need to show the article to Rahlys and Quaylyn right away,” Kaylya agreed. “It could be an important lead.”

“Klawock!” raven chortled flying across their vision.

“I think Raven wants to say hello,” Ilene said. “We practically ignored him when you got off the train.” They stepped out into the brilliant autumn day to find Raven sitting on the branch of a nearby tree.

*Greetings, Raven, I hope we can be friends,* Kaylya sent instinctively.

“Klawock…!”

“Raven is Rahlys’ familiar,” Ilene explained. “He found the Oracle of Light and brought it to her.”

“Raven must have been an incredible sight to my people. I’m trying to picture him flying over the Community of the High Council and The Devastated Continent.”

"He certainly did draw reactions!" Ilene laughed. Raven couldn't show Kaylya what he looked like to the people of Aaia, but he could do something even better.

"Oh, …how beautiful," Kaylya sighed as Raven telepathed bird's eye view images of the Golden Sea and Lavender Beach, The Crescent Mountains, and the Crystalline Landscape as he remembered them. A wave of homesickness for her world washed over her.

*Thank you, Raven, for your gift.*

"Look, Kaylya, I want to be frank with you; I had a bit of a crush on Rojaire while we were on the expedition, but I want you to know he never gave me an encouraging thought. Rojaire thinks only of you."

There was a quiet pause before Kaylya spoke.

"Be patient, my friend, one day soon you will meet the man who will love you incurably." She spoke the words as though they were prophecy.

---

Brakalar sat under the bright light of a glow globe in front of a glowing computer screen with maps and books strewed all around him. He looked up from his research to see the rune-covered chest sitting on the massive oak mantel, glowing softly in the semi-darkness that cloaked the rest of the room. It isn't the first time this puzzling phenomenon has occurred since his arrival on Earth, but despite all efforts he hadn't found any significance to it …other than perhaps the chest was mocking him for his failure to open it. At first he thought the sporadic momentary glow of the runes meant someone was searching for him and the chest, but long ago he had set up protective wards to prevent Rahlys or anyone else from locating him, assuming they thought to search. After a while, the runes on the chest went dark again and Brakalar went back to his studies.

Having turned his focus to acquiring information, he did so whole-heartedly. Taking a global view, he learned there were nearly 200 independent countries on the planet and the one he currently occupied was called the United States of America which was further divided into parts. He was living in the part called Louisiana. Rahlys, Ilene, and Raven were in Alaska which was also a part of the U.S.A. even though it wasn't connected to the rest of the country. *But is this the best country from which to launch my new life?* Brakalar wasn't so sure. He could learn other languages.

It quickly became evident that chaos was rampant around the globe. There were several autocratic governments in place, each one reputed to be more evil than the next. Most of the people lived with very little while their leaders lived lavish lifestyles. Some dictators had been overthrown; others threatened neighboring borders.

There were also several oligarchies with rigid class systems and rampant poverty. A few countries were monarchies, its ruler descended from the ruling family over generations, yet most of them also had elected officials that replaced most of the monarch's power.

Many countries were democracies, or so they claimed, with most of the power in the hands of the people. While this system offered its citizens the greatest personal freedom for fulfillment of individual potential, it was easily corrupted, oftentimes bringing it down.

*Perhaps the real question is where can I best slip into a position of power and remain undetected by Rahlys and her warriors?* Brakalar pondered over the question as he rose to fix himself another drink. He had taken a liking to brandy.

Earth was a world anchored in technology. Instead of telepathy, telekinesis, and teleportation, a worldwide communication system was achieved through the use of nearly three thousand large electronic brains put in orbit around the planet. Brakalar had installed both a computer and satellite TV in his study, drawing in all the necessary signals to access information.

Transportation was equally complex, and so diverse, encompassing land, sea, and air. There were trains, planes, boats ...and roads ran everywhere; there seemed to be a car for every person. Energy was in high demand, but no one drew energy from the elemental forces. Instead machines were developed to do all the work. Most of these energy producing machines burned primitive fuels such as oil, gas and coal; others were powered by sunlight, water, or wind. The machines to produce the energy were produced in factories ...as was nearly everything that was consumed here. The factories needed energy to build the energy producing machines as well as consumer goods.

And the population of the planet was unbelievably massive, seven billion. The population of Aaia before the Dark Devastation had been only half that.

There was also the matter of economics. Thus far he had taken what he needed ...food, clothing, material things, by simply teleporting the items to his home without even touching them. There were no pictures in the surveillance cameras that could link him to a crime; he was just one of many shoppers who walked the store isles without touching the merchandise.

*I guess my first major task is to establish an Earthling identity.* Fake ID's could be purchased, but he decided to technically create his own. Who would he become? Brakalar poured more brandy; it helped him think. *I guess America would be the best place for me to enter society since its population has the most diverse ethnic background. There are millions of illegal immigrants here already; I would just be one more. Let's see ... I need a name. These humans have such short life spans; I wonder how Theon handled living out the span of many lifetimes to their one. What I really need right now are computer programming and hacking skills. Then I need to explore this medium these people call science.*

## Chapter 12

# Aaia

The rest of the group looked on their faces crunched up skeptically as Theon skillfully skinned and gutted his kill with a knife he carried from Earth. The little hooved animal had plenty of fat on it; it certainly wasn't hurting for food. Theon's mouth watered.

"We're going to eat that?" Kiril asked.

"When's the last time you tasted meat roasted over an open fire?"

"But it's not a fish; it can walk and you killed it," Kiril said trying to wrap his mind around the concept.

"You have to kill it to eat it."

"But it is flesh."

"That's meat, boy. Make yourself useful will you and fetch my water container to rinse off my knife," he directed. Kiril readily obeyed.

Theon's first concern after killing the small animal was how he was going to cook it. Rojaire and Ollen solved that problem by finding some of the porous blue rocks that would burn. With dry grass for kindling, they soon had a fire.

"I'm going to climb up there and see where those creatures ran off to," Rojaire said walking off.

"I've butchered a lot of wild game with this knife," Theon said finishing up. Almost reverently, he placed the carcass on a large rock. Then he wiped off the knife with grass after Kiril poured water over it to rinse off the blood.

Theon directed Tassyn and Edty to place a large flat rock on a bed of coals at the edge of the fire for the cooking stone. Then he had them stack more flat rocks on edge around the back side of the cooking slab to radiate back more heat. When all was ready, he ceremoniously placed the meat in the makeshift, open-faced stone oven to cook.

"Hey, fellows…!" Rojaire shouted, from the narrow rocky cut. "You have to come see this; you won't believe it…!" the excitement in Rojaire's voice rang unmistakable.

Immediately the others took off for the slope, curiosity having got the best of them. Theon doubted he had the strength to climb up the long rocky slope to the narrow cut, so he held back until the others were out of sight before teleporting himself up to the top of the rocky mountain cleft. He suffered a twinge of guilt every time he secretly used the star stone to his advantage …but there had to be some concession for age. Just a few steps later Theon caught up with the rest of the men who stood in speechless awe as they gazed down on a huge fruitful valley with a broad river running through it gleaming in the sunlight in the distance, hills and plateaus, forests and meadows …and wildlife.

"It's Drak's Valley," Kiril said …the first one to speak.

"What are you talking about?" Theon asked, coming up behind him. "You've heard of this place before?" he questioned.

"Yes …well maybe. Drak gave me…." Kiril reached for his pack to show them the crystal floss map of the hidden valley that Drak had given him, but his pack was back by the fire.

"Drak said his chosen father's chosen father spent his life exploring the Crescent Mountains and claimed he discovered a great valley locked in by mountains with waterfalls and caves with precious gems."

"And you think this is that valley? How did he get here?" Rojaire asked. "The collapse of the lava tube wall is recent."

"According to Drak he scaled the mountain peaks. He gave me a map drawn on crystal floss. It's in my pack where we built the fire."

"Then go and fetch it, will you, and turn over the meat while you are there," Theon directed. Kiril, Tassyn, and Edty left to fulfill his directives.

Sunshine sliced through the narrow cut as the sun rose over the eastern peaks bathing the valley in golden light. The group waiting for the others to return soon moved over to sit in some shade as they continued to gaze out over the amazing scene below. A small herd of tall animals with patchy gray and gold fur and long necks grazed on tree leaves in the near distance. Theon pulled out his spyglass for a closer look.

"More plant eaters," Theon said focusing on them. "Since the valley is still lushly foliated, I can't help wondering what might be keeping the populations of plant eaters in check."

"Now that's an unsettling thought," Ollen said. "Anything that could bring down one of those things," indicating the animals in the distance, "could take down one of us."

Kiril returned quickly with a folded bundle of cloth in hand. He was alone, having left Tassyn and Edty still tending the fire.

"Has anything come after our meat yet?" Theon asked concerned.

"No...." Kiril looked around. "Are we in danger?"

"We don't know yet. Show us what you got."

Kiril unfolded the cloth woven of crystal floss on the rocky ground revealing the imprinted map inside. The men gathered around to take a look. "I didn't know crystal floss was real," Traevus said feeling it between his fingers. The men studied the map intently comparing it to what they could see of the large valley before them.

"Is this a treasure map?" Ollen asked.

"Sort of, I guess. These curved lines coming off the mountains are waterfalls," Kiril pointed out.

"Here's the river and this marking could be that plateau in the distance," Rojaire noted. "The shape of the drawing here looks like it could represent this end of the valley, but the map doesn't show a route leading into it. What do these symbols stand for?" he asked Kiril pointing to the numerous little loops that dotted the map. Most of the loops were drawn along the mountain edge of the valley, but there were also several placed near the hills and plateaus more centrally located.

"They are caves; Drak said the surrounding mountains are riddled with caves."

"That's a lot of caves," Rojaire observed trying to get a rough count of the loops. "This valley must be larger than we think. And there are supposed to be gemstones in these caves?"

"That's what Drak said."

Tassyn and Edty returned from the cooking fire in the little valley and rejoined them. "How is the meat cooking?" Theon asked digging for a report.

"I'm not sure," Tassyn answered respectfully, "I've never cooked meat before."

"What does it look like?" Theon asked.

"Well, it's kind of blackened on the side that was facing the fire and still pink on the other side. We turned it over as you said."

"Are we going to explore this place?" Edty asked still awed by the vista below.

"We wouldn't be explorers if we didn't, my friend," Rojaire said rising to his feet anxious to get started. "How much longer will it take that meat to cook?" he asked Theon.

"It will probably be a while yet. A good stout pole to hang the meat over the coals would help. I'll go back and tend to the cooking," Theon offered. The nearest small tree grew far downslope where more soil offered better anchorage for roots to take hold.

"We'll get that for you," Rojaire decided. "Kiril and Edty; you will stay with Theon. The rest of you come with me," Rojaire instructed them. Edty wanted to protest being separated from Tassyn, but refrained. Kiril swallowed his disappointment of not being chosen for the scouting party.

As the two groups prepared to go, Theon slipped Rojaire the star stone. *For protection…*, he sent before letting it go and headed back to inspect his roast beast with Kiril and Edty leading the way.

Rojaire secretly pocketed the star stone then turned to his unit, "Stay alert, watch around you, and stay close."

Both Rojaire and Ollen, more experienced explorers, still carried their packs, not liking to separate from their survival gear on the trail. They carried with them an assortment of tools, including implements to cut wood, but no weapons. Rojaire didn't know if he could draw enough energy from the elemental forces even with the star stone to stop a charging animal.

Nevertheless, he cautiously led his men down the long gradual slope. They quickly reached rocky soil that nurtured a variety of small bushy plants. Every few steps took them into taller, thicker, more varied plant life. The valley floor was still far below. Nothing moved around them; nothing charged at them along the way.

Soon they reached the tree they had targeted. The smooth-barked reddish-brown tree trunk supported branches of silvery-blue round leaves. It wasn't very tall, about twice his height. Rojaire decided to lop off most of the tree which would give them the stout pole that Theon requested.

"Keep watch while I saw through this," Rojaire instructed the others. "We don't want to be taken by surprise." He knew he sounded anxious even though he tried not to. It didn't take him long to make the cut and remove the top and branches. Task complete, he gazed through the brush toward the valley floor, now obscured by foliage. He longed to continue down and explore further, but forced himself to listen to his own voice of reason. They would rejoin the others and form a plan; they had to stay together.

Rojaire's team returned safely to the high little valley, filled with the aroma of roasting meat, to find Theon, Kiril, and Edty comfortably settled in a shady niche some distance away. The chef and fire tenders rose from their leisure and walked over to intercept Rojaire's scouting team when they appeared in the cut.

"What did you find? Were you attacked by wild animals?" Kiril asked still disappointed that he hadn't been assigned to the team to go exploring, but relieved he hadn't faced another animal stampede.

"All was calm," Ollen reported. "Nothing moved."

"What do you think?" Edty asked Tassyn siding up to him. "Is it safe?"

"We didn't encounter anything threatening."

"Here's the stout pole you requested," Rojaire said, handing it to Theon.

"For which I am grateful," Theon said appreciatively examining the staff. "Well, we don't need it for the roast, as it is close to done, but if you don't mind, I will put it to a far better use. This pole will make a wonderful walking staff."

"It's yours, wise one."

Theon tested his new walking staff as he strolled to the fire to check on the meat. The coals had nearly died out; but the meat looked ready to eat. He cut blades of grass for a hot pad and grabbed a leg cutting it away from the rest of the carcass. It came away easily. Lifting the small haunch to his mouth, he took a bite; the meat was incredibly tender and delicious.

"Dinner!" he shouted, stepping away to clear access to the roasted meat.

"Feast your choppers on this!" He took another bite, certain he could actually feel strength returning to his body as he devoured the fatty meat.

The others approached with uncertainty; Rojaire was the first to dive in cutting off another haunch. Ollen pulled a piece of exposed meat off the carcass and brought it to his mouth. "That's good," he said, pulling out his serving bowl and slicing off a large chunk.

Tassyn and Edty followed Ollen's example tasting it first to see if it was acceptable, then filling their dishes. Traevus and Kiril were slower to adapt, only pulling off a few nibbling bites until Theon and Rojaire came over for seconds; it was then they decided they had better get serious or miss out on eating. Reactions to the unusual meal were predominately favorable.

Having eaten their fill, the men found a shady cleft in the mountain enclosing the small valley to rest during the hottest part of the long Aaian day. The other option was to return to the lava tube, but everyone agreed they preferred being outdoors after travelling underground for so long. They mashed down grass to sit on and lay on. Theon placed his new walking staff on his lap, took out a small pocketknife, and started whittling on it. Everyone settled down.

"When the sun begins to descend toward the west we will head out," Rojaire said. "That will give us plenty of time to search out a place to camp before the period of darkness begins." Unfortunately, it would be many rotations yet before Seaa, the nearest star that shined like a distant sun during half the seasons finally arose.

"What if we are attacked by some of those wild animals?" Tassyn asked.

"We need to find a way to defend ourselves. When we reach the trees we will fashion some weapons. A staff like Theon's with a knife tied to its end can be deadly."

"How did all these creatures' ancestors survive?" Traevus wondered. "This continent was scorched clean."

"Somehow the mountains and caves must have saved them," Theon speculated. "The plants and animals in this valley have evolved over eons separate from the rest of the world. There's no telling what we may encounter now that we know the valley harbors life."

"Well, exploring this place is certainly going to be interesting," Ollen said. Rojaire couldn't agree more. In all truth, the men were indeed curiously excited over the adventure, regardless of some feelings of apprehension. When it came time to sleep, the men sought the relative safety of the lava tube after all. They slept in rotations with someone always keeping a watchful eye on the narrow cut through the mountain that led to the greater valley. Nothing came.

As the day started to cool, the men headed out, Theon carrying his walking stick. When they crested the cut, the long-necked tree grazers were no longer in sight. The explorers made their way down the slope to where Theon's walking cane had been harvested. There was no evidence of anything having investigated the site in the interim. A few more paces downslope and they were under the canopy of a forest.

"Let's construct some weapons, even if it's just a staff you can hit with," Rojaire said coming to a stop. The men set to work bringing out small saws and cutting tools while Theon armed with his staff and Rojaire armed with the star stone kept watch for anything that might creep up on them while the others were occupied in their tasks. When everyone felt minimally armed they continued on, the mountain slope leveling before them as they descended into the fertile river valley. All was quiet.

"Where did everything go?" Traevus asked after they had gone a long ways without encountering animal life.

"Don't let your guard down," Rojaire reminded them as they continued through the beautiful peaceful forest. They came across several reddish orange trees with low sweeping lateral branches offering fist-sized chocolate brown fruit. Theon plucked one to try it. "Careful," Rojaire warned. "You don't want to eat anything that may be poisonous."

Theon broke the fruit open and took a cautious nibble at the pinkish pulp that broke away from a central pit. It was tender and meaty and tasted sort of like avocado. He took another bite before discarding the rest then picked more of the fruit to eat later if he lived through the taste test.

Suddenly a small flying creature with disproportionally large lacy pinkish gray translucent wings and a furry body about the length of Kiril's thumb nail fluttered into view directly in front of him. Kiril yelped jumping back in alarm; everyone stopped and readied their make-shift weapons ready to confront danger. The flying creature, minding its own business, fluttered off into the forest ignoring the battle ready warriors. With the possible threat fluttering away, the men lowered their weapons scowling at Kiril.

"Did you see that? That thing can fly!" Kiril explained trying to recover his dignity after over reacting. He had never seen a flying creature before. "Why does everything have to come after me?" he muttered to himself.

The forest grew denser and taller as they neared the river. Massive bluish brown trees towered over them, their trunks too big around for two people together to encircle with their arms. The interlocking canopies of the trees blocked out the sky allowing little light to reach the forest floor. They could hear shuffling sounds in the high branches above, but the thick foliage prevented them from seeing the source of the noise. They moved on through the forest, glancing up frequently, fearing something would drop down on them at any moment. Gradually the forest thinned out and sunlight brightened the way. The sun had dipped greatly toward the west by the time they could see it again.

"I don't want to go in there again," Edty said glad to be done with the dark forest. Eventually they reached the wide expanse of rose, lavender, and dark purple gravel bed of the river.

"Well, we made it this far without being eaten," Tassyn said as they took a break. "Although I guess becoming food for something else is fair game after eating that other creature."

Across the braided stream they spotted the herd of long-necked animals again grazing on the trees at the edge of the forest. It looked like the same herd of six they had seen before. Now that they had a closer look at them, Theon determined that the herd consisted of one larger, older animal, three adults in their prime, another smaller one that looked like a juvenile, and a much smaller young one that was probably still nursing. The beasts continued grazing unalarmed by their presence; the men maintained what they hoped was a safe distance.

Theon observed the animals for a while. "As long as those creatures don't sense any imminent danger we are reasonably safe; but if they go on alert you can be certain that whatever they find threatening will also be threatening to us." Only Theon had any knowledge of instinctive animal behavior having lived for centuries, often in the wild, on Earth.

"Stay alert," Rojaire reminded them again. At least they could see around them, now. Rojaire did a lot of exploring, but he'd never had to contend with wildlife before; it was downright unnerving. The high distant western ridge was already casting a long shadow across the western edge of the valley.

"Bring out that map of yours again, Kiril," Rojaire requested. Kiril unfolded the map on the gravel bar and Rojaire and Ollen squatted to take a look while the others stood guard. "Where's the nearest cave?"

"Here," Ollen said pointing to a loop drawn on the side of a large plateau that dominated the south region of the valley, clearly in their view not far away. The cave marking faced the river.

"Let's go check it out."

The group followed the river where the air moved freely and their vision extended farther around them. The presence of animals suggested the possibility of human habitation as well, but so far there was no evidence of people living in the valley. If anything was watching they would be easy to spot out in the open, but it was preferable to being ambushed in dense brush.

Nothing threatened the explorers.

As they neared the plateau they left the river, hiking through mixed brush and trees and grass to reach the plateau's base. Following the contour of the land, they walked along the base of the rise looking for the entrance to a cave. They covered a great distance; the plateau's curve was now turning away from the river.

"Let's see the map again," Rojaire said after much walking and searching that turned up nothing. "We must be missing something, or the cave has collapsed in on itself." Kiril and Tassyn held the cloth map taut for Rojaire to view. "The loop marking the cave is higher up the slope rather than at the base." The men immediately began backtracking gazing upward. They hadn't gone far when Kiril sounded an alert.

"Up there …a flash of light," Kiril called out pointing.

"Take cover," Rojaire ordered. The men hid behind trees and bushes quietly waiting to see if they had been spotted. Nothing happened. In the intense quiet they could just barely hear the murmur of the flowing river some distance away.

"I didn't see anything," Ollen said after a long period of quiet.

"I didn't see anything either," Traevus added.

"Are you sure you saw a light?" Rojaire questioned Kiril.

"Yes."

"Did you see anything else?"

The sun was sinking behind the mountains to the west. "No, just a flash of light up high in the side of the hill, and then it was gone."

"Maybe you saw sunlight reflected off of something shiny," Theon suggested. "These caves *are* supposed to hold gem stones."

"I'm going up and take a look. Where exactly did you see the light flash?" Rojaire asked.

"Up there where those rocks stick out."

Rojaire started up the sloping side of the plateau searching out the easiest route to where Kiril pointed. The others, no longer hiding behind brush, watched anxiously as he made his way up. Then suddenly Rojaire spotted a cleft in the rocks beside the rocky protrusion. He approached cautiously and discovered the opening led deeper into the hillside. Pulling out a light to peer inside, Rojaire turned on his lamp and with his heart pounding stepped into a small cave.

It was empty.

"I found it," he shouted out to the others.

Rojaire watched over the group as they joined him. Upon entering the cave, the men gawked in amazement at the glittering walls and floor sparkling in the glow of his light.

"Diamonds…!" Theon gasped. The short climb up without the star stone had been hard on him, but he quickly regained his breath. "This is what you saw, Kiril, sunlight glinting off of diamonds. There's a fortune here." Only, there was no diamond market on Aaia; the diamond cave was merely a thing of beauty.

The cave, longer than it was wide, was large enough to accommodate them all. Rojaire stepped back out through the rock cleft onto the bit of ground in from of the entrance. The shadow of approaching night stretched across the valley. Would this land offer terror during the period of dark? Hopefully not, but they had found what he hoped would be a defendable shelter just in case. They needed wood for a fire …lots of wood.

Rojaire glanced toward Theon. It was obvious he needed to rest.

"Let's have Traevus, Tassyn, and Edty collect firewood. After dark we'll build a small fire outside the entrance to the cave to keep away possible predators. Stay close together and holler if you run into trouble. Theon and Kiril, you will stay here to guard the cave. Ollen, come with me; I want to take a look above us …before it gets dark."

"Kiril and I can haul the wood up by rope after you gather it," Theon offered. "We will need some fire starter, too," he reminded them. The men went to work.

Carrying their crude weapons, Ollen followed Rojaire up the steeper final climb to the top of the broad plateau. The distance wasn't great, but the route from the level of the cave up proved to be far more difficult than the gentler slope below. The going was slow and arduous, the men searching for hand holds to prevent plunging off the side. Finally they crested the top and stood on a relatively flat rocky field of mottled pink and rose stone and silvery grass.

There was still plenty enough light to appreciate the panoramic view before them. When they looked down they could see the men hard at work far below hauling lengths of firewood to the base of the plateau to be hauled up. Ollen and Rojaire searched the ground of mixed grass and rocks for animal tracks and scat, but found nothing. In a race against encroaching darkness, the two men set out to hike the distance across the top of the plateau to take a look off the other side, which was proving to be a lot farther than they had expected.

"The light is starting to fade; we better turn back," Rojaire decided.

"I agree; this place is bigger than we think?" Ollen said with plenty distance left to go.

The men turned around and hadn't gone far when something strange started happening. At first several, then dozens …hundreds … perhaps thousands of the delicately laced flying creatures they had encountered earlier fluttered around spreading over the plateau and landing on the sun-warmed rocks to roost for the night. Once settled in, the swarm became totally still effectively blending in with the rocky landscape.

"That was incredible!" Ollen whispered softly.

"They must feel safe up here, which is a good sign for us. Try not to step on them," Rojaire said as they gingerly tiptoed around the resting creatures.

By the time Ollen and Rojaire made it back to the cave it was nearly dark, but the men were still hauling in wood. A large stack of brush and tree branches were piled high to the far side of the entrance to the cave. "We have been stashing some of it inside too since we can't fit any more out here," Theon informed them while Kiril pulled up another load.

"All right, that's enough. Get back up here," Rojaire called down to Edty, Tassyn, and Traevus. He and Ollen helped Kiril hoist the last bundle of wood up. Soon, the others bringing materials they had gathered for kindling reached the security of the cave.

Night descended over the valley. There was a refreshing flow of air as the land began to cool.

"Good job, fellows," Rojaire praised them upon seeing the additional stack of wood inside.

"What did you find on top the plateau?" Theon asked.

"It was an incredible sight," Ollen said still excited. "As it got dark, thousands of those little fluttering creatures came in to roost on the rocks. When they stopped moving, you could hardly see them they blended so well into the landscape."

"Is that good or bad for us?" Rojaire asked Theon.

"Well, that depends…." Theon thought on it for a moment. "They may be up there to stay out of reach of predators, but what's preying on them…? The top of the plateau may just be a convenient place to rest."

"Let's build a little fire outside the door," Rojaire suggested. "We need to boil water for tea anyway."

The fire was built and tea was made. Theon brought out the avocado like fruit he had harvested and offered it around. Everyone decided to try it since Theon hadn't suffered any ill effects.

"You have the first watch, Edty," Rojaire told him. "Put some more wood on the fire." Edty stepped out of the cave under a star spangled sky to take watch.

"We need to talk about where we stand on telling the High Council about this valley," Ollen brought up unexpectedly as the men relaxed with their tea.

"What do you think would happen if the High Council learned about this place?" Traevus asked hypothetically. There was quiet as the men thought on it.

"Probably a team would come in and study the plants and animals, maybe even remove some …deciding where they should live instead," Ollen said sarcastically. His comment raised chuckles among the men.

"They could never get one of those long-necked creatures through the caves and tunnels," Tassyn said, his comment followed by laughter. It was a rare sound coming from Tassyn and contagious; they all laughed with him as they pictured such an undertaking.

"Maybe the High Council would decide to kill off all the wildlife to prevent them from spreading like a plague across the rest of the continent," Traevus said.

"Think about the valley strategically. You want to declare a new nation; what if there is retaliation?" Ollen offered. "This valley is a fortress; we control access, it's hard to get to, and it would be easy to keep secret."

"But is the valley safe, even for us?" Rojaire questioned.

Theon shook his head. "Just because a bear roams the woods, doesn't mean it's looking for a human to attack."

"What's a bear?" Kiril asked.

"Bears are big burly animals, furry meat-eaters with long sharp claws and sharp teeth that roam the forests on Earth. The fiercest ones live out on the tundra and the polar ice."

"Actually, the valley isn't so hard to get to from the interior," Rojaire informed them getting back to the topic. "We've been through the hardest part."

"But the High Council won't know that," Tassyn said.

"They won't know …if we don't tell them," Ollen growled. He scowled hard at Kiril, his expression harsh against the glitter of diamonds in the background.

Kiril became defensive, "I haven't written anything in my journal about the valley …yet," he said whispering the last.

"Finally, you are getting some sense," Theon mumbled under his breath.

The men discussed the valley's future long into the night. Edty's watch passed uneventfully and Tassyn took his place under the stars. By the time Kiril relieved Tassyn, most of the men were asleep.

Sitting alone by the fire under the stars, Kiril pulled his journal out of a pouch in his cloak and began to describe the wondrous valley.

# Chapter 13

# Earth

*The twins' first birthday; why couldn't it be my birthday?*

Leaf was not happy; birthdays took far too long to arrive. At least his birthday would come before Melinda's. When he asked Mommy about it she showed him on a calendar how many days before it would be his birthday and there were a lot, three more weeks she said. Melinda's birthday was much further away than that. Leaf was glad about that; he didn't want Melinda to leave.

The house was quiet, everyone else was still sleeping. Through the window, daylight barely dispersed the cloak of darkness. Leaf crept out of bed and peered wonderingly at Rock still sleeping soundly. *Why is Rock still sleeping when it's his birthday?* Of course Rock had to share his birthday with Crystal. How strange not to have a birthday of your own!

Leaf then went around the dividing wall to check to be sure that Melinda really hadn't left home yet. He found her sound asleep in her bed. Satisfied, he returned to his own room; Rock was still sleeping. *Should I wake Rock up and wish him a Happy Birthday?* Leaf stared at his little brother undecided. If only Rock were older, he thought, like able to talk. *At least the little fellow can run now.*

"What are you doing up already, Leaf?" Maggie said appearing in the doorway in time to prevent him from waking up Rock.

"I wanted to wish Rock a Happy Birthday."

"Let's let Rock sleep; it is hard work being only one year old. Do you want to help me plan for Rock and Crystal's birthday party?" she asked drawing him away from Rock's crib.

"Okay…." Leaf followed his mother into the family room.

"Oh, look it's snowing!" Maggie said. Sure enough, outside the big picture window, snowflakes spiraled down.

"Snow…!" Leaf ran to the window, awestruck. It had been forever since he'd seen snow! Snow was almost as wonderful as birthdays. "I need to go pee."

"Well, let's put a hat and jacket on you first…and you need something on your feet." Maggie dressed him quickly then released him. *I might as well take this opportunity to visit the outhouse.* Grabbing her own jacket she followed Leaf out the door.

The chilly and damp air made Maggie shiver despite her jacket. Leaf was already in the yard greeting the snow. She stepped out, a dusting of snow masking a thin layer of ice that covered the top step. Instantly her foot slipped out from under her sending her sailing through the air into a twisted fall. Maggie screeched as she…should have hit the ground.

Vince appeared in his bathrobe in time to see his wife suspended in air in a time-frozen fall just inches above the ground, her face contorted in fearful relief.

Leaf gently lowered his mother to the ground and ran to her.

"Oh, Leaf, my little hero," Maggie cried clutching Leaf in her arms and giving him a big hug. Leaf never knew what reaction to expect when his parents witnessed him using magic; their reactions have been notoriously mixed.

Vince made a move to come to her. "Careful, the steps are icy," Maggie warned.

"Are you hurt?" he asked in concern rushing down the steps regardless. By the time he reached her, Maggie was already getting up.

"I'm fine. Thank you, Leaf. I could have broken an ankle or a hip or even worse my neck. You're my super hero!" Maggie exclaimed kissing him on the forehead.

Leaf was delighted. Aunt Rahlys had been right; he didn't need a costume to be a super hero…but a cape would be nice.

---

"Traw is as much a mental challenge as a physical one," Quaylyn reminded Rahlys for the thousandth time. "You have seen how Leaf does it; he places himself mentally where he has to be to catch the glow globes." Rahlys felt she was no longer his prize student. Quaylyn had started training the three-year-old in earnest after he had shown such natural talent. Vince and Maggie had agreed to the training with some reluctance, with Melinda training with him.

The morning's dusting of snow had made the playing field treacherous. Although it had stopped snowing, the gray sky hung low and heavy.

"Draw energy to maintain your balance," Quaylyn instructed her.

Rahlys tried to concentrate.

**ANTHYA APPROACHES….**

Contact from Councilor Anthya was always sudden and unexpected.

"Quaylyn, a message from the Oracle, Anthya is coming!" Quaylyn immediately appeared by her side. "Do you think the High Council is calling you back?" she asked him.

"I don't know; I hope not," he said with all sincerity. Quaylyn was not ready to go home; he had not figured out how to convince Rahlys to return with him to Aaia.

"Maybe it is about Kaylya." Rahlys hoped so.

Suddenly Councilor Anthya appeared before them in a long flowing shimmering purple gown. It occurred to Rahlys that she had never seen Anthya actually dress like this in person, only in *non-permanent physical time.* Anthya had the beauty of Aphrodite herself with pale rose-white skin, long golden hair, and gentle gray-blue eyes.

"Greetings Sorceress Rahlys, Guardian of the Light, and Warrior Quaylyn. I bring word from the High Council." Although her greeting was formal her demeanor was warm.

"Greetings Council Anthya, how may we serve?" Rahlys asked falling into the traditional response for Anthya's world.

"I have come to offer you a mission if you choose to accept it. Since learning of Kaylya's presence here on Earth, the power of the Runes of the Crystal Table have determined it likely that Brakalar and the Rod of Destruction are also here on Earth."

It took the power of the runes for the High Council to come up with that? She, Quaylyn, and Ilene had come to that conclusion long ago, but so far their search had uncovered nothing.

"What do you wish for us to do?" Quaylyn asked. He knew appearances in *non-permanent physical time* tended to be brief, therefore information needed to be gathered quickly.

"Locate Brakalar and apprehend him so that he and the rod can be brought back to Aaia."

"What about Kaylya?" Rahlys asked.

"She is to join you on this mission as one of your warriors. When the mission has been accomplished, she will be granted Accepted One status. Rojaire currently leads an expedition to the Crescent Mountains on the Devastated Continent. When he returns, he will be informed that Kaylya is here."

"Will Rojaire...?" Rahlys started to ask, but Anthya was already gone. Rahlys wanted to ask her if Rojaire would be allowed to come to Kaylya when he returned, but Anthya didn't give her a chance.

"We will call a meeting of the Order of the Oracle in conjunction with the twins' birthday party. Everyone will be there."

---

"I don't like the idea of this at all," Elaine declared defiantly in protest of being teleported up the tracks. "It is unnatural."

"But that's where you are wrong," Ilene argued. "Teleportation utilizes natural mental ability. Steel locomotives are unnatural."

"Why can't we just wait to visit when there's a train running?"

"Because this is a special occasion; it's the twins' first birthday, and Rahlys has called a meeting of the Order of the Oracle. We can't wait for a train. You didn't mind it when Quaylyn used mental energy to boost you up hills. Besides, Jack Faulkner will be there," Ilene added to try and entice her. "I think he likes you."

"Oh please, the man is more decrepit than I am. I'm not looking for anyone to take care of." They were still arguing when Quaylyn appeared outside their apartment door. He knocked loudly and Ilene opened the door for him.

"Come on in, Quaylyn." With her back to her mother she jerked her head in Elaine's direction and oscillated her hand indicating to Quaylyn that her mother was iffy on the thought of teleportation.

"Greetings, my lady," Quaylyn said getting the message. Elaine smiled up at him as he took her hand and bowed to her slightly. "It is my great pleasure to serve you," he said. When he straightened up again the three of them were standing in Vince and Maggie's yard.

Startled, Elaine saw where she was and started to swoon. The chilled damp air made her shiver.

"Mother...!" Ilene cried in alarm.

Quaylyn caught Elaine in his arms and carried her to the porch. "She's alright," he said, having already mentally probed her. "Arriving so suddenly was a bit of a shock." He placed her down gently on the porch bench warming the air around her.

"Mother, are you alright?" Ilene asked anxiously, holding her hand and sending her positive healing energy.

"I'm alright," she reassured her daughter sitting up on her own quite recovered. "You forgot our coats," she barked at Quaylyn reproachfully.

"My deepest apologies; Ilene and I will go back and collect them …after we get you inside."

Hearing voices on the porch, Vince opened the door. "Hello, Ilene and Elaine, come on in. The party is just getting started."

"Ilene and I will be back in a moment. Elaine can explain," Quaylyn said grinning. With that, Quaylyn and Ilene vanished. Elaine shuddered to think she herself had vanished like that from her own living room only moments ago.

"I'm not going back that way," she gruffly proclaimed to Vince and went in to get warm. Vince closed the door behind them.

The family room was brightly decorated with paper streamers and balloons, some of which drifted across the floor like colorful tumbleweed responding to air movement in the room. A home-decorated cake with one candle graced the center of the family room table. Leaf seemingly jumped out of nowhere.

"It's a birthday party," he sang out gleefully jumping around in excitement. Rock, dressed in a new outfit, and Crystal, wearing a frilly pink dress, roamed around laughing at Leaf's antics. Melinda took numerous photos documenting the occasion for the family album.

"Elaine, my dear; it's so good to see you," Jack warmly greeted her rising from his chair and rushing over …or what passed for "rushing" in Jack's case… to intercept her. "Come over here and sit down by the woodstove. You look a little pale. Where's your coat?"

"Hello, Jack; I'm fine," but Elaine let him guide her to a chair by the stove. "Quaylyn zapped us over here without even giving us a chance to grab a coat. It's enough to give an old woman a heart attack."

"Elaine, welcome…!" Maggie and Rahlys called out while bringing dishes and utensils from the kitchen to the table. Kaylya brought Elaine a cup of herbal tea.

"Here is some hot tea to warm you from the inside. I'm so glad you could come, Elaine; I was so hoping you would."

"Thank you, Kaylya," she said, accepting the tea graciously.

"I don't know what is in it, but Kaylya's tea always makes me feel better," Jack said.

A chilly wave of fresh air accompanied Quaylyn and Ilene as they walked in with coats and presents, sending the drifting balloons dancing across the floor.

From there a classic family birthday party unfolded. Leaf had done his best to impress on Crystal and Rock the importance of the day. At best they were aware that something special was going on and it revolved around them. Maggie lit the one candle in the center of the cake. It was a mile stone for Maggie and Vince; they each held a child while Leaf climbed up on a chair to get on level, and everyone sang "Happy Birthday." Leaf had the honor of blowing out the candle. When the others clapped, so did the twins. They ate cake and home-churned ice-cream and Crystal and Rock opened numerous gifts with Leaf's help. Later, the new toys were hauled into the boys' room where Maggie set up the children to play without being underfoot, leaving the adults to clean up and visit. Melinda hung out with the adults for a while then retreated to her room.

When everyone was finally settled with full coffee mugs and tea cups Rahlys called the meeting of the Order of the Oracle to order. Rahlys conjured the crystal before them.

The membership of the Order of the Oracle had gradually grown over the years. Membership into the Order was not based on magical ability, but trust. Anyone trusted to maintain the integrity and secrecy of the Order was a member. The children became part of the Order at birth. Hence; Leaf, Rock, Crystal, Melinda, Ilene, Elaine, Maggie, Vince, Quaylyn, Theon, Kaylya, Jack, and Rahlys were now all lifetime members.

"I have received a message from Councilor Anthya," Rahlys announced to expectant faces. Kaylya felt a rush of dread chilling her blood cold; she had been waiting for and fearing such a message.

"What did she have to say?" Kaylya asked a bit tremulously.

"Councilor Anthya offered us a mission, naming Kaylya specifically as one of my warriors," Rahlys told the group. "The High Council came to the same conclusion we did. It is believed that Brakalar is here on Earth. Our mission is to find Brakalar and apprehend him so he can be returned to Aaia. When the mission is achieved, Kaylya will be granted Accepted One status on her world. She also said Rojaire is leading an expedition on the Devastated Continent, but the councilor vanished before I could ask her more."

The hope was readable on Kaylya's face. She had tried not to raise her expectations too high. "It's certainly more than I deserve."

"The only lead we have, assuming it is real, is the magazine article Ilene found," Rahlys reminded them, "so we should probably start our search in Louisiana."

"Brakalar will not be easy to find. His hideout will certainly be shielded," Kaylya reasoned. "We will have to lure him out into the open."

Rahlys focused on other worries. "Hopefully he hasn't found a way to open the chest; we must take him before he does."

*He hasn't....*

Everyone's attention riveted on Melinda standing in the entrance to her room. Her telepathed statement had been received by all.

"How do you know this, Melinda?" Rahlys asked gently.

*....because the essence of Droclum has not found me.*

"Melinda has terrible recurring nightmares," Maggie explained.

"When did these nightmares start?" Kaylya asked.

"Around the time Rahlys and Ilene returned from the expedition," Maggie offered. Melinda nodded in agreement.

"That is also about the time Brakalar would have arrived on Earth with the Rod of Destruction," Quaylyn calculated.

"Do you think there is a connection?" Rahlys asked.

Quaylyn thought about it. "Yes, I believe there could be a connection since both Melinda and the Rod of Destruction were ..."touched" by Droclum."

Melinda felt cold fear beading up and down her spine. She would not surrender to it; she was a warrior in training. It was time to be a woman.

"I didn't have a lot to go on," Ilene reported, "but I found another article about the disappearing flat screen TV in a local newspaper called the Daily Comet printed in Thibodaux, Louisiana. I also located the security worker, Fred Landry, on Facebook; he works at the local Wal-Mart. Apparently he's taken a lot of ribbing over the issue."

"Has anyone here ever been to Louisiana?" Kaylya asked.

Vince spoke up. "I have. My folks lived in south Louisiana for a few years while I was growing up. Mostly I remember bayous and cane fields ...and snakes."

"We need to send a team to investigate," Quaylyn said, "at least two people."

"We could send an expert on paranormal phenomena accompanied by an assistant," Rahlys suggested.

"What is paranormal phenomena?" Quaylyn asked confused.

"That's everything you do and take for granted," Vince answered him.

"Sending paranormal phenomena experts is a great idea," Ilene agreed. "I can print up some phony business cards."

*I'll design an artsy logo for it*, Melinda offered.

"That would be great! Who are we going to send?" Rahlys asked.

After some discussion it was decided that Vince and Rahlys would be the best choices. Quaylyn and Kaylya would be more likely to inadvertently make a social blunder due to lack of familiarity with the culture and Ilene and Melinda were too young to be convincing.

With autumn came the return of night and star gazing. As evening approached the sky cleared and the men decided to build a bon fire. The children were bundled up and everyone stepped out for some fresh air to watch the stars come out. Jack had also brought fireworks for the occasion which had Leaf all excited.

"Are you tired, Elaine?" Quaylyn asked solicitously. "I can take you home whenever you are ready."

Elaine had started dreading the inevitable trip back long ago; in fact, the mounting dread was biting into her enjoyment of the festivities. "I'm not going back the way I came," she said defiantly, "and don't you dare try to pull that stunt on me again."

"My apologies, Elaine, I'm sorry. I shouldn't have surprised you like that. It's just that I had hoped that once you saw that teleportation doesn't hurt, you would be more receptive to it. Again, I'm sorry; I promise I will never do that again …unless your life depended on it. You are welcomed to stay with us as long as you wish."

It was impossible for Elaine to remain angry with Quaylyn after such a humble, heart-felt apology. "Well, you're forgiven this time," she relented.

"The fireworks are about to start," Jack announced returning from the set-up zone and sideling up to the dwindling fire to warm up after gladly relinquishing control of the show to Vince. No sooner said and the first rocket zinged off bursting with a loud pop into a blooming spectacular of colored lights that sizzled away into smoke and ash. Kaylya and Rahlys held the twins while Maggie, Melinda, and Ilene kept Leaf safely corralled. One star burst of color followed another with Leaf jumping for joy after each display.

"…a lot of money going up in smoke," Elaine grumbled shaking her head in disapproval, but she couldn't resist going "ooh" and "ah" over the show like the rest of them. All too soon the fireworks were over. Ilene walked over.

"Are you ready to go, Mother?"

Before Elaine could answer her daughter someone shouted, "Look up at the sky!" Ilene and Elaine looked up to see a shimmering green curtain of wavering light cutting through the stars. Then suddenly a crown of undulating red light exploded directly overhead sending sheets of flickering quivering light streaming down from the heavens.

"Wow!"

Three more writhing whips of light cracked the sky in rapid succession … red, green, and white. In all her years Elaine had never seen northern lights so spectacular. All too soon the aurora faded out.

"Wow!" Ilene exclaimed. "It's like God said, 'you think what you did was a fireworks show, watch this!'"

"That did put our fireworks display to shame," Jack admitted.

That was a brilliant natural display of the power and beauty of the elemental forces," Quaylyn pointed out excitedly to Elaine. "See, there is nothing to be afraid of."

For some reason, teleportation was a lot easier for Elaine to accept after that!

"I think I'm ready to go home now," Elaine announced.

---

Using Melinda's carefully designed logo; Ilene produced business cards for Dr. Jeff Robertson, Director of Paranormal Phenomena at the Paranormal Phenomena Research Center in New York City and his Assistant Director Ms. Lucy Sutton. It didn't matter that such a place didn't exist; no one was likely to try and follow up on it. When all was ready, Rahlys conjured the Oracle of Light to her hand. The crystal would have the power to take them where they wanted to go without Rahlys having to envision the location in her mind.

"Are you ready?" she asked Vince standing beside her.

"I'm ready."

Holding the crystal tightly in the palm of her hand Rahlys formulated her thoughts. *Take us to the Wal-Mart store in Thibodaux, Louisiana …without anyone noticing our sudden appearance.* With her eyes shut to avoid distraction, she concentrated on the crystal and their goal, opening her eyes upon sensing her surroundings had changed; it certainly smelled different. She found herself standing in a public restroom stall; the stall door closed. Smart, Rahlys thought to herself, impressed with the crystal's ingenuity. Cautiously she opened the restroom stall door and was relieved to find a lady, not a man, primping in front of a mirror; at least she was in the women's restroom. She went to a sink and washed her hands; it would be expected behavior. Then exiting the restroom, she was relieved to find Vince leaving the men's room a short distance away.

"It looks like we are here," she said as they met.

"Yeah, I guess we should go to the customer service desk and inquire after Fred Landry." Bold lettering on one wall confirmed they were in Wal-Mart, but all Wal-Mart stores looked pretty much the same. When they passed a newsstand, copies of the Daily Comet and the Times Picayune confirmed they were in Louisiana.

"May I help you?" a female worker asked as they approached the desk.

"Yes," Vince said going into action. "I'm Dr. Jeff Robertson." He handed her a copy of his business card. "I would like to speak with Mr. Fred Landry, if I may, for a few moments."

"Hum, director of paranormal phenomena at the Paranormal Phenomena Research Center in New York City," she read ending in a chuckle. "I'll see if he is available." The store worker seemed beside herself as she moved away from the window and made an in-store call to what Rahlys and Vince assumed was Fred Landry's station. She was on the phone for over a minute.

"Maybe she is trying to convince him to see us," Rahlys said. The worker, still chuckling, returned to the window.

"He will be down in a minute," she said barely containing herself.

Meanwhile another customer approached the desk. Rahlys and Vince moved off to the side to give the customer access to the window. Several minutes passed before a tall heavy dark-haired man Rahlys recognized from the Facebook photos Ilene had shown them walked up. The female worker standing behind the desk still servicing a customer indicated Vince and Rahlys with a wave of her hand.

Vince stepped up to the plate immediately. "Mr. Landry, good afternoon; thanks for taking the time to see us," he said handing him a business card.

"Look, I know why you are here. I don't have anything further to say; I've had enough of this whole incident."

"Mr. Landry, believe me, I understand how you feel. We deal with skeptics every day."

"We are on your side," Rahlys assured him. "We believe what you saw may really have happened." This seemed to calm the security worker some.

"Is there a place we can talk in private?" Vince asked.

"We can go to my office," Fred Landry said relenting. He led them to a small office room lined with security monitors. He didn't offer them a seat; there weren't enough chairs for everyone to sit anyway. Vince scanned the monitors. Apparently a couple of digital security cameras were focused on the electronics department which included flat screen TVs.

"Look, I know what I saw," Fred said immediately on the defensive. "Like I don't have better things to do with my time than stage a hoax," he fumed.

Vince decided Fred could benefit from a little proof of their position on the matter. "Lucy, here, can move a pencil without touching it . . . just by using her mind."

"You're not serious?"

"Lucy, would you care to demonstrate a little of your talent?"

"I c-can try," Rahlys, acting the part of Lucy, stammered.

Vince reached over and pulled a pencil from a holder and placed it on Fred's desk.

"This ought to be good," Fred mumbled.

Rahlys, understanding what Vince was getting at, worked hard at looking like she was straining her brain to achieve this unbelievable feat. After nearly a minute of intense looking concentration the pencil rocked once. Fred Landry gasped. Rahlys gave it a little more intense looking effort and the pencil suddenly rolled several inches across the desk.

"Wow!" Fred exclaimed. "You guys mean business. What else can you do?" he asked looking at Rahlys.

Careful not to go overboard, Rahlys, with seemingly much effort, slowly rolled the pen back and forth across the desk a couple of times. Feeling Fred take the hook, Vince jumped in again.

"Would it be possible for us to see the footage of the disappearing TV?" Vince, playing the role of Dr. Robertson, asked.

"Ah, sure, I guess so. Do you believe someone took the TV by using their mind?"

"We believe it's a possibility."

Fred typed something using the keyboard in front of him and indicated which monitor they should watch. "Here's the video." The only thing that indicated they were watching recorded footage was a slight difference in the arrangement of the merchandise. "This is the item that vanished," he said pointing out a TV sitting on the shelf.

They watched the monitor in silence for several moments during which nothing happened, not a single shopper passed by. Then suddenly the TV disappeared from sight.

That gave Vince an idea.

"Let's assume that the person responsible for this came window shopping ahead of time. Can we backtrack the recording further and see what customers may have shown an interest in this model before it vanished?

"How far back do you want to go?"

"Let's try an hour prior to the TV's disappearance."

Fred complied backing up the recording. Again they watched the screen in silence. Fred fast forwarded repeatedly to when customers walked by, most not showing any particular interest in the television set.

And then Rahlys saw him.

*There he is,* Rahlys sent Vince in a telepathed message.

Vince glanced at Rahlys then studied the appearance of the man in the video, watching as Brakalar paused briefly in front of the TV set, and the video camera, before walking on.

They now had definitive proof that Brakalar was on Earth.

# Chapter 14

# Aaia

Dawn finally broke over the mysterious valley revealing a heavy mist, almost a light drizzle, hovering over the river. Rojaire was on watch, his third over the course of the long period of darkness. Nothing had threatened the men; the fire had been allowed to burn out long ago.

The others would be stirring soon. Rojaire rebuilt the fire with the last of the wood supply to brew tea and cook grains for a morning meal. They were almost out of water. He was tempted to make a trek down to the river, violating all rules about venturing out alone and not deserting your watch, but thought better of it. He would wait for the others to wake up.

Theon was next to make a move. "I see we've made it through the night. What does it look like out there?" he asked joining Rojaire outside the cave.

"It's damp, foggy. We need more water. I was thinking of making a trip to the river."

"Alone...?"

"I'll take someone with me. How did you sleep?"

"I slept as well as can be expected when sleeping on rocks ...even if they are diamonds." Theon stretched trying to work out the kinks.

"We should be thinking about returning to our mission goals, I suppose," Rojaire said a bit reluctantly. "We could make it to the end of the mountain passage in less than a rotation."

"…And pass up exploring this miraculous valley further?" Theon questioned. "We can return to the tunnels during the next period of darkness."

Ollen opened his eyes next and jumped right up. "I agree with Theon. This place is well worth exploring further."

"Then we will spend this period of light studying the valley and return to the lava tube again by nightfall," Rojaire conceded.

Before long everyone had risen and after a quick morning meal the men were eager to get moving again having had their fill of inactivity. They donned cloaks to shelter them from the dampness and carefully descended the slope down to the base of the plateau. The lingering moisture made the trail they had imprinted slippery underfoot. They hadn't gone very far after reaching level ground when they came upon fresh tracks deeply impressed into the soft loam of the forest floor.

"By Seaa's light, whatever made those tracks is certainly large!" Rojaire said with fearful concern.

"We may have found our meat eater," Theon said studying the tracks. "Look at those claw marks."

"What should we do?" Traevus asked ready to bolt to safety.

"Calm down; this animal is long gone…and it's moving in the opposite direction than we are headed," Theon noted.

"Could there be more than one?" The unmistakable tremor in Edty's voice reverberated in everyone's minds.

"There should be," Theon reasoned, "unless it's about to go extinct."

"Have your weapons ready," Rojaire ordered.

Theon was about to tell them a knife on a stick wasn't going to me a very formidable weapon against a beast this size, but thought better of it. "Just keep your eyes open, stay together, and make noise. A lone animal is not likely to attack a group of people. Plus, unless there are other humans living in this valley, whatever made these tracks probably won't recognize us as food."

"I hope it doesn't get to taste us," Kiril added.

By the time they reached the river, rays of sunlight pierced through the clouds driving off the misty fog. The rocky bottomed stream was shallow and braided with many exposed bars of rock and sand between strands of crystal clear flowing water, but the expanse of dry riverbed to each side spoke of times of greater volume.

"We should probably boil this water first before drinking it since there are all sorts of wildlife sharing the same water source," Theon recommended. "Just because the water is clear doesn't mean it's pure."

"What if we collected water from the waterfall?" Rojaire asked. "Wouldn't that water be out of reach of the animals living down in the valley?"

"Probably it would be okay coming down from the mountains," Theon agreed. We have been drinking the water up to now."

The group crossed the shallow stream; the waterfall they were headed toward flowed out of the western mountains. The sun quickly dried off rocks and foliage, the air becoming increasingly hot and humid. They soon entered more forest dominated by trees with hairy mottled yellow orange trunks and thick blue-green fern-like leaves that allowed dappled sunshine to reach the ground. The forest floor was littered with blue hard shelled nuts that had obviously dropped from the array of branches overhead. It was also obvious from the amount of cracked and discarded bits and pieces of shell that crunched underfoot, that something had been feeding on the nuts.

Ollen picked up a couple of the nuts trying to crack them against each other in his hand, but the shells were too hard. Placing one on a grayish-pink stone protruding from the ground he picked up a second loose stone and smashed the nut with it. The outer shell cracked exposing light blue meat inside. "Not bad," he said after giving it a taste test. The men gathered a bunch filling a harvest bag. Before long they saw some of the little creatures that considered the nuts a prime food source.

"Well, look at that," Tassyn pointed out, spotting the first one. A small blue fist-sized creature that was all teeth scampered up and down the outer trunk of a tree in nervous agitation over the presence of the men, sounding off a loud whistling alarm. Soon other little toothy creatures appeared running up and down trees and back and forth across branches joining in the whistling, their short bluish brown fur standing on end. Though noisy, none of the little creatures dared come any closer. When Kiril tried approaching one, it quickly vanished up the tree.

"Maybe they're upset we took some of their nuts?" Edty speculated.

The forest thinned and the trees were gradually replaced with thick bushes covered in large pinkish gray translucent flowers with petals so delicate, they swayed gently in the slightest breeze. At least the men thought they were flowers until suddenly hundreds of flowers took to the air. What they had at first taken to be flowers were actually a large flock of the little flying creatures they had already observed. As it turned out, the bushes *were* blooming, but the actual pink and white flowers were far less spectacular than the creatures that had been feeding on their nectar.

Eventually the forest and brush ended in grassland. The sun blazed hot overhead with the western peaks still quite some distance away. The valley stretched far wider and longer than they had originally estimated. They had expected to reach the western edge of the valley by high sun, but their destination still loomed far ahead. *At this rate we will never make it to the waterfall and all the way back to the lava tube by darkness,* Rojaire realized. *I hope there is shelter at the waterfall.*

According to Kiril's map three waterfalls joined the main stream that cut through the center of the valley. Assuming the landscape hasn't changed greatly since the map was drawn, one waterfall was located far to the north, another came out of the mountains to the northeast, and the closest one lay to the west. Which didn't explain the source of the river from the south. Setting out diagonally across the grassland, they planned to follow the western mountain range until they came to the waterfall. It was unclear what to expect as far as caves. On the map, adjacent to and south of the marking indicating the waterfall, numerous little overlapping loops like links to a chain marked the area; no one knew what the overlapping loops might mean.

"Maybe it is a whole bunch of caves," Tassyn offered.

A burst of movement caught their eye as the grasses started to sway, wavering with the absence of wind.

"Kurpers…!" Traevus shouted.

During the period of darkness the group had taken a stab at naming the species of animals they had encountered. Most of the names they had come up with were less than satisfactory, but in conversation, Theon had repeatedly referred to the little hooved creatures with silver fur as "kurpers" meaning "silvery" and the name had stuck.

This herd of kurpers was over twice the size of the one they had encountered in the little valley. The herd bolted upon perceiving the men, running away from them. Theon would have liked to have harvested another one to eat, but the animals were already gone.

The grassland ended as they continued to follow the mountain range north. Trees and brush dotted the land including several of the reddish orange trees laden with the fist-sized dark brown fruit they had already experimented with without ill effects. The men paused for a rest listening to the silence as they ate.

"I think I hear the waterfall," Ollen said after a while. The men listened intently; the sound was extremely faint, but Kiril, Tassyn, and Traevus thought maybe they could hear it too. Encouraged, the men started moving again, even picking up speed. After a couple hundred paces the others heard it too. It was not until they rounded a contour of the mountain that all was revealed. The men stopped abruptly and gaped awe-struck over the scene before them.

"Never in all my seasons have I ever imagined such a sight," Ollen declared quietly trying to take it all in.

"No need to imagine it; I think it's real," Rojaire said.

"Now we know what the overlapping loops on the map represent," Theon added.

"Is it human-made or the work of forces in nature?" Tassyn asked.

"I believe it's natural," Rojaire said, "Let's have a closer look."

The purple mountain cliffs opened up like a giant maw with stalactite teeth seemingly poised ready to devour the land. The floor of the huge open-faced cavern was only waist high from the valley floor, and at least a hundred strides long and twenty strides deep. The ceiling of the palatial cave rose three times higher than their average height with dozens of randomly spaced stone pillars reaching from ceiling to floor dividing the interior into suggested rooms. The cliff's rock base had eroded in layers that served easily as steps. Facing east northeast, the shelter provided cool shade from the midday sun. The waterfall cascaded down the mountain side at the far end, the little stream run-off flowing toward them before veering east to meet with the distant river.

"Will this do for shelter?" Theon asked Rojaire playfully.

"It will shelter us from the sun and the rain, but what about wild animals?"

"I guess we will just have to be vigilant."

They looked around walking through the enormous space. "I don't see any scat or other signs of occupancy," Theon said after closer inspection. "Perhaps the cave is too open to serve as a suitable animal den."

"Let's hope you're right," Rojaire said still ill at ease with the concept of wildlife.

After collecting water, the men settled down to sleep during the period of intense heat. The deep interior of the rock palisade was refreshingly cool. Kiril volunteered for the first watch. When he was later relieved from watch by Traevus, he chose a spot to settle in, but found that no matter how hard he tried to empty his mind he just couldn't sleep. Eventually he gave up trying.

"Where are you going?" Traevus asked as Kiril attempted to leave the shelter.

"I'm just going to the waterfall," Kiril grumbled.

"All right, just don't wander out of sight."

"I won't."

Kiril made his way down to the level of the stream runoff and strolled to the pool beneath the waterfall, already shaded by the western ridge. Kiril was not happy. He hadn't been allowed to make an entry in his journal since they discovered the collapsed wall of the lava tube. *It's not like I'm going to tell anyone about the hidden valleys; I can keep a separate private journal.*

Distracted by his own thoughts, Kiril picked up rocks and threw them into the water to relieve tension, but quickly became bored with the activity. He picked up a shiny round golden stone and absently rubbed the silky smooth stone between his fingers while he continued to sulk.

*Here I am in the most fabulous adventure of my longevity and the rest of the group forbids me to write a word about it,* he fumed. *It just isn't fair; how am I expected to keep so many details in my head. This valley is so incredible! I just want to describe all these wonders; these strange living animals, all the new varieties of plants, the cave of diamonds, and this stone pavilion. What's so wrong about that?*

Kiril almost tossed the golden stone he held in his hand as an expression of his fury ...except it felt so comfortably smooth between his fingers. *Why can't they see the importance of recording all this? After all, they are using my map!*

Kiril, lost in his personal tirade, hadn't notice the rest of the group gathering behind him. Then finally, becoming aware that he was no longer alone, Kiril turned around, startled to see the men staring fixedly at him.

"What...?"

"We can hear your thoughts," Theon told him.

"What ...what do you mean?" Kiril asked puzzled. He hadn't been exactly shielding his thoughts, but since telepathic communication was blocked on Lynnara, he hadn't thought it necessary.

"What's that in your hand?" Rojaire asked.

"Huh...? It's just a rock I picked up," Kiril said handing it to him.

"It's a star stone," Traevus said recognizing it.

"Where did you get this?" Rojaire asked examining it.

"I picked it up from right here," Kiril said pointing to the array of rocks at his feet. He had heard the stories and understood the significance of possessing a star stone. "Do you really think it's a star stone?"

Rojaire tossed the stone back to him.

"Well, there's one way to find out; try teleporting to the other side of the stream," Rojaire suggested.

"All right..." Kiril doubted it would work, but gave it a try, only to find himself immediately standing on the opposite bank. "Crystal shards, I did it!" he shouted with unbridled excitement, looking around amazed. Then suddenly he spotted what looked like a second star stone among the rocks bordering the stream and picked it up.

"Look, another one!" he shouted and tossed it across the stream. Traevus caught it and then tested it by placing himself on the opposite bank next to Kiril.

With two star stones already found, the men immediately started searching for more, following the little stream toward the distant river. For the longest no more star stones were found. Edty and Tassyn removed their boots and rolled up their pants legs to wade directly in the shallow stream. Silently, intent on their search, the men wandered far from the stone pavilion and were about to give up all together when Edty finally let out a whoop!

"Hey....I found one!" he shouted dancing in the water. Encouraged by another find, the rest of the men continued their search with renewed vigor. But as time passed and no more of the coveted stones were found, interest began to wane.

*This would be a good time to reveal the star stone Theon and I have kept secret till now,* Rojaire reasoned. He sent a tight mental message to Theon informing him of his intent. With so many star stones in play now, it seemed the right thing to do.

"I found one," he said pretending to pick it up from the rocks while holding the star stone concealed in his hand. To Rojaire's relief, no one questioned the find.

The men were getting tired, but with yet another star stone uncovered, they couldn't bring themselves to quit looking. Again a long time passed without another discovery; one by one the men gave up and gathered together on the bank of the stream to rest and eat. They now had four star stones amongst them; only Tassyn, Ollen, and Theon still lacked one of their own.

"You know, Rojaire, with these stones ...if those of us without one paired with those who have one, we could still make it back to the lava tubes before darkness," Theon said. He didn't really want to leave the valley, but he knew Rojaire wanted to return focus to the mission.

---

The sky brightened clear, promising another exceedingly hot day. Caleeza woke as the first light of a new dawn filtered down through the layers of crystal that sheltered her, the caverns cooled by an underground stream. She made her way to the surface where hardly a breeze stirred. The Crystalline Landscape glowed radiantly in the brilliant light of day.

Caleeza gazed about her at the towering jumbles of crystals extending to the horizon in every direction. For her it had become a crystal prison. She didn't really know how far she would have to go to reach the outer edge of the field of crystals since Sarus had placed her here when he brought her back, but she and Sarus had ventured deeply into the Crystalline Landscape before she had vanished and appeared on Earth. She also didn't know how far she would have to go to reach Mt. Vatre in the center of the Crystalline Landscape. The broken jagged caldera of Mt. Vatre loomed darkly in the distance.

Caleeza stared listlessly toward Mt. Vatre's ominous remains. *Should I try to reach it on my own? Would Sarus protect me if I attempted the journey to Mt. Vatre alone? Or should I try to escape the Crystalline Landscape all together by seeking its outer edge? Would Sarus let me go? Would he protect me along the way?* She had fallen victim to one of the crystals' invisible energy fields before. At the time, she and Sarus were all that remained of their seven member expedition. They had been unaware then of the dangers.

She had been lucky Caleeza realized. The energy field had transported her to a distant world across the galaxy, but she had arrived alive and in one piece. Other members of the expedition may not have been so fortunate.

When Caleeza had vanished from the Crystalline Landscape, Sarus was still composed of flesh and blood. Since her return, she had been unsuccessful at finding out what had happened to him. Sarus' mental energy, apparently all that is left of him, either can't or won't explain. He had brought her back to their world, but unfortunately she couldn't bring Sarus back to his former self.

Hunger drew Caleeza's attention. Having greeted the morning, she descended again to the crystalline cavern where she lived and located her harvesting bag. She found it nearly empty, rinsed out the last of the fruit, and ate it. It was hardly satisfying. She washed out the now empty harvesting bag and carried it with her back to the surface where the already blazing sun quickly zapped away the moisture.

"Sarus," Caleeza called out softly seeking a mental connection.

"Caleeza," she heard in response.

"Good morning, Sarus," she said greeting the emptiness surrounding her. She knew such sentiment meant little to Sarus, but it was part of her continuing effort to reach what was left of Sarus' humanity.

"Good morning, Caleeza," he responded dutifully.

"Have you ever been to Mt. Vatre?" Caleeza asked on a whim.

"My presence extends only through the Crystalline Landscape."

"Do you remember the mission assigned to us by the High Council of the Crystal Table?" There was a long pause.

"What was our mission?" he asked finally.

"Our goal was to reach the slopes of Mt. Vatre; we still haven't completed our mission."

"My presence extends only through the Crystalline Landscape," he repeated, but there was a hint of confusion. Did Sarus still harbor a sense of duty? She wanted to press the issue further, but decided to think on it first.

"I need to harvest food," she said changing the subject and grabbing her harvesting bag.

"I will place you where you can find food," he agreed, apparently willing to give up the topic of long forgotten missions. "Let me know when you are ready to return."

Caleeza found herself standing a short distance east of the Crescent Mountains. It was the closest Sarus had even positioned her to the mountains. Since the day was already heating up fast, she set to work quickly gathering food. After digging up a supply of ground nuts and picking zan fruit, she made her way down the side of a small ravine where a larger variety of berries and leafy vegetables could be found growing in the moister ground below. While harvesting, she thought about what Sarus had said. If his presence didn't extend beyond the Crystalline Landscape, could she escape from his control after all? What if she didn't let him know that she was ready to return to the Crystalline Landscape; would he still grab her? She had thought his range unlimited since he had brought her back from Earth? It was worth a try.

With her harvesting bag full, Caleeza sought shade from the scorching hot sun. Her first thought was to locate shade in the ravine, but since the mountains were so close, she decided instead to make her way toward them. Maybe she could find a cave to shelter her; if not there would be shade amongst the contours of the peaks. One thing she knew for certain; she would not call on Sarus to take her back to the Crystalline Landscape.

---

"It looks like the way is blocked," Ollen said. "The lava tube has collapsed."

Rojaire and his men were tired and ready for sleep. Travel through the lava tube had been uneventful after the adventures offered by the hidden valley.

"It was like that when we came this way the first time," Rojaire explained. "Our route is through here." The men stared at the entrance to a narrow cave that receded into the darkness with disdain. "I assure you, it's the way out."

"That's not a route; it's a hole in the wall," Theon moaned. "I thought you said the hardest part of the passage was over."

"It is except for this little stretch. Here, take the star stone to help you along."

Reluctantly, the men followed him through the tight space, Theon grudgingly leaving his walking staff behind. The narrow cave quickly shrank to a crawl space, forcing them to move along on their hands and knees. After a long arduous serpentine journey on their bellies, they finally emerged into a cavern they could stand up in.

Now the men were thoroughly exhausted, Theon near collapse despite help from the star stone. They ate quietly what they had harvested from the valley and the dried food they carried which sustained them.

"I guess we don't have to worry about the wildlife from the valley wandering out this far," Ollen said as he stretched out to sleep. Tassyn, Edty, and Kiril were already snoring.

"No, that's not likely," Rojaire agreed. "The same is true in the other direction." Traevus who had barely dosed off listened quietly to the discussion.

"Strategically," Ollen said, "the passage would be easy to defend; or we could even close it off if developments warranted it."

"If anyone from the Academy uses our mapped passage they will find the valley," Theon pointed out. "Perhaps we should close the passage before they ever get a chance to?"

Rojaire gave it some thought. "We would only have to close off the west end. If the passage doesn't go all the way through, the High Council will lose interest in it. That way we would still have access to the valley from the interior."

Without light to trigger them awake, the men slept long and hard.

After the needed rest, when everyone was ready, the team moved on. Rojaire assured his companions the worse was behind them. "The rest of the passage will be relatively easy."

"I can't believe you went crawling through that wormhole, Rojaire, in the first place," Theon said disgruntled. The long crawl through the wormhole had been extremely difficult for him. Every muscle and joint in his body ached. "What would you have done if you had come to a dead-end? There wasn't room through there to turn around."

"I would have crawled out backwards."

Theon limped along painfully, but did his best to try and hide it. *I should have stayed in the valley and let them go on without me.* Sensing Theon's need to do so, the group took frequent short rests. One cavern led to another, but fortunately all were large enough to walk through upright. Still the trek through darkness with only the light from their lamps to illuminate the way seemed endless.

When the men became weary, Rojaire coaxed them on. "We are almost there; it isn't far now." They had just entered a large cavern, the largest they had encountered so far. "We are only a couple of caverns from the exit." Encouraged, the men kept on walking. Eventually they entered a second cavern and then a third.

"I see light!" Edty exclaimed.

As they came around a bend, daylight spilled in at the far end.

"By Seaa's light, we made it..!" Kiril shouted unable to control his jubilance at reaching the end.

The men rushed to the exit only to back off as blinding sunlight made their eyes water. They hung around the broad mouth of the cavern giving their eyes time to adjust to the brightness.

At first they thought the light was playing tricks on their vision as they glanced out repeatedly into the brilliant sunshine. They could have sworn they saw the image of a woman walking toward them. As their eyes adjusted to the light, the image of the woman became clearer. Then finally Traevus recognized her.

"Caleeza," Traevus cried out rushing from the cave to meet her.

## Chapter 15

# Earth

*elinda…*

*No….*

The whisper in the dark exuded evil; once again Melinda sensed the taint of Droclum's horrific essence, faint but unmistakable. She tried to rouse herself awake to escape the nightmare, but without success.

*Droclum is dead! You can't hurt me.*

She thought this to be true. After his defeat, she had seen the pile of ash that had once been Droclum. Still she couldn't be certain the spectral that haunted her dreams couldn't hurt her; somehow she had to stand up to it.

*I will find you,* the essence of Droclum threatened.

Melinda fought back her fear. She found herself standing in a dimly lit hall, endlessly long, with brick walls that vanished in the distance at each end to a point, like a railroad track receding toward the horizon. Along the brick walls were numerous wooden doors each a different size and shape. There was no color; all was gray, barely illuminated by the unknown light source. It was time to open some doors.

*I am coming to you.*

Refusing to let fear paralyze her, Melinda rushed to the nearest door, small and square, but large enough for her to pass through. Bracing herself to face all kinds of horrors, she turned the handle; it was locked.

*I am coming to you.*

The taint was getting stronger …and closer! Desperately, with mounting terror, Melinda tried the long narrow door, the tall wide door, the round door, the triangular door, and the large octagonal one. All had different hardware, handles, locks, and latches. An endless array of doors presented themselves as she rushed down the endless hall trying each one. They were all locked.

*I am coming to you.*

Fear quickly turned to frustration. Taunted by the evil essence and the endless hallway, Melinda pounded on doors in anger. Sinister laughter rolled down the hall, an evil wave threatening to drown her.

Melinda knew what she was looking for. Rahlys, Quaylyn, and Ilene had described the rune-covered chest containing the Rod of Destruction in great detail. Droclum had created the evil relic and she could detect the taint of his essence. She felt certain the chest had to be hidden behind one of these doors. She stood her ground. In her mind she was shouting.

*Where are the keys to unlock all these doors?*

In timely response to her question, keys began to rain down on her. Keys of every description and size fell like hail from the undefined space above, the clatter of falling keys deafening on the stone floor. Hundreds …thousands …tens of thousands of keys fell from the emptiness above her. Keys pelted her head and arms, cutting and bruising her exposed flesh until blood flowed down her face and arms. The keys piled up around her as they continued to fall. Melinda struggled to climb above their crushing weight, to ride the avalanche, but was losing the battle to stay afloat.

*I am here.*

Droclum's horrendously foul essence overwhelmed her.

*No…!*

Melinda bolted upright in her bed, a cold sweat beading down her back, her breathing labored, and her heart beat racing. The room was dark and quiet; the late early winter dawn had not yet arrived, but faint light from the setting moon filtered through a crack in the heavy dark curtains that held back the intense chill pressing against the window pane. Gradually Melinda became aware that she held something hard and cold in her trembling hand. She looked down not knowing what she would find. Releasing the tension in her fingers slowly she opened her hand to find a thin strangely shaped metallic object. She held it up for a better view.

Melinda gasped in horror.

The strange object in her grasp was one of the unusual keys that had rained down upon her in the endless hallway in her dream.

---

Officer Gerald LeBlanc of the Louisiana State Police Department grimaced as he swallowed the bitter dregs of lukewarm overcooked coffee and tossed the empty coffee-stained mug on his desk in disgust. The steady drumbeat of pounding rain vibrated through the fogged-up windows of his cramped office. The weather had been so unpredictable of late, going from muggy warm to damply cold overnight. *Another three months and I can stay in bed on a morning like this.* Retirement was so close, yet at times could seem so far away, Gerald mused.

The phone rang interrupting Gerald's thoughts. Caller ID flashed the Boss' number. "Officer Gerald LeBlanc speaking," he said picking it up.

"Good morning. Listen, Gerald, I hate to send you out on a road trip in all this rain, but I have another case of disappearing objects for you."

Gerald almost moaned audibly, but caught himself in time. "Did another TV set go missing?" he asked instead.

"It's a bit more serious than that," the Boss said solemnly. "A titanium cutting laser machine disappeared from a science research center in Baton Rouge. The government wants to know if there is any connection between the laser's disappearance and the other cases of disappearance you have covered."

Gerald had been the butt of many jokes since being assigned to the disappearance cases and didn't know if he should take the Boss seriously.

"What have local investigators learned so far?" Gerald asked searching for information.

"Absolutely nothing; I would send you a case file, but basically it says nothing was found."

The boss gave him an address and contact number, then paused before going on. "Look, if you need help to investigate the case, I could send someone..." Gerald could hear the Boss' lack of confidence in him in his voice.

"I've got it, Boss, thank you; I'm on it," Gerald said gently returning the cordless into its recharge cradle.

He was totally aware that he had been given the disappearances cases because they were considered relatively unimportant. Gerald had long ago accepted that, but he felt insulted by the offer of help when the topic turned serious.

Gerald wheezed a bit and coughed to clear his throat. He knew he wasn't in the best of health, or in the best of shape, being considerably overweight, but he could still investigate a case. Reaching into a lower desk drawer he pulled out a deluxe size container of anti-acids, and poured a generous dose of tablets into his hand to extinguish his coffee-induced heartburn. Chewing the tablets, he grabbed his coat, hat, and umbrella from the coat rack by the door and headed out to his car in the pouring rain.

The windshield wipers whipped rhythmically to his thoughts as he made the long drive to the city. When reports of objects inexplicably disappearing started cropping up in Lafourche Parish, most of them were considered hoaxes. Sometimes the prankster even provided video of the disappearance. No one in the department had wanted the cases, preferring to focus on more serious crime. That left Gerald as the best candidate to deal with the files that spanned several months.

When the Boss assigned him to the project, he had also been provided copies of another series of cases that allegedly happened four years ago in the New Orleans precinct. The reported incidences in New Orleans were strikingly similar to the recently reported vanishing objects cases in Lafourche Parish today. The most striking similarity between the two time periods: a case of a furniture store reporting the disappearance of a bed. The most expensive item reputed to have faded out of existence: a diamond necklace that has never been recovered.

Gerald arrived at the research institute and found a parking spot. The rain had finally slacked off and the sky lightened to a paler shade of gray. He decided to take his chances and leave the umbrella behind. Locking his car and looking around, there was no evidence left of police tape if it had ever been present. Local police had already been all over it and had nothing to offer so a cap of secrecy probably covered the whole incident since there was no evidence to support a crime.

Upon entering the building Gerald was greeted by a perky young, dyed blond with a streak of purple, receptionist. “How can I help you?”

“I’m here to investigate the disappearance of a titanium laser cutting machine.” Gerald showed her his badge; he knew he was expected.

“Well then, Gerald, follow me. My name is Judy.”

Gerald wasn’t sure if he liked her lack of formality, but followed her down a hallway and through a couple of doors to a large modern metalworker’s shop that looked like a lab.

“The laser machine was here,” Judy said, pointing vaguely to the large empty area in the room.

It was indeed a big empty space, and Gerald realized he really didn’t know much about lasers, beyond those annoying little pointers of colored light. “What does it look like?” he asked as he tried to mentally fill in the gaping space. In response, Judy walked over to a computer terminal across the room and brought up a picture on the screen.

“It looks like this.”

Gerald joined her and examined the picture carefully. The shot was of the room with the laser machine in place. It did indeed fill in the empty area across the room. The bulk of the unit consisted of a level, four foot wide, eight foot long platform where the cutting was obviously done. The apparatus housing the laser itself fitted on a moveable arm that extended across the top of the cutting platform. A separate unit standing next to it offered controls that would be used to program the cut. It was big and bulky and heavy, not something that could be easily moved without anyone noticing.

"Why, do you suppose, someone would steal something like this?" he asked, but there was no answer. He looked up to discover Judy was gone; no doubt, she had returned to the front desk.

Gerald walked over again to the empty space; not a crumb had been left behind. The area was lab clean; not a scratch marred the polished floor. He pulled out a notebook and brainstormed some questions he would later research on the internet. What sort of items are made from titanium, he wondered?

He walked around the room. There was another exit, a wider freight door that led outside. He tried to open it, but it was locked. A camera was mounted above it. Gerald returned to the front desk where Judy tried to calm a professionally dressed woman in gray with red accents who was obviously under a lot of stress. When Gerald approached the woman gave him a disdainful stare.

"Was the camera over the freight door working when the laser disappeared?" he asked Judy.

"Yes, it was," the stressed lady answered before Judy had a chance to speak, "and the back door was securely locked. We provided the police with a copy of the recording. It shows nothing unusual happening until suddenly the laser machine is no longer there. A second camera keeps watch outside the building. That recording is totally uneventful. No one came anywhere near the freight door at the time of the disappearance."

"Leslie is department manager at the institute," Judy explained. "The loss of the laser machine has been stressful," she whispered. Gerald took the information in stride.

"Is there a night watchman?"

"No, we never thought we needed one," Leslie answered taking charge.

"I would like a copy of the surveillance tape of the twenty-four hours prior to the machine's disappearance, and I would like to take a look at the back exit from outside if I may. Could you have someone open the freight door for me?"

"Yes, of course."

As Gerald was about to exit the building he paused to ask one more question. "Where does one buy titanium?"

---

"Is Leaf still sleeping?" Vince asked, pouring a cup of coffee. Maggie, still in her bathrobe, fed Rock cereal, fruit, and milk.

"He was so excited about today being his birthday he had a hard time going to sleep last night," Maggie chuckled. "Crystal is still sleeping, too."

Melinda came in from outdoors stomping snow off her boots on the mat by the door. *I made four little snowmen for Leaf's birthday,* she telepathed, cheerily. A creative project in the brisk morning air was just what she had needed to cleanse the nightmare and thoughts of the strange key, secretly buried in the bottom of her jewelry box, from her mind.

Vince strolled toward the large picture window in the family room overlooking the porch, sipping and blowing on his coffee to cool it. Outside, four perfect little snow people nearly a foot high, with branch twig arms, chocolate chip eyes and noses, and red licorice mouths sat on the porch railing. They wore strips of cloth for scarves around their necks, curls of birch bark for hats, and even tiny wraps of bits of cloth at the ends of their stick arms for mittens. Falling snow swirled in the background.

*There's a snowman for each year of Leaf's life,* Melinda telepathed. She moved in beside Vince to inspect her work from inside. This would be how Leaf first viewed them. Melinda was pleased with what she saw.

"What about one to grow on?" Vince asked.

*He will find that one when he goes to the outhouse.*

Carrying Rock so he can see out the window, Maggie joined Vince and Melinda. "When is George supposed to bring over the big surprise?" Maggie whispered in case Leaf was awake and could hear.

"He said around ten. George is a good sport taking care of a puppy for us."

Vince had returned home from a trip to town the day before with a little puppy, her fur all solid white. To keep it a surprise, Vince had asked George ahead of time if he would keep the puppy overnight. To Vince and Maggie's delight, George had readily agreed.

"As long as it is only for one night," George had grumbled, while cottoning to the little thing that licked his hand and snuggled against him. Maggie had supplied a hot water bottle, an old windup alarm clock, and one of Leaf's unwashed shirts for a surrogate mother. Vince hoped the puppy and George were still friends after twenty-four hours.

Sounds of Crystal waking up in the next room filtered in. "I better go change her and get dressed myself," Maggie said putting Rock down to play.

"I'll make pancakes," Vince volunteered.

Leaf had been asking for a puppy for quite some time, but Maggie and Vince had postponed the addition of a dog until the twins were at least on their feet. Now that Crystal and Rock were toddlers, they had reconsidered. Maggie and Vince understood the close bond that existed between Melinda and Leaf, a companionship the twins couldn't replace quite yet because they were so young. Melinda would be turning eighteen in the spring; eventually she would venture out on her own. So they had finally decided a puppy might be just what Leaf needed. In time, a dog may prove to be a close, reliable companion. Therefore; today, Leaf's wish would finally come true.

---

Leaf woke up from a promising dream …something to do with the number four. Then he remembered.

"Today is my birthday," he breathed out with awe. "I'm four years old." Four was really getting up there, a giant leap beyond babyish one, two, and three.

A surge of excitement charged him with energy. Today was special; he could feel it. He sprang out of bed and rushed to the window. It was snowing. Leaf loved snow; the snow made the day even more special. After birthdays…and puppies…snow was his favorite thing. Glancing around the room he noticed that Rock was already gone from his bed. Was every one up but him?

With a wave of his hands and arms he was instantly dressed; pants, shirt, socks, the works. He knew his mother didn't approve of him dressing this way, but he didn't have time today to dress piece by piece. Leaf rushed out into the family room. It was toasty warm and filled with breakfast smells. "Happy Birthday, Leaf," his father greeted him, carrying two plates of blueberry pancakes to the table.

*Happy birthday, Leaf,* Melinda echoed telepathically, carrying a pitcher of orange juice. Across the room, Rock was pulling toys out of a cardboard box, scattering them around on the floor for the day. Leaf could hear his mother carrying on a one-sided conversation with Crystal in the next room.

"I have your plate of pancakes right here, Birthday Boy," Vince said, placing a plate of four neatly stacked sand dollar size pancakes on the table in full view of the four snowmen sitting outside on the porch railing.

"Hey, look at the snowmen!" Leaf climbed up on his chair and laughed; then he counted them, "…one, two, three, four…; there are four snowmen!" He laughed even harder over Melinda's cleverness. Vince and Melinda joined Leaf at the table.

Leaf had to examine his stack of four pancakes before he could eat them. Each pancake, he discovered, had four blueberries. With pride in his ability, he counted the berries in each and every pancake before drowning them in syrup.

"So, son, now that you are four, have you thought about what you would like to be when you grow up?" Vince asked by way of casual conversation.

"I'm going to be a warrior like Quaylyn," Leaf stated matter-of-factly.

Vince knew that Leaf did not mean a warrior in the sense of a US marine, but a warrior by Quaylyn's definition; a finely honed athlete of physical and mental conditioning and a master at drawing power from the elemental forces. Vince felt a mixture of fear and pride for his young son.

"I'm certain, one day, you will be a great warrior," he said solemnly.

"Good morning, Leaf, Happy Birthday," Maggie said upon entering the room. She placed Crystal in a high chair to feed her and gave Leaf a big hug.

"Mom, look at the snowmen."

"Yes, I see them. Melinda did a great job; four snowmen in a row are pretty impressive."

"And Dad made me four pancakes and look, four blueberries," he said holding up a little pancake dripping with syrup.

"Watch what you are doing; you are dripping syrup," Maggie pointed out. To alleviate the problem, Leaf shoved the culprit into his mouth, wiping his sticky hand on his shirt. Maggie sighed with a smile and went for a damp cloth to wipe sticky hands.

Realizing he was missing out, Rock abandoned the toys and made his way to the table. Vince grabbed the other high chair, pulled it up to the table, put Rock in it, and handed him a piece of pancake. Then Vince told them the story of the little boy who didn't have birthdays.

The original story had been a short and simple one that posed the question; if you don't celebrate birthdays, do you still get older? The telling of the story had become something of a tradition on family birthdays in the Bradley household and had evolved over time. New increasingly bizarre details were added to the story at each telling.

*But how did Jack make time go backward?* Melinda wanted to know.

"Did he go in a spaceship?" Leaf asked.

"His spaceship was a time machine," Vince explained.

The drone of an approaching snowmachine could be heard above the cheery commotion of family breakfast.

"Someone is here," Leaf shouted, nearly jumping out of his chair.

"I wonder who it might be," Maggie said, exchanging a secretive smile with Vince. Vince got up to let him in.

"It's Grumpy George," Leaf shouted, clapping his hands. The arrival of company when you lived in the woods was always an event.

"Stay ...and finish your breakfast," Maggie instructed Leaf as he got ready to jump down. "And don't forget to wipe your hands."

Leaf stuffed the last little pancake into his mouth and reached for the washcloth his mother handed him as George and Vince came through the door. Leaf jumped down and ran to George. "Grumpy George, Grumpy George ... guess what ...today is my birthday!" he announced as soon as he swallowed. Maggie still cringed when Leaf addressed him so, but George himself had long ago condoned it.

"Well Happy Birthday, little fellow. And how old might you be?"

"Four...," Leaf said, holding up four fingers.

"Four! Why you're practically a grown man."

"I know," Leaf agreed.

"Have some breakfast, George," Maggie offered.

"No, thank you, I've already eaten."

"...Coffee?"

"Yes, I would love some." At that moment the front of George's jacket squirmed ...and whimpered. Leaf's eyes opened wide. Then George's chest moved and cried again causing Leaf's eyes to open even wider.

"What do you have in your jacket, Grumpy George?"

"What...? Where...?" George asked, pretending to be unaware of the intensifying squirming and whimpering.

"There...," Leaf said, pointing to his chest. A quick scan of unguarded minds gave Leaf all the information he needed. "It's a puppy!" he shouted in jubilation.

"Is that what you call this overgrown puffball with legs?" George said unzipping his jacket to reveal a real life fluffy white ball of fur with two little pointed pink and white ears and four perfect white puppy paws that needed growing into. Amidst all that white, a tiny pinkish gray nose sniffed the air curiously while two intelligent midnight blue eyes studied the new surroundings. It was the most beautiful puppy Leaf had ever seen.

"Kept me awake all night, she did, whimpering for her master." George said petting the puppy with gentle affection. The puppy reciprocated by licking his hand.

"Who's her master?" Leaf asked, his heart longing to hold and pet the magnificent white puppy.

Taking his time, George lifted the puppy out of his jacket and held her up. Removed from her warm spot, the puppy squirmed and whimpered again. Then incredulously, George extended his arms toward Leaf.

"I believe her master …is you," he said, placing the furry bundle in Leaf's unbelieving arms.

The puppy was an armful for Leaf. Overwhelmed with joy, he dropped down to the floor to cuddle the puppy in his lap. The puppy, recognizing Leaf's scent from the shirt Maggie had provided, pawed around on his lap, sniffing and licking for clues. Leaf petted her, cooing reassurances. "It's okay; everything will be alright." Mentally reaching out to her, he could impart these reassurances more deeply. *I know you miss your mother, but I will take care of you.* The puppy began to relax in Leaf's possession.

"What are you going to name her?" Maggie asked.

"Keiluk," Leaf said without hesitation. Maggie, Vince, and Melinda smiled in agreement; they had all read the tales of Keiluk's adventures in Leaf's favorite storybook more than they cared to remember. "Your name is Keiluk," he told his little charge. "Keiluk, Keiluk," he sang, petting her.

"Keiluk, where did you find a name like that?" George asked.

"It means 'swift,'" Leaf explained, placing Keiluk on the floor as though he expected her to demonstrate. Glad to be finally free, Keiluk padded across the floor in an ever-widening circle around Leaf sniffing out her new environment. From his high chair Rock pointed to the puppy uttering sounds of inquiry. He wanted down to investigate so Maggie accommodated him. It was time for Keiluk to meet the rest of the family.

Rock boldly approached the furry ball of energy, but Keiluk didn't stay long enough in one spot for him to reach her. "Come, Keiluk, come," Leaf called her. To his great pleasure she responded to his mental nudging. "Good, girl," he praised her putting his arms around her.

Cradled in Leaf's lap, Rock was finally able to gain access to Keiluk and stooped down to pet her. He chortled over the softness of her fur and the roughness of the little tongue that licked his hand. Then the toddler reached out and roughly grabbed ahold of Keiluk. "No, no, Rock …gentle…," Leaf intercepted. "One more," Maggie said, taking Crystal down from her high chair. Resisting the mandatory face and hand wash before release, Crystal escaped from Maggie's hold and immediately ran over to join her brothers. Keiluk jumped out of Leaf's lap to intercept her. Upon seeing the rambunctious tail-wagging puppy plowing toward her, Crystal stepped back letting out a shriek. After a couple of backward steps she fell over onto her diapered bottom. Immediately, Keiluk was all over her, pawing her, sniffing her and licking her delicious unwashed hands and face. Leaf was there in a flash to mediate, and Crystal's shrieks quickly turned to cackling laughter.

Once Crystal was back on her feet, Keiluk strode around and then started to squat. Vince, who was standing close by, grabbed the puppy by the scruff of her neck and gently tossed her out the door in one fell swoop.

"You will have to teach her to go outside to use the bathroom," Vince explained. "That means you will have to take her out regularly until she can indicate to you when she needs to go. Here, put on your coat, hat, and boots, and go watch over her. Bring her back in in a few minutes."

Leaf rushed to get dressed ...the slow way with everyone watching... and ran out the door to find Keiluk.

He found Keiluk exploring all the wondrous smells of firewood, old boots, bird feeders, and windblown fresh snow the porch had to offer. A wet spot on the porch indicated the urgency had passed. Still, she would have to learn to leave the porch.

"Come, Keiluk, come," Leaf called, urging her to follow him down the two low steps to the packed snow trail below, but Keiluk proved reluctant to take the plunge from the solid footing of the porch to the questionable snow-covered steps. Taking no arguments, Leaf teleported her into the soft powdery snow on the side of the trail. He laughed at Keiluk's comic effort to right herself and shake off the snow. Feeling bad about dumping her in the snow, he ran to her and cuddled her in his arms in apology.

"Come on, Keiluk," Leaf directed after receiving a forgiving lick on the face, "come on," he said slapping his leg for emphasis. Keiluk pulled herself together and started to follow Leaf down the outhouse trail, but stopped after a few steps and started to whimper; she really wanted to get back where it was warm.

Vince followed George out to see him off. "Thanks again, George."

"It's your problem now," George chuckled, "and Happy Birthday again, Leaf. Enjoy your new puppy." He started up his snowmachine. "Have fun," he told Vince and waved goodbye driving away down the trail.

"You better bring her back in now," Vince told Leaf, "she is probably getting cold."

---

Later that afternoon, Quaylyn, Rahlys, and Ilene arrived for cake and ice cream. Leaf excitedly presented his new puppy which they greatly admired taking turns holding and petting her. Wallowing in all the attention he and Keiluk were getting, he proudly showed them the food and water dishes that had come with her and the bag of puppy food. And there was more; his mother brought out a chocolate birthday cake with four colorful blazing candles. On top the cake, Happy Birthday and a crude image of a dog were drawn in white icing. Leaf gazed into the dancing flames while everyone sang, and then he blew out the candles, which kept relighting like magic. Cheese and crackers, cookies, cupcakes, chips and dip, and an assortment of other tantalizing party snacks as well as a stack of presents seemingly appeared by magic. Soon Keiluk was hard pressed keeping up with all the food crumbs that fell to the floor. Boisterous adult talk and laughter competed with youthful squeals and chatter as children and puppy scattered ribbons, paper, and toys.

That evening when the children had finally been put to bed, Ilene pulled a folded sheet of paper she had run off from her computer from her pocket. "I found another disappearance case in Louisiana. It looks like Brakalar is still trying to open the chest," she said handing the article to Quaylyn.

"What disappeared this time?" Rahlys asked, the new topic of conversation dampening the mood of the evening.

"A laser cutting machine that can cut through titanium," Ilene informed them and handed the page to Rahlys.

"Do you think he will be able to open the chest with this?" Rahlys asked Quaylyn with alarming concern after reading the article.

"I don't know; I hope not," he said scanning the article then handing it to Vince. "If it works, he may have already opened it. We will have to monitor the news carefully for anything unusual or unexplained."

"Almost everything in the news these days is unusual or unexplained," Maggie mumbled.

"This Investigating Officer Gerald LeBlanc's name has been reported before," Vince said, scanning the article. "Maybe we should pay him a visit and find out what he knows."

"Yes and Rahlys can demonstrate, once again, her profound ability to move a pencil," Maggie said, her statement lightening some the heavy mood that had descended on their celebration.

# Chapter 16

# Aaia

"Caleeza," Traevus cried out to her, drawing her attention.

Caleeza looked around stunned at the sound of her name. A male figure was running toward her from the mouth of the cave; and she couldn't help but think he looked familiar.

"Caleeza, greetings, how can I serve you?" Traevus greeted reaching out toward her.

"Traevus…," she gasped astonished, gazing into his radiantly pleased face and reaching for his proffered hands, hands that were real flesh, solid and living.

"What happened to you? Why did you leave us?" Caleeza asked, obviously still puzzled by his disappearance from their expedition seasons ago. "We searched for you for many rotations, but we couldn't find a clue to your whereabouts."

"I was taken by the Band of Rogues. I tried repeatedly to escape; to warn you, but Stram was too powerful."

"They must have been the men I saw you with through Raven's telepathed images."

Traevus didn't quite follow this, but there would be time later to go into details. There were so many experiences to be shared. "Where are Caponya, Selyzar, and Sarus?"

"Caponya and Selyzar vanished in the Crystalline Landscape… and Sarus… Sarus…." Caleeza didn't know how to explain what happened to Sarus.

By now the rest of the group all stood outside the cave watching.

"Come," Traevus said not waiting for an answer. "Let's get out of this hot sun and I'll introduce you to the others; one will not need an introduction."

"Ollen," Caleeza cried out in delight upon seeing him.

"It is a joy to my heart to see you again," Ollen greeted her.

"Oh, Ollen how is Cremyn? Is she alright?" Caleeza watched as his demeanor shifted from joy in finding her to deep personal sorrow.

"She didn't make it; I buried her on a hillside." Caleeza was struck by grief over Cremyn's loss and struggled for control as Ollen led her into the cool depths of the cave." The cave proved exceeding dark after the brightness of outdoors, and Traevus produced a glow globe to light the way. Caleeza gazed at the floating light in shock.

"How did you do that?" she asked in amazement. "No one can draw energy from the elemental forces on the Devastated Continent…." Caleeza had almost added "except Sarus" …when she stopped herself.

"And we don't call it the Devastated Continent anymore," Kiril spoke up. "The continent's name is Lynnara."

"Does the High Council sanction this?" she asked immediately.

"Not exactly, but we are working on it," Kiril explained. Theon gave him a sharp kick warning him not to say more.

"All will be explained in due time," Ollen assured her as he guided her to a suitable rock to serve as a chair and motioned for her to have a seat. Grouped together, everyone found comfortable perches on which to sit and Ollen started in on the introductions.

"This eldest of elders beside me here is Theon."

"You're Theon…?" she asked incredulously. The man seated beside her did indeed look older than time unimaginable.

"Greetings, Caleeza. It is my pleasure to serve; I believe we embrace mutual friends in Alaska." His wise aging eyes studied her warmly, appreciative of the friendships they shared.

"You're really Theon," Caleeza exclaimed examining him closely. "Where are Rahlys and Ilene who were supposed to be with you?"

"They have been safely returned to Earth," Theon reassured her, suppressing a pang of longing for his daughter. "The expedition that went out to find you ended abruptly seasons ago."

"So what are you doing here?" Caleeza asked.

“The same might be asked of you,” Rojaire pointed out, rising to stretch his legs.

“I’m Rojaire, the leader of this group. It is my pleasure to serve. And here we have Tassyn, Edty, and Kiril,” he said pointing them out as he walked around introducing them. There was something familiar, Caleeza thought, about the first two men he introduced, but she didn’t say anything.

“I was also on the expedition to find you,” Rojaire continued, coming up behind her. “Strangely we have found more of you on this excursion than we did back then. I hope you will enlighten us some.”

“Well, I can try, but some events that have happened are difficult to explain…some are inexplicable,” she added softly.

“Give us a try; remember we have also been to the ruins of the Temple of Tranquility and to the Crystalline Landscape. You will find us a very receptive audience,” Theon explained. “Ollen has already covered his portion of the expedition, so perhaps you could pick up the story from there,” he suggested in an effort to help.

“Well, after Ollen left with Cremyn for Lavender Beach, the rest of us continued our hike across the interior toward the center of the continent. The absence of Ollen and Cremyn were heavily felt, casting a gloom over downhearted spirits. We were a desolate, dispirited group, but Sarus strove to instill purpose and drive back into our mission. As leader, Sarus took Cremyn’s disappearance and subsequent loss of mind the hardest, but he reminded us we were on a mission and failure was unacceptable. Once again, reaching the slopes of Mt. Vatre became our focus.

“The journey went smoothly for a while, and then deep in the interior Traevus suddenly disappeared; it was another devastating blow to moral. Again for many rotations we searched for one of our own, but without finding a clue. As far as we knew, he had simply vanished from existence.” Caleeza noticed a growing uneasiness in Tassyn and Edty as the story unfolded.

“But Traevus is here. I’m the one who is still in the dark as to what happened.”

Traevus tried to fill in the gap with minimum damage to his friends. “We thought the continent was uninhabited, but there was a wandering group of rogues roaming the area. As I said before, I was taken by Stram, the leader of the Band of Rogues,” Traevus said. “Tassyn and Edty had the misfortune of being under his leadership.”

“But how was this leader of rogues able to take you without anyone else detecting anything?”

"Well, Stram had in his possession a star stone that made it possible for him to draw enough energy from the elemental forces to whisk me away without leaving a trail."

"A star stone…?" Caleeza stopped, gazing up at the glow globe lighting their intimate circle in the dark cavern.

"Would you like a cup of hot tea, my lady?" Traevus asked gallantly, deftly producing a cup, water, and dried herbs. While nodding her head in affirmation, he poured water into the cup and drew energy which he directed to the water, bringing it to a boil. Quickly he dropped in the dried herbs and let it steep.

"So you have one of these star stones," Caleeza surmised eyeing the steaming cup and pointing to the glow globe. "What does it look like?"

Traevus pulled the star stone he carried out of a pouch and showed it to her. The smooth golden stone glimmered faintly in the light of the glow globe.

"Where did you find it?" Caleeza asked fascinated.

"We will talk about that later, "Rojaire said handing her the hot cup of tea. Caleeza took it gratefully. "To get to the point, Stram was a tyrant and he met his demise when he attempted to draw energy in the Crystalline Landscape.

"That proved not to be a good idea," Tassyn added.

"So what happened to him?"

"Boom…!" Edty interjected softly, making an expansive motion with his arms.

"Eventually your team must have given up on finding Traevus," Rojaire said to get her back on track. "So where's the rest of your team? And how did you get from here to Earth and back again?" he asked impatiently. Caleeza turned around and glanced up at Rojaire not sure what to say.

"Easy there, Rojaire, let her tell her story," Traevus intervened.

"Forgive me, Caleeza; I didn't mean to rush you," Rojaire said contritely. "Please continue."

"Yes, we finally moved on, but the unexplained mystery of Traevus' disappearance on top of what had happened to Cremyn cast a terrible gloom over the expedition. There were only four of us left; still we forged onward …and eventually we arrived at the field of crystals." Caleeza sipped her tea while everyone waited expectantly for her to continue.

"We could hardly believe what we were seeing," she continued, "the massive jumble of crystals stretched to the horizon, a seemingly impenetrable obstacle to reaching our goal. There was much discussion amongst us about turning back, but Sarus never considered it; he was determined. We feared the crystalline landscape may be dangerous; still we agreed to follow him. Without further study of what lay before us, we forged on, the beauty that confronted us surpassed only by the difficulty of the terrain." Nods of agreement responded reflectively to her words. "But, of course, you have seen it."

"We have all experienced it except Kiril here," Theon clarified.

"Did you know that the crystals form force fields that can transport a person across the galaxy?" Caleeza asked.

"We have come to suspect as much," Rojaire said. "Is that what happened to you?" Caleeza continued her story without answering the question.

"Caponya was the first to vanish, but because of the previous disappearances of Cremyn and Traevus we didn't make the connection between her disappearance and the crystals right away. But then when Selyzar vanished too, we could no longer doubt what was happening. But by then we had pushed deep into the Crystalline Landscape with the slopes of Mt. Vatre far closer than the outer edge of the field of crystals. Now only Sarus and I remained; and we had endured so much." Caleeza paused reliving the agony and despair while the others quietly waited for more.

"Helpless in saving Caponya and Selyzar, Sarus raged at the elements; he raged over his failure to protect the expedition and over the dismal prospects of our survival. With failure and doom in our hearts we stubbornly pushed on. Mt Vatre loomed darkly on the horizon, yet the field of crystals still stretched endlessly before us.

"Then suddenly a seismic shock wave shook the ground. The intensive ground shake threw me off balance; my foot slipped and I fell, or so I thought, but I didn't land on crystals. In what seemed like the next instance in time I was standing on this vast frozen landscape on Earth. Of course, I didn't know it was Earth at the time." She paused once again to sip tea and collect her thoughts, giving her enthralled audience a moment to absorb the enormity of the event.

"The Crystalline Landscape transported you through time and space to Earth?" Kiril gasped. "I thought only the powers of the Runes of the Crystal Table could do that!"

"There are others who have vanished in the Crystalline Landscape," Rojaire said, no longer capable of holding back, "but only you have returned." Rojaire didn't want to utter Kaylya's name. Dare he hope to ever see her again?

"Hold on there, Rojaire! We're just getting to the good part. I want to hear about her visit with Vince and Maggie," Theon interjected. He turned to Caleeza, "We were informed through the Oracle of Light that you had been on Earth, but weren't given any details," he explained to Caleeza.

"I agree with Theon," Ollen said thoroughly enjoying the tale. "Don't leave out any parts of the story; you take all the time you need." The others nodded in eager agreement.

"…more tea?" Rojaire asked in way of apology.

"We will all have some tea," Theon said.

"Are you hungry?" Caleeza asked. "I have a harvest bag of food," she said offering it.

"We also have some preserved food," Ollen said bringing it out. Soon the group was drinking tea and picnicking on a pleasing variety of snacks while Caleeza related her adventures on Earth.

"The cold was intense and it took all my energy in the fight to stay warm. But the worst part was leaving Sarus alone in despair and not being able to let him know what had happened to me." Caleeza described her long cold trek across winter white tundra, meeting the musk-oxen, the caribou hunters, and the long road that crossed the vast North Slope of Alaska. She told them about the ride with Trucker Stanley, the old trapper cabin where she found warm clothes and food, the charitable man who bought her a hotdog, the secret ride in a camping trailer, and passing through a community that lit up the night sky.

"The next morning I found a strange trail made of wood and steel and followed the path of rails through tundra and forest, over hills and valleys and across mountain ranges. Eventually the trail led me along a great river through open forest when I felt the use of magic. Someone had drawn energy from the elemental forces. I did a mental scan to trace the source; and incredibly, I found the ability in a little boy."

"That would be young Leaf Bradley. He was only two short Earth-years of age when I saw him last; and he could communicate telepathically even back then," Theon reminisced. "Leaf, a wizard; I would love to see how he has grown."

"Melinda and Leaf were always together, at least until the twins were born."

"I knew Maggie was carrying twins!" Theon jumped up in delight, momentarily forgetting his aches and pains until they quickly reminded him. "… a boy and a girl?" he asked suppressing a groan.

"Yes, a boy named Rock and a girl named Crystal."

"Rock and Crystal…" Theon chuckled despite the pain.

"Their chosen mother Maggie and chosen father Vince work hard caring for so many," Caleeza added, a smile lighting her suntanned face and violet eyes as she recalled them fondly.

"By Seaa's light," Ollen exclaimed, "...one chosen mother and one chosen father caring for how many new persons?"

"Four, which I learned is not all that uncommon on Earth."

"So how did you return from Earth?" Rojaire pressed once again.

"Yes, of course," Caleeza said. This would be the most difficult part of her story to explain. She brushed her orange unkempt hair out of her eyes and away from her face, searching her mind for a lead in.

"I thought of Sarus every moment I wasn't struggling to survive; it crushed my soul to think of him left alone and in despair in the vast and dangerous crystalline landscape, a despair that I knew my disappearance would only have worsen. I loved Sarus deeply in my heart and wished greatly to assure him I was all right. I desired to communicate with him so intensely, I started hearing him speaking to me from the Crystalline Landscape in my dreams, but the Sarus who spoke to me in dreams seemed more ethereal and detached than the Sarus I knew. Over time, he convinced me that our connections in my dreams were real and he promised to work on bringing me home."

Caleeza's listeners sat in spellbound silence, only their breathing could be heard. The men were tired from the long difficult passage through the caves, but there would be no sleep until Caleeza's tale was complete.

"Maggie and Vince told me the story of Droclum's defeat by Sorceress Rahlys, the Guardian of Light, and believed Rahlys may be able to help me return home. Unfortunately Sorceress Rahlys was on an expedition, accompanied by Theon and his daughter, and a raven, to search for the lost expedition on the Devastated Continent. Of course, that lost expedition was us.

"I related these things to Sarus in my dreams.

"Then one night, Sarus informed me that Councilor Anthya's expedition had reached the Crystalline Landscape. He urgently worked to bring me back so I could warn the members of the expedition to stay away. He said he would send the raven back to Earth as a test."

Rojaire listened carefully; the facts as given were incredulous. *Can Sarus actually control the forces in the Crystalline Landscape to transport people through space/time contingents?*

"So when the raven returned outside Vince and Maggie's home, I knew Sarus would eventually succeed in bringing me home. A short time later I was suddenly there, standing alone and barefoot in the Crystalline Landscape."

Eyes lowered to her feet covered in crystal floss moccasins; she was barefoot no longer.

"I called out to Sarus over the empty landscape of crystals and he appeared, but it was only a projected image of Sarus. I told him how much I loved him, but he hardly remembered the feeling at all." Caleeza's demeanor saddened with the telling. "He wanted me to go to Councilor Anthya and warn the expedition of the dangers, and then he would send everyone back, including me, to assure everyone's safety out of the Crystalline Landscape."

"So it was Sarus who brought our expedition to an abrupt end." Rojaire hadn't meant to speak out loud. "But you didn't join us."

Caleeza fought back tears, "I couldn't leave him." She paused to collect herself. "I loved him and I needed to understand what happened to him, so I begged him to let me stay. His physical self was gone, but remnants of his consciousness remained. I described to him what our relationship had been like, and he recalled it. I described the troubles and misfortunes we had endured together, and he remembered them. By some osmosis Sarus had become a part of the crystals, and I feared for his humanity. In the end he agreed to let me stay …until the next expedition arrived."

"You must contact Sarus," Rojaire said.

"No!" Caleeza shouted, louder than she had intended. "No, please; I fear, if I summon him, he will take me back among the crystals. I don't want to go back."

"But there are others who have vanished in the Crystalline Landscape."

"Sarus has searched for Caponya and Selyzar, but has been unable to locate them.

Caponya and Selyzar are not the only ones missing," Rojaire explained. "Councilor Brakalar also vanished in the Crystalline Landscape …and Kaylya."

"…Councilor Brakalar! Was he looking for us too?"

"Take it easy, there, Rojaire," Theon coaxed again. There would be more stories to tell before rest could come, Theon realized. "We just found Caleeza; we don't want to lose her again. We need to give this Sarus thing some thought. Kaylya disappeared long before Sarus arrived at the Crystalline Landscape."

"Who's Kaylya?"

"…the love of my heart," Rojaire said simply and stepped away for a moment, leaving an aura of long and deep sadness.

Theon took over telling the story.

"There were nine of us on the mission to find the lost expedition with Councilor Brakalar in command and Councilor Zayla his second; also with us, Councilor Anthya, Warrior Quaylyn, Sorceress Rahlys, my daughter Ilene, Raven, Rojaire here, and myself."

Theon described their journey to the Sooty Caves, and how Rahlys had drawn the ruin-covered chest from the black stone that had once cradled Quaylyn in suspended animation . . . which only led to another story. He told her about the key to the chest that contained the Rod of Destruction that Rojaire had found and given to Brakalar and how he, Rahlys, and Brakalar met up at the ruins of the Temple of Tranquility.

"Obsession over gaining possession of the powerful relic the key alluded to, had taken over Brakalar's mind. Brakalar approached us charged with rage and demanding rights to the chest by virtue of possession of the key, which he waved angrily in the air, the key drawing him toward the chest.

"I held the chest in my arms in hopes of keeping him from it, the runes covering its surface glowing, and the discordant song the chest emitted piercing in response to the dark flows of energy defending the ruins. When Brakalar drew closer, the key left his hand in a stream of smoky mist and melded into the rune matching its shape on the chest, and the seamless chest sprang open."

Theon told how he and Brakalar had struggled for possession of the dark and powerful rod and how Brakalar had overpowered him; how Zayla had then arrived on the scene and tried to reason with him.

"Brakalar thirsted for power and the Rod of Destruction would make him more powerful than he had ever dreamed of before. Refusing Zayla's help, Brakalar waved the deadly weapon around threateningly and released its force. The dark ray struck Zayla . . . surrounding her, reducing her to ashes in just heartbeats." Theon hoped it had been that quick remembering Zayla's horrible muffled screams.

"Then Quaylyn and Anthya arrived and took possession of the rod from Brakalar and returned it to the chest. When the chest lid closed, the key fell out of the rune engraved on its surface and melted away into the stones of the temple."

Caleeza shuddered, vividly recalling the horrors of the ruins of the Temple of Tranquility and what had happened to Cremyn. The news of the councilor's death was shocking; her death at the hands of Councilor Brakalar even more so.

"The ruins are a horrible place," Caleeza said softly. "What did you do after escaping the temple ruins? What happened to Brakalar?"

Theon cleared his throat. "Brakalar was relieved of command of the expedition, and since Zayla was gone, Anthya took command with Quaylyn as her second. In all fairness, Brakalar was grief stricken over what he had done. He knew, of course, he would be stripped of his position as councilor of the Crystal Table when we returned to the Community of the High Council."

"But you said Brakalar disappeared in the Crystalline Landscape."

"He found an exit." Seeing the look of confusion on Caleeza's face, Theon attempted to explain. "Since Rojaire told us about Kaylya's disappearance, we were forewarned of the danger. So Anthya devised a safety mechanism of sorts using pebbles which we tossed before us, to test the terrain, so to speak. Once tossed, if we heard the ping of the pebble dropping on the crystals, the distance between was considered safe to cross. If the pebble vanished instead of landed…," Theon shrugged. "Sorceress Rahlys located an energy field this way and Brakalar took advantage of it, managing to take the chest containing the Rod of the Destruction with him."

For the longest no one spoke, everyone reflecting on all they had heard.

"At least he doesn't have the key," Rojaire added after a while, having rejoined the group. "It's gone forever."

"Let's hope so," Theon said, pushing himself up off his hard seat, "but I have my doubts. Now if you will excuse me I'm going to find a comfortable place to lie down." He located a shelf of smooth stone and laid out his cloak for bedding.

Outside the cool, dark cavern, Aaia's late summer sun burned hotly in the white gold sky. It would be some time yet before she crested the mountains casting some merciful shade.

Theon's departure from the group set the others in motion. Tassyn and Edty soon followed Theon's example. "Where do you think all those people who disappeared went, Tassyn?" Edty asked his buddy, in a troubled whisper, when they were comfortably settled.

"I don't know, Edty. We may never find out."

"I don't want to go back to the Crystalline Landscape," Edty confided. "Promise me we won't go back there."

"Don't worry; we aren't going back there. Now get some sleep." Tassyn's reassurance was all Edty needed; almost instantly he was asleep. Tassyn lay awake listening to Edty's snoring while thinking about all that had been said.

Kiril, however, darted off to a distant secluded corner to update his notes. Bent over his work lit by his headlamp with notepad and stylus in hand, he hurriedly spilled out recollections from all he had heard before he could forget anything. When he was done, he placed the notes in his journal and packed them away before laying out his cloak to sleep on.

Ollen, Traevus, and Caleeza sat by the entrance to the cave, just out of reach of direct sunlight, and intermittently gazed out over the parched terrain and then at each other, amazed at being back together again. They were members of the lost expedition, but they were here, with their lives still ahead of them.

"What did the High Council say when you returned and told them about Cremyn?" Caleeza asked Ollen. Ollen looked away from Caleeza's probing violet eyes.

"I never returned to the Community of the High Council," he confessed.

"What did you do?" Caleeza asked surprised.

"I just wandered off on my own, lost in grief. Eventually I settled in a beautiful valley, build a shelter and a kiln, put up food, and lived alone until this bunch came walking in."

"We found Ollen living quite well on his own," Traevus admitted, "just lonely. By the way, the valley Ollen settled is now called the Cremyn Valley with the Cremyn River flowing through it. And the Cremyn River empties into the Zayla River which empties into the Golden Sea at Lavender Beach."

"Does the High Council condone you putting your own names on things?" Caleeza asked intrigued. "Kiril called the Devastated Continent Lynnara."

Traevus and Ollen weren't sure what to say. "The High Council named the Zayla River," Traevus told her. Caleeza knew nothing of the passage through the mountains and the hidden valley. They were sworn to secrecy about their alliance and goal to free Lynnara from the rule of the High Council and form an independent nation.

"Don't you like the name Lynnara?" Ollen asked playfully.

Eventually everyone settled down to rest except Rojaire. He paced through the caverns until a shadow grew along the edge of the mountain. Then he stepped out and wandered far from the group following the mountain's slow growing shadow, occasionally climbing over rocky debris, totally lost in his own thoughts.

For Rojaire, the continent's interior along the eastern ranges of the Crescent Mountains was familiar territory. There were no kurpers or large-clawed beasts roaming around here. Before him lay only expanses of yellow and orange zan fruit bushes and ground nuts growing sparsely in the coarse lavender soil cut by shallow ravines so narrow they were unnoticeable from a distance.

But the turmoil in his heart blinded him to the harsh beauty of the interior. The possibility of finding Kaylya consumed him. In his heart he longed to go immediately to the Crystalline Landscape and try and contact Sarus, whatever his state of being, and beg a search for Kaylya; but practical reasoning cancelled such folly. He would have to complete this current mission first.

Eventually Rojaire reached a trickle of a waterfall, its runoff quickly swallowed by the thirsty streambed. Quenching his thirst, he seated himself on a grassy spot by the side of the trickling stream. Finding Caleeza was an unexpected development and one of merit, as was finding Ollen, but Rojaire doubted Ollen, who had developed a brash independence, would return with them to the Community of the High Council. They will take Caleeza with them; therefore the secret of the secluded valley will be revealed to her. Will she be willing to keep the secret?

He could lead them around the point of the Crescent Mountains to return to Lavender Beach, but the distance was far too great. The journey would take a season and Theon would never make it. But Rojaire was also concerned about Theon making it back through the difficult cave tunnels that connected them to the lava tube. Rojaire knew if he got Theon back to the valley in the mountains, he would never leave.

As far as the mission was concerned, they had reached their goal. They had successfully made their way from the continent's coastal region to the interior going through the Crescent Mountains. He had never promised the route would be easy. It was time to take his companions home. Then he could decide what to do next.

With a start, Rojaire awoke beside the trickling stream, surprised that he had fallen asleep. He stood up, brushed himself off with his hands, and groggily made his way to the tiny waterfall. Catching some water in his hands, he threw it on his face in an effort to dispel his drowsiness and headed back to join the others. According to the lengthening shadow, he had slept for a long time.

When Rojaire arrived back at the caverns, he found the group outdoors gathering food, exploring the area, or just enjoying the open air and wide open space after the dark, enclosed caves and tunnels. When they saw him coming, they gathered together to hear what he may have to say. Theon strolled toward him, meeting him part way. Rojaire was relieved to see Theon looking well-rested and moving about.

"So what have you decided, boss?" Theon asked. Rojaire didn't answer right away and they walked together in silence.

"What do you see as your future, Theon?" Rojaire asked metaphorically … compassionately. "Where do you want to be, my friend; I will do my best to take you there."

"Well, Rojaire, to answer both your questions; I see my future in that great valley we found enjoying roast kurper. My aspirations at this point are small compared to yours, my friend. Listen, I know you want to search for Kaylya, but I hope you manage to put your priorities in order."

"We have met our goal; it is time we turn back." Rojaire smiled, knowing it was what Theon wanted to hear.

By now everyone had gathered together and Rojaire spoke to the group.

"I wish to congratulate you, and thank you, for the success of our mission so far. We have achieved our goal of mapping a passage through the Crescent Mountains...," There were gasps of surprise; from Caleeza over learning the true purpose of their mission and from the others over their surprise that Rojaire had revealed it. "...and we have found two members of the lost expedition. So, if everyone is ready," Rojaire studied their faces, only Caleeza looked puzzled; "it is time for us to turn back."

"We are going through the mountains?" she asked amazed.

The hike back started out easy at first. Caleeza marveled at the large, long meandering caverns of purple stone, each larger than the one before, as they made their way deep into the mountains. "The route isn't this easy the whole way," Traevus warned her.

Still it was a long time before they left the last large cavern and entered the narrower cave system beyond. Caleeza liked it less and less as the walls closed in tighter and tighter, her disquieting claustrophobia increasing exponentially. They paused frequently to rest and eat, but Rojaire quickly pushed them on to cover as much distance as they could before stopping to sleep. By the time he finally called a halt in a cave large enough for all of them, the group, exhausted from the arduous trek, dropped down in whatever space they could find to rest, Theon unable to suppress a painful moan.

They were still a long way from the distant lava tube. The long serpentine stretch of cave tunnel that would require the team to crawl on their hands and knees, and sometimes bellies, lay before them; it was the leg of the journey Theon dreaded the most. Tired as they were it wasn't long before the group settled down and extinguished the lights. Soon the sonorous chorus filling the cave indicated most of the companions were sleeping.

Ollen, knowing Rojaire was probably doing more worrying than sleeping, spoke to him softly in the darkness. "Crawling back through to the other side will be extremely difficult for our revered but ancient friend. What do you think the chances are of a person successfully teleporting to the lava tube from here with a star stone?"

"I don't know. I guess it would depend on the ability of the person in possession of the star stone, but I can see where you are going with this. It would help greatly if Theon could teleport there." He had already given Theon possession of his star stone to help him along the way. "Someone would have to go with him to assure his safety."

"Perhaps the straight distance isn't as great as we think considering all the twists and turns Kiril recorded on the way here and we have four star stones in our possession," Ollen reminded him.

"We'll give it a try," Rojaire agreed. "Get some sleep; we have a long way to go yet to reach the valley."

After everyone was up and moving in the little well-lit cave, Rojaire offered his proposition. "Theon, remember the place where the lava tube was blocked and we slipped into the thin hole in the wall?"

"Vividly, and I wish I would never had slipped through that hole." Theon thought longingly of the walking staff he had been forced to leave behind.

"I want you to concentrate; picture that location in the lava tube in your mind; do you think you can teleport there?"

"From here?"

"Yes, and if you think you can, I would like to send Ollen and Traevus with you, in case there is anything waiting at the other end, that is if Edty will loan Ollen his star stone."

"Sure, no problem," Edty agreed handing Ollen the stone.

"What could possibly be waiting for them at the other end of the tunnel?" Caleeza asked.

Her question was answered with silence. Since the men weren't quite sure what they should reveal, no one spoke up to answer.

"Fine," Caleeza mumbled to herself, "I will find out when I get there."

"Any time you're ready," Rojaire said to Theon.

"We'll have dinner waiting for you," Theon assured the others when they were ready to go. While the others watched anxiously, Theon and his companions focused their thoughts on their targeted destination. They pictured in their minds the lava tube with the blocked end and the questionable opening into the cave tunnels with Theon's walking staff propped up against the rock wall next to it …mentally placing themselves there.

Heart flutters later, Theon, Traevus, and Ollen vanished from the little cave leaving Rojaire, Kiril, Caleeza, Tassyn, and Edty to navigate the serpentine tunnel, with only Kiril still in possession of a star stone in case of need.

"All right," Rojaire exhaled after the trio was gone. "Now let's catch up with them." With another sigh of relief, he led his remaining crew toward their destination.

The configuration of the cave tunnel presented many challenges, requiring much bending and stooping along the way. Eventually the tunnel funneled into a crawl space. The journey was grueling for Caleeza; the physical exertion minor compared to the claustrophobia that plagued her. The restricted space kept her on the edge of panic, beading cold sweat along her spine. She feared the ground would start to shake or their lamps would go out at any moment leaving them in solid darkness. She felt the weight of the mountain pressing down on her and feared it would drop, crushing and suffocating her, or the exit would be forever blocked and she would never again see the light of day. Time seemed endless. She struggled to maintain calm as she pushed her body forward. The occasional glimpses of Kiril and his light ahead and Edty coming up from behind did little to comfort her. Somehow she managed to press on. When she thought she could bear it no longer, she heard Rojaire's distant shout from up ahead proclaiming that he had reached the exit. Caleeza shed silent tears of relief as she struggled on.

By the time Caleeza finally reached the broad lava tube she was trembling. Rojaire was there to help her out of the narrow slit of a tunnel into the larger space. Once out she tried to stand, but her legs buckled under her. In one smooth fluid motion, Rojaire caught her and lowered her gently to the floor of the lava tube.

"How can I serve?" he asked concerned over her extreme stress. He reached for his water container handing it to her. Caleeza gratefully took a drink.

"Just give me a moment," she said breathing hard. "I'll be all right. I have a fear of tight spaces." Rojaire could only imagine what the passage through the tunnel must have been like for her.

"If it is all right with you," Kiril said after Edty made it out of the tunnel into the lava tube, "Tassyn, Edty and I would like to scout up ahead." They knew the opening to the valley was relatively close and were eager to rejoin the others. Rojaire gave them the go ahead and Kiril handed Rojaire his star stone, "In case you need it," he said.

Caleeza took a few deep breaths relaxing her body; soon she was ready to try standing up again. This time, with a little help from Rojaire, she managed to stay on her feet. With each step, Caleeza felt a bit more stable. Thanking Rojaire for his concern, she assured him she could manage on her own and they walked on. It was a long stroll, but the way was clear and they were walking upright.

"Your men have great respect for you," Caleeza said as she and Rojaire hiked the lava tube together.

The comment disturbed Rojaire; he knew he hadn't been totally forthright with his men concerning the star stone he and Theon had carried at the start of the mission. Revealing the stone's presence was not the same as honesty. When Rojaire failed to respond, Caleeza tried a different topic.

"I sense a bit of secrecy about where we are going," she said broaching the subject carefully. "Am I in for a big surprise?"

"...Oh definitely," Rojaire said tantalizingly. "This continent offers wondrous surprises."

"...And you have seen them all."

"Far from it ...I've seen more than most. About Sarus...," Rojaire said desiring to learn more about Sarus and his connection with the Crystalline Landscape. "Do you think he can be contacted again?"

Caleeza chose her words carefully. "I understand your desire to have Sarus search for the woman you love so deeply." She took a breath before continuing. "I don't know if it is possible for you or anyone to make contact with Sarus' mind. He may have already forgotten all that I worked so hard to help him remember."

It was not what Rojaire wanted to hear.

Eventually, Caleeza saw a splash of sunshine spilling into the tunnel in the near distance and the sweet kiss of a current of fresh air brushed her cheek, lifting her spirits. When they finally reached the wide lava tube opening, Caleeza gazed out amazed at the panoramic view of the small grassy blue-green valley under a golden sky hemmed in by steep purple mountain slopes, and broke into a pleased smile.

Below them, a short distance from the rock spree sloping down to the valley floor, the rest of their companions were gathered around a kurper roasting on a spit over an open fire. Looking up, Theon spotted Rojaire and Caleeza framed in the lava tube opening and shouted.

"I told you we would have dinner ready for you when you got here."

## Chapter 17

# Earth

When Vince entered the cabin with an armload of wood he found Leaf and the twins jumping and shrieking playfully in the family room, Maggie darting about the kitchen in a baking/cooking frenzy, and Melinda laboring in vain to put the house in order. Kaylya and Jack were coming for a visit.

Vince dropped the armload of wood for the cook stove by the door and stepped back out.

The cabin, heated by the baking hot cook stove, zinged with noise and activity. Beaded steam rolled down chilled sunny, winter windows as the aromas of baking bread, freshly baked molasses cookies, and simmering moose pot roast competed for dominance in the rooms. A tea kettle whistled noisily on the stove, bouncing Nerf balls rattled cups and spoons left on the table, and Keiluk joyfully barked her puppy bark, happy to be part of the fun family, when for Maggie the noise and activity in the enclosed cabin surpassed sustained tolerance levels.

"All right, enough …enough," Maggie shouted above the ruckus, removing the whistling tea kettle as Vince brought in the container of water he had filled at the spring.

The children paused in their movements, the last Nerf ball rolled harmlessly off the table onto the floor, and since things had come to a stop, Keiluk ceased barking. "Melinda, could you help me please, get the kids dressed and take them and the dog outside to play for a while?" Maggie asked grabbing hold of two toddler sized snowsuits with mittens attached.

"Calm down," Vince coaxed Maggie, "Jack and Kaylya wouldn't want you to work this hard over their visit. I'll help you get the twins into their snowsuits."

Maggie took a releasing breath or two. "I'm sorry," she managed to smile, "I just want everything to be perfect."

"Everything is perfect," Vince reassured her, kissing her gently on the forehead as he took a toddler-sized snowsuit from her.

Children and dog spilled out the door into winter-bright sunshine. Having passed the shortest day, the sun rose a bit higher and shone a bit brighter than just a few weeks ago, but still lacked any real warmth to bask in. Keiluk, no longer timid about snow, was the first off the porch, running off a short distance before going into a squat.

The snow around the porch area, littered with woodchips and twigs, was well packed by snowmachines and human foot traffic. Beyond the heavy traffic area the sun's rays gleamed off a sparkling white three-foot snowpack through which several rough and narrow Leaf and Keiluk made trails wove aimlessly through the deep snow. Boy and dog zipped out and headed down one of the winding snow paths in merry chase, leaving Melinda with the little ones.

Melinda looked about at the brightly cold winter day with longing in her heart. She wasn't immune to the beauty that surrounded her; the artist in her noted the weave of tree branches laden with snow against a stunningly blue sky, the stark blue shadows bluish cold against the brilliantly white snow, the gentle snow-softened contours of the hills and creek, and the vibrantly black strutting raven on the woodshed roof.

*Hello Raven ... How are you doing today?*

"Klawock...!" Raven chortled.

*I have nothing for you,* Melinda had to admit. *I didn't know you were out here.*

Disappointed, Raven flew off.

Watching him go, free as a bird, only intensified her longing. Melinda wasn't unhappy living with Vince and Maggie; she knew she was loved by everyone around her, but she couldn't just hide out here for the rest of her life minding kids. In a couple of months she would be eighteen, a woman.

*When spring arrives, I will venture out on my own,* she decided for the hundredth time.

"Da...," Crystal said pointing to Rock, already across the clearing. Crystal captured Melinda's attention telepathically, transmitting her desire to follow.

Early on, Melinda had been faced with the dilemma of whether or not to encourage Crystal to use her budding telepathic ability by responding telepathically. But she had decided long ago that avoiding telepathic communication with Crystal was foolish. She doubted Maggie and Vince were even aware that Crystal possessed telepathic abilities.

*I'm coming,* she telepathed smiling and reached for the little girl's hand, leading her to Leaf and Keiluk's network of snow trails.

Rock, in an attempt to catch up with Leaf and Keiluk, stumbled in the churned up snow left in their wake. By the time Melinda and Crystal reached him, Leaf and Keiluk were headed back to the clearing, Keiluk in the lead with her puppy tongue hanging out.

"Watch…!" Leaf shouted out as soon as he realized he had an audience. They all watched expectantly as Leaf levitated his body several feet up over a section of undisturbed snow, and then dropped down feet first into it, sinking up to his neck. As a grand finale, Leaf made his escape by drawing energy and exploding the snow away from his body leaving behind a meteor impact crater in the snowpack.

*It wouldn't be wise to let Mom and Dad see you doing that, Melinda advised Leaf.*

Rock, greatly impressed by Leaf's snowy blast, grunted with arms up for Melinda to pick him up and toss him in the snow, a game they'd played before.

Melinda obligingly lifted the little boy up and gently placed him into the nearby snow bank. Rock's light weight coupled with the density of the snowpack, plus the added floatation of his snowsuit prevented him from sinking very deeply. He wallowed playfully in the snow laughing and slapping at the glittering ice crystals, gradually packing a deeper, broader depression with his thrashing movements.

When she offered Crystal a turn to be dropped into the snow bank, the little girl backed off. Thinking he was being helpful, Leaf levitated his little sister up over the deep unpacked snow, then from a height of nearly a foot he dropped her. The height provided enough momentum to send the shocked expression on her little girl face disappearing beneath a powdering of snow. Quickly realizing his mistake, Leaf brought Crystal back up, holding her suspended in midair until Melinda could come to the rescue.

Crystal's shocked expression coated in ice crystals quickly turned to screeching rage, the heat of her anger melting the ice crystals from her face as Melinda snatched her from the air, comforting her in her arms. The howling brought Maggie and Vince out on the porch to investigate.

*She fell in the snow,* Melinda explained.

Crystal chose to explain further by pointing to Leaf accusingly and scrunching up her little face, renewing her howling rage.

"I'll take her," Maggie offered, meeting Melinda across the small packed clearing. "Did Leaf make you fall in the snow?" she asked Crystal taking her into her arms. Deciding that was close enough to the truth, Crystal nodded her head still crying out her indignation.

"I'm sorry," Leaf said, knowing an apology was in order.

"Well, greetings everyone; we didn't expect to find the whole family outdoors."

The snow incident was immediately forgotten with the arrival of Jack and Kaylya.

"Welcome…! It's so good to see you two," Vince said, already off the porch and in the yard giving Kaylya a hug and shaking Jack's hand.

"Kaylya…! Jack…!" Maggie exclaimed giving them each a three way hug that included the now contented little girl.

"Maggie, you look as radiant as ever," Jack greeted her.

"Hi Crystal," Kaylya greeted the toddler. "You sure have grown a lot since the summer." Crystal stared at the strange lady, not recognizing her. *Are your brothers behaving themselves?* She telepathed the message confidentially and soon had an unmistakable mental reply.

*No, Leaf bad.*

Then Leaf and Keiluk came running up. Leaf and Jack were established buddies.

"Hey, Jack, this is my dog Keiluk; I got her for my birthday; I'm four now," Leaf announced proudly holding up four fingers.

"Well congratulations, Leaf. Yes, indeed, that looks like a fine dog you have there," Jack said, looking over the obviously still growing white puppy that sat patiently by Leaf's side.

Finally Melinda and Rock joined the circle.

"Melinda, good to see you," Kaylya said, putting an arm around her. "And young Rock…," she added, picking him up in her arms.

"Let's take the party inside," Vince said, "I rushed out when we heard Crystal crying and didn't put on enough warm clothing to stay out long."

---

Bright sunshine, deceptively warm coming through doubled paned windows, streamed in with a promise of lengthening days …and dare one hope… spring. While chopping vegetables for a pasta salad she was preparing for the gathering at Vince and Maggie's, Rahlys glanced repeatedly at an unfinished watercolor sitting on a table easel a short distance away. She had stayed up late into the night working on it, trying to capture the luminosity of a full moon on snow-laden spruce boughs and bare birch branches.

"If you don't watch what you're doing, you're going to chop off a finger," Quaylyn cautioned coming up from behind and startling her.

"If I do, it will be your fault," she mumbled, jumping back at his unexpected touch. "What's up?" Rahlys asked looking into his eyes.

"I've been thinking about Brakalar. There has to be a way we can flush him out."

All Rahlys' efforts at seeking out Brakalar through the Oracle of Light had failed. Brakalar had, no doubt, invoked powerful protective shields to prevent detection. They could only hope that Brakalar had failed to open the rune-covered chest concealing the Rod of Destruction.

"The sooner we apprehend Brakalar, the sooner we can return to Aaia," Quaylyn said gently moving her darkening, once blond, hair aside and planting a kiss on her soft warm exposed neck.

Quaylyn's statement, however, had left Rahlys cold; she tensed and pulled away out of his embrace.

"What are you talking about?" she asked not at all pleased. "You said you weren't here on a mission for the High Council of the Crystal Table; you said you were here for me."

"I am here for you," Quaylyn assured her. "That doesn't mean we can't eventually return to Aaia."

Rahlys recalled the fear of never returning to her own world while on the expedition to the Devastated Continent, and her joy and relief upon returning, secretly vowing never to leave her home world again.

"I can't," Rahlys said simply.

"What do you mean, you can't?" Quaylyn asked confused.

"I can't return to Aaia," she said placing what was left of the fresh produce back into the root cellar. Quaylyn watched in silence; her statement threatening all his hopes for the future.

"Why can't you…?" he asked finally.

How could she explain the feelings of vulnerability from being trapped on a distant world? With what words could she relate to him her innate need to be where the sky was blue and the forest green …at least part of the time… and where individuals make their own decisions about their own lives?

"I don't belong on Aaia; I belong here. This is my home; I don't want to leave. You lied to me, Quaylyn," she said facing him. "This isn't about us; it's about bringing Brakalar to justice. That has been your mission all along."

"No, that's not true," Quaylyn denied, "We didn't even know Brakalar was on Earth until things started to disappear."

Silence ensued over hurt feelings.

"I love you," Quaylyn said breaking the silence. Rahlys did not rebuke Quaylyn's declaration of love.

"I love you, too."

"...But not enough to return with me to Aaia."

Rahlys didn't know how to answer him. How could she love him so much and not be willing to go with him to the end of the heavens?

*Quaylyn, Rahlys, we have arrived,* came the telepathed message from Kaylya, *and so has Ilene.*

*We will be there shortly,* Rahlys assured her, careful to disguise the disquieting emotions stirred up by her and Quaylyn's discussion.

The boisterous play and merry chatter that greeted Quaylyn and Rahlys upon arriving at Maggie and Vince's log home did little to dispel the troubling thoughts that plagued Rahlys' mind.

"Rahlys, it's so good to see you ...and Quaylyn," Jack greeted them heartily.

The warm companionship of her friends only served to punctuate her reluctance to go away with Quaylyn. This was her world; she did not want to let it go, not now, perhaps not ever. Lured by the rich comforting aroma of hot chocolate, she followed Maggie into the kitchen and grabbed a mug from the cabinet.

"Let me heat that up for you," Maggie said moving the pot of leftover hot chocolate over to the warm part of the stove before Rahlys could grab it. "Is everything alright between you and Quaylyn; you look a bit piqued."

"Things are fine; it smells great in here," Rahlys said although she didn't feel hungry at all.

"Doesn't it...?" Ilene agreed coming for a warm-up of hot chocolate.

"Have you found anything else that might be Brakalar related through the news media?" Rahlys asked Ilene.

"Nothing at all; if Brakalar managed to cut open the chest, he hasn't taken any noticeable action yet."

"I don't believe any laser on Earth will cut through Droclum's enchantment," Kaylya said having walked in on their conversation, thereby leaving the men with the children. "The key will resurface again somewhere, and the recipient will be chosen by Droclum's essence."

Kaylya's prediction sent chills down Maggie's spine.

"You guys keep saying a person has to be able to visualize a place before invoking magic on it," Maggie said. "If that's true, Brakalar must have seen the laser cutter at the science institute before taking it. Perhaps if you could find out who introduced the laser cutting machine to Brakalar in the first place, you would have a lead as to his whereabouts."

---

"Whew…!"

Officer Gerald LeBlanc shook rainwater off his umbrella before closing it to enter the low two story wood-sided police station. The arthritis in his hands and the rust on the umbrella's release mechanism made closing the umbrella harder than he cared to admit.

"Good morning," a couple of his co-workers greeted him in passing. Upon entering his office he dropped the umbrella into a large cream colored ceramic vase boasting a large blue flower on its surface, which served as a receptacle for it by the door, and hung up his coat and hat on the rickety coat rack, a ritual he had performed for thirty plus years now. Just two more months and I can retire he sighed as he tore another page off his calendar. With a ton of vacation time owed to him, he wouldn't have bothered to come in today, especially in the rain, except for an appointment he had reluctantly agreed to.

Settling into his chair Gerald opened a file drawer, pulled out a bottle of antacid tablets, took a handful, and removed a file pertinent to the upcoming meeting with Dr. Jeff Robertson, Director of Paranormal Phenomena at the Paranormal Phenomena Research Center in New York City and his assistant Lucy Wright. Dr. Robertson claimed on the phone he may know who was responsible for some of the items that have reportedly disappeared … including the laser cutting machine. Gerald doubted the truth of the claim, but couldn't take the chance that it was all bogus and not meet with the guy. Solving the mysterious cases would be a sweet crowning glory to his career, instead of the cases making him the laughing stock of the department.

With a wishful sigh, he opened the file and glanced over his skimpy, unhelpful notes. Through his research, he learned that titanium could be purchased like any other metal in four by eight foot sheets and rods of varying thicknesses and diameters and was used in the construction of an endless array of products from airplane parts to prosthetic limbs; and thus, providing no clue to the intended purpose of the purloined laser cutter.

Then this Dr. Robertson called. *How can anyone be a doctor of spooks and magic?* Gerald shook his head; the worst of it was he came to work in this kind of weather for the meeting. Although any lead as to what was going on would be greatly appreciated, Gerald didn't believe paranormal phenomenon was the explanation.

Quaylyn and Rahlys did a surveillance mission ahead of time and decided that the ailing, retiring police officer with low self-esteem would be a better target for their purpose than the gruff high-strung lady at the science institute. Regardless whether or not their plan worked, it could be a fascinating finale to the police officer's career.

"Officer LeBlanc…?"

Gerald looked up to discover a rugged outdoorsman looking uncomfortable in a suit and a color challenged young woman with mossy grayish brown hair standing in front of his desk. He hadn't seen them come in which startled him.

"Yes…?"

"I'm Dr. Jeff Robertson and this is my assistant Miss Lucy Wright," Vince said introducing himself and Ilene who was playing the role of Lucy this time instead of Rahlys.

"Yes, of course, won't you have a seat;" Gerald said indicating two padded metal folding chairs.

"Thank you," Vince said taking a seat. Ilene did the same.

"On the phone, you claimed to know something about the sudden disappearance of merchandise in our local stores." Gerald decided to get right to the point; there was nothing to gain by pussyfooting around.

"We know who the culprit is," Vince said, being just as direct and presented Gerald with a photo of Brakalar that Quaylyn had impressed mentally on Vince's computer and printed off for this meeting. "His name is Brak Alar and we have been looking for him for quite some time," Vince said; all of which was true.

"How do you know this man is responsible for the disappearances?" Gerald asked looking up from the photo of a stern dark man.

"We worked with him at the institute," Vince explained slowly making a tale of it. "Brak's abilities are exceptional and he is a very gifted clairvoyant I might add."

"What kind of abilities?"

"Well, for instance, Brak can make objects move just by thinking about it," Vince said with much enthusiasm. "But even more than that," Vince said, leaning forward to stress the importance of his revelation, "Brak can teleport objects instantly from one place to another using his mind." Vince leaned back as though to say; now, isn't that incredible?

"Mr. … Dr. …" Gerald stuttered in exasperation.

"Call me Jeff."

"Jeff… you can't possibly expect me to believe that this Brak fellow," Gerald said tapping the photo with his hand, "is taking merchandise out of our stores…using his mind!" Gerald was nearly shouting at the end.

Ilene, aka Lucy, gave Vince, aka Dr. Robertson, a reassuring glance indicating she was ready.

Ilene had exhibited a possible talent for healing in regards to her father five years ago during the heat of battle with Droclum; and Councilor Anthya had worked with Ilene to develop her talent during their stay in the Community of the High Council. So when Quaylyn returned to Earth, he could not accept Ilene's claim that she could not communicate telepathically or work the simplest feats of telekinesis. That just could not be; after all, she was Theon's daughter. Over the ensuing months Quaylyn had worked rigorously with Ilene to ascertain her potential. This would be her first public performance.

"Brak Alar is not alone in his ability to manipulate objects with his mind," Vince said indicating Ilene. "Although not as talented as Brak Alar, if we may borrow a pencil, Lucy would like to give a little demonstration of what we are talking about."

Gerald tossed them a pen. "This will do," Vince said taking the cap and pocket clip off and setting it on the desk. All eyes turned to Ilene.

The patter of rain encroached on the silence that followed as the two men watched and waited in anticipation as Ilene strengthened her focus on the pen. Ilene struggled to gain control of her heart beat and breathing, both running wild with anxiety over the possibility of failure. As the image of the pen strengthened in her mind, she began to relax.

Vince suppressed a chuckle watching her, recalling how Rahlys had worked so hard to make what she could do so easily, seem difficult. Ilene, on the other hand, didn't have to pretend. Although Vince appeared outwardly relaxed; in truth, he was not. He found himself straining with very fiber of his being to help Ilene succeed.

After some time, Gerald shook his head in disdain. This was all a waste of his time …a waste of a day. Gerald was ready to deem it all a freak show, and a failed one at that, when the pen rolled toward him across the desk.

Vince struggled not to whoop with joy.

"She blew on it," Gerald rationalized after a stunned moment.

No one responded. *If he needs more I will give it to him,* Ilene thought to herself. Ilene continued to concentrate on the pen while Vince held his breath. After a moment, the pen vanished from sight right in front of their eyes, leaving empty space on the desk where the pen had been.

Gerald jumped back in alarm, "How did you do that?" but recovered quickly feeling foolish at being so gullible. "What are you trying to pull here? I don't have time for magic tricks. Unless you have some concrete evidence that stands up to reasonable logic this meeting is ended."

"We know for a fact Brak Alar was on site shortly before a TV disappeared from your local Wal-Mart," Vince said giving him some facts. "We paid Fred Landry, the Wal-Mart security guard a visit; he was glad to have someone actually believe him.

"Do you have a copy of the surveillance tape showing the TV's disappearance?" he asked Gerald.

"Yes, right here." Gerald reached into the folder and pulled out a disc. He fed it into the computer unit on the floor by his desk and rotated the monitor on his desk so they could all view it.

"Brak Alar passes by the TV about fifteen minutes before it vanishes," Vince explained when the recording started playing showing an empty aisle. Gerald glanced at the time of disappearance noted in the file and scrolled the recording back to the approximate time of Brakalar's expected appearance. Soon Brakalar strolled into view. Gerald paused the recording and compared the photo Vince had provided with the security surveillance image. It did indeed look like the same man, but still it didn't prove anything.

"The thing is this," Vince tried to explain. "In order for Brak Alar to teleport an object from a given location, he must first visualize both the object and the location. Now that's not a real problem when the object of your desire is in a department store where anyone can freely walk through, but the science institute isn't open to the public freely walking through its workshops. Chances are someone at the institute has had some contact with Brak Alar and may even know where he is."

"I've watched the security recording from the location, and no one was inside the workshop at the institute for a full twenty-four hours before the laser cutter's disappearance."

"Then Brak Alar was there earlier than that."

"You're certain of this…?" Gerald asked still skeptical.

"Absolutely…!"

"What is your interest in all this?" Gerald asked Vince sounding as grumpy as he felt.

"I just don't want to see anyone get hurt. Brak Alar has the potential of becoming a very dangerous man."

"Is he a radical Muslim?"

"No, not that I know of," Vince said suppressing a smile. *I wonder how he would respond if I told him Brakalar was from another world.*

"So what do you want me to do?" Gerald knew this wasn't a stance fitting to a police officer, but frankly it didn't really matter anymore. He was sixty days from retirement. With an increase in prestige unlikely and ridicule already abundant, he had nothing to lose by going along with this lunacy. There was always the chance that something interesting would develop.

Vince sensed he had an ally and leaned forward in earnest. "Find out who associated with the Science Institute recognizes Brak Alar's photo. The closer we can narrow down the playing field, the better chance we will have of locating him," Vince said with complete sincerity.

"Where did the pen go?" Gerald asked finally.

"Look in the top drawer," Ilene informed him. Gerald reached over and pulled the drawer open.

Once the drawer was open, Ilene mentally latched onto the pen and floated it up into the air, gently landing it back on the desk.

Gerald didn't comment at first, staring intently at the pen, now at rest.

"I'll see what I can find out," Gerald said at long last, even though he knew it would mean another trip into the city which didn't please him one bit.

## Chapter 18

# Aaia

"The time has come for us to leave," Rojaire said solemnly, his pronouncement not unexpected. The departure had been delayed as long as practical, with excuses such as making sure that those staying behind would be safe and comfortable no longer holding merit. Further exploration of the valley, with the help of Kiril's map, had uncovered a large defensible cave not far from the stone colonnade by the waterfall where the star stones had been found. Rustic beds, tables, and chairs now furnished the new dwelling.

"It's so beautiful," Caleeza whispered, standing off from the others, looking out over the valley from the mouth of the cave. Most of the spectacular valley remained unexplored. *How far does it go? What is at the other end?* Caleeza couldn't help but wonder. The valley's mystery tugged at her heart as much as the thought of reentering the underground tunnels repelled her.

"We need to decide what we should take and what should stay here," Rojaire said when no one else spoke.

"I'm not going," Caleeza announced loudly turning toward the others.

"Caleeza ...what are you saying?" Traevus asked shocked by her decision. "You have been gone..."

"I want to stay," Caleeza said definitively, she had made up her mind. Sarus had not attempted to communicate with her since joining the group, and enough time had passed that in all likelihood he no longer remembered her at all. Sarus and the Crystalline Landscape were now truly merged as one. "I have no desire to explain all that has happened to the High Council and no desire to crawl through any more caves."

"Are you sure you want to stay here? It could be a long time before anyone returns from the outside," Rojaire made clear.

"This valley is intriguing and I intend to explore it, besides these fellows are going to need a healer around to take care of them," she added.

"The decision is yours, of course," Rojaire said. "And like with Ollen, we won't reveal your whereabouts or confirm your existence, if at all possible. Let's just hope no one thinks to ask if we found any sign of the lost expedition."

That left only Kiril and Traevus returning with him. The largest part of the passage through the mountains remained before them. They would only need enough provisions to see them through the Crescent Mountains to the western coastal region of the continent.

"As for the star stones...," Rojaire began as they pooled together their resources. "I want to make a confession."

The companions turned questioning looks toward him; Theon looked down and said nothing. The star stones had become important tools shared by the group to facilitate work. They had searched for more of the magic liberating stones, but without success.

"Not all the star stones we share were found here," Rojaire started to explain. "Theon and I had one in our possession before we left the Community of the High Council."

There were many surprised looks.

"It was given to us by Inventor Sulyan; how he acquired it, I do not know. We didn't tell you about it because of the previous situation with Stram; we didn't want anyone to feel threatened. Mostly the stone was used by Theon to help him along. So when Kiril and then Edty found star stones in the valley, I took the opportunity to expose the one we already had by pretending to find it in the creek," Rojaire confessed. It felt good to come clean.

All was quiet for a while.

"Well, Rojaire, seeing as you have treated us all fairly, there's no reason for us to hold it against you," Tassyn offered, easy to forgive.

"I can see how at the time, you might have seen it as the right thing to do," Traevus said, "but I appreciate you finally confessing up to us. I would hate to think I couldn't trust you."

"Now take it easy there," Ollen intercepted. "The man has cleaned his conscious; and as Tassyn said, you have all been treated fairly. Without the star stone Theon may not have endured the trip, and since no one knew about it, there could be no fear of anyone taking it." The others readily agreed with Ollen's logic.

"I am late in joining you," Caleeza said carefully, "but I can see the bond of respect and trust that has developed among you. Don't fracture that by fighting over this."

Caleeza was right of course, as both men knew. Before long, Rojaire and Traevus bowed their heads respectfully placing a hand on one another's shoulders.

"We will leave three star stones here, the same number that were found," Rojaire decided getting back to business, "and take one with us, which Traevus will carry, in case of a bad situation on the way back."

Before long, the travelers had their packs full with enough food to make it through the underground passage and a bare minimum of tools. Most of the tools and equipment they had carried in would be left for the first colonists. Theon watched carefully as Kiril made a quick final entry into his journal and packed it away in a pouch inside his pack. When all was ready, everyone decided to accompany Rojaire, Traevus, and Kiril to the opening in the lava tube to see them off.

Morning's long shadows still covered much of the valley floor as they headed out following a shorter, easier, more direct route they had found to the cut in the eastern ridge. Along the way, clouds of the large fluttering creatures with translucent laced skirts for wings flittered from plant to plant drinking dew off the foliage. As the group approached, the now familiar valley dwellers casually flew off to another nearby bush, barely disturbed by their passage.

"What beautiful twirling bits of life!" Caleeza marveled for the hundredth time.

"They look like a cross between a jellyfish and a moth," Theon said in good humor, but his comparison was completely lost to Caleeza who had never seen or heard of either.

"Life forms of Earth," Theon explained. Theon could come up with terms to approximate 'jelly' and 'fish,' but there was no correlating word on their world for 'moth.' Caleeza laughed over the mental image she drew of a fish made of jelly.

"I will call them callelas," Caleeza decided producing her own word derivative meaning "twirling life."

The naming of the callelas was a heart-lightening moment for the companions, saddened by the prospect of saying goodbye. Otherwise it was a solemn hike to the little grassy valley, now known as Kurper Valley, because of the initial encounter with the animal there and the two significantly important roasted kurper feasts they had shared below the open portal in the mountains.

By the time they arrived at the cut that led up to the little valley, the sun burned hotly over the peak of the eastern ridge. All too soon they had reached the point of departure. Everyone knew once they said good-bye, it would be a long time, if ever, before they would see their friends again.

Theon, first in longevity, made the hard first move turning to Rojaire and placing a hand on his shoulder.

"Travel safely, my friend ...May you serve well ...and stay away from my daughter!" Theon shouted at the end to cover fought-back tears.

"I won't be anywhere near your daughter," Rojaire shouted back just as boisterously. "But I will be back, Theon, and you had better be here, alive, with that sarcastic attitude...." Now it was Rojaire's turn to fight back tears.

"When you see Captain Setas, would you give her a message from me?" Theon asked.

"Of course, what's the message?"

"Tell her, 'Seek heart, not soul.'"

"Seek heart, not soul," Rojaire repeated. "What does it mean?"

"She will know what it means."

"I will give her your message," Rojaire promised and moved on to carry out personal farewells with the others as Kiril took his place beside Theon.

"Here, I want you to have this," Kiril said handing Theon the folded crystal floss map.

"Thank you," Theon said sadly accepting the map.

"You will need it; I won't."

Theon could hear the discontent in Kiril's choking voice. Kiril turned away quickly so he wouldn't have to look Theon in the eye.

"What is wrong with you?" Theon asked demanding Kiril's attention.

"I want to stay."

"Well, you can't; Rojaire needs someone to return with him, or the High Council will start to suspect something. He can explain away Tassyn, Edty, and me, but it would be a lot harder explaining the defection of a loyal student of the Academy. Besides, you haven't finished your training yet."

"I will be back," Kiril said defiantly.

"Of course you will," Theon agreed solemnly. "Of that I am certain and your map will be here waiting for you," Theon assured him.

"What will I tell Drak when he asks about the map?" Kiril asked, suddenly worried about the inevitable dilemma he would eventually face.

"Well, I can give the map back to you right now, but your first instinct was probably the right one; the map will be a lot more useful here …and safer I might add. The solution I think would be to tell Drak the truth, as long as you're sure he can be trusted to keep our secret. After all, he gave you the map and believed in the valley's existence long before our discovery."

A smile of relief crossed Kiril's face; Theon's authority as First in Longevity of the newly established colony granted him the permission he needed to confide in Drak.

"Well don't worry about us," Ollen told Traevus loud enough for all to hear. "The five of us have everything we need right here. Why, by the time you return, we will be a thriving community."

"That I doubt not after having seen what you accomplished alone in the Cremyn Valley," Traevus agreed.

"And you have chosen to stay with these men," he said facing Caleeza.

"This is where I belong for now," she confirmed. "I will be able to make him comfortable as time progresses, thanks to the star stones," she said glancing briefly at Theon. Caleeza's ability to heal had already proven extremely helpful during the few rotations of light and dark they had worked together setting up living quarters for the group staying behind. She did not add out loud her own need to think about what the future held for her before returning to the greater outer world. All she understood at this point was that she no longer wanted the High Council to determine her future for her.

"What about Sarus?" Traevus asked her, the unexpected question shaking up her newly found contentment.

"Sarus the man is no more," Caleeza said softly. "A little of Sarus' essence may still exist, but for the most part he has melded with the Crystalline Landscape."

Traevus tried to understand the meaning, even the possible significance of Caleeza's statement as Tassyn and Edty wished him a safe and speedy trip home.

Finally with all their farewells played out, there was nothing left to say, and Rojaire, Traevus, and Kiril climbed the rock scree up to the lava tube portal that led to the passage through the mountain. While they climbed, Theon drew a little energy from the star stone in his hand, and focusing on the journal in Kiril's pack, transferred the journal from Kiril's pack to a pouch in his cloak.

*Sorry my friend; one day you will understand.* Theon regretted the need to pull the deception, but in the long run it would make Kiril's life easier. If the High Council read his journal, there would be far too many questions to answer. *It will be here when you get back,* he promised Kiril silently.

The three travelers reached the opening, turned, and stood for a moment framed in by the ragged edges of the collapsed rock wall. With their hearts weighed down with the sadness of departure, they gazed down at the friends they were leaving: Theon, Ollen, Caleeza, Tassyn, and Edty, the five would-be colonists. Both groups wondered if they would ever see the other again. Then the travelers waved a final farewell and turned away, quickly vanishing from sight around a curve.

Kiril's first impulse was to turn and dash back to Kurper Valley to rejoin the others, but he forced himself to continue to follow Traevus and Rojaire through the lava tube. For the longest, the men hiked in silence sadly lost in their reflections of the departure.

They made swift progress through the broad lava tube that sloped ever so gently downward toward the fresh water cavern they knew awaited them. Eventually they reached the hole in the lava wall that led down a natural, albeit a bit rough and unstable, stone stairway. By the time the companions finally reached the cavern of trickling streams of water and many dead-end tunnels, they had gotten over the worst of their gloominess and were ready for rest and nourishment.

Traevus drew energy with the aid of the star stone and dried places for them to sit in the damp cave. They drank and ate to the soothing murmur of the stone fountains flowing around them, the water dribbling in through cracks and crevices in the rock walls then exiting the cavern again through cracks and crevices in the rock floor. Once the men were relaxed, the conversation reached tentatively back to the colonists left behind, but now with a hopeful note for the future.

"We will have the opportunity to return with more settlers, perhaps enough to sustain a tiny community," Traevus offered.

"We will definitely need more women to join us," Kiril added.

"We will have to convince the High Council to allow Lynnara to be colonized, but how? It will require some creative thinking." Traevus noticed Rojaire was not contributing to the conversation. "What do you think, Rojaire?" he asked breaking into his thoughts.

"...definitely," Rojaire said, agreeing to whatever they were talking about.

Rojaire had been oblivious to their discussion, his mind absorbed in formulating totally different plans in his head. He would return to the valley, but not to settle. He would ask Caleeza to return to the Crystalline Landscape with him, but with or without Caleeza's help, he would find a way to contact Sarus and search for Kaylya.

"If you are ready, let's move on," Rojaire said eager to start his search.

They quickly readied themselves, leaving the watery cavern behind and slowly crawled their way through the long rough series of low rocky caves that frequently brought them to their knees. The group was ready to drop from exhaustion by the time they finally reached the long narrow cavern veined in crystal and gold.

"We can get much needed sleep here," Rojaire announced, the weariness evident in his voice. The tired men quickly found suitable spots to do just that.

The remainder of the journey through caverns and lava tubes progressed speedily, and remained fortunately, uneventful. With no sense of night or day, only distance held them back.

*Returning always seems to go faster than going*, Kiril reflected, as they started out from the intersection of lava tubes where they had stopped to sleep. From here the clearly marked lava tube pathways would lead them out. *Is it the lack of anticipation and wonder over what to expect that speeds things up*, he wondered?

After time unknown, the travelers finally emerged from the lava tube passages into a narrow rock-strewn crevice hemmed in between towering walls of stone. A sliver of sky above revealed a star-studded night. *The stars,* they whispered in mental relief to themselves as they gazed up with primordial awe at the heavens, and then moved on seeking wider open spaces.

---

Captain Setas woke to a new dawn filtering in through the living botanical walls of her small bedchamber. She moaned softly as she rose, drawing what feeble healing energy she could still muster to warm the stiffness in her ancient joints. Once in motion, she strolled out to her gardens, her bare feet absorbing the morning coolness of the paving stones.

An observer from far off might have imagined a nymph, a sylvan creature anointing each botanical wonder with her nurturing touch. On closer inspection, all nymph-like illusions dissolve into shriveled leathery-skinned antiquity. Stepping lightly down the path, her white gauzy gown billowing in the air currents, Setas glided through the perfumed morning mist greeting each delicate flower unfurling their velvety petals to the strengthening daylight.

Captain Setas plucked dew drenched clusters of fruit for her morning sustenance and drank generously of the fresh cool spring water flowing from a hollow wooden pipe stuck into the rocky reservoir at the foot of the hill. Then with her thirst quenched, she set to work. Standing still with her arms outstretched, she seemingly began to sing softly, but actually murmured a spell, a melodic incantation to summon her little enchanted workers.

A tiny light suddenly appeared twinkling beside her, then two more, and soon tens, hundreds, thousands of tiny twinkling lights undulated like an aurora around her. With a single graceful wave of her hand, Setas sent her swarm of pollinators out to do their work.

As her little workers darted off toward their task, Setas thought of the last group she had ferried across the Golden Sea. *Did Rojaire's group plant the tree seeds I entrusted them with?* Of course the tree varieties she had given them were all wind pollinated and wouldn't need her little swarm of workers to eventually bear fruit.

Following the babbling brook that accommodated the spring's runoff to the sea, Captain Setas gingerly descended the paving stone steps down to the lavender-blue beach where frothy gold-tinted waves cascaded against the exposed tideline. Here the sea attacked the sandy shore, unprotected by rocky protrusions or sheltered bays. Dark rusty-gray clouds driven by a refreshing breeze ruffled across the western sky, the east lit now by the rising sun. A storm was brewing; not only could she see it in the angry sky, but she could feel it in her fragile bones and stiff joints. As though on cue with her thoughts, the wind picked up a little, pressing her airy gown against her legs and jostling her stark white hair.

There hadn't been any further contact from the Academy or the High Council since Rojaire and Theon passed through. She considered that a good thing. The less contact she had with the outside world the better, and in her opinion, the High Council and their puppet the Academy were the worst of the outside world.

"Seek heart, not soul," Theon had spoken, denoting acceptance of an alliance. But whether it was an alliance of only two, or a more far reaching network, she wasn't sure. She suspected some kind of coercion between Theon and Rojaire. Not surprising considering there had been only animosity between Theon and Councilor Brakalar when she had ferried the previous expedition across.

What ever happened to Brakalar, she wondered? And why is his disappearance so shrouded in mystery? Brakalar had provided Rojaire and his men secret passage to the Devastated Continent. Why had an Accepted One in such a high position instrumented such a clandestine act? Long ago there had been a woman with Rojaire, Kaylya was her name, Setas recalled. She also never returned.

With the storm fast approaching, Captain Setas realized it was time to turn around. Lost in her musings, she had gone a lot farther than she had intended and the storm was rolling in faster than she had expected. The sky darkened as clouds pulled a heavy dark curtain across it, shutting off the sunrise lit eastern sky. As the wind picked up, the waves grew in height and fury crashing against the sand and rocks. She had been walking into the wind coming out and now fortunately had the wind to her back.

Suddenly Setas halted her rush for shelter and turned laughing heartily into the fury of the elements, her laughter competing with the mounting roar of the wind.

"What a fool I have been letting the High Council brainwash me over eons into calling Lynnara the Devastated Continent! And Alaia, my own island world!" she shouted. *To think, it took the brass and daring declarations of new person Kiril to shame me into new awareness.*

"Lynnara … Alaia Island…," she shouted to the mournful wind, repeating the names over and over again, enjoying the feel of the melodic syllables in her mouth, the tangent sweetness of the sounds to her ears, and relishing the delicious taste of freedom the name invoked in her heart. It had been a long deprivation.

"Alaia Island… and Lynnara… I anoint you!" she shouted with increasing volume into the approaching storm. As though in response, not so distant lightning forked beautifully against the dark cloud backdrop. The resulting thunder rumbled and roared in applause.

"Good, I'm glad you agree with me," she cried out defiantly to the elements as the first heavy raindrops felted her head and arms. Setas headed back to the security of her shelter with a gladdened heart.

It was almost time for her to make another run to Lynnara to check on the explorers; hopefully the storm would pass quickly and the waters would calm before her scheduled appointment with Lavender Beach.

q

The storm the travelers had been watching approach from the west hit full force not long after they arrived at Ollen's shelter in the Cremyn Valley. The men arrived tired, hungry, and wet. They had journeyed a long distance since they left their friends behind in the secluded valley, stopping seldom to actually sleep. They were overdue for an extended rest.

Rojaire, Traevus, and Kiril inspected the open stone structure, taking note of the contents of the numerous clay pots and storage vessels that lined the walls and shelves. Nothing had been disturbed. Many of the stoneware containers were empty, but some still contained dried grains, fruit, and nuts they had left behind seemingly so long ago. Ollen's stores had been ample, more than the explorers had been able to take with them.

"Looks like we have everything we need to wait out the storm," Rojaire said as they began to settle in. The men changed out of their wet clothing and Traevus drew energy to dry them. Outside the shelter the storm continued to rage, but inside the men were cozy and warm.

"It's certainly roomier for three than it was for seven," Traevus said recalling that they had all gratefully taken shelter from a rainstorm the last time they were here. Any mention of the others always brought a quiet thoughtful moment.

"I'll set out some empty pots to catch rainwater," Traevus offered.

Rain and wind pounded the shelter throughout the long Aaian day, the storm releasing its load of pent up fury. As boredom set in, Kiril decided he was long overdue in updating his journal on the, so far, uneventful return trip toward home. He reached into the pouch of his pack where he always kept it and was startled when his groping fingers failed to locate it. A little irritated, Kiril pulled the pack closer to him and peered inside rummaging through it; the journal was not there. Becoming alarmed, he frantically pulled items from his pack …a change of clothes, some dried food, his drinking cup, a cutting tool. Even though he couldn't have missed something as large as the journal among so few possessions, at the end he stood up dramatically and turning the pack upside down, shook it out furiously, shocked over the loss.

"The journal; it's gone!" Kiril growled angrily throwing down the worthless empty pack.

"Well, at least we won't have to worry about the High Council getting ahold of it," Traevus muttered unsympathetically.

"It was you who took it," Kiril accused pointing a shaky finger at Traevus.

"I did not," Traevus answered firmly also standing up in his own defense. "I don't know anything about your missing journal."

"And neither do I," Rojaire said ready to intervene if necessary. "Are you sure you packed it?"

"Yes, I'm sure I packed it. What am I going to do without the journal?"

"I'm sure you are capable of presenting the council with a fair and amiable report of our journey without relating anything that could be threatening to Lynnara's future."

"You know what happened to the journal," Kiril accused.

"No, but it is my guess, someone else felt as we do about the information it contains."

With some effort, Kiril gradually calmed down; he knew Rojaire was right. Now that they had actually left behind a little colony, the degree and value of freedom and independence the group aspired to begin to register with Kiril. Revolution was far more than daringly calling Lynnara and Alaia Island by their true names against the High Council's wishes. They had taken on an important responsibility with far reaching possibilities. A sense of truth and purpose had embedded itself deep into Kiril's consciousness, and he was ready to concede to the wisdom of secrecy.

But he had put so much work into his journal. He sure hoped the journal would be waiting for him when he returned to the secret valley.

By the time the storm finally passed it was night. The clouds parted unveiling a distant celestial light that washed out all but the brightest stars and bathed the Cremyn River Valley in soft luminosity. Night wouldn't be as dark over the next season. For there in the eastern sky Seaa, the nearest star, glowed brightly in the storm-washed night sky.

The appearance of Seaa denoted the end of Aaia's hot sweltering summer as the near star tugged the planet farther away from her sun, bringing cooler, more pleasant temperatures. Seaa wasn't nearly as bright as the sun, but it blazed far brighter than any of the other stars or the reflected light of Aaia's tiny moon. The star's proximity to their solar system and its effects on the seasons placed Seaa in a category all its own.

Rojaire gazed across the starlit valley. "Let's go," he told the well-rested restless explorers. All agreed there was no reason to linger. Everyone was more than ready to go.

The first obstacle they faced right from the start was crossing the rain-swollen Cremyn River. Without discussing it with anyone, Traevus drew energy and placed himself on the opposite bank, but Rojaire and Kiril didn't carry star stones.

"Catch...!" Traevus shouted out to Rojaire and sent the star stone, reflecting starlight, arching toward him. Rojaire catch it deftly.

"That was putting the star stone at risk," he shouted back to Traevus.

"Would you rather swim?"

Rojaire didn't answer. He glanced at the star stone and Kiril standing beside him, "I can take us both across," he told Kiril.

After successfully crossing the river, they followed it to the beginning of the river canyon area where they were forced to climb uphill to circumvent the narrow ravine filled with rushing water. It was from the crest of this hill they had first spotted Ollen's shelter.

They made remarkable progress navigating the hills by Sea's light, only occasionally pausing to rest. Little was said throughout the night; the three men, hearty and fit, channeled all their energy into the hike. By the time the sun rose again, they were descending from the hills in the region where the Cremyn River entered the Zayla River Valley.

All focus was on reaching Lavender Beach to intercept Captain Setas as soon as possible. They weren't sure where they were on the timing, but if they just missed her it would be three long rotations before the captain would check the beach again.

"Where did all the water go?" Kiril asked puzzled when they returned to the banks of a greatly reduced Cremyn River. Rojaire laughed heartily.

"Amazing, isn't it," he said. "Apparently the river has a second underground outlet to the sea."

It was obvious the travelers were exhausted. Rojaire would have liked to push them further, but called a halt so they could get some rest and sleep.

---

Captain Setas loaded the last of the solar charged crystals in the control pedestal and closed the little access door. The handmade wooden ferry of her own design was ready to go. She had woven vines into a sturdy mat stretched over her control station; the mat pegged into uprights anchored into the polished wooden railings to provide her some shade. The bare wooden oval deck gleamed brightly in golden sunshine as she eased the little craft with its long pointed prow out of the protective bay into open water.

The sea, still charged with residual energy from the storm, rolled gently in the direction of Lynnara. Setas adjusted the ferry's speed, never fast regardless of conditions, for the most comfortable ride. As the journey progressed, the sea surface continued to lay down until eventually the surface of the water stretched smooth as the finest crystal floss reflecting golden in the sun lowering toward the western horizon. Finally, the natural breakwater was in sight and she nosed the ferry's pointed prow into the protected bay that opened to Lavender Beach. Bone weary, she rammed the pointed prow into the lavender sand and shut off the crystal-driven engine. As usual, the beach was deserted.

---

Rojaire slept restlessly with visions of Kaylya haunting his dreams. She seemed so close, closer than he had felt her presence in endless seasonal changes. Was it his growing obsession to find her, his renewed hope and faith that she was still alive enacting the desired results in his mind? At some point he did finally fall asleep, for when he opened his eyes again the sun blazed high in the east. They should have been on the trail again by now.

They left the hills following the tiny stream across the broad funnel-shaped Zayla River Valley to its confluence with the Zayla River. Their cloaks protected their skin from the burning sun, but the heat was oppressive. The peak of the day was not the best time to hike, but in his opinion they had no choice. Captain Setas' next scheduled return to Lavender Beach could be soon. They didn't want to miss a rendezvous; it would be a long wait for her next trip if they did.

When they finally reached the Zayla River, they found it had blossomed from the trickling brook that normally could be jumped across, to a wider, fast flowing stream that filled her gravelly bed, drowning foliage that had deigned to grow too close. But they didn't need to cross it; from here, they had only to follow it down the flourishing valley to the coast. They took few breaks, taking only an occasional opportunity to sit in patches of shade provided by taller brush. Fortunately, the closer their approach to the coast, the more refreshing the breeze moving ashore from the Golden Sea became.

"Do you hear that?" Kiril asked, pausing to cock one ear toward the still distant beach. Traevus and Rojaire also stopped to listen and they all heard the low distant hum.

"The ferry boat…!" Rojaire shouted and took off running. Then remembering he was currently in possession of the star stone, he transported himself as far as he could in leaps to reach the beach before it was too late.

---

Setas stretched to relieve tense muscles. *I will have my supper and take a nap before making the trip back by Seaa's light to Alaia Island on the night tide,* she decided.

Retrieving her dinner safely stored in a compartment built into the bow, she was just about to settle down on the open deck to eat and watch the sunset when she heard someone shouting her name in the near distance. Using the tiered storage units built in the bow as steps she walked out onto the broad flat base of the boat's thick prow for a better look. Soon she could make out someone thrashing through the brush like prey trying to outdistance its most deadly predator.

Her sense of preservation immediately went on alert. Quickly she stepped back down to the deck and pushed the start lever on the control pedestal in case she needed to make a desperate escape and climbed back up to the prow for another look.

Then Rojaire burst into full view, red faced and breathless, and came to a stop before her. Nothing appeared out of the brush behind him.

"Captain Setas…!" Rojaire gasped once he knew she had spotted him.

Captain Setas stood on the wide base of the ferry's prow waiting while Rojaire walked the rest of the way to the beach, still fighting to catch his breath.

"I thought you were running for your life," she croaked scornfully when he reached her. "Greetings, rogue explorer, how may I serve you?"

"Greetings, Captain Setas," he gasped bowing respectfully. "I humbly request passage for Traevus, Kiril, and myself to the Community of the High Council."

Setas looked out beyond Rojaire, but didn't see anyone.

"They're coming," Rojaire assured her. "I also carry a message from Theon."

Setas stepped back down to the deck and shut off the engine to hide her inner reaction to the news of a message from Theon. Rojaire walked up the anchored prow to join her.

"What's the message?" she asked after hitting the switch to silence the engine.

"Theon said to tell you, 'Seek heart, not soul.' He said you would know what it means."

Setas' dry weathered face crackled into a brief smile despite all her efforts to suppress it. "Yes," she said, touching her heart, "and so do you."

# Chapter 19

# Earth

New March snow fell heavily over the quiet, sopped-in upper Susitna Valley, already deeply buried under a winter's mantel of snowpack. One thing Rahlys knew for certain, winter was far from over. Turning away from the spirit-dampening view, she shuddered to think how much solar energy it was going to take to melt all the snow away.

"I guess we can't expect to see spring any time soon," she said rejoining Quaylyn and Kaylya at the dining room table after refilling their coffee cups. The rustic birch table and chairs, built by the same crafty woodsman who built Rahlys' log cabin, took up the southeast corner downstairs. Two windows, one facing east and one south, let in the day's leaden gloom, brightened only by the white falling snow.

**OFFICER LEBLANC HAS ARRIVED.**

The oracle's message was not unexpected. Now that Vince and Ilene had been successful in carrying out their part of the setup, it was time for the warriors of the Oracle of Light to follow up.

"He's there," Rahlys informed the others.

"Then let's begin," Quaylyn said calmly.

Focusing her thoughts, Rahlys conjured the crystal from its beaded pouch and directed it to the center of the table. The slowly spinning crystal, with its multi-colored lights glowing softly from within, brightened the gloomy day.

Concentrating on the purpose of the scrying, Rahlys called on the power of the Oracle. As she continued to focus on it, the crystal slowed its spin to a crawl. Above the table before them the Oracle projected a scene of Officer LeBlanc in front of the science institute, three thousand miles away. The sun shone warmly in a land where spring had indeed arrived and they could feel the warmth and smell the blossoms in their minds.

"This is incredible," Kaylya whispered in case she could be heard in the Deep South. "I can even feel the warmth of the sun on his skin."

"You don't have to whisper; he can't hear you," Quaylyn assured her. "You are doing great, Rahlys; now relax a little and let the scene unfold," Quaylyn coached.

They watched as Gerald LeBlanc, carrying a blue folder, entered the building and ambled over to the reception desk, manned by the same overly friendly young woman he had encountered on his first visit *…what was her name?…* 'Judy' he read off her name tag.

*I can even pick up his thoughts,* Kaylya gasped.

"Good morning, Gerald!" Judy said recognizing him instantly. "Have you found our laser machine thief yet?" she asked cheerfully.

"Not yet, but I could use your help."

"Of course, anything for you, Officer Gerald," she said flirtatiously.

Ignoring the come-on Gerald placed his folder on the counter and pulled out the image of Brakalar. "Do you recognize this man?" he asked handing it to her.

"Oh, yes, that's Dr. Simon," she said without hesitation. "He was here about a month ago attending a seminar on robotics and artificial intelligence."

"You have a good memory for people, I see," Gerald conceded honestly impressed.

"Why, thank you, Officer Gerald," she cooed obviously pleased that he had recognized her talent.

"Would you have a phone number, address, email address for Dr. Simon?"

"Of course, but you can't believe that Dr. Simon stole the laser cutter?"

Judy typed something and stared at her computer screen for a while. She hit more keys and a puzzled look took control over her cheery face. Then she typed something else and gaped at the monitor in disbelief.

"I just don't understand; he's not in the system," she said giving up.

"When was the seminar held?" Gerald asked not willing to give up so easily.

"Let's see; here it is, it was on February 21st and there were seventy-four scientists in attendance.

"That's a lot of faces; and you remember Dr. Simon in particular?"

"Yes, well, Dr. Simon was a little peculiar, he didn't really fit in, and he asked some really strange questions," Judy said trying to pin point what was so different about him.

"Strange questions…?" *Don't all scientists ask strange questions,* Gerald thought, but kept it to himself? "What kind of questions?"

"Well, to start with, he came up to the desk and with all seriousness asked if I was human or android."

"Maybe that was his idea of a pick-up line," Gerald offered. "After all, you did say it was a seminar on robotics and artificial intelligence."

"Yeah … well then, in all earnestness, he wanted to know what percentage of life forms on Earth had artificial intelligence. I mean, he referred to Earth like it was an alien planet or something," Judy added indignantly.

"Perhaps he was trying to be humorous."

"I don't think he knows the meaning of humor. If you ask me, he was dead serious." Gerald found her testimony fascinating.

"How did Dr. Simon arrive at the seminar, do you know?"

"I guess he arrived in a car like everyone else."

"What I meant was did he arrive alone or did he come with someone else?" Gerald clarified.

"I'm not sure, but the surveillance tape from the parking lot…and over the front door there," Judy said pointing to the camera eye watching them right now, "can be easily retrieved. Come have a seat," she said invitingly, tapping the unoccupied chair behind the desk beside her. Gerald readily took her up on her offer.

In front of him a separate surveillance screen, split into six frames, showed feedback sent from six cameras in and around the building. A FedEx delivery woman entered the building, handed Judy a package that she signed for, and then left in her delivery truck. Gerald watched the whole proceeding from camera feedbacks displayed on the monitor.

"Can you find the recording of Dr. Simon arriving for last month's seminar?"

"Sure I can," and true to her word, Gerald was soon watching Brak Alar a.k.a. Dr. Simon entering the building. The recording was so clear; Gerald couldn't resist looking up to make certain it wasn't happening in real time. Judy and Gerald watched the screen together as Dr. Simon approached the desk in the recording.

"See, I checked him in, gave him a name tag and directed him to the meeting room. I don't understand why he isn't in the address book," Judy said still dismayed.

"According to the recording, he entered the building at 7:53 a.m.," Gerald said. "Let's look at the recording of the parking lot around that time and see if we can spot his vehicle, maybe get a license plate number.

"Alright…," Judy readily complied. Soon they were watching scientists arriving, one car after another, for the 8:00 o' clock seminar. In groups of two and three they climbed out of their shared rental cars and cheerfully strolled up to the front entrance. Gerald scrutinized the attendees who climbed out of each vehicle that drove up, but Brak Alar hadn't arrived in any of them. Therefore, he was blown away when suddenly he saw Brak Alar approaching the building.

"Stop it there," Gerald said. He pointed to an image in the paused recording showing Brak Alar strolling across the parking lot. "That's him. Now slowly, back up the recording so we can follow him back to his vehicle." Judy readily complied. Gifted in facial identification and computer savvy too Gerald noted. "That's a girl; good job."

With anticipation, followed by shock, they watched Dr. Simon/Brak Alar slowly take step after step backward, all the way to the deserted far back corner of the parking lot, screened in by flowering trees …and then vanish.

"What…?" Gerald and Judy shouted together, equally stunned by what they saw.

"Run that back forward again!" Gerald exclaimed his eyes glued to the spot where Brak Alar had vanished. Immediately the time clock on the recording was running forward once again and to their astonishment Dr. Simon appeared just as instantaneously as he had vanished in the back corner of the parking lot where no one was likely to notice and proceeded to amble up to the front door.

"How did he do that?" Judy asked, still gaping at the monitor in disbelief. Without being told, she manipulated the recording replaying the appearing and disappearing act over and over again. No wonder the guy can't be traced Gerald thought silently.

At that moment, a couple walked in through the front door and stopped at the counter. Judy rose from her chair to address them. While she was diverted, Gerald had time to think. What he had seen here far surpassed what had been demonstrated in his office by Dr. Robertson and his assistant. The possible significance of all this was overwhelming. Who was Dr. Simon and where did he come from? Gerald intended to contact Dr. Robertson and ask some hard questions.

Far away in the northern Susitna Valley, Rahlys, Quaylyn, and Kaylya followed all this, including access to Judy and Gerald's current thoughts and emotions, and knew Judy spoke truthfully. One fact was certain; there were now two people outside their group who knew something that they would be unable to explain. What they did with this information was a real concern.

"I think Brakalar is attending seminars to learn about the state of science on Earth, probably to eventually use this knowledge to his advantage," Quaylyn surmised.

"He may also have a hard time separating science from science fiction if he has been watching movies," Kaylya explained. "Watching movies is a big past time in the villages and I remember being confused for a long time as to what is real."

"So Rahlys, let's have Gerald find out when the next seminar will be held," Quaylyn suggested.

"How do I do that?" Rahlys asked uncertain how to proceed without detection.

"Just reach for his signature and break into his thoughts, implanting the idea as though it were his own."

"That's coercion; bending a person's will," Rahlys protested.

"You're not asking him to kill someone or change his morals; you are just having him ask a question which he is likely to eventually think of on his own anyway.

"Would you rather see Brakalar take over the world with the Rod of Destruction?" he asked when she still hesitated.

Rahlys focused her mind on Gerald's signature, touching it ever so softly, gently nudging her own thought in. Gerald's face lit up with his strategically new idea. The couple moved on and Judy returned to the chair next to him.

"When's the next seminar?" Gerald asked right away.

"The institute sponsors a seminar or two every month. The next one is Saturday, the topic ...String Theory and Multiverses. These are all day affairs from 8:00 to 4:00 with an hour break for lunch."

"That's just two days away. Has everyone planning to attend the seminar signed up all ready?" Gerald asked.

"Yes, the registration period ended yesterday."

"Has Dr. Simon registered?" Gerald asked although Judy was already looking up the information.

"Yes, he has," she announced triumphantly.

"And what is the address on the registration form?"

“There aren’t any addresses here; all I have is a roster of names.”

“Well, thank you, Judy, you have been a big help,” Gerald told her sincerely.

“You’re very welcome.”

Gerald stood up and prepared to leave, reaching for the blue folder containing the photo.

“Officer LeBlanc,” Judy addressed him formally, “do you think Dr. Simon is an alien …I mean like a *real* alien… like one from outer space?”

“I don’t know,” Gerald said honestly, “but let’s keep what we’ve seen just between the two of us for now. We wouldn’t want word to get out to Dr. Simon that we are on to him.”

“Our secret…,” she whispered back.

Rahlys held the connection until Officer Gerald LeBlanc left the building. With a sigh of relief, she relaxed her focus. The crystal lost some of its brightness and wandered off about the room.

“We have our work cut out for us,” Quaylyn said simply when no one else spoke. “We must plan very carefully; if Brakalar detects anything, even the slightest anomaly, he will bolt and we will lose him again,” he warned.

“Then we will have to be on site and take him by surprise,” Rahlys concluded, weary from the long scrying.

“He seems to be getting a little lax the way he just dropped in at the science institute,” Kaylya observed.

“Part of that may be because he thinks our expedition is still on the Devastated Continent,” Rahlys surmised.

“We need to think this through carefully.” By now Quaylyn was pacing the room in thought, the crystal following him like a tiny glowing aura. “We can’t afford to make a mistake.”

---

When Gerald returned home after his long day, he hung up his jacket and changed into his slippers, then tried to call Dr. Jeff Robertson at the Paranormal Phenomena Research Center only to learn that the business card and the phone number were bogus. “Damn…!” he exclaimed slamming the phone back into its charger. “How could I have been so stupid, not checking his credentials before this?”

Going to the kitchen, he reached into the refrigerator for a beer. For thirty years he had ended his work day with a good cold beer. Would he still enjoy that beer when he retired? He hoped so.

Taking the beer to the living room, he sat down in his favorite easy chair, put his feet up, and turned the TV on low for company. Sipping on his beer, Gerald went over the facts of this particular case in his head.

It all started with the disappearance of the laser cutting machine at the science institute in Baton Rouge. He still didn't understand how the laser cutter fitted in the picture. Then a man claiming to be a research scientist of paranormal phenomena comes to my office with an assistant to try and convince me that magic is real. They give me a photo of a man they say goes by the name of Brak Alar and claim he may be the one who took the laser cutting machine. Turns out the researchers are frauds, but the magic may be real!

*On Saturday I will be looking for a man with two known alias, Dr. Simon and Brak Alar, a man who can pop in and out of a place like in a sci-fi movie and is the prime suspect in the disappearance of merchandise in the area.*

How do you stop and question someone who can just vanish on you, he wondered? Who are these people? Why are they so secretive? Where did they come from? How did they get here? Gerald was startled by his sudden realization that he was indeed considering an otherworld origin as a possibility.

There were even more important considerations. Is Brak Alar a.k.a. Dr. Simon dangerous? Were the other attendees at the seminar in danger? Should he have backup when he confronts Dr. Simon for questioning? He could hear the laughter in the department now if he were to ask for backup. "Old Gerald here needs support to interrogate dangerous Martians."

No, he had to handle this himself. *I'm not totally without support.* The thought of Judy, a bouncy young woman with a memory for faces and an ease with computers, as his partner brought a smile to his face, but his smile quickly faded. *Am I inadvertently placing Judy in danger? I will confront Dr. Simon in the parking lot before he even enters the building.*

Following well-established habit, Gerald finished his beer, and then went upstairs to take a shower. When he came back, he put a frozen dinner in the oven. Then Gerald did something that was unusual for him; he broke away from his usual routine by opening a second beer and instead of going back to his recliner in front of the TV, he stepped out onto the back patio.

The spring night was surprisingly warm, the air unusually dry, and the stars shone brilliantly in the clear night sky. He wasn't generally a star gazer, but tonight he felt an irresistible urge to gaze up into the vast unknown.

It was a rare quiet moment for the three women to visit without interruption from the children or intervention from the men. Jack was flying down to the lower forty-eight to visit family for a while and Vince and Quaylyn had volunteered to take Jack to the airport. The toddlers were down for a nap and Leaf entertained himself quietly in the boys' room. A quick peek into the room verified that Leaf had also fallen asleep on the floor with Keiluk by his side. Melinda had taken off walking in the woods on snowshoes.

"Melinda seems to desire plenty alone-time lately," Maggie worried. "But the nightmares have apparently stopped."

"Well, that's good, but I still wonder what may have triggered them in the first place," Rahlys reflected. "As for spending time alone in the woods; that I can relate to entirely. I did the same thing growing up, approaching womanhood. There is so much to think about at that age … one's whole future."

"I know what you mean," Maggie agreed. "Growing up I used to take off roaming through the streets of Seattle to get away from everyone and think."

Rahlys smiled knowingly. She remembered a much younger Maggie full of street smarts when they met, and Rahlys was country innocent.

"I know Melinda is lonely and desires to go out into the world," Maggie said, but lack of speech and a secret background are serious hindrances. She can communicate with us telepathically, but that could present problems in the 'real world.' If she reclaimed her true identity, she would have five years to account for and explain to the rest of the world. Claiming amnesia isn't going to work; she would still have to describe the circumstances around her when she supposedly recovered her memory. The worse part of it all is; some aspects of what happened to her are nearly inexplicable without revealing the Oracle of Light." The three women, bonded by friendship and concern for Melinda's future, pondered on the complexity of the problem.

"What's going on with you and Quaylyn, Rahlys?" Maggie asked changing the subject. "You thought no one has noticed, didn't you, but things have obviously cooled a bit between you."

"Quaylyn wants to return to Aaia."

Maggie's heart lurched; it was her greatest fear that Rahlys would leave again, maybe forever.

"And what did you tell him?" Maggie asked tenuously.

"I told him I don't want to leave."

Rahlys was saved from further explanation by the sound of snowmachines approaching. It would be Vince and Quaylyn returning. Because of Quaylyn's unbounded fascination for Earth's mechanical wonders, Rahlys had purchased a snowmachine for Quaylyn to follow Vince around on.

The three women rose as one and headed out the door into bright sunshine sparkling on snow to greet the men and carry in supplies.

"So Jack is off?" Maggie asked Vince giving him a kiss after the machines were shut off and the men had dismounted.

"Yes, Jack is on his way and we got everything on your grocery list."

"Good job," Maggie praised him giving him another kiss.

"I got something for you," Quaylyn said pulling out a box of chocolates and handing it to Rahlys. She couldn't resist the dimpled smile that always warmed her heart. Accepting his offer of embrace, she gave him a warm welcoming hug and thank you kiss.

**ROJAIRE APPROACHES….**

Rahlys jerked involuntarily in Quaylyn's arms in response to the message.

"What is it?"

"The Oracle … a message … Rojaire's coming." Rahlys announced. All eyes turned toward Kaylya.

"What…? When…?" Kaylya gasped, the color draining from her face.

"Any moment now…."

Kaylya began to totter and Vince gallantly stepped up offering her gentle unobtrusive support.

"Take a deep breath," he advised her. Kaylya finally did so and followed it with a second intake of air while focusing on calming her rapidly beating heart.

*Would he recognize her? Would she recognize him?*

And then he was there.

Rojaire opened his eyes to snow-covered forest glistening in dazzling sunlight that blinded him to the sight of Kaylya standing only feet away. The air surrounding him felt colder than the brilliant sunlight would suggest. Gradually his weeping eyes discerned humanoid shapes standing all around him. Then coalescing out of the glare, Kaylya … his Kaylya … emerged.

Vince let Kaylya slip out of his support and approach Rojaire unencumbered. Kaylya wanted to run, but her feet felt leaden, each step toward him taking a lifetime. She didn't notice as the others left the scene to give them respectful privacy. Her only focus was on Rojaire standing before her.

Kaylya loomed real before him. He reached out to touch her his arms aching to hold her, to absorb this new reality of Kaylya returned. But when he took a step forward, the soles of his sandals slipped precariously on the unfamiliar hard-packed snow.

Kaylya caught him in her arms, restoring his balance. She gazed deeply into his dark eyes full of mystery, her heart seemingly pumping out of her chest as she searched for the man she once knew. Within those depths she found Rojaire's strength of character and sense of purpose …and his undying love for her.

"Kaylya…," he whispered softly. The sun haloed her auburn hair framing the delicately smooth chestnut skin and gold-flecked eyes that had haunted him for so long in his dreams, moist eyes that now spoke so much. He saw her undefeatable spirit, her unfathomable goodness, and the pain of separation she had endured sheltered under the brimming joy of reunion.

"Rojaire…," she whispered in return, touching his strongly chiseled, ruggedly handsome face. She touched his chest and he placed his hands over hers. She found his heart beating as rapidly as her own.

"Love of my heart," he whispered, afraid to speak louder and scare her spirit away.

"Love of my heart," she whispered, her throat too choked with emotion to say more.

Rojaire took her into his arms and they firmly embraced burying their joyful tear-stained faces in each other's shoulders. For now it was enough … in fact, all that they needed. They had so much to share … in due time … in due space.

When Rojaire began to shiver in the cold air, Kaylya drew energy, creating an aura of warmth around them.

The sun was already reaching for the western horizon with the promise of a spectacular sunset when Kaylya finally brought Rojaire in to present him to the others. The happiness they exuded filled the room, embracing them all.

"Sorceress Rahlys, Guardian of Light, it is my honor to serve," Rojaire greeted bowing to her in near reverence, which made her laugh. She could remember Rojaire speaking those same words, at one time, with mocking scorn. "I have come to help you take Brakalar."

"Greetings, Rojaire," she said hugging him warmly. Then she held him out at arm's length looking him over carefully. The dashingly cocky rogue adventurer boldly met her gaze. "Your arrival is timely," she said. "Your offer of help is greatly appreciated. I may indeed have use for your services."

"Warrior Quaylyn, how satisfying it is to meet with you here," Rojaire greeted his fellow Aaian.

"It is indeed good to see you again, Rojaire," Quaylyn greeted in Earthly informality. "And how fairs our friend Theon?" he asked.

"He was alive and well when I left him."

It was with great pleasure that Rojaire finally met the members of the Bradley family. He had heard so much about them from Theon, Rahlys, and Ilene on the journey to find the lost expedition and then later from Caleeza who had also spent time with the family on Earth. Rock, Crystal, Leaf, and Keiluk swelled the room with youthful activity. Before all the introductions were over, Melinda returned from her snowshoe hike through the woods.

"Where's Ilene?" Rojaire asked inquiring over Theon's daughter.

"She's lives in town where she works in her mother's gift shop," Kaylya informed him.

"And our glorious flying friend, Raven…?

"…off in the woods somewhere."

It was fun to visit, but before long Quaylyn had the group focused on the business at hand. Their countdown for intercepting Brakalar, now only a few hours away, was approaching rapidly.

---

Rahlys called the meeting of her warriors to order and quickly explained to Rojaire what little they had discovered about Brakalar's presence on Earth.

"We have been unable to locate Brakalar's hideout, of course, but we have been able to confirm his presence in a couple of locations. We now know that Brakalar is expected to attend a science seminar tomorrow morning in Baton Rouge, Louisiana, a city far south of here," she explained.

"I hope it's warmer there than here," Rojaire commented.

"Actually it is," Kaylya told him and described the scrying she had participated in.

"So what is the plan?" Rojaire asked.

"Well, now that you are here, there will be four of us to close the net," Rahlys said. "This increases considerably our chances of success in capturing Brakalar and decreases Brakalar's chances of escaping through a gap. Still it will not be easy."

"And where do we deposit Brakalar after we have him in our net?" Rojaire asked.

"We've discussed that at length," Quaylyn said and have decided the best place to contain him would be the traw playing field."

"You have a traw playing field?"

"There is already a concealment dome in place over the traw arena," Quaylyn explained. "That will make it easier for Rahlys, with the help of the crystal, to quickly put in place a confinement field over it once Brakalar is inside."

"Sounds like it might work," Rojaire said with his old familiar swagger. Silently Rojaire began formulating a few plans of his own.

---

Rahlys, Quaylyn, Rojaire, and Kaylya approached the science institute from different directions; four unobtrusive pedestrians enjoying the warm early morning Louisiana sunshine. The heavily sweet fragrance of blooming magnolia trees and azalea bushes that served as a privacy screen along the property's edge perfumed the warming air. Parked toward the center of the parking lot Officer Gerald LeBlanc sat in his unmarked black sedan waiting, while inside the science institute Judy kept a watchful eye on the surveillance screens.

Attendees of the seminar began to show up, one or two cars at a time turning into the tree-lined parking lot, most parking as close to the front entrance as possible. The observers watched as aspiring scientists spilled out of parked cars with laptops, note bags, and briefcases in enthusiastic anticipation of the seminar.

Kaylya transported herself inside one of the empty parked cars to wait for Brakalar's arrival. Quaylyn sat facing the parking lot on a park bench provided in the institute's tiny flower garden pretending to be engrossed in texting something on his cell phone. Rahlys strolled into the front parking lot on foot as Rojaire made his way to the other end of the parking lot through a service lane that squeezed through around the back of the building. More cars arrived and the increased milling about of people offered cover as Rahlys strolled along the front of the building while keeping furtive watch on the corner of the parking lot where she expected Brakalar to materialize.

Then suddenly the moment they had been waiting for arrived. Brakalar appeared in exactly the same location he had the month before. Only those watching for him noted his arrival. Unaware of all the eyes on him, Brakalar casually strolled across the parking lot toward the entrance.

Rahlys knew she would have to act fast to keep the element of surprise on her side. She and her warriors would have to entrap Brakalar before he had time to transport away, keeping in mind that he would know something was up as soon as he detected a draw on the elemental forces.

She paused in her stride as she noticed Rojaire coming up from around the corner. All the members of her team were ready and in place. Immediately she gave the subtle pre-planned hand signal.

At her signal, the four warriors drew heavily on the elemental forces and cast their net. Brakalar jerked to alert and Rojaire sprinted to close the distance between them.

In one fluid thought, Rahlys rapidly drew… more rapidly than ever before… the energy needed to make the capture, scooping Brakalar up and transporting him to his waiting prison, immediately activating the shielded sphere surrounding the traw playing field. But when Rahlys and her team cast their invisible net, two men vanished from the science institute parking lot.

In less than an eye blink Rojaire and Brakalar arrived on the snow-covered traw playing field in the remote Susitna Valley under a cold gray sky, the bright sunshine of the day before already a distant memory.

Rojaire, still in motion, tackled Brakalar, bringing him down into the deep snow. The unfamiliar cold crystalline snow covering his arms and face came as a shock to Brakalar. Charged with panic and desperation, he drew energy from the elemental forces, throwing Rojaire off with ease, but not before Rojaire could determine if Brakalar carried the Rod of Destruction. The two men quickly regained their feet and faced off.

"Rojaire…! I see you made it out of the Crystalline Landscape." Without taking his eyes off his opponent, Brakalar probed the space around him looking for an escape route. As he expected, it was heavily shielded. Rojaire sensed Brakalar's probe.

"You aren't going anywhere, Brakalar. It's just you and me."

"What are you doing here …looking for another free pass to the Devastated Continent?"

Rojaire let the sarcasm wash right over. "I am here to see that you face the High Council and accept a sentence of service for the severing of Zayla's longevity …and turn in the Rod of Destruction," Rojaire said, staring at the man who had helped him in his quests by making passage to Lynnara possible. Of course Brakalar had profited from Rojaire's explorations of the continent in the acquisition of relics.

"Never…," Brakalar sneered. "How dare you confront me with demands? Since when have you been on the side of the High Council?"

"Since you became a despicable power grabbing murderer…."

Quaylyn, Rahlys, and Kaylya arrived outside the invisible shielded sphere that surrounded the traw field above and below ground. As they had suspected, Rojaire had been trapped with Brakalar.

"Rojaire…!" Kaylya cried out in despair.

"I have to get him out of there," Rahlys said also concerned for Rojaire's safety.

"You can't drop the shield and allow Brakalar to escape," Quaylyn put into words, sparing Kaylya the painful need to do so.

"Quaylyn is right," Kaylya's voice trembled. Rahlys could see it was an agonizing decision for Kaylya to make. "Rojaire chose the situation he is in; we will have to let him work it out."

"What if Brakalar has the Rod of Destruction?" Rahlys asked.

"If that's the case, we are in as much danger as Rojaire," Quaylyn said bleakly.

By now the snow that had clung to Brakalar's skin and clothing had melted from his body heat, leaving him wet and cold. In a rage he pulled energy into a fireball and sent it hurling across the frozen medium like a bowling ball aiming it as much at the hated snow as his adversary.

"Rogue…! You will always be a rogue…," Brakalar hollered in anger.

Kaylya, Quaylyn, and Rahlys watched helplessly as the fireball scored a trench to Rojaire's feet … and beyond… sending up searing billowing steam.

Rojaire dove out of range of the blazing missile and quickly scrambled through the knee-deep snow to escape the scorching steam. He managed to scuttle behind the protection of the nearest snow-covered stone pinnacles rising up from the arena floor before Brakalar released a second, third, and even fourth fireball, quickly warming up the surrounding air and turning snow to steam that filled the dome, defining the otherwise invisible shield.

Spotting shadowy movement, barely discernible through the foggy mist, Rojaire drew elemental energy, hurling a sledge hammer of force aimed toward the retreating shape, but Brakalar managed to shield against the blow.

Rojaire knew Brakalar would prove a formidable opponent having received warrior training from the councilor at the Academy long ago. He could sense Brakalar's draw on the elementary forces and did the same for his own protection.

"Where is the Rod of Destruction?" Rojaire shouted out into the fog.

"You will never find it," Brakalar growled struggling through what was now mostly deep icy slush since the ground beneath was still frozen, not allowing snowmelt to drain. "I will never surrender it."

"Then we fight till one of us no longer serves the living;" *or until I change your mind without sacrifice of longevity*, Rojaire added silently.

"You're making a big mistake, Rojaire. If we worked together, we could be kings on this world."

"And just what do you plan on offering your subjects," Rojaire shouted back, drawing energy to strike from the abundance of molecular forces around him "… control of their lives …servitude?"

Rojaire hurled the lance of force in the general direction of Brakalar's voice. An explosion sent shock waves through the air as the missile hit the ground behind Brakalar sending up a spray of slush and frozen ground.

As another fireball arched his way it became apparent Brakalar was using the same strategy.

"I offer them survival, safety. These people only understand enough about the workings of the universe to get them in trouble."

"So you have appointed yourself as Earth's savior, is that it, Brakalar?"

"You are a rebel as well as a rogue," Brakalar taunted. A fireball connected with the boulder that had been in front of Rojaire, shattering it and sending out rocky shrapnel, but Rojaire had already moved on, escaping injury.

The thickening fog prevented the anxious warriors outside the shielded arena from seeing any further details of the battle. Only flashes of light were now visible as the foes attacked each other viciously in an effort to gain dominance.

"What's happening?" Kaylya asked after long moments had passed with more flashing fiery streaks and muffled explosions. Her voice quavered a bit despite all her effort to control it. Kaylya was as ashen gray as the overcast sky, all color having drained from her face. Rahlys doubted she took a breath as she stood anxiously by waiting for information regarding Rojaire's fate.

"I intend finding out," Rahlys said summoning the crystal to her hand. "I can go in without dropping the shield." Before Quaylyn could object, Rahlys was gone.

Rahlys arrived in the arena unnoticed, a strategy she planned on taking advantage of. Her first concern, besides assuring Rojaire's safety, was ascertaining whether or not Brakalar carried the Rod of Destruction. The abundant residue of spent magic in the confined dome confused her senses as she sought out Brakalar and Rojaire's locations. Blinded by the fog, she called on the power of the crystal, still in her hand, to be her eyes. Suddenly she could see clearly, as though the fog wasn't there. She located Brakalar just as he launched a horrific lance of force across the arena.

Rojaire tried to dodge the blow, but it clipped his right shoulder. A thud followed by his cry of agony let Brakalar know he had hit his mark. Rojaire braced his right arm grimacing with agonizing pain as he changed his position. He was certain his shoulder was broken. At last he reached the cover of another outcrop of rock pinnacles.

"You can't win, Brakalar! Even if you kill me Councilor Anthya will take you back to Aaia."

Rojaire moaned; shouting only made the pain worse, but he refused to surrender to it. Ignoring the pain in his shattered shoulder, Rojaire prepared a retaliating shot. Despite his injury, he continued to move among the rock outcrops. As he sprinted, he released a barrage of fiery shots in Brakalar's general location whenever an opening presented itself, shattering the tops of the rock formations around his last known position …and beyond.

*There is something familiar about the layout of the land*, Brakalar reflected as he paused against a rock face to catch his breath.

Brakalar ducked in an effort to dodge the rain of sharp shattered rock flying toward him from first one direction and then another. He struggled futilely to magically deflect the deadly missiles, managing to deflect some, but not all. A flying shard of sharp rock connected with Brakalar's chest, knocking the breath out of him and throwing him backward into the cold slush.

Rojaire quietly changed direction and stealthily returned to his original position before pausing to rest after expending such large amounts of energy. He waited for Brakalar to make a move.

"Rojaire…" Rahlys called out to him. "Cease firing."

"Rahlys…?"

Rahlys rushed to Brakalar's side. He was still conscious, but unmoving. The shard had pierced his chest, barely missing his heart.

"Don't move," she cautioned Brakalar. "I can help you."

"No…" Brakalar croaked. "Let me die."

"I can't do that," Rahlys said, "Zayla would not want your life to end like this."

Releasing the crystal, Rahlys mentally probed his chest searching for the point of greatest stress. She didn't dare remove the rock shard until she could staunch the flow of blood and heal the damage.

"I … will … not … live …" Brakalar said, the words low and raspy. They would be his last.

Finding the rock shard's deepest point of entry, Rahlys drew heavily on the power of the Oracle of Light twirling above them and her own healing energy, directing it where it was needed….

…but she met resistance.

"No…" Rahlys cried out in despair, drawing even more energy from the Oracle as she felt Brakalar's life forces slipping away.

Rojaire finally regained enough energy to risk making a move. Rahlys had not answered him. There had been no retaliation or sign of Brakalar, and the mist was beginning to thin.

Then he heard Rahlys cry out. Rojaire rushed toward her; jabs of sharp pain cutting through his shoulder with every step.

Locked outside the dome Kaylya and Quaylyn waited anxiously. As they watched it became apparent that the cloud of water vapor was slowly clearing in the dome as the temperature balanced again with the continuous exchange of air from the outside.

"How long is it going to take?" Kaylya breathed anxiously turning to Quaylyn.

"All we can do is wait for the mist to clear."

When Rojaire reached Rahlys he found her slumped over Brakalar's lifeless body. "Rahlys, are you all right?" he asked alarmed, arousing her with his touch.

"I couldn't save him," Rahlys cried overcome with grief. "It didn't have to end this way."

"A man who wishes death cannot be healed," Rojaire explained gently helping her to her feet despite the pain in his shoulder. His concern was for Rahlys; his shoulder would heal long before Rahlys' troubled heart. Ever so gently he led her away from Brakalar's lifeless body. "You can lower the shield."

Rahlys hesitated only briefly before complying.

Rojaire, sensing the lowering of the shield, led Rahlys out of the traw arena… right into Kaylya's crushingly relieved arms.

---

Officer Gerald LeBlanc was indeed surprised when the men in his precinct threw him a surprise retirement party. He had arrived quietly to clean out his desk and turn in his keys, but when he opened the door to his office he was greeted with cheers and well wishes.

The last two months of his service had been uneventful. There had not been any new cases of vanishing merchandise and nothing previously reported had been recovered. Furthermore, he and Judy had reviewed the recordings of that inexplicable morning in the science institute parking lot a thousand times over.

Two men had vanished before the camera that day: Dr. Simon and the man who was about to tackle him. Judy was unable to identify the second man that had vanished, nor was he the bogus director of the nonexistent center for paranormal phenomena. They had watched for Dr. Simon at the next scheduled seminar, but he did not appear.

Gerald never reported the bizarre incident at the science institute on that warm spring morning to his superiors; there seemed nothing to gain by doing so.

---

The air in the cabin tingled with emotional tension … love and heartbreak … pain and sorrow; but Rahlys had made her decision and Quaylyn had accepted it gallantly. The days of cloudy gloom had parted and strong spring sunshine reached deeply into the rustic log home, begging to cheer Rahlys and Quaylyn's battered emotions. Later today Quaylyn, Rojaire, and Kaylya were going home.

"I love you, Quaylyn, and I will always be your friend, but I cannot go with you." She knew no words she offered would ease the pain she caused him, but the words were true and sincere. "I need to be here, for now. My own people need me more than Aaia's. They will have you." Rahlys fought back tears but managed a little smile that softened Quaylyn's heart. Even more important to her personally, although she didn't say so to Quaylyn, was being here for Maggie, watching the children grow, and being a part of their lives. Instead, Rahlys continued with what she thought would matter most to Quaylyn.

"We still haven't located the Rod of Destruction; if it should surface, I will need to be here to secure it. Hopefully I will find it before anyone else does." Quaylyn didn't take the bait.

"I will never forget you, Sorceress Rahlys," *love of my heart* he added silently to himself, looking deeply into her pale blue eyes that reflected her soul.

"It is possible, you know, depending on where Brakalar hid the rune-covered chest containing the Rod of Destruction; that it may not surface in your lifetime. The chest has magic of its own that may conceal it until someone turns up with the key," Quaylyn reasoned. Rahlys knew Quaylyn might be right, but she couldn't take the chance that he was wrong.

---

Everyone turned up in Vince and Maggie's yard to say good-bye to Rojaire, Kaylya, and Quaylyn. The sun shone brightly, even warmly, on the gathering of the extended family of the Order of the Oracle.

The playful shouts and squeals of children playing mixed with the chatter of twittering birds in the budding birch trees at the north end of the garden. Vince, Maggie, Melinda, Rahlys, Quaylyn, and Ilene planted the carefully prepared rows of their new communal garden, drying out in the warm late spring sunshine. At the edge of the garden Rojaire, Kaylya, Jack, and Elaine watched over Leaf, Crystal, and Rock darting about in the sparkling sunlight, with Keiluk watching over them all.

This spring, Vince had purchased a rototiller to work the ground and with Rahlys and Quaylyn's help drawing energy from the elemental forces to blast out large rocks and tree roots; they soon had a large garden plot. Maggie had been composting kitchen and plant waste for years now, and a darkly rich composted hill of new dirt had been added to the soil.

"We should think about raising chickens," Maggie announced, standing up to straighten her back after scattering a row with carrot seed. "Composted manure is great for gardens. And it sure would be wonderful to have fresh eggs."

"Sure, Leaf will be old enough to tend to chickens soon," Vince agreed. He and Melinda patiently struggled with a pea fence they were building out of poles and string.

"What…? He's only four years old," Ilene protested setting in cabbage and broccoli starts Melinda had started indoors in southern exposure windows. But Rahlys knew what Vince meant; Leaf was mature beyond his years and growing fast, and he was learning quickly how to use his magic with discretion.

The family group celebrated Melinda's eighteenth birthday two weeks ago and to their relief, she did not rush off as they had feared. But Rahlys knew, as well as Maggie and Vince, that when Melinda was ready she would leave, and that was likely to be soon.

Rahlys glanced over to where the children were playing after a series of zealous squeals. As usual Leaf and Keiluk were the center of attention when it came to action, but the twins were growing and developing rapidly, personalities coalescing. Rock and Crystal complimented each other perfectly with Rock proving to be as boldly adventurous as Crystal was thoughtfully contemplative. The two were always together and Crystal was definitely in charge.

These people were her love ones … her family, Rahlys reflected, her aching heart warmed by the thought. She was glad she was here to watch over them.

Jack had been shocked by the turn of events during his visit with family in the lower forty-eight. While he was gone, the Order had defeated Brakalar, his body returned to Aaia. And Kaylya had been right; her Rojaire came for her just as she said he would. Now Kaylya was leaving.

"Will I ever see you again?" he asked Kaylya sadly. Jack felt like he was losing a daughter.

"If it is possible," Kaylya said gently. "You will always be with me. Thank you for all you kindness." Kaylya touched his heart sending him strength as she kissed him tenderly on his tear-streaked cheek. Only Rojaire and Kaylya's abundant happiness dispelled some of the pain in saying goodbye.

"Aaaarrrk…!" Raven called out from the woodshed roof.

"Da…," Rock called back pointing to his feathered friend, but Raven chose to remain aloof.

"Ba…ah," Crystal answered Rock also pointing to Raven.

The twins continued to converse in a language of their own while Leaf and Keiluk ran circles around them.

Ilene had wanted to return to Aaia to see her father, but Elaine's own heart-rendered pleas to her daughter had won out. Rojaire had assured Ilene that Theon was doing well and sent his love, but he had made no mention of the wondrous valley in the Crescent Mountains during his stay on Earth, not even to Kaylya. There had been so much to relate to one another, the omission had not been noticed, and Rojaire feared that if Rahlys learned of the valley, so would Councilor Anthya through the Oracle of Light. Therefore, he had decided to say nothing, not even to Kaylya, until it was safe.

Ilene approached Rojaire and Kaylya to say goodbye and ask a favor. Kaylya and Ilene had become close friends, often sharing Rahlys' guest cabin during visits. They had also shared the anguish of separation from someone they loved. "Would you give this letter to my father, if you should ever have the opportunity?" Ilene asked.

"Of course…," Kaylya said taking the letter.

"I will see to it that your letter gets delivered," Rojaire promised with a look of determination.

Ilene felt certain that he would.

**ANTHYA APPROACHES….**

It was the moment Rahlys dreaded; too choked up to speak, she telepathed the message to the others.

Vince, Maggie, and Melinda left their gardening to say their final goodbyes.

Alone in the garden, Quaylyn turned to Rahlys taking her hands, still covered with dirt, into his own. "I will miss you Sorceress Rahlys, Guardian of the Light. If you should ever need me, just call; I will forever be in your service."

"Thank you," Rahlys whispered, tears spilling over. With herculean effort, she regained control. "I'll keep that in mind; who knows what trouble I might get into."

Quaylyn took her into her arms and held her gently.

Then Anthya appeared before them, her flowing gray gown shimmering in the sunlight.

"Greetings, Sorceress Rahlys, Guardian of the Light, Warrior Quaylyn, Warrior Rojaire, Accepted One Kaylya…."

For Rahlys, the rest was a blur of pain and heart-ache as formal greetings were exchanged…. And then all too soon… Anthya, Rojaire, Kaylya … and Quaylyn … were gone.

## Other Book by Cil Gregoire

***Crystalline Aura***

Book One of the Oracle of Light

ISBN: 978-1-59433-137-4 — eBook ISBN: 978-1-59433-169-5

When a magic crystal is released by the retreating Susitna Glacier in Alaska, and the Dark Orb is unearthed by the flooding of New Orleans in the aftermath of Hurricane Katrina, an ancient battle, brought to earth twelve thousand years ago, is rekindled. Rahlys, disillusioned with urban life, the commercial use of her artistic talent, and an unfaithful boyfriend, returns to Alaska and purchases Trapper Bean's log cabin in the pristine wilderness of the Northern Susitna Valley, seeking peace and solitude to paint. Peace and solitude are challenged when a raven, formerly tamed by Trapper Bean, brings Rahlys a strange crystal that glows softly from within with multi-colored light. When Rahlys takes possession of the crystal, she takes possession of Sorceress Anthya's powers, and a classic struggle between good and evil unfolds. Filled with the natural beauty and magic that is Alaska, Crystalline Aura compels us to believe in the unbelievable, and in the magic within ourselves.

***Anthya's World***

Book Two of the Oracle of Light

ISBN: 978-1-59433-300-2 — eBook ISBN: 978-1-59433-301-9

Droclum is dead, but artifacts of his evil remain. Rahlys and a chosen few of her warriors join Anthya and Quaylyn on an expedition to the Devastated Continent, to search for the seven members of the lost expedition, and to explore the island continent, transformed by the catastrophic eruption of Mt. Vatre. Meanwhile back on Earth, Vince and Maggie are immersed in unique challenges of their own. Anthya's World intricately weaves a powerful tale that spans from Alaska's North Slope and Upper Susitna Valley to a world across the Milky Way Galaxy.

www.ingramcontent.com/pod-product-compliance
Lightning Source LLC
LaVergne TN
LVHW050618100826
845148LV00011B/1641

* 9 7 8 1 5 9 4 3 3 4 9 5 5 *